PRAISE FOR
DEIRDRE MARTIN'S ALL-STAR DEBUT,
Body Check

"A story that will delight lovers of sports heroes."
— *Romance Reader* (4 hearts)

"Ms. Martin's story is sparkling in creativity and spunky dialogue. It melts our hearts, not the ice, and uncovers the true meaning of the word *winner*. What a delight."
— Suzanne Tucker, *Old Book Barn Gazette*

"Heartwarming." — *Booklist*

"The promising Martin gives this debut story punch by adding a realistic feel for the high-stakes, high-pressure world of major-league hockey." — *Romantic Times*

Titles by Deirdre Martin

FAIR PLAY

Deirdre Martin

BERKLEY SENSATION, NEW YORK

This is a work of fiction. Names, characters, places, and incidents either are the product of the author's imagination or are used fictitiously, and any resemblance to actual persons, living or dead, business establishments, events, or locales is entirely coincidental.

FAIR PLAY

A Berkley Sensation Book / published by arrangement with the author

PRINTING HISTORY
Berkley Sensation edition / February 2004

ISBN: 0-425-19457-4

BERKLEY SENSATION™
Berkley Sensation Books are published by
The Berkley Publishing Group,
a division of Penguin Group (USA) Inc.,
375 Hudson Street, New York, New York 10014.
BERKLEY SENSATION and the "B" design
are trademarks belonging to Penguin Group (USA) Inc.

PRINTED IN THE UNITED STATES OF AMERICA

For T. Edward Connors,
the Merv to my Eva

THANKS TO:

My editor, Allison McCabe, and my agent, Elaine English,
for their hard work and faith.

Binnie Syril Braunstein, publicist extraordinaire.

Steve Haweeli, president of Wordhampton PR,
for giving me a glimpse of what
goes into doing PR for a restaurant.

My husband, Mark Levine,
for his hockey expertise and willingness to read
the manuscript numerous times to make sure I
"got the hockey stuff right."

Paula Epps for use of her impressive collection
of New Age and occult books.

Susan Lerner, for her insight and compassion.

Daniela Gobetti for her book, *Dictionary of Italian Slang,*
and Roland Delicio for *Merda!*
The Real Italian You Were Never Taught in School,
both of which were invaluable resources.

Mom, Dad, Bill, Allison, Beth, Jane, Dave and Tom
for all their love,
support and patience.

CHAPTER
01

Some women fantasize about being wed on the beach at sunset as the warm surf gently laps at their bare, tanned feet. Others picture floating down the aisle in a cloud of ivory tulle. Theresa Falconetti's dream wedding was exchanging vows at St. Patrick's Cathedral, followed by a horse-drawn carriage ride to a reception at The Plaza Hotel.

And now it was happening.

Gazing rapturously into the eyes of her true love as two proud, white stallions conveyed them up Fifth Avenue, Theresa couldn't believe her good fortune. One year ago, she had been the co-owner of a struggling PR firm. Now she was the wife of Miles van Dusen, architect, equestrian and collector of Sumerian pottery. They met at the wedding of Elizabeth Taylor to Nicholas Cage, one of Theresa's premiere clients. All Miles had to ask was "Fancy a prawn cocktail?" and Theresa was smitten, the deep, sonorous tone of his voice its own aphrodisiac. By the time the lemon sorbet was served, she knew he was The One.

"Happy, my sweet?" Miles murmured into her hair as the cool night air embraced them.

"Ecstatic." Theresa sighed, laying her head to rest on his shoulder.

"Theresa?"

"Yes, beloved of my heart?"

"Geez. That's a new one."

Startled, Theresa blinked. She wasn't in a horse-drawn carriage, but an Aeron chair. And the person calling her name wasn't the imaginary Miles van Dusen, but Janna MacNeil, her business partner.

"You okay?"

"Fine, fine," Theresa replied breezily, mortified at being caught conjuring a romantic fantasy so riveting it unmoored her completely from the present.

"Walking up the aisle again, huh?" Janna observed wryly.

"Maybe," Theresa said, anxious to steer the conversation back to business. "You said you had a lead on a possible new account?"

"It's a restaurant," Janna said as she sipped her coffee, a mutual addiction. This had been their routine ever since opening FM PR two years earlier: come to the office, check in over coffee, then split up and get down to work.

"A restaurant," Theresa repeated thoughtfully. "Since when do we handle restaurants?"

"Since our accountant told me we need to drum up as much business as we can."

Theresa sighed. "Hit me."

"It's a mom-and-pop place in Brooklyn," Janna began, reading the details from a piece of paper on her oversized desk, which dwarfed her. At five feet tall, with short blond hair, she was the physical opposite of Theresa, whose long legs and dark curls made her the envy of countless women. "It's got a strong local following, but the new owners, two brothers, are looking to expand the clientele," Janna continued. "They want to start pulling in the foodies from Manhattan." She raised her head to look at Theresa. "Are you free this afternoon?"

"I think so."

"Then would you mind going out there and meeting with these guys? I've got to meet with Mike Piazza."

"Mike Piazza? Of the Mets?"

"No, Mike Piazza the *plumber.* Of course Mike Piazza of the Mets." Janna looked hopeful. "If we could get him, it would be huge."

Theresa sank back in her chair. It always seemed to work out this way: Janna meeting celebrities, Theresa dispatched to check out what was probably a glorified pizzeria. Before starting their agency, Janna did PR for one of the NHL's New York franchises, the Blades. Theresa had haunted her long and hard about meeting the team's hottest new player, Alexei Lubov. She still suffered nightmares when she recalled what happened when her wish was granted: She and Lubov had gone out, and he had tried to rape her. When she dared to press charges, Theresa's self-esteem and reputation were nearly destroyed, but she persevered, and finally settled out of court. She used the money to set up the firm with Janna and swore off professional athletes entirely, except for a friendly relationship with Janna's husband, Ty, the former captain of the Blades. Well, Janna could deal with Mike-Piazza-the-Met, that was more than fine by her. "What time do the Brooklyn brothers want to meet?"

"Around two."

"That's doable. Where's the restaurant?"

"Bensonhurst."

"Really?" Theresa was surprised. She was born and raised in Bensonhurst. Her family lived there still, constantly making it clear they wished she did, too. Bensonhurst . . . She wracked her brains, trying to figure out what family restaurant Janna might be talking about. And then it hit her.

"You're sending me to Dante's, aren't you?"

Janna glanced away guiltily. "Yes."

"I don't *believe* you!"

Dante's was the restaurant where the Blades held all their private parties. One of its co-owners was Michael Dante, a third line winger for the team. He'd made a lasting impression on her two years ago when he asked to buy her a drink, failing to realize he didn't have his two front teeth in. At Ty and Janna's wedding, he'd hounded her endlessly to dance. She had a hard time being around him, since he reminded her of everything she'd like to forget: an athlete who refused to take no for an answer.

"You tricked me," she accused.

"I know," Janna confessed. "But I knew it was the only way to get you to agree. Besides, his brother will be there, too."

"Can't you switch your meeting with Piazza so that you can handle it?"

"It's business, Theresa." Janna sounded weary, despite the early hour. "Besides, you're better at this stuff than I am."

Theresa regarded her friend warily. "Better at what stuff?"

"Assessing potential clients, deciding what direction to go with a campaign, if they decide to hire us. You *know* you are. I'm better at the ego-stroking and damage control."

"If that's the case, then let me meet with Piazza and you can go *stroke* Michael Dante."

"That's funny, Ter. You know, I've never understood what you have against him. He's a nice guy."

"A nice guy who reminds me of every Italian Brooklyn boy I grew up with and moved to the city to avoid."

Janna gave a small grimace. "Well, try to keep an open

mind when you're meeting with them, please. We could really use this account."

"I'll be the consummate professional," Theresa assured her, while mentally stockpiling rebuffs to use on Dante if he tried flirting with her. She'd meet with him, fine. They needed the business, so she'd do it.

But she didn't have to like it.

"Dante! Off the ice."

At the sound of his coach's voice, Michael Dante abruptly cut short his rink-long sprint, and with dogged determination skated over to the bench where Ty Gallagher sat, stopwatch in hand. Michael was close to throwing up from sheer physical pain and exhaustion, Gallagher having insisted the entire team sprint up and down the ice until he told them to stop. That had been twenty minutes ago—after a practice that had already been an hour and a half long.

"What's up?" Michael panted, grateful for the momentary respite. He wished he could collapse onto the bench beside Ty, but knew it would be seen as a sign of weakness. Instead, he bent over with his stick across his knees, trying to steady his breathing and get rid of the stitch in his side that zapped him with pain every time he inhaled.

"You're slowing down," Ty barked. "You started out fine, but the last couple of sprints, you've been dragging your ass. Out partying last night?"

"No." Michael knew there was an edge of defensiveness to his voice, but he couldn't help it. If Ty had his way, they'd all be tucked up in bed by nine with a glass of warm milk, even though there'd once been a time when *he'd* availed himself of all the fruits Manhattan had to offer.

The difference was Ty had still managed to excel on the ice. He was one of the NHL's legendary players, with

four Stanley Cup wins to his credit. Two years ago, as
their captain, he'd led the Blades to their second Cup in as
many years, before shocking the hell out of everyone and
retiring while still at the top of his game. Last year, the
Blades didn't make the playoffs, and when their beloved
coach, "Tubs" Matthias, was killed in a car crash over the
summer, Kidco Corporation, who owned the team, lured
Gallagher back by making him the highest-paid coach in
the NHL. He was also perhaps the toughest, a dedicated
but relentless SOB who pulled no punches with his players and brooked no bullshit, either. Judging from the skeptical expression on his face, Michael guessed that Ty
thought he was lying.

"I kid you not," Michael swore. He was breathing easier now, enough to stand upright. "I was home last night."

"Why's that?" Ty needled. "Every bar, restaurant and
dance club in the city closed?"

Jesus wept, can you cut me a break here? Michael
pleaded in his head. Ever since Ty had taken over the
team, Michael's off-ice activities had been a bone of con-
tention between them. Ty thought that Michael led "too
active" a social life. He claimed it showed a lack of com-
mitment to his chosen profession. But that was bull.
Michael had been a professional hockey player for ten
years, and he knew it was possible to be a dedicated
player *and* have a decent social life. What the hell did Ty
want from him? He was a single guy, for Chrissakes. And
New York was his town. He was born here, learned to
play hockey here. . . . Hell, he still choked up when he
thought back to the first professional hockey game he
ever saw. He was six years old, and his father, whose idea
of sports was bocce ball, took him to Met Gar to see the
Blades play the Rangers. He'd known then and there that
he wanted to be one of those tough guys magically flying
down the ice. And he'd made his dream come true.

When the Blades acquired him in a trade with Hartford

three years back, he'd reveled in coming home to the city, and the city did nothing to hide its unabashed love for him in return. He was their own "Mikey D," the local boy made good. So what if, like Ty once cracked, "He'd never met a photo op he didn't like?" He was a people person. He liked meeting New Yorkers, talking to them, finding out what made them tick. And not just the rich ones who showed up at charity events and swanky parties, either. Michael liked talking to the people he met on the subway. People who approached him when he was out doing his grocery shopping. Normal, hard-working people who reminded him of where he came from should his ego start getting the better of him. Good people. New Yorkers. Where was the problem in that?

Still, his coach's insinuation that he was slowing down bugged him. He knew he'd never be a marquee player like Ty had been. But he was a solid hockey player, a grinder, an old-school third line winger. He was the guy they sent out to pound on the other team's defensemen. When the tide of a game needed to be turned, he was the one they relied on. He might not be the fastest skater in the world, but he was renowned for his relentless, crushing forecheck and his refusal to ever back down. "A formidable physical presence," that's what the *New York Post* had called him his first season back. So what was Ty trying to tell him? That he was losing his juice?

"Tell you what," Michael said, glancing back at his teammates, a number of whom looked as physically sick as he had felt just minutes before. "I'll concentrate on picking up the pace, okay?"

"*Concentrate* is the operative word here," said Ty. "I don't have a sense you're really focusing on what you're doing."

"I'm trying."

"Well, try harder. Or else you're going to find yourself watching van Dorn."

Paul van Dorn. Golden boy. Rookie. The second coming of Christ at training camp. Fresh out of college, van Dorn was acquired in the Lubov trade and was among the youngest players on the team. He didn't yet have a permanent place on the roster. But all that could change if Michael, or any of the other players, got sloppy or slowed down. And van Dorn knew it. He seemed to take sadistic pleasure in needling some of the guys about being "old men." But with Michael, it was more personal. "I thought old Italian men liked to sit in their gardens and look at their tomatoes," he'd once cracked while Michael was killing himself on an exercise bike. Another time he'd asked Michael if he needed help dressing. *Arrogant little Wasp prick.*

Michael nodded at what Ty said and skated back out onto the ice.

The coach was right: He wasn't focused at all today. Instead, his mind was on the meeting he was having later in the day in Brooklyn. He wanted Theresa and Janna's PR help to bring in more customers to the restaurant he and his brother, Anthony, had inherited from their parents. Unfortunately, Anthony was the patron saint of sullen, older siblings. He was also the head chef at the restaurant and was horrified at the idea of changing *anything*. To him, change was bad, period. Anthony had had the same hairstyle for twenty years and had held on to his '70s threads for so long, they were now back in style. Michael loved Anthony, but his narrow-mindedness and inflexibility often drove him to despair. He knew that when he got to the restaurant that afternoon and told Anthony they'd be sitting down with a PR person, his brother would start foaming at the mouth. Pots and pans would be hurled and the sanctity of their parents' vision invoked. Michael could deal with that later. Right now, he had to deal with muscles screaming for relief in his legs.

Joining his teammates, he gave it his all as they sprinted up and back, up and back. . . .

Theresa muttered to herself as she hustled down Eighty-Sixth Street on her way to Dante's on Twentieth Avenue. She was feeling guilty that she was in Bensonhurst, but had no intention of visiting her parents. She kept imagining bumping into her mother coming out of Cuccio Brothers Cheese or Santoro's Pork Store. After feigning a heart attack, her mother would launch into a tear-jerking soliloquy about how her only daughter had time to come to Brooklyn for work, oh yes, but God forbid she see her family more than one Sunday a month. The fantasy encounter was so real Theresa had started defending herself out loud. If that wasn't a testament to how easy it was for her family to get under her skin, she didn't know what was.

Dante's. She could have put her foot down and demanded Janna do it. But Janna seemed so stressed of late. Not that she wasn't stressed herself. The idea that their agency might not make it kept her up at night watching bad TV, sucking her into the twilight world of infomercials and square-headed, self-righteous televangelists. She sighed. There were worse things in life than meeting with professional athletes. Unemployment was one of them.

Rounding the corner of Twentieth Avenue, she marveled at how little it had changed since she was small, the mom-and-pop stores of her childhood still intact. Dante's was the same as she remembered it, a veritable Bensonhurst institution with a decent-sized dining room and an ample, traditional menu that featured everything from spaghetti and meatballs to osso bucco. Up until her father was diagnosed with lung cancer eight months ago, her parents used to go to Dante's every Thursday; their "date night" as they called it. But now Poppy was too tired and too sick to go anywhere. Once again, guilt gripped her. Maybe she *would* stop by the house when she was done and surprise them.

She pushed open the large, carved wooden door to the restaurant and slipped inside, out of the warm September air. The lights and air-conditioning were on, but there was no one behind the long, polished wood bar, and every linen-covered table in the large room was empty. Trying hard to ignore the bad paintings of Venetian gondoliers and photographs of local priests gracing the red walls, she loudly called out, "Hello?" A minute later, Michael Dante appeared through the swinging steel doors of the kitchen. He was scowling, but upon seeing her, the tensions melted from his face, replaced by a big smile. *Here it comes,* thought Theresa.

"Theresa. It's great to see you."

Theresa smiled politely. "Nice to see you, too. I see you're wearing all your teeth today."

"For you, a full mouth," he kidded back. Theresa noticed him subtly checking her out and bristled. *Get over it, ice boy. I'm through with your kind.*

"So . . ." she began, eager to get the ball rolling so she could leave as quickly as possible. "Should we wait for your brother to arrive?"

Michael's scowl returned. "That won't be necessary," he said, ushering her to a table for two adorned with a red and white checked tablecloth. "You want anything to drink? Pellegrino, a glass of wine?"

"Pellegrino would be great," said Theresa, watching his back as he sauntered away and slipped behind the bar. Objectively speaking, he was not unattractive: black, tousled hair, tan skin, and green-blue eyes, which seemed to change color depending upon what he was wearing. A decent body, too: strong arms and a muscled chest tapering down to a perfect V at the waist.

Filling two glasses with ice, over which he poured

mineral water for both of them, Michael tried to hide his
disappointment at the change in Theresa's appearance.
She was still gorgeous, but looked nothing like he remembered—or fantasized about. Clad in black from head to
toe, her long, wavy hair was pulled back in a sleek bun,
and her eyes were obscured by those chic, heavy-framed
glasses all the hip people seemed to favor nowadays. Her
manner was different, too. Polite, formal. How could this
be the same woman who, just two short years ago, was
fun, flirty, and enjoyed cursing at him in Italian? *Maybe
she wasn't The One after all.*

"Here you go." Michael handed Theresa her Pellegrino
and slipped into the chair opposite her. "So," he said.

"So."

"You look nice today," he noted.

"Thank you," Theresa replied politely, having been
taught from a young age that when someone pays you a
compliment you acknowledge it, whether you like the
person or not. "So, what can I do for you?"

Michael opened his mouth, then closed it, clearly
thinking better of what he intended to say.

"My brother and I need your help. We want to turn
Dante's into an upscale, Manhattan-style restaurant."

"Okay," said Theresa, intrigued as she took out a legal
pad and pen. "Tell me what you have in mind."

She listened carefully as he outlined the reinvention he
envisioned. Just as she was about to ask him if they
planned any renovations—*boom!*—one of the kitchen
doors flew open and out stormed an older, 1970's version
of Michael, pointedly glaring at them as he strode across
the restaurant and out the front door.

Theresa turned to Michael questioningly. "Was that—?"

"My brother?" Michael supplied. "Yeah, that was him,
all right."

"He doesn't seem very happy."

"He's not. He thinks upgrading the restaurant is a car-

dinal sin on a par with jarred gravy and *Godfather III*."
Michael shook his head dismissively. "Don't worry about
him. I've got him covered."

"Do you mind if I ask you a personal question?"

"You can ask me lots of personal questions."

Theresa squirmed. "If upgrading the restaurant is going
to cause your brother to throw an embolism, why do it?"

Michael looked uncomfortable. "Because it's time. My
mom died last year, and she always talked about how she
wished the place was just a little bit . . . better. I've been
waiting to see what Anthony would do, but it's obvious
that if I don't step in, things are never going to change. So
here I am." His expression was playful as he leaned toward her. "Anything else you'd like to know?"

Theresa pushed back out of range, hoping he got the
message. "Why do you want FM PR to represent you?"

"Well, for one thing, it's all in the family, so to speak."
Theresa assumed he was referring to his connection to Ty
and Janna and not, she hoped, some imaginary union between them in the future. "Plus, Eddie James Jackson told
me that you, personally, were the best at spinning PR
straw into gold."

Eddie James Jackson. Now there was a name from the
past. Jackson was an actor on *The Wild and the Free* when
she was still with the show. Theresa managed to convince
the soap press he was the daytime equivalent of Robert
DeNiro—no small feat considering Jackson had the emotional range of a wood chip, and his character was an
alien masquerading as a nightclub owner, sent to earth to
hunt new breeding stock for his planet.

Theresa chuckled. "You know Eddie?"

"He's a big hockey fan." His eyes held hers. "Big fan
of yours, too." Theresa looked away. "Guess I'm just one
of many." Dante smiled.

"Don't," Theresa admonished, concentrating on her
legal pad. Easing the conversation back to business, she

posed the question she'd meant to ask before they'd been interrupted. The answer was they were planning to expand both the dining area and the banquet room within the next couple of months.

"What about decor? What have you got in mind there?"

"I don't know." Michael looked around the restaurant blankly. "Some more paintings, I guess. A couple more pictures."

"If you want to attract a more upscale clientele," Theresa began gently, "the restaurant may need a more . . . polished . . . look."

"Okay." Michael drained his Pellegrino like a man needing fortification for what might come next. "What else?"

"Staff."

"What about them?"

"How many, how old."

"I'm not sure how many," he admitted. "I'll have to ask Anthony. As for how old, most of them are probably in their sixties now. A few might even be in their seventies. They all started working for my father when they were young men," he finished proudly.

Sensing that this might not be the time to tell him the staff might need some renovating as well, Theresa turned to the most important issue of all: the menu. "The food has got to be exceptional if you want to draw from the other boroughs."

"It is."

"You're sure it is or you hope it is?"

"It is," he repeated. "You know it is. You've eaten here."

"That was over a year ago." *At Ty and Janna's wedding, when you were such a noodge pestering me to dance I wanted to stuff a piece of lasagna in your mouth just to get you to shut up and leave me alone.*

"Well, nothing's changed. If anything, the food's gotten better." He jumped up from the table. "Hang on a minute, I want you to taste something." He disappeared into the kitchen, returning a minute later with a small dessert plate that he placed in front of her.

"What's this?" Theresa asked suspiciously, staring down at puffy pancakes drizzled with honey.

"Just try it," Michael urged. "Go on."

Uncomfortable with being watched, but trapped, Theresa reached for a fork and cut off a small piece of the pancake, popping it in her mouth. It was good. Okay, it was very good. No, she had to be honest, it was great. If he wasn't there she'd scarf down the whole thing.

"Well?" Michael folded his arms across his chest, awaiting her reply.

"BTS," she declared rapturously.

"BTS?"

"Better than sex."

Michael laughed. Now *that* was the Theresa he remembered: blunt, funny, unself-conscious . . . obviously, the girl who haunted his dreams was still in there somewhere, lurking behind the crisp, clipped demeanor. Hopeful of bringing out more of her real personality, he leaned toward her.

"Careful. Your roots are showing, and I'm not referring to your hair."

Theresa's eyes narrowed. "What?"

"Your Brooklyn accent," Michael said affectionately. "It was there in full force just a moment ago. As for BTS," he added with a devilish grin, "are you sure about that?"

Theresa's expression darkened. "*Zoccolo! Come sei sciocco,*" she muttered under her breath, just loudly enough for him to hear.

Michael's heart swelled. She'd called him a tasteless clod! In Italian! God, he adored her. "I try," he replied.

"You succeed," she snorted, putting her guard back up. She took another small bite of pancake, unable to resist.

"What are these anyway?"

"Ricotta fritters. My maternal grandmother's recipe. I'll have to tell Anthony you enjoyed it."

"Is he the pastry chef?"

"He's the everything chef."

"Well, he's got a winner here; I have to hand it to him. No wonder my mother loves the desserts here."

Michael looked confused. "Your mother—?" He tilted his head this way and that, studying Theresa. "Wait a minute," he said, light beginning to break behind his eyes. "Falconetti? Natalie and Dominic are your folks?"

"Yup."

"I never made the connection. They haven't been here for a while."

"No," Theresa said, her chest constricting as she thought about why. "My dad's sick."

"Jesus, I'm sorry to hear that," Michael said, sitting back down. The way he was looking at her, so full of compassion and concern, was unnerving. She much preferred when he gazed at her like she was a centerfold. "Give them my and Anthony's regards, will you?" he continued. "And if there's anything we can do . . . ."

"Thanks," Theresa said quietly, afraid that if they stayed on the topic of her father, she might tear up. "I need a copy of the menu, if you can spare it."

"No problem."

The front door of the restaurant opened and Anthony reappeared, his demeanor still surly.

"Hey, come over here a minute," Michael called out to him in a coaxing voice as his brother stormed back towards the kitchen.

"Vaffanculo!" Anthony shouted back over his shoulder

before disappearing once again through the swinging steel doors.

Theresa winced. "Ouch."

"Sorry about that," Michael apologized, looking mortified that his brother had just told him to do the physically impossible in mixed company. "Anthony can be overly emotional."

"They have pills for that now, you know." When her quip didn't even register a smile, she decided to be direct. "Is he going to be okay with my developing a PR campaign for you guys?"

"He'll be fine," Michael replied in a voice taut with self-control. Theresa didn't want to think about what was going to happen when she left the restaurant. She could already see the headline: HOCKEY STAR DROWNS BROTHER IN VAT OF OLIVE OIL, GOES ON LAM WITH NOTHING BUT DENTURES AND FRITTERS. It was going to be ugly.

"Are *you* okay?" she asked, surprising herself.

"Fine," Michael replied brusquely. He jerked his head in the direction of her legal pad. "So, what are your services going to cost me?"

She wished he hadn't used the phrase "your services." It made her sound like a hooker. "Well, normally we'd charge thirty-five hundred dollars a month, but since you're a friend of Janna and Ty's, I'll make it twenty-five hundred."

"So that would be thirty-thousand for a year."

"Yes."

"That's enough for a down payment on a house."

"Do you want to buy a house, or do you want the best PR services money can buy?" she asked suggestively.

His mouth curled into the hint of a crooked grin. "So you're the best, huh?"

"Buy my services and see."

Michael chuckled appreciatively. "With a sales pitch

like that, how can I resist?" He extended his hand across the table to shake hers.

"You're on for a year, Ms. Falconetti."

As delicately as she could without appearing impolite, she withdrew her hand from his. "You won't be disappointed."

CHAPTER

02

Michael found Anthony in the kitchen, at the far end of one of the two long, stainless-steel tables in the center of the room, mincing walnuts on a giant cutting board with a full-size mezzaluna. *It was bad enough Anthony made such a jackass out of himself, storming in and out of the restaurant,* Michael fumed. *But telling me to go screw myself when I'm trying to conduct business? And in front of a woman? That was crossing the line.*

The rest of the kitchen staff were happily chatting among themselves while they prepped for that night's menu. Michael's ire cooled temporarily as he took in the swirl of intoxicating scents around him: sauce cooking, foccacia baking . . . nourishing smells he associated with the sweetness of childhood, when both his parents were alive and running the show. Jesus, he missed them. Especially now, when he could use their help dealing with his bullheaded big brother. His eyes shot briefly heavenward. *Mom, Dad, give me the strength not to snap and bust his jaw.*

"Anthony." His tone was a call out, though he hadn't meant it to be. He tried to sound more casual. "Can I talk to you a minute?"

Anthony shrugged, not bothering to make eye contact. "Talk away."

"Alone."

"We're working here, Mike. Some stuff's got to be ready when we open at five-thirty."

"I KNOW," Michael replied, ignoring the implicit jibe. "All I'm asking for is five minutes."

"I don't have five minutes."

"Make it," Michael threatened.

Sighing theatrically, Anthony put the mezzaluna down. "Yo, listen up everybody." The staff stopped what they were doing. "Everyone take five so my brother the hockey star can talk to me in private."

Michael saw the questioning glances exchanged by the staff, but all did as they were told, trooping one by one out of the kitchen. Anthony sauntered over to one of the massive industrial stoves and began absently stirring one of the huge vats of sauce with a giant ladle.

"I'm all ears."

"Good. Number one, I didn't appreciate your immature behavior when I was trying to conduct business."

"Business I want no part of," Anthony reminded him, putting down the ladle and moving along to the wall of ovens, forcing Michael to follow.

"We'll get to that in a minute. Number two: Don't you ever curse at me like that again, especially not in front of a woman. Where the hell were your manners?"

Anthony smirked. "I guess I forgot them."

"Yeah, well, next time remember them or I'm going to kick your rude ass from here to Hoboken." Michael watched as Anthony carefully tipped open the door of an oven to check on the foccacia. "Ma always said you shouldn't open the oven while the bread was baking."

The oven door slammed shut. "Who died and made you fucking head chef, huh?" Anthony snapped.

"Anthony." Michael's voice was imploring. "Look, I don't want this bad blood between us—"

"Then keep your nose out of the restaurant, Mike."

"I can't. Mom and Pop made me co-owner."

"And what? All of a sudden I'm too fucking stupid to run things? I've been running the restaurant for years."

"I know that. But—"

"But what?" Anthony returned to the table where some walnuts still lay intact and resumed chopping, violently. "Look, why don't you stick to what you do best, and I'll stick to what I do best? You're a hockey player. Go play hockey."

"I'm also co-owner of the restaurant," Michael repeated stubbornly. "Besides, Mom wanted to upgrade the restaurant. I'm just trying to honor her wishes."

"Mom wanted to *expand* the restaurant, not upgrade it," Anthony countered. "There's a difference."

"If we're expanding, we may as well upgrade, too."

Anthony's expression bordered on the mutinous. "No offense, baby bro, but what gives you the right to walk in here and change things around? I seem to remember that while you were off at college and playing for Hartford, I was the one sweating here in the kitchen with Mom and Pop, learning the ropes. You might own half the restaurant, but you don't know shit about what goes into making it run."

"You're right," Michael conceded humbly. "I don't." Out of the corner of his eye, he spotted a tray of almond cookies cooling. He went to grab one, but Chef Eagle Eye was already one step ahead of him.

"Eat one and I'll chop your hand off. They're a special order for Saint Finbar's. You know that bastard Father Clementine: He'll count every freaking one."

"He's still there?"

"Oh yeah." Anthony frowned. "Still comes in here every Sunday night, too."

"Know why? Because the food is great."

"Well . . . yeah." Anthony shot him a glance that said, "Why state the obvious, you moron."

"Which is why I had the meeting with Theresa." Michael took a step closer to his brother. "You're a great cook, Ant. That's why this place has such a huge local following. But don't you think it's time to get the word out?" Anthony continued chopping. "We're sitting on a gold mine here. You know that, or you wouldn't have agreed to an expansion. A little advertising, a little sprucing up, we could probably double the traffic in here within a year. We could pull in the food fanatics from the city. Word of mouth gets around. Before you know it—*baboom!*— you're getting mentions in *Gourmet, Food & Wine*, maybe even a review in the *Times*. Wouldn't you like that?"

"No."

"No?" Michael echoed incredulously. *"No?"*

"No offense, Mikey, but business is fine. We're packed every night. We start trying to pull in all those Park Slope yuppies and before you know it, the regulars won't be able to get their tables. People who have been loyal customers for years are gonna write us off. I don't want that to happen."

"It won't."

"How do you know?"

"Because I know. Trust me."

"What, is that what the PR woman told you?"

"No, I just know."

"You just know." Chopping completed, he grabbed a large stainless-steel bowl from the shelf below the table, tilting the walnuts into it. "You've been a professional hockey player for ten years, you don't know dick about cooking or the restaurant business, but you *just know.*

Well, let me tell you what *I* know. Mom and Pop never intended this place to be some fancy, schmancy *trattoria,* where people have to pay twenty bucks for a bowl of pasta and gravy. And *that's* what you're talking about turning it into."

"You don't know that, Anthony," Michael insisted.

Anthony's response was an unintelligible grunt.

"Let's just wait and see what the PR people come up with and we'll talk about it then." He sighed. "*C'mon,*" he said, jostling Anthony's shoulder. "Try to have an open mind."

"I already told you: I don't want anything to do with your PR bullshit. How much is this going to cost, by the way?"

"Don't worry about that," Michael assured him. "I've got it covered."

"No, tell me," Anthony insisted, wiping down the cutting board and the mezzaluna blade. "I'm curious."

"Thirty," Michael admitted reluctantly.

"Thirty K!" Anthony exclaimed. "What are you, *ubatz*?"

"Wait and see," Michael insisted. "It's going to pay off big time and you know who's going to reap the rewards? You and me."

"My life's rewarding enough," Anthony said, sauntering over to a row of cabinets where he pulled out a bag of candied citron. "But hey, you want to piss your money away, you go right ahead. Thirty K," he chuckled to himself. "*Madonn'.*" He carried the citron back to the table, and tearing the bag with his teeth, shook the contents out onto the cutting board and began dicing again with the mezzaluna. "So that PR woman, Theresa. She's the one you've got the hots for, right?"

Michael frowned. "Could you be a little more respectful, please?"

"Oh, I'm sorry, is my blunt language offending your delicate sensibilities?"

"Vaffanculo!"

Anthony laughed. "Look whose trash-talking now." He popped a piece of citron into his mouth. "Seriously, she's the one, right?"

"Yup."

"So what's the deal? You hiring her to do all this PR crap because you really care about the restaurant, or because you wanted an excuse to see her?"

Michael shook his head in disbelief. "I had no idea *she* was going to show up. It could just as easily have been her business partner." Of course, he would never tell Anthony that in hiring FM PR, he was well aware his path would cross more frequently with Theresa's. Not that it seemed to matter.

"Besides," he added, taking some citron for himself. "She doesn't seem to like me."

"Maybe because you're an arrogant, meddling jackass," Anthony suggested.

"That could be it. We know her folks: Dominic and Natalie Falconetti."

"The Falconettis." Anthony paused, trying to place the names. "Veal sorrentino and fettucini alfredo, two slices of olive-oil cake afterward with espresso. They haven't been here for a while."

"The old man is sick." Suddenly Michael had an idea, his eyes scouring the kitchen. "In fact . . . I was thinking of stopping by and saying hello to them before I head out for the game tonight. Would you mind putting together a care package for me?"

"You sure you got time? I could drop by there tomorrow morning."

"I want to do it."

Anthony's eyes crinkled as he smiled at his little brother and winked. "Yeah, of course you do. Just let me finish up with this citron and I'll fix a nice little plate for each of them."

"I appreciate that."

"Now can I call my staff back in?"

"Go ahead," said Michael. "And make sure you tell them great changes are on the way."

Anthony ignored him.

"Any messages?"

Theresa drummed her nails impatiently on the glass-topped reception desk while Terrence, FM PR's receptionist, took his sweet time closing the *Vanity Fair* he'd been absorbed in. Delicately licking his right index finger, he began thumbing through the small pile of messages on the desk before him, reciting to her.

"Let me see: your mother; Gail Tudor at *The Wild and the Free*, who said she can't do the celeb softball game because that's the day she's getting her ta ta's done like they're not already fake as her tan, thank you very much; your mother; Lou Capesi from the Blades office; your mother; oh, and lest I forget, your mother." Terrence's gaze was withering as his eyes rose to meet hers. "Time to phone home, ET."

"No comments from the peanut gallery, please," Theresa returned dryly. "Is Janna back from meeting with Mike Piazza yet?"

"No, though she should be in any minute. Anything else?"

"Nope. Go back to your Tom Cruise pictorial."

Anxiety mounting, Theresa walked down the hall to her office and quietly closed the door behind her. Kicking off her shoes, she settled down behind her desk and dialed her parents' number, preparing for the worst. Either her father was back in the hospital, or she had been spotted walking down Eighty-sixth Street earlier in the day and her mother was going to accuse her of familial treason.

"Hello?" Her mother's voice was tense.

"It's Theresa, Ma. Terrence said you called three times. Everything okay?"

"You're interrupting my show."

Her show. *Guiding Light*. God forbid anyone came between her mother, Josh and Reva. "So tell me fast," Theresa said, relieved that she hadn't been seen in Brooklyn. "What's up?"

"I was calling to remind you about coming to dinner on Sunday."

Theresa pinched the bridge of her nose. "Have I ever missed Sunday dinner, Ma?"

"No, but I just wanted to remind you."

"Consider me reminded."

"Also, Cousin Angelo's daughter's third birthday is coming up."

"Uh huh."

"There's going to be a party. With a clown."

"Now there's an enticement."

"Always with the mouth." Her mother sighed.

In the background, Theresa could hear her father asking her mother who was on the phone.

"It's Theresa!" her mother yelled. Theresa winced, holding the phone away from her ear.

"Is she coming to little Gina's party?" her father shouted, trying to be heard over the television.

"Guess," her mother shouted back.

"Hey!" Theresa exclaimed defensively. "I didn't say I wasn't coming!"

"Are you?" her mother demanded.

"No. But only because I'm busy."

"Is she saying she's too busy?" her father shouted.

"Of course," her mother shouted back. "She's always too busy."

Theresa closed her eyes. "If you know I'm busy," she trilled sweetly, "then why do you even bother asking?"

"Because I was hoping that just once, you might make more time for your family."

"I guess Miss *Cosmopolitan* has better things to do," her father noted loudly.

"I have to go now, Ma." Theresa's voice rang with false cheer. "Love you and daddy. See you Sunday."

Mother of God, she thought, as she hung up the phone, *was she allowed to have a life?* The once-a-month Sunday family meal was never enough. Her mother wanted her to follow in the traditional pattern where your extended family was your entire social life, and weekends were an endless round of communion parties, birthdays, anniversaries. Any excuse for a family get-together. It *had* been fun as a kid, always having cousins around to play with as well as aunts and uncles who doted on you like you were their own. But now that she was an adult, she didn't have time for that whole smothering Italian-American *thing*. She had friends from high school who had never left the neighborhood. Cousins, too. They'd married boys they'd gone to school with, boys who were just like their fathers and their brothers and their uncles. And they all lived within ten minutes of their parents and siblings. Their whole life revolved around *la famiglia*—which was *fine,* if that's what you wanted.

But Theresa never had.

When she was in high school, she'd take the subway into Manhattan every chance she could and just walk around, exploring. Bookstores were her favorite: the Strand and Partners & Crime in the Village, where she could gorge on mysteries. And the Public Library on Forty-second Street. God, she loved that place—still did—with its reverential silence and implicit promise of transformation. Those trips to Manhattan were what helped her realize she wanted to go to college and major in English. Her family actively encouraged her dream. So why was it, now that she'd carved out a successful life for herself, they held it against her, accusing her of getting too big for her britches and forgetting about her roots? She didn't get it. Didn't parents want their children to spread their wings and fly? Why were her folks always trying to drag her back down into the nest?

She suspected part of it was because she was still single. So what if she ran her own business, lived in the city, and occasionally brushed elbows with the rich and famous in the course of her work? In her family, what mattered was getting married and having babies. Her mother and sister-in-law were constantly on her case, offering to set her up with friends of cousins and neighbors, always wanting to know if she'd met anyone "nice"—a polite code word for "Italian." *Too bad I don't like Michael Dante,* she mused. *He'd be right up their alley.*

Michael Dante . . .

Thankfully, the meeting hadn't been as uncomfortable as she'd expected, though she was displeased she'd let her guard down even momentarily, and the bizarro older brother was a little unnerving. She tried to recall if she'd met Anthony at Ty and Janna's wedding or any Blades functions, but came up blank. He must have been hiding in the kitchen the whole time. Pondering the Dante account, her gaze was drawn to the small Miro lithograph hanging across the room, which led her to thinking about the artwork—if you could call it that—at the restaurant. God, was it awful. How could she tactfully suggest a new look? Yawning, she glanced up at the clock. Quarter to five. Resignedly, she picked up the phone to call Lou Capesi, when a knock sounded at her door and Janna stuck her head inside.

"Got a minute?"

"Of course." Theresa put the phone back in the cradle. "How did it go with Piazza?"

Janna gave a big thumbs-up, smiling broadly. "I think he's going to have us work for his charitable foundation."

"That's *great!*" Theresa hadn't realized how tense she had been. Hearing Janna's good news, she could feel her hunched shoulders slowly lowering.

"How'd it go at Dante's?"

"Well, the good news is he committed to a year, not a month-by-month."

Janna perched on the edge of the desk. "That's fantastic."

"The bad news is the brother, who's the head chef and runs the place, had a total conniption about my being there and wants nothing to do with any of it."

"You'll just have to work around him."

"I hope I can work it, period," said Theresa uneasily. "I've never handled a restaurant account before. I think I might be in over my head."

"You'll be fine."

"What if I'm not?"

"Ter, we don't have a choice," Janna said grimly. "We need the money."

"Right."

Janna gazed thoughtfully into space. "I think I might know someone at the Food Network."

"That would be great. Maybe we could get them on some talk show or something."

"Yeah, let me think about it." She pushed off the desk and settled down in a leather chair identical to the one in her own office. "So, it was just you and Michael?" she noted coyly.

"Yup."

"And—?"

"Dante's is now one of our clients," said Theresa, refusing to take the bait. Though it did make her wonder . . . "Do you think I'm a snob?" she asked abruptly, swinging back and forth in her chair.

"When it comes to Michael Dante, yes. He's a really nice guy and you know it."

Theresa stopped swinging. "I'm done dating jocks."

"Not every jock is a potential rapist, as I can attest."

"And as I've told you, you got the only good one." The phone line on her desk lit up and she held her breath. *Please, Terrence, take care of it, especially if it's my mother again.* The light went out. *I knew there was a reason I loved you, Terrence.* She looked to Janna. "So what did you want to talk about?"

Janna took a deep breath. "I got a call this morning from someone named Ted Banister."

"Sounds like a soap opera character."

"He's a lawyer. Representing the Butler Corporation."

The Butler Corporation. All the tension that had melted from Theresa's shoulders came screaming back with a vengeance. Butler was a huge international advertising agency currently in the process of gobbling up PR firms like M&M's. In the two years since she and Janna had opened their office, Butler had bought out three small PR firms and buried two small ad agencies. With money and clout to burn, it was clear they wouldn't rest until they owned every boutique agency in the city.

"Let me guess: They want to buy us out," Theresa deduced blandly.

"I assume that's the case, but of course Banister wouldn't come right out and say so on the phone. He wants to meet with us here Friday morning."

"And did you tell him to go take a leak in his hat?"

"I wish," Janna replied. "No, I told him to stop by around ten. Should be interesting."

"Mmm." Theresa resumed swinging in her chair, more slowly this time. "Why would they be interested in *us*? We're not that big."

"No, but we've got some professional athletes and TV people on our roster."

"Jesus. How long do you think the meeting will take?"

"I have no idea. Why?"

"I have to be at the celeb softball game at noon."

"I'm sure we'll be done by then. If not, you can go when you need to, and I'll wrap things up."

There was an edge of uneasiness in Janna's voice that Theresa found contagious. "I don't like this," Theresa confessed.

"I know," Janna agreed. "I'm afraid he'll offer us an obscene amount of money we'd be insane to turn down, or else he'll blatantly threaten to ruin us. But we'll hang tough, right?"

"Damn straight," Theresa replied without hesitation.

But whether they truly believed what they were saying was another matter.

Hurry, hurry, hurry!

Hustling through the small crowd of fans outside the players' entrance at Met Gar, Michael promised to sign autographs afterward, praying the team wasn't already on the ice for the pregame warm-up. If they were, his ass was going to be grass. Tearing down the long concrete hallway leading to the locker room, he was hurriedly calling out hellos to various Met Gar staff. *Shit.* Most of the guys had already left, but a few were still dressing. *Thank God.* If he could dress really fast and get out on the ice with them, he'd be okay.

"Hey, hey, Mikey boy, nice of you to show up," quipped Dennis O'Malley, the team's backup goalie, his melon-sized head bobbing up and down in time to the music blasting from the locker room sound system. "We were starting to wonder if you forgot how to get here."

"Or if you forgot to set the alarm before you took your afternoon nap," added rookie van Dorn. "I hear you old guys need lots of sleep."

Pointedly ignoring him, Michael went to his locker, peeled off his street clothes and began frantically dressing for the warm-up. But by the time he was done, the stragglers who had still been putting on their uniforms when he came in had already left. Grabbing his stick, he headed out to the ice to join the rest of the team. Their captain, Kevin Gill, just shook his head when he spotted Michael. Ty Gallagher stood behind the bench clutching his ever-present clipboard.

"You're late," he called out as Michael hit the ice, skating slowly and deliberately to give his body a chance to warm up, even though he was pretty sure anxiety had pushed his resting heart rate up a notch or two already.

"Sorry, coach," he called back.

"Get over here."

Michael skated to the bench. "Yeah, coach?"

"You owe me fifty bucks," Ty informed him.

"What?"

"Fifty bucks for every five minutes you're late. We talked about it last week."

Michael frowned. "Right." He remembered it now that Ty mentioned it. Otherwise? Zip, gone, out of his head. *Jesus. Wasn't he a bit young to be going senile?*

"Stop taking the subway and start using the car service, Mike. That's what it's there for."

He toyed with massaging the truth and telling Ty he was late because he'd been going over plans for the restaurant with Theresa—plans that would benefit his wife, Janna's business—but then decided against it. The reason he was late had nothing to do with the subway, and everything to do with Theresa's parents, who could talk the ears off a brass monkey. They were lovely people, welcoming and warm, but trying to get out of that house was like trying to escape from Sing Sing. Three times he'd tried to politely make his exit and three times they managed to detain him. By the time he hit the subway, he knew he'd be late. Even so, he was glad he'd gone to visit them. Very glad.

"Yeah, all right," he muttered, joining the parade of players already circling the ice.

Muscles loosening, he headed toward one of the pucks scattered on the ice and began practicing his stick handling. He'd been at it less than a minute when van Dorn sidled up to him and stole it, seemingly under the mistaken impression that the fans and little kids gathered around the Plexiglas were there to see him, so superior was his expression. *Schmuck. They couldn't care less about you.* Michael waved to a couple of familiar fans, and grabbing another puck, flipped it over the glass to one small girl in particular who looked completely enraptured. It was a feeling he remembered well, one he always tried to tap in to when he was out there, that sense of magic.

Michael looked around at the rapidly filling arena, where a sense of anticipation was beginning to build. He could still remember exactly where he sat that first time his pop took him here for a game: high up in the blue seats, or the "nosebleeders" as Pop liked to joke. Back on the ice, Dallas's players were starting their own warm-up.

"Hey, how ya doin'?" Michael called out to a former teammate from Hartford, Duncan Lee, who'd been traded the same year as Michael.

"Doin' good," Lee replied. "Yourself?"

"No complaints. Give my regards to Andrea."

"Will do."

Once the game started, all notions of friendship would be put aside as each team focused on winning. But for now, during the warm-up, players who were once teammates weren't averse to a little catching up as they circled opposite each other. Picking up the pace a bit, Michael glided past his nemesis, who refused to be bested and went tear-assing down the ice at warp speed. *Nice one, Mr. Ivy League. What'll you do for an encore?* Finishing their three-on-two drills, Michael and the rest of the guys formed a circle and started shooting at the goalie to help warm him up. Michael was easily passing a puck back and forth with one of the team's defensemen, Barry Fontaine, when he heard Ty call out his name again. Changing direction, he skated over to the bench.

"Don't tell me you want the money now," he ribbed Ty.

A hint of a smile shadowed Ty's face. "After the game would be fine. No, I just wanted to let you know you're a healthy scratch tonight. You can watch from the skybox if you want."

Ty's words hit like a blow to the solar plexus. Michael knew his pain must have been obvious because Ty, who rarely explained his decisions, did this time. "We need more speed on the ice against Dallas."

"Who are you dressing instead?"

Not van Dorn, please Jesus, not van Dorn . . .

"Fabian."

There wasn't much Michael could say. Fabian was a great skater and he wasn't.

"Anything else?" he asked.

"Ask La Temp to come over here."

"Will do."

Ty nodded curtly, signaling their conversation was done. Feeling oddly numb, Michael skated up to the team enforcer Guy La Temp, told him the coach wanted to see him, and continued circling the rink, the eager faces of the fans smearing into a blur as he obsessed on what had just happened. He couldn't remember the last time he hadn't dressed for a game. It had to be at least two years, and even then, it was because of a sore hamstring. A healthy scratch . . . shit. He wished he could be a bit more zen about it and convince himself that in the grand scheme of things, sitting out one game was but a drop of rain in the ocean, but that wasn't his nature. He *did* take it personally, whether it was meant that way or not.

The warm-up ended. Heart heavy, Michael followed his teammates and the coach back off the ice and into the locker room. As Ty talked about strategy and Kevin tried to get them pumped up, all the guys not playing that night slipped out of their uniforms. Trying not to feel self-conscious, Michael changed back into his street clothes right along with them, painfully aware of the excitement emanating from Jim Fabian, who'd been with the team two years and still didn't have a regular spot in the lineup. Michael was just finishing combing his hair when van Dorn came up to him, snapping gum and looking every inch the trouble-making little prick.

"Got the ax, huh?" the youngster chuckled as he took off his jersey.

Michael just stared at him, noting contemptuously how van Dorn looked like he'd just stepped out of a Tommy Hilfiger ad.

"Maybe you should think about retiring and save yourself the pain and humiliation of eventually losing your spot on the third line to me."

"And maybe *you* should kiss my ring," Michael snapped back, shoving his Stanley Cup champion ring right in the pubescent wonder's face. Still infuriated by van Dorn's mocking chuckle, Michael shoved him as he went past. "Outta my way, frat boy."

"*Arriverderci,* gramps."

The urge to wheel around and pound that pretty little face into chop meat was strong, but Michael fought it, choosing instead to wish his teammates good luck while he and Guy La Temp headed toward the elevator that would take them to the skybox. They didn't wait for the others, not wanting to share the ride with van Dorn. Neither of them said a word as the elevator ascended. But as they walked through the opening doors, La Temp turned to Michael. "This sucks," he grumbled.

That said it all.

CHAPTER

03

Theresa and Janna were prepared for Ted Banister to sell them on the idea of Butler Corporation acquiring their business.

They weren't prepared for him showing up with a hottie in tow.

Both women arrived at the office early to get a head start on work. Despite protests that they were "ruthless slave-drivers hell-bent on exploiting his gentle nature," Terrence went out to pick up a tray of muffins and croissants they'd ordered from a nearby bakery. When he returned, he made a great show of plonking the tray down in the middle of the conference room table, declaring, "I give and I give and I give, and what do I get?"

"Health insurance," Theresa replied.

That shut him up.

Watching Janna raise then lower the conference room shades at least half a dozen times, Theresa knew her friend was nervous. But she also knew the minute Banister strolled through the door, Janna would morph into the

ultimate professional, all hints of anxiety completely sub-
merged. This transformation always amazed Theresa, who
was less skilled than Janna at masking her emotions. This
was why they'd agreed that Janna would do most of the
talking. Theresa still squirmed with embarrassment whenever Janna told the story of how, when they worked together at *The Wild and the Free,* Theresa had quietly
voiced the desire that one network exec's arms would
blacken, wither and fall to the ground, only to find out
that he was Sicilian, too, and had understood every word.

Definitely better to let Janna do most of the talking.

Theresa was both anxious and irritated. Like Janna, she
was afraid Banister would come in, and using corporate
doublespeak, threaten to blow them away. But she was
also resentful of the sheer greediness of Butler Corporation. Did they have to own *everything?* Couldn't they
leave a couple of the smaller firms, like theirs, alone?

Ted Banister arrived promptly at ten, looking distin-
guished in a steel-gray, Italian silk suit and Bally shoes as
he flashed a smooth, nonthreatening smile no doubt per-
fected over years of corporate dealings. Theresa reckoned
him to be about fifty, judging by his mane of well-
groomed silver hair and the deeply grooved crow's feet
around his eyes. By his side, looking just as polished but
completely uncomfortable, was a young, handsome man
somewhere between twenty-five and thirty whom Ted introduced as his nephew, Reese Banister.

"Reese recently graduated from Harvard Law and is
eager to learn the ropes. I hope you don't mind if he sits
in on our meeting."

"Not at all," Janna assured him, ushering both men into
the conference room.

Theresa followed right behind, closing the door. Since
Janna was now in pro mode, she had no way of telling
whether or not Janna really *did* mind if Reese was there.
Theresa couldn't take her eyes off of him. He was preppie

gorgeous, with pale blue eyes, a strong jawline, and blond, sun-kissed hair that probably came from time spent playing touch football on the beach at Hyannis or Martha's Vineyard. He smiled at her shyly as he took the seat opposite. She acknowledged him with a polite nod of the head, as she settled back in her chair to hear out his uncle Ted.

Banister began by saying, "I'm here today because Butler Corporation has been watching your business since its inception two years ago. It's very impressed with the client roster you've managed to assemble in that short time. Clearly, the two of you are extraordinary business-women."

"Thank you," said Janna.

"Yes, thank you," Theresa echoed. Her gaze drifted across the table to Banister the Younger. He was staring at her. Flustered, she looked away, turning her attention back to Janna.

"We appreciate the compliment," said Janna, "but I'm sure you didn't come here to feed our egos."

"No, of course not." Banister coughed uncomfortably. Perhaps he was unused to Janna's form of directness. "I'm here to tell you Butler Corporation would very much like you to join their corporate family."

Janna folded her hands in front of her. "Now why would we want to do that, Mr. Banister?"

"Because such a partnership would be mutually benefi-cial."

"How?" Theresa interjected.

Both Banister and Janna swiveled to look at her, Janna's expression warning her not to start whispering an incantation to turn him into poultry.

Meanwhile, Ted Banister was smiling warmly at her with all the sincerity of a politician. "Allying yourself with Butler would afford you—how shall I say—a safety net which you currently lack. Since you'd be part of a larger organization, there would be less pressure on the two of you individually to secure clients simply to meet your monthly expenses."

"Interesting," Janna murmured. "What else?"

"You'd have the kind of extensive support staff you now lack: personal assistants, secretaries, artists . . ."

"But wouldn't *we* be support staff, in essence?" Janna countered. "I mean, we're talking about a buyout, aren't we? Theresa and I would become employees of Butler."

"Technically, true. But you'd maintain a great deal of independence," Banister insisted.

Janna and Theresa exchanged wary glances.

"Go on," said Theresa. She watched as the older man glanced pointedly at his nephew, who up until that second had still been concentrating all his attention on her. Or maybe he'd been eyeing the muffins in the middle of the table. *Shoot,* thought Theresa.

"I think what my uncle is talking about is this," said Reese, casually reaching for a brioche. Theresa's heart sank. It *had* been the baked goods, not her. "You'd be free to specialize in the areas you find most appealing and lucrative."

"But we'd still be employees no matter how you choose to frame it," said Janna.

"Interesting way of looking at things," Ted Banister noted, tugging thoughtfully on his chin. "Suppose I told you that in order to acquire your company, Butler Corporation would be willing to pay a substantial multiple of earnings?"

"Can I have that in English, please?" Theresa asked bluntly. Across the table, she caught the look of amusement on Reese's face, and flushed. *He thinks I'm witty,* she thought, feeling very pleased with herself. Maybe he did like her better than the brioche.

"It means they're willing to pay us more than we're really worth," Janna explained.

Ted Banister laughed coldly. "That's a little blunt."

"It's also a little true," Janna rejoined.

"I realize this might be a bit much to take in right now." Banister slid his card across the table to Janna. "Why don't you think about what we've discussed and give me a call in a few days if you have any questions?"

"Thank you, we will." She glanced at both Banister and his nephew. "Can I get you gentlemen anything else? Some more coffee?"

Ted Banister's smile was reptilian. "I'm fine, thank you." He turned to Reese. "Shall we?"

Reese hurriedly swallowed the bite of pastry in his mouth and rose, rounding the table to join his uncle. Theresa and Janna rose, too, and together they led the two Banisters out to the lobby, Theresa acutely aware of the younger man's appraising gaze. *Goddess of Undergarments,* she prayed, *don't let me have visible panty lines.* After cordially wishing both men good day, they hurriedly reconvened to Janna's office for a postmortem, closing the door so that Terrence couldn't hear what they were saying.

"Well, that was short and sweet," said Janna with a pronounced frown. "So what did you think?"

"I don't know," Theresa admitted. "What do you think?"

"That they'll try to bury us if we turn down their offer."

"How much do you think it will be?"

"A lot." She didn't sound happy.

"The nephew was cute," Theresa noted lamely, apropos of nothing.

"Yes, I noticed the two of you making eyes over the muffin tray."

"Hardly," Theresa sniffed.

"Well, thank God that's over," said Janna, massaging

the back of her neck. She glanced at her watch. "*And* you won't be late for the softball game."

"Lucky me." She watched Janna. "You gonna be okay?"

"Of course. You?"

"Totally," Theresa scoffed. But neither would quite meet the other's eyes.

Theresa wasn't a big softball fan, probably because she'd never been to a game when she wasn't working. By the time she got back to the office in the late afternoon she was exhausted, and wanted nothing more than to shut her door and steal fifteen minutes for a power nap. But just as she was preparing to close her eyes, Terrence buzzed.

So much for recharging her batteries.

She pushed down the intercom button. "Yes?"

"That *extremely* adorable blond boy who was here this morning is back to see you," Terrence murmured breathily into the phone.

Theresa immediately perked up. "Reese Banister?"

"Uh huh."

"And did he hear the less than professional way you just described him?" Theresa chided, doing a quick check of her office to make sure it wasn't too much of a mess.

"Give me some credit, please," Terrence replied in a low but indignant voice. "He's in the lobby area thumbing through an issue of *Men's Health*."

"Did he say what he wants?"

"Something about wanting you to bear his children. It was too graphic, so I blocked the rest out."

"You're treading on thin ice, Terrence. I hope you realize that."

"Yes, but you love me anyway. Shall I send him back?"

"Please."

She released the intercom button, and rising, smoothed the front of her slacks before pinching some color back into her cheeks and hurriedly applying a coat of lipstick. God, was she pathetic or what? When the anticipated knock sounded, she squared her shoulders and stood up straight. Physically, she felt more than presentable. But her emotional state was another matter. Her insides were buzzing like an excited school girl's.

She opened the door. "Reese." She didn't need to fabricate a smile. "This is a surprise."

"Not a bad one, I hope." He returned her smile with one of his own that left Theresa feeling distinctly fluttery. "Can I come in?"

"Of course."

Standing in the doorway, she watched as his eyes traveled over every surface in her office, stopping when he got to her Miro lithograph.

"You like Miro?" he asked, sounding surprised.

Theresa didn't know whether to be flattered or insulted as she nodded. "Do you?"

"A great deal." He continued surveying her office, then became aware of what he was doing and stopped. "I'm sorry," he apologized. "You have such an interesting office, so many books and things, I couldn't resist checking it all out."

"It's all right." She took a step toward him. "What can I help you with?"

"After we left, it dawned on me we'd forgotten to give you some info we'd brought with us about Butler Corporation and its most recent acquisitions."

"Oh. So you stopped back with it. How nice." Theresa smiled again, this time to hide her disappointment. *Business. He's only here on business.*

Sitting down, Reese opened his briefcase on his knees and extracted the paper in question. Theresa feigned scanning it, even going so far as nodding her head thought-fully. Who was she kidding? There was no way she could concentrate with him watching her. She put the paper down on her desk.

"I'll be sure to share it with Janna," she said. He smiled. She smiled. Then an awkward silence descended. Theresa, never good with uncertainty, rushed to fill the vacuum.

"So, you're entering the family business?" she asked.

Surprisingly, Reese seemed grateful for her interest. "I'm sure you could tell at the meeting this morning how enthused I am about it."

"You don't want to be a lawyer?"

"That is *exactly* what I'm saying."

"Then why are you?" Theresa wondered aloud.

"Why am I what?"

"Why are you a lawyer?"

Reese sighed, leaning back in the chair as he wearily ran a hand through his hair. "Because that's what good blue bloods do. They become politicians or lawyers." He looked embarrassed, almost furtive, as he quietly con-fessed, "What I really wanted was to be a photographer."

"You're kidding. I wanted to be a writer," Theresa blurted, wondering if that was the sort of thing you should confess up front to a virtual stranger who could possibly give you three beautiful, towheaded children and a sum-mer house on the Cape. Well, hell, he'd just told her what his dream had been, right? The polite thing to do was reci-procate. She could see his interest was piqued.

"So why didn't you pursue it?" he asked.

Theresa shrugged, feeling self-conscious now. "I still write for myself. And PR allows me some creativity in terms of writing press releases, which I enjoy." She cast around for the right words with which to explain why she wasn't this month's selection for Reading with Ripa. "But when I graduated from college, no one bothered to tell me there wouldn't be a job waiting for me at *The New Yorker*."

Reese laughed appreciatively. "I hear you. The same people didn't tell me that when you get a poli sci degree at Harvard, you don't go on to become Ansel Adams. Or if you try, it's certainly not going to provide you with a living wage."

Theresa scrunched up her nose. "Not a very fair world, is it?"

"No, it is not." Curiosity informed his face. "What do you like to write?" Against her will, Theresa could feel her cheeks turning crimson.

"I've embarrassed you," Reese noted softly. "I'm sorry."

"No, it's all right," Theresa hastily assured him. "It's just been a long time since anyone has asked me about my writing. It caught me off guard."

"Tell you what," Reese proposed. "I'll tell you what I like to photograph, and you tell me what you like to write."

"Deal."

They laughed together then, the easy laughter of two people who feel completely simpatico. *God help me,* Theresa thought. *He's handsome, artistic, smart . . .* After swapping artistic confessions, another small, strained silence descended, but this time it was Reese who ended it. "I guess I should be going," he said with what sounded to Theresa like reluctance.

Give him your phone number. Now. Theresa's brain urged action. But she remained frozen. Scared.

Reese tugged uncomfortably at the collar of his shirt. "So, um, as my uncle said, if you and Janna have any questions, feel free to give us a call." He fumbled for a card in the breast pocket of his blazer, a move Theresa found charmingly inept. "Here," he said, handing it to her with a shrug. "Call anytime."

"I will. I mean, if I—we—have any questions." *Give him your damn number!* her brain howled at her. She flashed a quick smile, glad he couldn't read her thoughts, and showed him to the door.

"Can you find your way out?"

"I think so."

"Enjoy the rest of your afternoon," Theresa said, thinking, *Just give him your number, fool!!!*

"You, too," he answered. He walked halfway up the hall, then stopped and turned around. Theresa held her breath. *Please ask me out for coffee, pleeeeasssee.*

But whatever it was he planned to say, clearly he thought better of it. Looking sheepish, he turned back around and continued down the hallway.

Two days later, Theresa found herself enjoying a crisp, fall breeze as she descended from the subway platform atop the Eighty-sixth Street station and walked east to her parents' house on Bay Twenty-sixth Street. Before leaving Manhattan, she had gone crosstown to Balducci's to pick up the special Pernigotti soft nougat her father loved. It was out of her way, but Theresa didn't mind, since it seemed to make him so happy. If she couldn't please him by marrying a nice Italian boy and having kids, at least she could bring him his favorite Italian candy.

Going to dinner at her parents' house always made her anxious. It wasn't that she didn't love seeing them, because she did. And you'd never hear her complaining about her mother's food; it was the one time each week she actually enjoyed a home-cooked meal, being somewhat immune to the kitchen herself. But it was hard to see the robust man her father had been wasting away with cancer. Hard, too, to deal with her family's unwillingness to validate all she'd achieved professionally. Deep down, she knew they were proud of her. She just wished they'd throw her the occasional bone by coming out and telling her so, rather than teasing her in a way that made her feel defensive.

Still, it felt good to be out walking her old stomping grounds. All over Bensonhurst, families were preparing their post-Mass, Sunday afternoon meals. Theresa passed house after house that looked just like her parents: small brick homes with wrought iron fences and postage stamp-sized front yards. Theresa liked the way each house strove to make itself unique, whether by painting the fence, creating an ornately sculpted topiary, or putting a statue of the Virgin Mary or St. Anthony on display. Her parents had broken with tradition somewhat, their front yard featuring a row of waist high, perfectly shorn hedges *and* a statue of St. Francis, whom her mother loved because of his kindness to animals. When Theresa was young, the statue had mortified her; she saw it as proof of her parents' failure to fully assimilate despite being second generation Americans. Now it comforted her in an odd way she didn't really want to think about.

Rounding the corner of her parents' street, she recognized her brother's Explorer parked outside their house and frowned with disapproval. Phil lived ten minutes away, tops. Why couldn't he, Debbie and the kids walk over? It was gorgeous outside, a perfect day for a stroll. But she knew her brother: If she brought it up, he'd accuse her of being a "wacko environmentalist." That was the problem with Phil—with all of them, actually. They couldn't understand why anyone would *think* differently than them, never mind lead a different kind of life.

Passing through the gate, Theresa walked the six steps up to her parents' tiny stoop and pushed open the front door, which was never locked on Sunday. There in the living room, her father sat in his Barcalounger watching the Giants game, a canister of oxygen on the floor beside him.

And on the couch were her brother, Phil, and Michael Dante.

Theresa stared at Michael, dumbfounded.

"Um . . ." She struggled to find her voice. "No offense, but what are you doing here?"

Michael looked to his left, then to his right, then back at Theresa questioningly. "Are you talking to me?"

"Who are you, Travis Bickel?" She turned to her father. "Dad?"

"Mmm?" Her father's eyes, huge and distorted behind his thick glasses, were glued to the TV set. "Your mother and I invited him," he replied distractedly.

"What?" Theresa spluttered. *"Why?"*

Her brother shook his head disapprovingly. "Whatever happened to 'Hello, how ya doin',' maybe taking your coat off?"

"Butt out," said Theresa.

Phil nudged Michael in the ribs. "Nice girl, huh? Talks to her brother like that."

Michael's hands went up in a gesture of surrender. "Hey, I don't want to get in the middle of anything here."

"Too late," Theresa mumbled. Grim, she slipped out of her coat and hung it on the coat rack by the front door. Then she sidled over to her father's chair. "I bought you some nougat," she cooed.

Her father glanced up into her face appreciatively. *"Cara mia.* How sweet."

Her voice dropped down to a whisper. "But you're not getting it until you tell me what he's doing here." She jerked a thumb in Michael's direction.

Her father looked back and forth between her and Michael in bewilderment. "You two know each other?"

Oh, that was rich. That was good. She turned to Michael with what she hoped was a storm brewing in her eyes. *You are going to rue the day you ever cooked up this little scheme, Puckhead.*

Michael obviously had no trouble reading her expression, because he volunteered to answer the question— fearful, Theresa assumed, that if he didn't come clean she would soon divest him of more than his teeth.

"Theresa's agency is putting together the PR campaign for Dante's."

Theresa's father nodded, impressed. "Is that so?"

"Yes, it is," Theresa replied. "Now tell me why you invited him."

"Because he's a very nice boy," her father declared. "He stopped over here at the beginning of the week with some food from the restaurant for us and wanted to know all about how I was feeling. They noticed we hadn't been to Dante's for a while."

"So—?"

Her father shrugged. "It was your mother's idea. Ask her."

"Fine. I will."

She spun on her heels and was heading toward the kitchen when Phil called out her name. "What?" Theresa snapped, stopping dead in her tracks in the dining room, where the table was all set and ready to go.

"Hand over the nougat."

Doubling back to the living room, she fetched the bag of nougat from her purse and hurled it at her brother like a baseball. "She's got some temper on her, that one," she heard him say to Michael as she disappeared into the kitchen.

The tableau greeting her was one she'd seen a hundred times before: her mother standing at the counter, arranging the ingredients for the antipasto on a platter with the precision of an artist, while her sister-in-law, Debbie, stood at the kitchen table, putting together a salad. Farther down the table, Theresa's niece, Vicki, and nephew, Philly Junior, ages seven and nine respectively, sat coloring. Baby Carmen, three months old, sat gurgling in a baby

seat on the floor. When the two older children spotted
Theresa, they jumped up and ran to embrace her.

"Aunt Theresa! You're here!"

"Aunt Theresa, you look beautiful!"

"Hey, rugrats." She leaned over to kiss both of them
and without prompting, slipped off the phalanx of silver
bracelets encircling her left wrist and handed them to
Vicki. This was their own little tradition: Whenever
Theresa came to Sunday dinner, she would give her
bracelets to Vicki to wear for the duration of her visit. The
little girl loved slipping them on and off and playing with
them.

"Hey, Ma." Theresa gave her mother a kiss on the
cheek, doing the same with her sister-in-law.

"Did you meet Michael?" her mother asked, glancing
slyly at Theresa out of the corner of her eye.

"Ma, I already know Michael. He's a client." She was
working hard to keep the annoyance she was feeling out
of her voice.

"He's single," her mother continued, rolling up a piece
of cappicola and putting it on the plate.

Theresa looked at her sister-in-law imploringly, but it
was clear she wasn't going to get any assistance from that
quarter. There was only one possible rejoinder. "So?" It
was pathetic, but right now she couldn't think of anything
else to say.

"So he's nice. And *Italian*," her mother practically
sang.

"*So?*" Theresa repeated.

"Forget it, Ma," her sister-in-law called out to
Theresa's mother. "She don't wanna hear it."

"No, I don't," said Theresa. "Did it ever occur to you
two busybodies that I might not want to go near a professional hockey player with a ten-foot pole?"

"I don't know why you still act like it was such a

trauma," said Debbie offhandedly as she sliced a cucumber. "I mean, it's not like you were actually raped."

Vicki looked up from her coloring. "Mom, what's—"

"Nothing," Debbie cut in. "You just concentrate on your coloring."

But to Theresa, who felt as though her sister-in-law had just kicked her in the teeth, it *was* something. She crouched down beside her niece, stroking the girl's thick brown hair.

"Vicki, would you and Philly mind going into the living room to play for a few minutes? I need to talk to Mommy and Grandma privately."

"Ooookay." Vicki huffed, reluctantly picking up her coloring book and crayons as she followed her brother out of the room. Theresa waited until she was certain they were out of earshot before sliding into the chair Vicki had vacated. Debbie was family. They'd known each other for years. So why was she so worried her voice might crack with anger?

"What you just said really hurt me, Deb."

"But—"

"Let me finish." Theresa could feel the walls of her throat closing in. *Please, God,* she prayed, *let me be able to get the words out without crying.* "Have you ever had a man force his tongue into your mouth when you didn't want him to?"

Debbie was silent.

"How about having a man grope your breasts against your will, or stick his hand up your skirt to try to shove a finger inside you?"

"Theresa." Her mother's voice was anxious.

"That happened to me," Theresa continued in a quivering voice. "I was also punched in the face and called a bitch and a whore. But according to you, none of that counts."

Debbie's eyes darted away as her face colored red with mortification. "That's not what I said."

Theresa began to tremble. "No, but it's what you implied, whether you realize it or not."

"*Cara.*" Theresa's mother's voice was gentle as she approached her from behind and placed two loving hands on her daughter's shoulders. "No one doubts that little Russian *farabutto* hurt you, or questions why you might have a hard time trusting. But Michael's not like that."

Theresa turned to look up into her mother's eyes. "How do you *know?*" she asked plaintively. "He brings you a plate of ziti and you know his life story?"

"I just know," her mother insisted stubbornly.

"Well, I don't," Theresa replied. "And I would appreciate it if you quit playing matchmaker."

Her mother muttered something under her breath—a prayer for Theresa's obstinate soul, no doubt—and doubling back to the stove, handed her the now completed plate of antipasto. "Would you bring this out to the table and call the men into the dining room?"

"Sure."

Theresa took the tray and did as her mother asked, gratefully accepting her sister-in-law's apology on her way out of the room. She went to help her father out of his chair, but he was already being aided by Michael, whom, she noticed, took the not-so-subtle opportunity of sitting down right across from her at the table. Maybe her mother was right, she thought, as her father led the family through saying grace. Maybe Michael wasn't "like that." But Theresa wasn't about to risk finding out.

"So, Ter," said her brother, heaping his plate high. "Did you know Michael plays for the Blades?"

"No, I didn't," deadpanned Theresa. "I just moved here from Mars. Tell me more."

"He's a successful, famous athlete but he still lives in

Brooklyn," her father added, his eyes flashing with significance.

"Maybe he's not successful enough to afford the rent in Manhattan," Theresa pointed out coolly.

"Or, maybe he hasn't forgotten where he comes from," said Phil.

"Whoa, folks, please," Michael appealed as he looked around the table. "Let's get off the subject of me and talk about something interesting here, like who's going to make it into the Superbowl."

Theresa's family seemed to take the hint, and for that she was grateful. Talk of football led to talk of individual players, and Michael had her family laughing until they damn near cried telling them about the time he and some of the Blades tried to take on a couple of the Giants in an impromptu touch football game.

Was he always this entertaining or was he putting on a show for her approval?

Whichever it was, she was forced to admit he seemed able to hold his own on any number of subjects and appeared to have a never-ending supply of amusing stories, which he told with great flourish. He also appeared to be an all-around good guy, even going so far as letting little Vicki crawl all over him during dessert, despite her mother's protestations. Even so, it creeped Theresa out that he was even *here*. It was like one of those bad, B-grade horror films where someone seemingly innocent worms his way into a family, only to turn around and dismember them in their sleep a few months later.

Every once in a while, Michael's eyes would seek hers for some kind of confirmation, which Theresa would pointedly ignore, giving him the look Janna had christened "The Ball Shriveler." She wanted to make her displeasure at his presence clear. It was icky. Deceitful.

And it wasn't going to work.

CHAPTER

04

"Mind if I walk with you to the subway?"

To Michael's mind, it was a simple enough question, but Theresa looked as though she were deciding the fate of nations while she buttoned up her coat.

"Sure," she finally said, her voice noncommittal as she waited for him to finish up his good-byes to her family. Walking up Eighty-sixth Street together, Theresa's pace was closer to a sprint than a walk.

"What's the big rush?" Michael asked, hustling to keep up.

"I don't want to miss my train."

"You won't." He checked his watch. "You have a few minutes left."

Theresa said nothing. He might be wrong, but Michael could swear she looked kind of annoyed, the way she had all through dinner. He knew he had some explaining to do. "Theresa, I swear to you, I did not bring your parents a care package to worm my way into your family."

"Right."

"Look, I brought your parents some stuff from the restaurant because it felt like the right thing to do. And I won't lie, I was hoping that maybe, the next time they talked to you, they'd mention I'd been over and say what a nice guy I was."

"Or invite you for dinner so you could ambush me, and I'd have no way of escaping."

"No. *No!*" He put his hand over his heart. "I swear on my mother's grave that is not what I was thinking."

"No?" Her left eyebrow was practically touching the sky. "Then what *were* you thinking?"

"I never expected a dinner invitation. And when it came, all I could think about was how I hadn't had a Sunday family dinner since my mom died. I was so thrilled I didn't stop to think how it might look to you," he said quietly. "I'm sorry, Theresa."

That seemed to do it. The truth always did. Theresa slowed her pace and her expression relaxed.

"You and your brother don't have any family?" she asked.

"Yeah, we do, but it's not the same. My mother was always the one who did Sunday dinner. She was the best cook."

"Hmmm." She seemed to be mulling this over. "You should have checked with me first to ask how I felt about it," she said, almost sounding apologetic.

"I'm sorry." He peered at her, trying to get those big, almond-shaped green eyes of hers to look directly into his. But she wouldn't. Jesus, she was stubborn. Her eyes remained fixed straight ahead.

"Apology accepted," she said.

Delighted to have reached a state of détente, Michael was eager to keep the ball rolling. "So we're friends now?" he ventured.

"I wouldn't go *that* far," Theresa returned in a tone bordering on affectionate.

"No?" Michael asked, thrilled to witness the return of a more playful Theresa. "How far would you go?"

"Depends. I—"

She stopped herself. Michael could actually see it happening, Theresa willing herself to stop flirting with him. It was like a curtain fell over her face. The transformation was startling, the more so because he didn't understand it.

"Let's stick to business, Michael, okay?" Her tone was brisk.

Michael deflated. *Business. Sure.* "So how's the PR stuff coming?"

"It's coming. I'll call when l have everything ready and we can arrange a time to meet."

"How about we talk about it over dinner one night this week?" he asked politely.

"I don't think so."

"Coffee?"

"No."

No, no, always no. What the hell is her problem with me? "Look, do I have bad breath or something?" he blurted.

Theresa looked at him as if he'd just escaped from Bellevue. "What?"

He followed her up the steps leading to the subway platform. "Can I ask you something?"

"Sure."

"What do you have against me?"

She stared at him.

"Seriously," he continued.

"I don't have anything against you," she assured him, backing away slightly.

"So, then, what's the deal? One minute ago, we were having a nice conversation. Now you won't even go out for coffee with me. What gives?" She peered at him over the top of her glasses, the better for him to feel the full effect of her reserve, or so he imagined.

"Don't take this the wrong way, Michael. But I don't go out with guys whose last names end in vowels."

"What?" He peered at her quizzically. "Did you just say what I think you said? You won't go out with anyone Italian?"

"That's right."

"Why the hell not?"

"Because it's been my experience that Italian guys are not my cup of espresso, okay?"

"You've got to be kidding me." Utter disbelief overtook him. "What the hell is wrong with Italian guys?" he demanded. Beneath his feet, he could feel the platform beginning to vibrate; the train was coming. He didn't care. He'd get his answer before she hopped aboard if it killed him.

"Answer me, Theresa, c'mon!"

Her expression was pained as the train slowly pulled into the station. "They're macho, arrogant and rude. With the exception of their own mothers, they treat women like second-class citizens."

"WHAT!" He was yelling but he couldn't help it. Disbelief was losing the battle to outrage.

"You heard me."

"Have you ever been out with an Italian guy?"

"Yes."

"When?" he challenged.

"In high school."

"So you dated one stupid goomba in high school who treated you badly and you write the rest of us off? Give me a break!"

"The train's here, Michael, I have to go."

He watched as she stepped onto the train and slid into a seat right by the window. Unable to contain himself, he walked up to the train car and began pounding on the glass.

"You're wrong, Theresa."

The doors rolled shut and the train slowly began moving. Michael moved along with it.

"You're wrong! Not all Italian guys are Tony Soprano!" he shouted, still banging on the window. She had reached into her bag and cracked open a book. Maybe she was ignoring him, but the other passengers were staring. "You think you can stereotype *me*?" He was jogging along side the train car now. "Wait and see, Theresa! I'm going to make you see what you've been missing! I'm going to wear you down until you agree to coffee with me! I! AM! GOING! TO! WEAR! YOU! DOWN!"

He halted, catching his breath as the train sped out of sight. *Macho, arrogant and rude?* How dare she say that to him! He couldn't believe it. Suppose he'd said all Italian women have big hair and get mustaches after the change? She'd have cut his balls off! But it was okay for her to lump him in with every stupid *paisan* who ever drove a Camaro and wore a gold horn around his neck? Talk about unfair.

Well, he had a mission now, didn't he?

A challenging, off-ice mission.

Turning up the collar of his coat, he bounded back down the subway platform steps and hailed a cab to take him to his own apartment in Park Slope. He was going to prove to that narrow-minded, cynical woman that not all Italian men were created equal. He was also going to draw the real Theresa out of hiding for more than a few seconds at a time if it was the last thing he did.

The question was how?

"*Took your vitamins* this morning, huh?"

Michael turned from where he was pulling up his jeans to see van Dorn watching him from his own locker across the room.

"Bite me," said Michael, zipping up his fly.

"If I did, at least I'd be using all my own teeth."

Michael suppressed a smirk as he slid a long-sleeve T-shirt over his head. "All that proves is you're not a pro yet, kid. I wouldn't go bragging about it." That seemed to shut van Dorn up—for now.

This morning at practice, Michael had kicked ass on the ice. So much so that Ty commented on how focused he seemed. The irony, of course, was that his mind was on the Theresa problem the entire time. *Who knows?* he thought as he finished dressing. Maybe his anger over her refusing to give him the time of day was something he could channel into being a "more productive" player. It certainly seemed to do the trick this morning.

"Hey, Mikey," called out backup goalie Dennis O'Malley, clad only in a towel, which was threatening to fall to the floor at any moment. "Wanna grab a bite?"

"Nah, I gotta talk to Gilly about some stuff."

"You free tonight?" O'Malley continued.

"Yeah, why?"

"VH-1 is having some party and they invited a couple of us to come down. You game?"

"Sure. Leave the vitals on my answering machine and I'll see you there."

"Cool. Ciao."

"Ciao, Denny."

He dragged a comb through his still-wet hair, then went in search of Kevin Gill, the team's captain. Kevin had been happily married to the same woman for fifteen years and had a great family. Michael admired Kevin and thought he might be able to give him some valuable insight into how the female mind worked.

He found Kevin lying face-up on a massage table, his left thigh being kneaded by the team's top massage therapist.

"Hey, Gilly. Got a minute?" Michael approached the table.

Kevin chuckled. "Does it look like I'm going anywhere? What's up?"

Was it possible he was a total loser asking Kevin's advice on this stuff? Michael cleared his throat, stalling for time. Well, he'd find out in a minute or two. "I need your input on this woman I'm interested in."

"Anyone I know?"

Michael hesitated. Kevin did know Theresa. He was Ty's best friend, after all. And thanks to the sexual assault case a few years back, the whole team at the very least knew Theresa's name. Kevin was there the first time Michael had offered to buy Theresa a drink and she turned him down, and he'd been there at Ty and Janna's wedding when she'd repeatedly refused to dance with him. If he told Kevin who it was, chances were he'd tell him to get the hint and move on.

"No one you know," Michael lied.

"What's the problem?"

"This girl—this woman—won't go out with me. Not even for a cup of coffee."

Kevin gave a small growl of pain as the trainer moved farther down his leg and began massaging his shin. "Any idea why?"

"She says she never dates Italians."

"Huh?" Kevin looked bemused. "That's a new one."

"I know that if she'd just give me half a chance, she'd realize we could really hit it off. But I'm not sure how to get her to see that."

Kevin closed his eyes. "You know, when I first met Abby she didn't want anything to do with me."

"Really?" This was good to know. It made Michael feel hopeful. "So what did you do?"

"I wooed her." Kevin's mouth curled into a smile of remembrance. "I sent her flowers, I turned up where I knew she'd be. I was a real pest."

"And she fell for it?"

"Not right away." Kevin opened his eyes. "In fact, I remember her threatening to call the cops to have me arrested for stalking. But eventually, she was flattered. Or maybe just tired." He turned his head to look at Michael. "I can't believe you need advice—a dog like you, out on the town every night."

"Yeah, I get around. But I haven't had a serious relationship in . . ." He paused, trying to think of the last steady girlfriend he'd had. *Christine? No, that was four years ago. So, it had to be Dory. Dory was before he met Theresa.* "Two years."

"What happened?"

Michael shrugged. "She wanted to get married. I didn't."

"So you've just been screwing around since then?"

"Pretty much."

"Well, if you're serious about this woman, try wooing her in some way."

"What if it doesn't work? I mean, she seems like a pretty tough nut to crack."

"If it doesn't work, it's not meant to be."

"I guess," said Michael unenthusiastically. He went to the head of the table and patted his friend's shoulder. "Thanks for the advice, Kev. I appreciate it."

"Let me know how it turns out. Oh, and Mikey?"

"Yeah?"

"Don't be late for warm-up tomorrow night. Ty's loaded for bear."

"Gotcha."

Woo her. Two simple words, a not-so-simple woman. He had a gut feeling that flowers might be coming on too strong when it came to Theresa. But there were other weapons in the romantic arsenal he could use.

Though it was not yet nine, Theresa's morning had already been a nightmare. Not only did she wake up to find she had no hot water, but the subway was late, and some lollypop in a sky-high pair of Jimmy Choo's had stepped on her left foot, nearly severing her pinky toe. By the time she limped into the office, she was in a foul mood.

"Aren't we Little Mary Sunshinetti this morning," Terrence noted as she hobbled into reception.

"Don't start with me," Theresa warned.

"Maybe this will help." Terrence tapped the top of a small, white box.

"What is it?"

"Do I look like John Edward?" Terrence drawled. "It came for you about five minutes ago."

Intrigued, Theresa approached the box, and with Terrence watching, carefully opened it. Inside was a large, luscious square of tiramisu, along with a small white envelope, which she immediately extracted and opened. "Surrender, Theresa," was all it said. Theresa smiled, delighted in spite of herself as she slid the card back inside the envelope.

"Well?" Terrence demanded impatiently. "Spit it out. Inquiring minds want to know."

"It's tiramisu and it's none of your business who it's from."

Terrence's lips pursed in cool assessment. "Oh yeah? Well, I know a thing or two, Madame Mysterioso, and that is that you are *sweet* on whoever sent you that darling little cake."

"Wrong."

"Take it from one who knows you: Your sour little face lit up like a G.D. roman candle when you read the card. It's been a lo-o-o-ng time since I've seen you smile like that."

"I was smiling because I love tiramisu," Theresa insisted.

"Uh, huh, and Boy George is engaged to Rosie O'Donnell. Nice try." Terrence pulled the box toward him and looked inside. "Are you going to eat it? Because if you're not, I'll take it."

"Yes, I'm going to eat it," Theresa replied with fake annoyance.

Terrence pushed the box back her way. "A minute on the lips, a lifetime on the hips," he trilled.

"Tell me," said Theresa, closing up the pastry box. "Would you like me to fire you *now,* or should I wait until Friday?"

"Wait until Friday. That way my entire weekend will be ruined."

"Friday it is, then."

Walking to Janna's office, Theresa found it hard to keep from smiling. Loath as she was to admit it, she was charmed. But being *charmed* was different from being *impressed.* And she was *not* impressed. Not in the least. Unless, of course, he *meant* her to be charmed, in which case she wasn't. Whatever Michael Dante wanted her to be, she was the opposite.

She arrived to find Janna looking like she was about to lose her breakfast.

"What?" Theresa asked, concerned. "What is it?"

"You will not believe who I just got off the phone with."

"Who?"

"Robert Turner."

Theresa groaned as she deposited the pastry box on Janna's desk along with some papers and pulled up a chair. Turner was Janna's ex-boyfriend, a poet whom Theresa had hated on sight when their paths first crossed well over five years ago. He was pretentious, spoke in a fake French accent and claimed to be a "poet of the people." He was also a jerk.

"What did he want?" Theresa asked, dreading the answer.

Janna's eyes met hers, stunned. "Aegis Press is publishing a book of his poems."

"What?" Theresa knew she had just squawked like a deranged parrot but she couldn't help it.

"They're doing in-house PR," Janna continued, "but he wants to hire us to do some as well."

"You could tell him no."

Janna was already shaking her head. "We need to make as much money as we can right now." She peeked inside the pastry box, then looked at Theresa. "Did you buy this on the way to work?"

"I'll explain in a minute. Do you have any forks?"

"Sure." Janna opened her lower desk drawer and pulled out two plastic ones from a box she kept there while Theresa dragged a chair over to the desk. Janna handed Theresa a fork and they both dug in.

"Mmm, this is outrageous," Janna murmured, gulping down some coffee. "Theresa, you have to handle Robert. Please. I cannot sit down and listen to him talk for hours about his struggle as an *artiste*. I'll put a bullet in my brain, you know I will." She slumped in her chair. "I can't believe Aegis is going to publish him. He's awful."

"I remember," Theresa said, taking another bite. "Maybe he's improved?"

"Maybe." Janna ate some more. Theresa didn't blame her. It was that good. Plus, the prospect of dealing with Robert—"Call me Ro-*bear*"—Turner could drive anyone to stress eating.

"What do you want me to do?" Theresa asked.

Janna took another forkful. "I guess you'd better call him back and set up an appointment."

"And what do I get in exchange for this incredible act of kindness?"

"My undying gratitude."

"And—?"

"I'll let you finish this tiramisu." Janna threw her fork

into the garbage. "What's the mystery behind this heavenly pastry?"

Theresa heaved a sigh. "It's from Michael Dante."

"He sent this?" Janna went misty-eyed. "That is so romantic."

"What?" Theresa scoffed. She'd show Janna how romantic it was. She proceeded to tell her the whole sordid tale of how Michael had taken advantage of her parents, weaseling a dinner invitation by bringing them a plate of food from the restaurant. She did *not* tell Janna how she almost fell back into her old habit of mindless flirting as they walked to the train station. Janna would latch on to that like a terrier on a plump, juicy ankle. When she was done, she sat back triumphantly.

"I think you're wrong about Michael," Janna said quietly.

Theresa blinked. She had fully expected Janna to agree that it was wrong of Michael to surprise her like that at her parents' home. "*Excuse* me?"

"I know him better than you, Ter, and I'm sure his bringing food to your folks was completely on the level."

"He *admitted* he was hoping they'd put in a good word for him!"

"Well, he's honest. But he has a big heart. Ty once found him giving out care packages of ziti to some of the homeless guys who congregate around the entrance to Penn Station."

"So nominate him for sainthood," Theresa interrupted.

"He's no saint, that's for sure. He's got a wicked temper."

"Tell me about it. I thought his head was going to pop off on the train platform when I told him I don't date Italian guys."

"I don't blame him."

Theresa's heart sank in dismay. "You're supposed to be supportive of me, not him. That's what best friends do."

"You're being arbitrary and unfair. One cup of coffee with Michael Dante wouldn't kill you."

"Yes, it would. Besides, he's a *client*. I want this relationship to remain strictly professional, thank you."

"You mean like mine and Ty's did?" Janna asked, eyeing the last small bite of cake. Theresa pushed the box to Janna and handed over her fork.

"You and Ty were different," said Theresa.

"How?"

"You liked Ty. I don't like Michael." *I won't let myself,* she added in her head.

"But you like that he sent you a present," Janna crooned.

"Shut up, will you, please?" Theresa said with a sigh. This whole exchange was reminding her of a bad after-school special, teenage girls teasing each other into revealing secret crushes. . . . If she *were* flattered that Michael had sent her the pastry—which she wasn't— Janna was the *last* person she'd admit it to. Janna would go running to Ty and Ty would say something to Michael at practice and then it would be all over. It would be *exactly* like high school.

She watched as Janna finished the cake and tipped the empty box and remaining fork into the trash. Obviously, the tiramisu was made by Michael's brother, and that bode well for the restaurant. If she did her job right, Toothless Michael the Noodge and Chef Anthony the Nut were going to be elevated to a level they never dreamed of. She could already imagine the review in the *New York Times,* the four-star rating . . . and it would all be because of her hard work and creativity. And the food, of course.

"Theresa?"

Blinking the daydream away, she turned to her friend. "Mmm?"

"I'm sorry to push you about Michael. I know you hate

it. It's just that it's been so long since you've gone out with anyone, and he's such a nice guy—"

Theresa made a zipping gesture across her lips and Janna shut up.

The subject was closed.

Three days and three more dessert deliveries to the office forced Theresa down to the gym at Chelsea Piers for an hour-long session on a cross trainer. Between the tiramisu, sfogliatelle, olive-oil cake and almond cookies, she didn't want to think about how many calories she had ingested. She had to hand it to Michael: He was persistent.

Not to mention creative; other guys might have tried flowers or perfume.

She increased both the exertion and elevation level on the elliptical. Perspiration seemed to be pouring off her in buckets, rivulets running between her breasts and down her back. *Just ten more minutes to go,* she thought, as she mopped her dripping face with a towel and took a large gulp of Evian. She tried to resume reading the book she'd brought, but the truth was that she could never concentrate on words when she was working out. She wound up reading the same paragraph over and over. She wished she'd brought her Walkman with her. At least then she could zone out listening to music.

She was panting her way through her final four minutes when she thought she heard someone say her name. She looked up to see a blond vision looking buff and delectable and standing only a few feet away from her.

Reese Banister.

"I didn't know you worked out here," he said. He was wearing gray sweat pants and a plain white T-shirt.

"Yeah . . . I . . . do," Theresa managed breathlessly. *This is not happening. I am not standing here on this ma-*

chine with no makeup on, drenched in sweat and stinking to high heaven, in front of this man. It is a hallucination. If I blink once, he will go away.

She blinked.

"What are you reading?" he asked with interest.

Shit.

"Um . . . uh . . ." Theresa stopped peddling in an effort to catch her breath. Mortification had struck her mute. She could barely form words. She sounded like a grunting idiot. In a few seconds, he would realize this and turn away from her in disgust. Quickly, she handed her book to him.

"Wuthering Heights," he read out loud. "Hooked on the classics, huh?"

"I like to read it once a year," she told him, her breathing beginning to normalize somewhat.

"So you're a romantic," he murmured.

Theresa could feel herself blush straight up to the roots of her sweaty hair. "I guess."

"Have you ever seen the movie? he asked. "You know, the original, with Laurence Olivier and Merle Oberon?"

Theresa nodded, her heart pounding wildly. She adored that movie. She could quote huge chunks of dialogue from it. Her impersonation of Cathy flinging herself across the rainy moors howling "Heathcliff!" was famous. "You've seen it?" she ventured.

"Oh, yeah," said Reese. He looked almost bashful. "I love old movies."

"Me, too," Theresa confessed.

"Name your favorite."

Theresa shook her head, tongue-tied. "I couldn't. There are so many."

"Top three, then," Reese goaded.

Theresa thought hard, trying to ignore the glare from a nearby woman who clearly thought she should surrender the cross trainer. "*Gone with the Wind* is definitely up there," she said slowly. "*Strangers on a Train* . . . *Casablanca.*"

"You can't say *Casablanca*. Everyone says *Casablanca*."

"I was unaware there were rules to this game."

"That's the only one," Reese promised.

"Okay, then. *A Streetcar Named Desire*."

Reese's eyes lit with unexpected surprise. "That's in my top three, too!"

"What are your other two?" Theresa asked.

While Reese contemplated the question, Theresa grappled with the excitement welling up within her. They shared so many common interests, interests she never thought she'd find embodied in one man. Like a flower long buried under snow, Theresa could feel herself thawing and preparing to bloom. It was a feeling she hadn't experienced since before the Lubov incident. She gratefully welcomed its return.

Reese snapped his fingers. "Got it! *Bridge Over the River Kwai* and *Zulu*."

"Those are *guy* films."

"So? They're great."

"I'm not sure I agree."

"Well, we'll just have to have our own film festival some time and see who's right."

Theresa blushed again, prompting Reese to cough uncomfortably. Looking apologetic, he handed the book back to her. "Sorry I interrupted your workout."

"No, it's okay," she said, patting the back of her neck with a towel. "I was almost done anyway."

"You don't look like you need to work out."

"Believe me, I do. If I didn't go to the gym my butt would have its own zip code." *What was she saying?! Here they'd had a nice, relaxed, intellectual conversation—he'd even flirted with her, if she wasn't mistaken—and she had to ruin it by putting herself down like some self-deprecating twit?? Time. To. Shut. Up.* Theresa tried to be cool as she reached for her Evian bottle and drank deeply. Unfortunately, the water went down the wrong pipe. She leapt off the cross trainer coughing and spluttering.

"Theresa! Are you all right?" Reese asked, alarmed.

"Fine," Theresa wheezed, humiliated. *Slow breaths, take nice slow breaths, then run away as fast as you can.*

"You sure you're okay?" He looked genuinely concerned.

"Fine, fine," Theresa croaked.

"I was wondering . . . have you and Janna had a chance to look at that memo I gave you?"

Business. "We've looked at it," she told him, "but we haven't had a chance to discuss it."

"Oh, okay. That's fine. Ummm, maybe you and I could get together over drinks Friday night?" he asked casually. "To talk about it," he added. And then said shyly, "And other, more important things like writing and photography and old movies. Are you free?"

Not business! "Sure!" The urge to resume coughing and spluttering returned, this time from sheer disbelief. "I mean, I think so. I mean, I have to check my PalmPilot and get back to you." *I mean, I should just nod and be quiet!*

"Great." His smile was infectious. "What if I give you a call at work to finalize plans?"

Theresa nodded. "That sounds good," she said.

"Okay, then. I guess I'll see you Friday." He pointed in the direction of the rowing machines. "I'm going to work out. Have a good night."

"You, too," said Theresa, collecting her things and heading straight to the locker room to shower.

I have a date, she thought, amazed. *Maybe it's time.*

CHAPTER
05

Fall was in the air. Theresa could feel its invigorating bite, and every tree she passed proudly displayed its new wardrobe of oranges, reds and yellows. For most people, the new year began in January. But for Theresa, it always started in the fall, when the hot, dreamy days of summer officially ended and everyone was forced back to the realities of work or school. To her, autumn was a time laden with possibility. Normally, spending a glorious day like this on a non-Sunday trip to Bensonhurst would dampen her spirits.

Not today.

She was meeting Reese Banister for drinks tonight. She imagined his face illumined by flickering candlelight as his sensitive blue eyes unlocked the secret of her soul. . . .

Stop.

Now was not the time to fantasize.

She had arrived at Dante's and had work to do.

The door to the restaurant was open, and she ducked

inside. It had been a month since she'd last seen Michael, running like a lunatic beside her train. In the interim, she'd been busting her butt coming up with a good plan for putting Dante's on the map. Her gut instinct was that Michael—irritating as he was—would be open to her suggestions. It would be an uphill battle with his brother. As her eyes adjusted to the light, she saw Michael sitting at the same table as last time.

But he wasn't dressed casually in jeans and a tennis shirt.

This time he was wearing tight black polyester pants and a sleeveless white undershirt known in some circles as a "wife beater." Around his neck was a giant, gold Italian horn. On his left hand, an ostentatious pinky ring. On his right wrist, a braided gold bracelet thick as a dog collar. His hair was slicked back and a toothpick dangled suggestively from his lips.

"Hey, babe," he crooned as she approached the table. "What took ya so long?"

Theresa bit her lip, but it was no use; she burst out laughing. "What on earth—?"

"Wha? I'm an *Italian* guy, right? So I figured I'd bedda start lookin' and actin' da part." He slouched down his chair, opening his legs wide. "Lookin' good today, sweetcakes. My wife's working late. Wanna go out dancin'?"

"Stop it," Theresa begged.

"Stop what?"

"Fine." Theresa slid into the seat opposite him. "I was wrong. Now cut the wiseguy act. You're giving me the creeps."

"Okay, baby. Anyting for you." Michael straightened up in his chair, removing the toothpick from his mouth. "Better?"

"A bit." Theresa found herself smiling. "You need your head examined," she told him.

Michael grinned. "It got a reaction out of you, didn't it?"

"I suppose," Theresa admitted begrudgingly.

Michael noticed her eyes do a circuit of his body, pausing to admire his bare biceps. He held up his right arm, making a fist and flexing his arm. "You wanna cop a feel, baby? Be my guest."

Giggling, Theresa reached out to briefly touch the rock-hard muscle.

"Nice and hard, huh?" Michael asked.

"Oooh, very hard," Theresa snorted, playing along.

"Just the way the ladies like it," Michael confided. "Wanna touch the other one?"

Theresa started to speak, then stopped, heat rising to her cheeks. *Stop,* a voice in her head warned. *Stop now. This is exactly the kind of behavior that got you in trouble in the first place. Stop flirting. Stick to business.* "Let's discuss the restaurant instead, shall we?" she returned lightly. But even as she said it, she was having a hard time keeping her eyes off his body. And that bracelet! "Where did you get that jewelry?"

"The horn is Anthony's. The ring and the bracelet belong to my cousin Paul."

"Or Paul*ie*," Theresa replied quickly, "as he's probably known."

Frowning with disappointment, Michael slouched again and shoved the toothpick back between his lips. "You're doin' it again, angel."

"Sorry," Theresa muttered grouchily, relieved when he grabbed a flannel shirt off the back of his chair and covered up the well-sculpted arms and shoulders she'd never noticed before today.

Divested of his toothpick, he smiled playfully. "So, now that you know what an innovative, witty, and non-stereotypical Italian male I am, will you have coffee with me?"

"Let's talk business first, all right?" Theresa craned her neck past him to peer at the kitchen doors. "Will your brother be joining us?"

"No, Lurch is hiding in the kitchen waiting for you to leave. Later, I'll tell him what we discussed, and he'll curse me for tampering with the purity of our parents' vision."

"Sounds like you two have a great relationship."

"We do. In between the name calling and occasional fist fights." Michael gazed at the walls of the restaurant. "Let me guess: The first thing you want us to do is build a big bonfire, and torch the pictures of Frank, the Pope and the gondoliers."

"Nope," Theresa replied cheerfully. "I want you to keep the decor."

"You do?" Michael pushed back in his chair, surprised.

"Yup. It's homey, which is how we're going to spin the restaurant: as an unpretentious family place where customers can get good, traditional Italian food at decent prices."

Michael peered at her dubiously. "Are you yanking my chain?"

"No." Theresa laughed, smiling. "Look, there's a trend right now toward comfort food. People want stuff they remember from childhood, or from their imagined childhood: meatloaf, macaroni and cheese, spaghetti and meatballs, you name it. You guys are going to become *the* name in Italian comfort food."

"So we don't have to change the menu?"

"Not exactly."

Michael looked confused. "How are we going to pull in new customers if we don't have a new look or a new menu?"

Theresa beamed. "Specials."

"Specials," Michael repeated blankly.

"You're going to have something special two or three

times a month, tied to the calendar. The first Friday night of every month could be family night; kids eat free and adults have unlimited salad and breadsticks. In December you could offer a big, traditional Italian dinner on Christmas Eve. January? A Superbowl party. Romantic candlelight dinner on Valentine's Day. A Mother's Day special in May." Theresa found herself getting excited. "We'll tie specials into the community. Next September, you could run a special connected to the Santa Rosalia festival. There will never be a holiday or local event for which Dante's isn't doing something special."

"Starting when?"

"Now." She checked Michael's expression, hoping to see the enthusiasm she was feeling reflected back at her. Instead, he looked like he was suffering from a bad case of indigestion. "What's wrong?"

"When you say specials . . . will Anthony have to make special dishes?"

"Sometimes, like for Christmas Eve and Valentine's Day. In the summer, you guys could make up special picnic baskets to go with biscotti, cured olives, some panini."

Michael looked doubtful. "I don't know."

"I do," Theresa said confidently.

"This will bring in the real foodies?"

"In time. I'm going to start by sending out a press kit to every magazine and newspaper writer under the sun who has anything to do with food. I've already compiled a list of about three hundred."

"Three *hundred*?"

"And that doesn't even include radio and TV personalities who we want to try to get in here to review the restaurant. I'm telling you: One thumbs-up from Joan Hamburg at WOR and you'll have a line out the door, guaranteed. When's the construction being done for the expansion?"

"March, I think. We're open in April."

"Hmmm." Theresa nibbled the tip of her pen. "That means we might miss the chance to do Easter dinner here, depending on when it falls. We'll have to check the calendar."

She stopped talking, giving him time to let it sink in. Michael remained silent.

"You look shell-shocked." She laughed.

"Don't get me wrong," Michael answered carefully. "Everything you're laying out sounds great. It's just Anthony. He's going to blow a gasket. I can hear it already: 'Mom and Pop never ran monthly specials, yada yada yada.' "

"You said you could handle your brother."

"Oh, I can. I was just hoping I wouldn't have to resort to firearms."

They both laughed, and for a split second, it struck Theresa how ruggedly handsome he was. But as quickly as the thought came, she made it disappear. She had blonder fish to fry.

Theresa hesitated. "There is one more thing."

Michael waited.

"You need to update your wait staff."

Michael stared at her.

"You need to get some younger waiters and waitresses to reflect the diversity of customers you'll be pulling in."

"Theresa, all the guys who work here worked for my dad, they—"

"I know that, Michael. They're all old men."

"Why can't that be part of the restaurant's old-world charm?" Michael challenged. "If you want me to convince Anthony to put together picnic baskets and prepare baccala on Christmas Eve and Christ knows what else, we have to leave the wait staff alone."

"We'll talk about it another time," Theresa placated. She glanced down at the notes she'd typed up. That seemed to cover everything for now. "Any questions?"

"Is there anything *I* can do?"

"Actually, there is. Since you're the man about town, you need to start talking up the restaurant every chance you get. And if you know any Italian celebrities who might be willing to come to the reopening, that would be great as well."

"I'll see what I can do." Michael ran his hand through his hair, grimacing when it came away greasy, which made Theresa grin. "Did you enjoy the pastries I sent you last week?" he asked casually.

Theresa decided to tease him, just a little. "Those were from you?"

"Did you like them?"

She couldn't lie. "Yes."

"Good." Nervously, almost distractedly, Michael began playing with the toothpick lying on the table in front of him. "When would you like to go for coffee?"

Groaning, Theresa cradled her head in her hands. "Michael."

"It's not a difficult question, Theresa. All you have to do is say yes."

"Let me think about it, okay?"

"What's to think about?"

Theresa bristled with annoyance. "Don't push, Michael. I don't like it."

"Fine, I won't push. But I don't see what the big deal is."

Of course you don't. You weren't sexually assaulted by a hockey player. You don't wake up in the middle of the night in a cold sweat feeling smothered because he pushed himself on top of you . . . and you don't recall the taste of blood in your mouth after he cracked you across the face . . . his saliva drying on your breast. . . .

"Theresa?"

She forced a smile. "Sorry. I was zoning out."

The disappointment shadowing Michael's face almost

made her feel sorry enough to have coffee with him. Almost. But he was pushy. If she agreed to coffee, the next thing you know he'd be on her about dinner, and then . . . she shuddered.

"I have to go," she said abruptly, gathering up her things. "I'll be in touch again soon. In the meantime, if you need any help with Anthony, let me know."

"Sure, no problem," Michael said glumly.

Theresa hurried out the door and back into the brisk air, where she could clear her head and concentrate on more important things.

Like what she was going to wear when she met Reese Banister.

"*Mikey! What a* surprise!"

Michael smiled as his cousin Gemma drew him into an embrace, crushing him against her as the overwhelming scent of her patchouli perfume, strong and musky, tickled his nostrils. Gemma ran the Golden Bough, a New Age shop in the Village. He'd come to see her because he was desperate for female advice.

Gemma was the black sheep of the family. Not only was she thirty-one and happily single, but she'd committed the cardinal sin of moving into the big, bad city, far from Brooklyn and all that was pure in this world, or so his family thought. Worst of all, she was a *stregh*—a witch. She'd explained it to him once, all about paganism and white magick and Wicca. Michael had teased her about worshipping furniture, but his feeling was that if it made her happy, who was he to criticize?

The rest of the family took a less charitable view. Gemma was rarely invited to family events for fear their sainted grandmother Nonna Maria might find out she'd "gone over to the dark side" and promptly keel on the spot. Anthony now made the sign of the cross whenever he saw her. None of it seemed to phase Gemma, who had always been Michael's favorite cousin, even if she was a bit, well, spooky. When they were kids, Gemma was always freaking him out, accurately shouting out who was on the other end of the line when the phone rang, or predicting things before they happened. One time, Gemma airily announced to him, "You're gonna fall and go to the hospital." Five minutes later, he tripped and fell down the steps at Nonna's and had to get five stitches to his chin. At the time, he was certain she'd somehow made him fall. Nowadays he was content to admit some things simply defied explanation and leave it at that. It wasn't an area he cared to delve into too deeply.

"Sit down," Gemma urged, leading him to one of the tall stools behind the counter. A few customers were silently browsing the book section, which Michael noticed carried books on everything from astrology to Zoroastrianism. He didn't mind the books. It was all the other stuff, the tarot cards and the crystals and the incense and the candles, that gave him the willies. Maybe it was a case of "You can take the boy out of Catholicism, but you can't take the Catholicism out of the boy." He wasn't sure. All he knew was that just being there made him feel slightly uncomfortable, like he was doing something vaguely sinful. It was ridiculous, but he couldn't help what he felt. Or smelled. The cloying sweetness of incense wafting through the small store was so strong he knew that by the time he left he'd have a whopping headache.

He turned to his cousin, her forehead wrinkled as she concentrated hard on staring into his face, eyes narrowed.

"What?" he asked, alarmed.

She touched his wrist lightly. "You're in pain?" she asked with concern. "Someone's hurt you?"

Jesus H, did she have to start in with the witch stuff right off the bat?

"In a way," Michael admitted. "There's this girl—I mean woman . . ."

He proceeded to tell her all about Theresa, pausing only when one of the customers came to the counter to pay for a book on Santeria. Michael jokingly asked if she'd read the sequels on the Nina and the Pinta, only to be punched in the shoulder by his cousin. The customer awarded him such a look of condescension that had he been a dog, he would have slunk away with his tail between his legs. When the shop was empty again, Gemma listened carefully as he finished his story, nodding thoughtfully.

"Let me ask you a question," she finally said.

"Okay."

"Why do you think this girl has changed so much since you first met her? You said that when you were first introduced a few years back, she was easygoing and funny. But now she's stiff and formal and looks like a schoolmarm."

"A *HOT* schoolmarm," Michael felt compelled to point out.

"Whatever. What do you think is going on?"

Michael felt uncomfortable. "It could have something to do with what happened to her." He checked Gemma's expression to make sure she knew what he was referring to. "But why does she need to hide? When I fed her some of Anthony's pastry, the *real* Theresa came out. But the minute she realized it, bam! It was back to cold fish Theresa."

"She's obviously trying to protect herself."

"Ya think?" Michael retorted.

"So, maybe you should leave her alone," said Gemma, pointedly ignoring his sarcasm.

"I can't."

"Why? Why do you refuse to accept that she doesn't want anything to do with you?"

"Well . . ." Michael scratched his left ear distractedly, trying to formulate an answer not only for Gemma, but for himself. "Because I just have this *feeling* I can't shake, that if she would just give me a chance . . . trust me . . . let her guard down . . . she'd see we were right for each other somehow. I don't know how to explain it."

Gemma's mouth gave way to a knowing smile. "It's called intuition, Mikey. Everyone has it. But some are more willing to pay attention to it than others."

Michael rolled his eyes. "Don't get all airy fairy on me here. Just tell me what you think I should do."

Gemma sighed. "I'm not sure. Hold on a minute." Reaching down, she pulled out a small, purple velvet bag from beneath the counter.

"What's that?" Michael asked suspiciously.

"Tarot cards," she informed him, removing a deck from the bag and placing it on the counter.

Michael groaned. "Gemma, c'mon, you know how I feel about this stuff."

"Indulge me." She handed the cards to him. "We'll just ask one question at a time and see what they say. Think of a question, then shuffle the deck as many times as you want. When you're done, put the deck down and turn over the top card."

"Okay." He held the cards tight in the palm of his hand, thinking. "Is Theresa the one for me?" he asked quietly. He began shuffling the well-worn cards, surprised to find he was somewhat nervous. "I swear to God, if you tell anyone in the family I did this, I will hunt you down," he threatened his cousin.

"Concentrate on the cards and the question, Michael," Gemma urged. *The cards and the question. The cards and the question.* A number came into his head: *thirty-three.* His uniform number. Shuffling the cards thirty-three times, he put them down on the counter as instructed and turned over the top card. There was a picture of a couple dressed in medieval garb, holding hands in front of what looked like a preacher or a judge. "The Lovers" it said in flowery print beneath them. His eyes darted to Gemma's, hopeful. "That's good?"

"Very good. The card symbolizes love, beauty, the beginning of a romantic relationship. Maybe even marriage, eventually."

Michael felt vindicated. "See? It's in the cards. Literally."

"The cards you think are a bunch of bull," Gemma pointed out.

"Maybe not," Michael admitted, encouraged. Maybe there was something to this mystical mumbo jumbo after all. "Can I ask another question?"

"Be my guest."

He picked up the cards again, this time closing his eyes. "When will it happen?"

He waited for another number to appear in his mind. *Thirty-three.* Okay, so maybe thirty-three would be the only number that ever came to his mind. That was fine with him. He shuffled the deck more slowly this time, turning over the top card when he was done. The card was upside down. "Nine of Wands," he read aloud, checking out the illustration of a peasant in tights alongside a cart loaded with nine long pieces of wood. He looked at his cousin expectantly.

"Well . . ." she began hesitantly.

"What?" Michael was growing alarmed. "What is it?"

"Reversed, the Nine of Wands indicates obstacles, adversity, delays. Lots of problems, lots of barriers to overcome." She winced. "Sorry."

"I knew these cards were bullshit," Michael muttered darkly.

"It doesn't mean you're not going to get her," Gemma assured him. "It's just not going to be easy."

"Great." Michael sulked.

Gemma's gaze was sympathetic. "You really like her, don't you?"

"Yeah, I really do," said Michael. "She's smart and funny. A little bit cranky, too, but that's okay, I can cope with cranky. And she's gorgeous—*Madonn'* . . ."

"Well, then you've got to have faith it's going to work out." Gemma began putting the cards back in their velvet bag. "What does Anthony think of her?"

Michael pulled a tortured face. "Don't get me started on Anthony."

"What? Why?"

He told Gemma all about Dante's, including Theresa's suggestions and his brother's reluctance to change anything.

"You have to go easy with Anthony, Michael. He's very sensitive."

"Who isn't?" Michael scoffed.

"I mean about the restaurant in particular."

"Well, so am I."

"It's different. Dante's has been his whole life. He's poured his guts into it. Now all of a sudden you step in and want to change things around? No wonder he's upset."

"Are you saying I don't have a right to improve things?" Michael demanded, feeling defensive.

"Not at all. I'm just saying be sensitive to his feelings. You've seen and done things he never has, maybe never will. He's jealous of you. All he's ever had is Dante's, and he's afraid you're somehow going to take it away from him. Be gentle with him, Mike."

"Yeah, yeah, I will," Michael promised. He found the idea that Anthony might be jealous of him bizarre, but he supposed it could be true. All those times Anthony got on his ass about being a wussy college boy and a dumb jock . . . Michael always assumed it was Anthony's way of putting him down. But now he saw there might be a different way to interpret it.

The incense was starting to make his temples throb. Hopping down from his stool, he leaned in to kiss his cousin's cheek. "I should run. I've got a million things to do today."

"Wait. Let me give you something."

Gemma hustled out from behind the counter and went to the front of the store, returning with two large, thick candles, one white, one red. "Burn them and think thoughts of Theresa. They're to attract love."

"Don't you have a spell I can recite or something?" Michael ribbed.

"I do, but I know you won't do it."

Squirming with embarrassment, Michael gently thrust the candles back at his cousin. "I can't take these, Gemma."

"Afraid you might get what you want?" she asked, refusing to take them back from him.

"No, afraid people might think I'm a total whackjob."

"Thanks a lot." Gemma sniffed, looking mildly offended. Not wanting to hurt her feelings, Michael told her he'd take the candles and waited while she rolled them in protective tissue paper and put them in a bag.

"One more thing," she said.

Michael shifted his weight impatiently. "If you're gonna tell me to dance beneath the moon naked and howl like a wolf, you've got the wrong guy, okay?"

"You're a big, fat idiot, you know that?" Gemma shook her head affectionately. She pressed a stone into his hand. Smooth, milky white, it was the size of a jawbreaker. "That's moonstone. Also known to attract love."

"And what the hell am I supposed to do with it?" Michael lamented. "Use it as a doorstop?"

"Just carry it in your pocket. It's not kryptonite, it won't kill you."

"What do I owe you for all this?"

"You can give my love to Nonna. Tell her I miss her," Gemma said sadly.

"Hey, you know you're always welcome by me and Anthony."

"I know that," she said, squeezing his shoulder. "Now get out there and get Theresa. Just remember: It's not gonna be easy."

After visiting his cousin, Michael took advantage of having the day off. He shot back to Brooklyn, stopping first at his own place in Park Slope to drop off the candles and moonstone. Then he headed to Bensonhurst, letting himself into Anthony's house, which was once his parents' house. He and Anthony had a standing rule that either could walk into the other's place at any time. Not that Anthony ever did. Anthony hadn't been to Michael's apartment since helping him move in three years before. Walking through to the kitchen, Michael poured himself a cup of coffee from the ever-present Mr. Coffee on the counter.

Glancing around, he felt nostalgia envelop him like a well-worn blanket. If he closed his eyes, he could almost hear his mother humming while she stood at the stove, her happiness an invisible but omnipresent ingredient in every dish she prepared. He'd never known anyone as easygoing or as happy to be cooking. Nothing daunted her. He could remember nights his father would be about to burst a blood vessel when something had gone wrong at the restaurant, a vegetable delivery that was late or some dish that hadn't turned out the way he wanted. It was always his mother who was able to calm him down and make him see that in the grand scheme of things, one burnt eggplant didn't merit that much *agita*. Growing up, he always thought his father was the strong one. Now he knew it was his mother.

Coffee prepared, he wandered back out into the living room to wait for his brother. It wasn't only the kitchen that remained unchanged. Everything in the house was the same as when his parents were alive. The couch with its faded green slipcover was still under the picture window. The TV still sat atop a lace runner on a table that had once been Nonna Maria's. Jesus, there was even hard candy in the glass dish on the sideboard. That candy was probably older than he was. He wondered when, or if, Anthony would ever get around to redecorating. There had to be a part of him that wanted to make the house his own.

Sighing, Michael took a sip of coffee. Anthony would never redecorate. It wasn't who Anthony was. He could already hear him protesting: "But *why* would I want to get rid of the couch? It's perfectly good." Anthony had lived his whole life in this house, and would probably die in his bed upstairs. Michael never understood why Anthony had never gotten around to getting a place of his own. How did he stand being a grown man, living with his parents? It had embarrassed Michael, but obviously Anthony didn't feel the same way, and neither did their parents. Every time Anthony made overtures about leaving, their mother would talk him out of it. It was a little game they played. But once their father died six years ago, the game was over. There was no question Anthony would stay on. Michael had always felt guilty over his relief that Anthony was shouldering most of the burden of taking care of their mother—not that she needed it. Right up until the day she died, she worked in the kitchen at Dante's, teaching Anthony everything she knew, then crowing with pride to whomever would listen when he surpassed her. It struck Michael that Anthony had to be feeling pretty lonely these days without Ma, both at home and in the restaurant. Keeping Gemma's advice in mind, he resolved to be patient with his brother, even if Anthony wound up threatening him with a carving knife, or worse.

He heard the back door open. "Hey, Ant! In here."

"Mikey?" Anthony called back, sounding surprised. "Just let me get my coat off and pour myself some joe and I'll be right in."

Michael listened to the sounds of Anthony moving around the kitchen. He wasn't sure whether Anthony was aware of it or not, but just like their mother, he was humming to himself. *Sounds like he's in a good mood. Maybe this won't be too awful after all.*

"Hey." Anthony sat down, joining Michael on the couch.

"Where ya been?"

"Had to take Nonna to the dentist."

"Why didn't you tell me?" Michael asked, feeling guilty. "It's an off day. I could have taken her."

"I was going to ask, but you shot out of the restaurant so fast after talking to—what's her name?"

"Theresa."

"I didn't get a chance to."

"Sorry about that." He took another sip of coffee. "Nonna's teeth okay?"

"The few that are hers, yeah. You two should go together. Maybe Doc Collins would give you a two for one deal, since neither of you has a full set of choppers."

"You're funny as cancer, Anthony, you know that?" Unable to resist, Michael continued. "You ever think of redecorating this place?"

"What for?" Anthony replied.

"Because this room has looked the same since the Nixon administration."

"So? The furniture's still in good shape. What the hell do I care if it's in style or not?"

His brother was so predictable.

Anthony took a long, slow, deliberate sip of his coffee,

his eyes glued to Michael's face. "So, you wanna tell me the latest PR bullshit Theresa has cooked up for us?"

"It's not bullshit," Michael informed him. "It's great."

"Yeah? Tell me how great it is."

Keeping it as simple as he could, Michael outlined Theresa's plans for monthly specials. Unnervingly, Anthony's eyes never wavered from his face. Michael wasn't even sure he blinked. When Michael was done, Anthony spoke one simple word.

"No."

Michael steeled himself. "What do you mean, no?"

"I mean, no, N-O, I'm not going to do this."

"Anthony—"

"A traditional Italian dinner on Christmas Eve," Anthony jeered. "Forget it. Christmas Eve is sacred, Mike. You know that."

"It can still be sacred."

Anthony snorted in disbelief. "How, if I'm in the kitchen up to my ass in fucking squid?"

"Easy. We close at ten. That still gives everyone enough time to get to Midnight Mass and eat dinner."

"Oh, and when am I supposed to cook our family dinner? In my sleep?"

"Aunt Gavina could do it this year."

Anthony bit down on the knuckle of his left index finger, horrified. "God forbid." He shook his head. "This isn't gonna work, Mike."

"Yes, it is, Anthony." He could hear the stubbornness creeping into his voice and struggled to remain focused on Gemma's advice. "It's not really that big of a departure, Ant. All it takes is a little planning."

"And a lot of hard work." Anthony was incensed. "What the hell makes you think I want to stand in the kitchen on Valentine's Day, preparing flourless chocolate cake for some fucking Park Slope yuppies, no offense? Does this PR lady have any idea how long it takes to prepare a Christmas Eve feast? Does she know how long it takes to cure those olives she thinks we should put in summer picnic baskets? I don't have time for this, Mike."

"So we'll hire some additional staff."

"We?"

"Fine, me, I'll lay out the money, how's that?"

Anthony was unyielding. "Fine, since you're the one who seems hell bent on messing with a good thing."

"Good things can turn into great things with a little care and planning," Michael retorted. He stared at his pig-headed brother. "I don't understand you. I don't understand why you don't want the restaurant to get the recognition it deserves."

"Because unlike you, I don't need the approval of the public. I love to cook. The restaurant lets me do that. I don't need it to be the most popular restaurant in the world."

"Yeah, well, maybe I do," Michael replied warily. He took another sip of coffee, making a sour face. It was losing heat. He liked his coffee hot or not at all. Disgusted, he put the cup down on the coffee table. "I can't do this without you, Anthony."

Anthony laughed bitterly. "No shit."

"Can we at least give it a try?"

Anthony's expression was cool. "On one condition."

"What's that?"

"If you expect me to slave away in the kitchen, turning out little orange and black Halloween cupcakes and fuck knows what else, then I expect you in the front of the house whenever you're in town and don't have a game, making sure everything is running smoothly. And when you do have a game, I think you should get your ass back to Brooklyn as soon as you're done at Met Gar to help me."

Their eyes locked. One second, two seconds, three. Finally Michael broke contact.

"After games is off limits," he informed his brother. "I need time to unwind. Plus I'm entitled to a life."

"Glad one of us is," Anthony muttered.

Michael snorted derisively. "How's the weather up there on the cross, Anthony?"

"Screw you, Mike."

"Have we got a deal?" Michael repeated.

"Yes," Anthony assured him. "You mentioned you were off today, so you may as well come down to the restaurant." Wicked glee twinkled in his eyes. "That won't be a problem, will it, Mike?"

"Nope." Michael stood up, afraid if he stayed a second longer he'd grab Anthony in a headlock and throttle the life out of him. "Gotta run, Ant," he said hurriedly as he zipped up his bomber jacket. "Places to go, people to see."

"Toodle-ooh, Mikey. See you later."

Smiling tersely, Michael leaned over and patted his brother's shoulder. Maybe he was crazy, but Michael could have sworn he heard his brother laughing as he closed the front door.

CHAPTER
06

When she and Janna were roommates, Theresa could always count on getting the unvarnished truth about her wardrobe. If a pair of pants made her normally slim legs look like tree trunks, Janna told her. If a blouse was too low cut, or a pair of shoes not quite right, Janna always came up with the perfect alternative. It was a service Theresa performed for Janna, too, making it rare for either of them to walk out the door looking anything less than expertly put together. But now that Janna was married, Theresa was forced to rely on her own judgment, which suddenly felt shaky.

It had been ages since she'd been out with a man.

She didn't want to send the wrong message.

She wanted to look polished yet casual. Attractive yet not provocative. After staring into the abyss of her closet for what felt like hours, she'd finally narrowed it down to two outfits. One was super casual: chinos, flats, turtleneck and her favorite suede jacket. The other was a bit more urban: a knee-length black satin skirt, channel quilted with red stitches and trimmed in red contrast stripes. Theresa loved this skirt, not only because it hugged her in all the right places, but because it was lined in red satin, making her feel just the slightest bit sexy without anyone else knowing. It was sporty without being slouchy, especially if she topped it with the tight, black, cable-knit sweater from DKNY that Janna had given her for Christmas the previous year.

Still undecided, she perched on the edge of her bed with a sigh of resignation.

Ridiculous, the way women tortured themselves over what to wear. God knows most men never gave it a second thought. The image of Michael Dante in his *guido* getup flashed through her mind, and she chuckled to herself, wondering where he'd come up with those awful polyester pants. Was it possible they were *his*? No, they couldn't be. In real life, he seemed to dress okay: tennis shirts and jeans. Chinos and pullover sweaters. She closed her eyes, trying to recall the sight of him in a tux at Ty and Janna's wedding. She vaguely remembered thinking he looked sort of handsome, but then, all Ty's teammates had that day. The formal wear lent even the goofiest of them an air of dignity.

Annoyed to be thinking about Michael, she turned her thoughts to Reese, feeling an ache of anxiety in her chest. They were meeting at the Harvard Club. The Harvard Club! Talk about upscale and exclusive, not to mention *impressive*. She imagined herself on the phone with her mother a few weeks from now, boasting about her new smart, successful boyfriend. "He graduated from *Harvard Law*," she heard herself saying, proudly. Apart from his not being Italian, there wasn't much with which her parents could find fault.

Still, Theresa found his pedigree unnerving. She was plagued by a vision of walking through the doors of the club, only to set off an alarm and an announcement sounding eerily like John F. Kennedy that blared, "Non-blue blood on premises. Non-blue blood on premises. Eject. Eject." *Stop,* she scolded herself. *You're being ridiculous. Being a graduate of NYU ain't exactly peanuts.*

But it's not Ivy League either.

Truly anxious now, she rose from the bed, and picking up the chinos, held them against her with one hand while plastering the turtleneck against her chest with the other, examining her image in the full-length mirror on the back of her bedroom door. Too casual? Glancing back over her shoulder, she looked at the shoes she'd picked out to go with the outfit. The suede jacket, too. The outfit was laid back but confident. It said: *I like myself and I hope you do, too.* Or, perhaps it said: *I don't think enough of you to get dressed up.*

Groaning, Theresa threw the pants and shirt back on the bed and went to inspect her makeup for the third time. It looked fine. Grinning like a hyena, she checked her teeth for rogue seeds or flecks of spinach. Her teeth were fine. She was fine. All she had to do was stop her brain, put on her damn clothes and get out the door.

She hustled back to the bed and forced herself to make a decision. "Sorry," she told her chinos and turtleneck, returning them to the closet. She was going with the outfit that would make her feel the most confident. That meant the skirt and sweater.

Once dressed, she did a final inspection of herself from head to toe. She had to admit, she looked pretty darn good. Her hair seemed extra full and curly, her complexion rosy-hued and healthy from a nice, long run in Central Park earlier in the day. Her mother always complained that her glasses obscured her beautiful eyes, but Theresa didn't agree. If anything, the sophisticated, super chunky frames drew more attention to them. So what if she didn't really need them? They made her feel safe. That's what mattered.

As for perfume, she decided to forego scent until she knew Reese better.

If she got to know him better.

God, please let me get to know him better.

With that simple prayer on her lips, she went to the Harvard Club.

She found him standing beneath the club's crimson awning waiting for her. His face broke into a slow, pleased smile as he watched her approach.

"You didn't have to wait out here for me," she said, not failing to notice the quick, appreciative sweep his eyes did of her body.

"I wanted the pleasure of escorting you inside," Reese murmured, offering her his arm. "Some people find this place intimidating the first time they come, especially if they're not grads. I didn't want you to be scared off."

Grateful, Theresa took his arm and allowed him to guide her inside to the main bar, with its memorabilia-packed crimson walls and gorgeous, horseshoe-shaped mahogany bar. So far, so good. Her presence hadn't triggered the JFK blue blood alarm. Even better, no one at the surrounding tables was looking at her as if she didn't belong. Theresa heaved a huge, inward sigh of relief.

"Martini?" Reese asked as he pulled her chair out for her at a small, square table.

"That would be great."

Her gaze followed him as he walked to the bar to order for them, his gait relaxed but confident. How was it that he had anticipated her trepidation in crossing the threshold of this bastion of wealth and privilege? Was she that transparent? Or was he one of those rare, sensitive men acutely attuned to the feelings of others? Theresa suspected the latter.

Reese returned to the table with two tall martini glasses and a very mischievous smile.

"What?" Theresa prompted.

"I bought you a present."

"Reese!" Theresa exclaimed, embarrassed. "You didn't have to do that."

"I wanted to. Besides, I think you'll get a kick out of it."

He reached down into the leather satchel at his feet and pulled out a book, handing it to her. It was Vincent Canby's *The New York Times Guide to the 1,000 Best Movies Ever Made.*

"I believe *The Bridge Over the River Kwai* is in there," Reese teased.

"Is that so?" Theresa flirted back, thumbing slowly through the pages. "I guess I'll just have to rent it and see for myself what all the fuss is about."

For two hours they talked, conversation flowing effortlessly from one topic to the next with no awkward pauses, no long, stubborn silences, no well-placed coughs of discomfort. At first she thought the ease might be alcohol induced, but then she realized they were only on their second martini.

No, the chemistry had nothing to do with booze.

They were twin souls, artists, believers in love and beauty and truth. They were Hammett and Hellman, Steiglitz and O'Keefe. Spurred on by his unwavering interest in all she had to say, Theresa felt herself dizzyingly brilliant. She was witty and wise, a veritable Oscar Wilde with bon mots falling from her lips like gems. She was Dorothy Parker, Joyce Carol Oates and Susan Sontag all rolled into one.

"I can't believe how easy you are to talk to," Reese eventually marveled.

The wonder in his words had Theresa purring inwardly like a contented cat.

Buoyed by his compliment, she returned one of her own. "You're very easy to talk to, too." She paused, her fingers running up and down the stem of her martini glass. "This might sound crazy, but I feel as if I've known you for years."

"I know," Reese agreed, looking relieved. His hand moved out from beneath the table to cover hers. Theresa's immediate impulse was to pull her hand away, but she fought it. If she wanted a relationship, she had to learn to trust again. That meant being able to give affection as well as receive it. She kept her hand still.

"I've never told a woman so much about myself so early. I hope I haven't put you off. Or bored you."

"Are you kidding?"

Reese appeared to be a lot of things—son of privilege, disgruntled neophyte lawyer, compromised artist—but boring wasn't one of them. Theresa had been held rapt by his stories of growing up the youngest of three sons in Upper Brookville on Long Island. She loved hearing about Harvard, and the atmosphere at the club certainly helped. It seemed only natural he would open up to her about his slow, painful journey from dreaming of being a photographer to succumbing to rationality and family pressure and going to law school.

"If you really hate practicing law, you can always do something else," she suggested.

"Well, the thing is, I don't know if I hate it yet, if that makes any sense. I haven't been at it long enough." He shrugged diffidently. "If I'm terrible at it, I'm sure Uncle Ted will let me know."

"And what about your photography?" Theresa enquired playfully. "Who tells you if you're terrible at that?"

"You."

Theresa laughed. "Does that mean I'll one day get to see the Reese Banister collection?"

"One day—if I can read one of your short stories."

Theresa suddenly felt shy. "We'll see about that. Maybe you should show your photos to your uncle instead."

"I don't think so," said Reese tersely. "As you might imagine, he thinks it's a huge waste of time." With his free hand, he lifted his martini glass to his lips and drank. "Speaking of Uncle Ted, where are you and Janna on Butler's proposal? If you don't mind me asking."

"Honestly? We've been too busy to even talk about it."

"Want to know what I think?"

Theresa laughed. "You represent Butler! I already know what *you* think."

"Now, wait, that's not fair," Reese protested with a grin.

Theresa found herself adoring the way his eyes crinkled up when he smiled.

"My *uncle* represents Butler Corp. *I* am merely learning the ropes and observing."

"In an impartial manner, of course." Theresa grinned back.

"Absolutely."

"Go on, then," she shrugged, taking a slow sip of her drink. "Let me hear your completely objective, unbiased opinion."

"I think you ladies should take the money and run. Ninety percent of all small businesses go under within the first three years of operation. Selling to Butler will allow you to keep doing what you do best, with a top-notch support system in place. You'll no longer have to worry about carrying your own rent or health insurance."

"We'll also be employees of Butler."

"What's so wrong with that?" he said with mock hurt, making a gesture towards himself that said "I'm one, too."

Theresa tried for a serious expression. "Reese, Janna

and I both worked long and hard to be self-employed. The thought of giving up our autonomy . . . I just don't know."

"Hey, it's just my opinion. You don't have to agree."

Theresa checked his face to see if his expression matched the neutrality of his words. They did. "But you think we're nuts if we don't at least entertain the idea."

"Absolutely. They're offering a lot of money, Theresa."

"Money isn't everything."

"That's true," Reese agreed. "But having enough of it can free one to pursue one's passions. Like writing, for instance."

"Or photography."

Reese raised his glass. "Amen." His hand squeezed hers. "Tell me you'll at least think about it."

"I'll think about it," Theresa promised, surprised to find herself feeling mildly irritated the conversation had turned to business. Eager to deflect further comments or questions, she asked him to finish the story he'd started about being thrown off the crew team.

Reese resumed his tale.

He was a good, descriptive storyteller, but Theresa found it harder and harder to focus. One part of her brain was taking in what he was saying and directing her body to respond with the appropriate smile, laugh, or question. The other part was picturing them hand in hand, walking along the beach, eating dinner at her mother's house, raising children. She knew she was jumping way ahead of herself, but she couldn't help it. The impulse to imagine a future with him was irresistible, especially since there was such a spark between them. It was there in the way he looked at her, like she was a gorgeous puzzle he was eager to solve, and in the warmth of his hand atop hers, which she was now getting used to, and actually enjoying.

He *had* to be as aware of it as she.

Could he be The One?

Before they knew it, the bar was closing and they were drifting towards the door.

"Where do you live?" Reese asked, once again taking her hand. Theresa let her fingers curl around his. It felt good. Right. So much easier than she thought it would be.

"Fifty-ninth and First. You?"

"Eighty-ninth and Park."

"Swank-ky," Theresa teased.

"Want to split a cab?"

"Actually, I feel like walking." The words came out more quickly than she intended. And they were true—she was a ball of energy and excitement, and a walk would help her run through and analyze everything that was said between them tonight. But there was something else. She didn't want to deal with the possibility of his suggesting she invite him up for a nightcap.

Reese checked his watch. "It's awfully late." He looked concerned. "I'm not sure that's such a good idea."

"I'll be fine," Theresa assured him, hoping he didn't notice she was a walking contradiction of fear and desire. They pushed through the front doors and stood beneath the club's awning, hands still entwined. "Thank you for a wonderful evening," she said softly.

"No, thank you." He brushed his knuckles tenderly against her cheek. "Can I call you?"

"Of course."

He seemed to hesitate. "I need to ask you something."

"Go ahead."

"I don't want to make you uncomfortable, but you're beautiful, Theresa. You must know that."

Overcome, Theresa looked down at her feet.

"I would love to take some photographs of you some-time. Nothing fancy, just some black and white shots done in different lighting. Your cheekbones alone . . . ." He trailed off.

"I don't know," Theresa murmured shyly, raising her head. "I have to think about it."

He squeezed her hand. "Do that."

"I will," Theresa promised.

Reese rocked back nervously on his heels. "Well, then . . . good night."

Theresa's heart fluttered expectantly as she anticipated his kiss. But it didn't happen, at least not the way she expected it to. Instead of kissing her on the mouth, Reese leaned in and pressed his lips tenderly to her forehead. In an instant, fear and desire turned to relief and disappointment. Releasing his hand from hers, he murmured, "I like to take things slow. I hope you don't mind."

"Not at all."

Enchanted, she watched as he hailed a cab and hopped inside. As its taillights faded to two glowing red pinpricks of light, Theresa reached up and touched her cheek where Reese's hand had been.

He was so gentle and tender.

So honorable and kind.

And he thought she was beautiful.

Happier than she could remember being in months, she floated all the way home.

"Okay, now tilt your head to the left a little. That's right."

Blinking against the glaring lights in Reese's makeshift photo studio, Theresa did as he asked. At first, the thought of being photographed had terrified her. It was such an intimate process. But Reese had worked hard putting her at ease, carefully explaining to her how everything worked and letting *her* dictate the poses she was comfortable in. She had almost bolted when he'd asked her to remove her glasses and let her hair down, but after thinking about it, she acquiesced in the name of art. Reese wanted to capture *her,* her essence. That meant there could be no hiding. No disguises. Allowing herself to be truly seen was terrifying at first, but then it felt wonderful. To her surprise, she found herself reveling in the attention.

He'd been photographing her for close to two hours now, and she was tired. Reese must have sensed it. Sympathy played across his boyish face as he put down his camera and came to where she sat against a dark blue backdrop.

"You okay?" he asked, stroking her hair which he' d arranged around her shoulders like a gorgeous, silken mantle.

Theresa closed her eyes, nodding.

The feel of his hand on the back of her head . . . the warmth . . . it was soothing somehow. Reese paused, then his fingertips began to feather lightly across the nape of her neck. The soothing feeling faded, replaced by something much more primal she hadn't allowed herself to feel for a long, long time.

She held her breath, waiting to see what would happen next.

Taking his time, Reese's fingers found their way to her earlobe, his touch remaining light as air. Yearning filled her, sharp and sweet.

He was torturing her, couldn't he see that?

If he could, then he was obviously enjoying it, as he began running his hands up and down her arms. Theresa swallowed nervously as her skin responded to the demand in his touch, her nerves pulsing and alive.

"Tell me something," said Reese.

Theresa opened her eyes.

"Are you afraid of me?"

She searched his face. "Why on earth would I be afraid of you?"

"Because you seem a little nervous," he murmured, taking his thumb and slowly, tantalizingly, running it back and forth across her bottom lip. "And I just want you to know . . . that you never have to be afraid of me. I'll never hurt you."

"I know that," Theresa whispered.

"Good." Her lower lip continued tingling from his touch as he extended his hand to her and she rose, facing him. Eyes never wavering from her face, he wrapped his arms around her waist. Tentative, Theresa reached out and did the same. She half expected him to evaporate in her arms. But he didn't. He was solid. Real.

And he wanted her.

"I'm not sure this is a good idea," she managed, her breath hitching.

"Why not?" Reese pulled her closer to him, the distance between their lips mere inches now. "Is this so frightening?"

"No, but . . ."

She was unable to finish the sentence as he leaned forward, closing the gap between them with the faintest brushing of his lips on hers, their mouths barely touching. Moaning softly to himself, Reese pulled her even closer. Theresa's lips parted on a sigh as he put his mouth full on hers, pressing hard as he nipped at her bottom lip. Gasping, her mouth opened beneath his in complete submission. He tasted faintly of wine, but there was something else there, too, sweet and feral at the same time, that she wanted to lap up and roll around on her tongue and taste. Heart thundering in her ears, she slid her hands up under the back of his Oxford shirt, caressing the center of his warm, silky back tenderly. Reese groaned as their soft, lingering kisses turned into sleek, demanding glides of tongue against tongue.

Feverish, he tore his mouth from hers. "Tell me if you want me to stop," he whispered thickly.

Theresa shook her head no.

He nodded once, then resumed kissing her. Theresa felt

heat exploding low in her belly as one of his hands found its way to the hair at the nape of her neck while the other went to cup her bottom. They were both breathing hard now, the still, silent air around them punctuated with their soft moans and sighs. The way he was making her feel . . . sacred, cherished—and for the first time in over two years, gloriously alive . . . filled her with a sense of gratitude she had to give voice to. She pulled back and looked lovingly into Michael's face.

"Thank you, Michael," she managed in a voice just above a whisper. "Thank you for—"

She jerked awake, disoriented.

She wasn't in a photo studio, but in her own room, in her own bed. And there was no Reese and no . . . Michael. But her nipples were hard, and the heat inflaming her body was real. "Just a dream," she muttered, drawing her blankets tighter as she curled back up into a little ball. "Doesn't mean anything."

But even half asleep, a small part of her wondered.

The next morning, Theresa could hardly wait to get to Janna's for brunch so she could dish about Reese. The Blades were on a road trip, and it had been ages since they had been able to carve out "girl-time" together. The game plan was brunch, followed by an afternoon of watching videos on Ty's huge HDTV.

What is it with men and electronics? Theresa mused as she rode the elevator up to Janna's apartment on the fifty-second floor. She recalled a boyfriend in college who would pace like a caged animal each month as he waited for the next issue of *Stereo Review's Sound and Vision* to arrive. When it came, he'd read it cover to cover, drooling over speakers.

She didn't get it.

Entering the apartment, Theresa was greeted by the enticing aromas of coffee brewing and muffins baking. "Oh my God, that smells great," she marveled as Janna took her coat.

"I hope you brought your appetite. I'm making us an omelet, too," said Janna, ushering Theresa through the huge glass-walled living room into the state of the art kitchen.

Before Janna moved in, the apartment was a high-tech bachelor's paradise, all steel, chrome and glass with no personal warmth. Janna had added some life to it. Strategically placed plants and pots of herbs were everywhere; there was artwork on the walls, and opulent Oriental rugs graced the highly polished marble floors. Theresa always felt a pinprick of envy when she visited. Ty and Janna seemed to have it all: a beautiful home, a great relationship. She knew from Janna they had to work at it, since Ty wasn't the most emotionally expressive of men—unless it came to hockey, which Janna jokingly referred to as "his mistress." Even so, they seemed so simpatico, so happy. *I want that,* Theresa often thought longingly.

And maybe now, with Reese she would find it.

"It still amazes me you *like* to cook," Theresa marveled, sidling up to Janna, who had just started chopping basil. Careful of her fingers, Theresa reached out and took a taste. It was tart but not too bitter.

"It still amazes me you don't," Janna returned.

"I know," said Theresa, resting her elbows on the counter. Since Janna was a control freak when it came to cooking, she knew it would be pointless to ask if she should help. "It just seems like so much work for so little payoff."

"The payoff is nourishing the people you love," said Janna, scooping the basil from the board and reaching for a colander full of mushrooms.

"You sound like my mother."

"Your mother's right." Theresa watched as Janna's

small, nimble hands made short work of the mushrooms. "I bet she's also the reason you don't like to cook."

"What do you mean?" Theresa asked.

"I think it is so important for *you* not to be like her that you deliberately reject anything that even resembles domesticity."

"Tell me more, Dr. Freud."

"You know what I mean." Dumping the mushrooms into a bowl, Janna reached next for a small block of fontina cheese, giving her friend a concerned once over. "You look tired."

A Mona Lisa smile played across Theresa's lips. "I was out late last night," she said cryptically, knowing it would get Janna's attention.

"With?" Janna asked, her gaze divided between Theresa's face and the cheese she was now cutting into cubes.

"Reese Banister."

Janna's eyes darted quickly to Theresa's. "You're kidding, right?"

"No." Theresa wasn't sure why, but she felt mildly wounded by the hint of incredulity in Janna's voice. "You yourself said you noticed us making eyes at each other at that first meeting."

"Yeah, but I never thought—" Janna seemed to stop herself, taking a long break as she concentrated on finishing the cheese. "I guess I don't know what I thought," she concluded lamely.

"He's wonderful," Theresa gushed, determined to make Janna see him through her eyes. "He's smart, tender, considerate and artistic."

This time Janna didn't mask her skepticism. "Whoa, slow down, sister," she ordered. Crossing over to the fridge, she pulled out half a stick of butter and a carton of eggs. The butter she set to melting in the skillet atop the stove. She broke six eggs into a large metal bowl and began beating them.

"I want to hear everything," she told Theresa.

So Theresa told her everything, ending with the mutual confession that they felt like they'd known each other for ages. Through it all, Janna listened intently. By the time Theresa was through, the omelet was done, the fresh blueberry muffins were sprung from the oven, and the coffee was poured and creamed. Theresa sat down at Janna's table with a satisfied sigh and waited for her friend's response.

"He sounds perfect," Janna said dryly, biting into a muffin.

Theresa felt her hackles rise. "I know that tone of voice, Janna. What's wrong?"

"Don't take this the wrong way, Ter, okay?"

Theresa nodded, feeling her shoulders knotting.

"Did the subject of the Butler buyout come up?"

"Yes."

"In what context?"

"Reese wanted to know if we'd given any thought to the proposal, and I said we'd been too busy to talk about it." She slashed away at her omelet. That was the smallest, most insignificant part of the evening. Why was Janna focusing on it? Then she realized. "You think he's using me, don't you?" she asked.

"I didn't say that."

"No, but you do," Theresa accused, now sure of it. "You think I'm so desperate for a man I can't tell whether someone wants me for *me,* or for their own *agenda.* You think I'm too stupid to see the difference."

"Theresa." Janna's voice was gentle as she put down her knife and fork. "I don't think that at all."

"Good, because it's not the case. We really connected, Janna. I don't know how to explain it without sounding crazy, but it was like some *soul* thing." She looked to her friend for confirmation. "Didn't you feel that with Ty?"

Janna nearly choked on her omelet. "No! With us, it was some *sex* thing. The soul stuff came later, after I stopped thinking he was just an arrogant, uncooperative jackass." She glanced down at her plate, breaking off a piece of muffin. "I'm sure Reese is all you say he is—"

Theresa frowned. "But."

"There's something about him," Janna continued thoughtfully. "I don't trust him."

"Why? Because he's a lawyer?"

"Because he's a lawyer being retained by a company who wants to swallow us up."

"One thing has nothing to do with the other," Theresa insisted. "You're confusing who he is with what he does, Janna. That's not fair."

"Maybe," Janna allowed. "But I still think . . ." She trailed off. "Never mind."

"No, tell me. You're my best friend and I want to know what you're thinking."

"I was turned off when he showed up unannounced with his uncle. I felt like we were being ambushed."

"Go on," Theresa urged, pausing for a sip of coffee.

"Who brought up the Butler buyout when you were having drinks last night?"

"He did," Theresa admitted reluctantly.

"And that doesn't bother you?"

"Janna, we were talking about work. People *do* talk about work in the course of getting to know each other, you know. It wasn't like he just brought it up out of the blue."

Janna's gaze was steady as she drank some coffee. "Did he offer his opinion about what he thought we should do?"

"Of course he did. He's a lawyer. Lawyers always offer suggestions whether you want them to or not."

Janna was unblinking. "Let me guess: He thinks we should sell."

"Are you surprised?"

"None of this bothers you?"

"No, because unlike you, I'm able to separate who a person is from what they do."

Janna wasn't buying it. "I don't know. There's something about his bringing it up that I find unethical."

"My friend, the moralist," Theresa snickered.

"Don't make fun, Terry. You know I believe in gut instinct. And mine tells me—"

"That there's more to him than meets the eye," Theresa finished for her, pressing her lips into a hard line.

"I guess," said Janna, sounding deliberately noncommittal.

"Well, then, we've got a problem here."

"Because your gut tells you the opposite," Janna deduced.

"Absolutely. I don't want to sound completely nuts, but I think he might be *The One*." The mere words brought a suffused glow of warmth to her body.

Janna, meanwhile, was staring at her as if she *were* nuts. "What about Michael Dante?" she asked.

"Oh my God." Theresa's head dropped down to her chest in mock defeat before she snapped it back up again. "What are you, his agent?"

"I don't see Reese Banister wooing you with homemade pastries and sweet little notes."

"That's because Reese isn't desperate and insane." Once again, the image of Michael in his "Italian" outfit came to mind and against her will she found herself suppressing a smile.

"What?" Janna pressed.

"Nothing."

Janna snatched the muffin basket from the center of the table and held it hostage. "Tell me or the carbs are history, baby."

In her best bored voice—because, really, it was a boring little story, and kind of pathetic when you thought about it—she told Janna about Michael's sensitivity lesson.

"He went through the effort of finding hideous jewelry and clothing and you won't even have a cup of coffee with the guy?" Janna couldn't believe it. "Jesus, Theresa. You *are* heartless."

"And you're relentless. Stop shilling for Michael Dante. He's a nice guy, but he's not my type. Repeat: Not. My. Type."

"Because—"

"Yes," Theresa cut in tersely, "and because he's simply not what I want in a man."

"Okay," Janna conceded, backing off. She put the muffins back in the middle of the table. "You know what's best for you."

"Thank you for acknowledging that." Theresa took another bite of her muffin. "Maybe you and Ty and Reese and I could go out for dinner sometime."

"Actually, Ty and I are planning on having a small cocktail party in a couple of weeks, nothing fancy."

"Can I bring him?"

"Why do you think I brought it up?"

Happy thoughts filled Theresa's head until she realized who most of Ty's associates were. "Will Michael Dante be there?" she asked.

"No. Nobody from the team is coming. Well, only Kevin Gill and his wife, and maybe that new rookie van Dorn and his girlfriend so Ty can build him up a bit, help him acclimate to New York. Otherwise it will be Lou and his wife, and my sister Petra and her girlfriend. As soon as we have a definite date in mind, I'll let you know."

"Then I can't wait," Theresa said, relieved. "I know once you get to know him, you'll really like him, Jan. Wait and see."

CHAPTER

07

"I'm sorry, miss. Mr. Banister appears to be out."

Theresa blinked twice, staring at the doorman as if he'd just spoken Esperanto.

"I—that's not possible. He told me to meet him here at six."

The doorman raised his palms plaintively. "You saw me buzz his apartment. There's no answer. Would you like to leave a message?"

"No, I'll stop back in a little while. Thank you."

Stunned, Theresa walked out the lobby and headed west on Eighty-ninth toward Central Park, wondering what to do. Reese had invited her to come by before Ty and Janna's cocktail party, so she could see some of his photos.

Yet here she was at the appointed hour being told he wasn't in.

Could he have forgotten?

The question bit at her as she tightened the silk scarf around her neck against the cool breeze. Now October, the nights were getting colder. Soon it would be time to break out the hats and gloves.

Where the hell was Reese?

Walking down the quiet, tree-lined street, oblivious to everything around her, she came up with a couple different scenarios. The most obvious was that he'd completely forgotten. She found that hard to believe; they'd spoken just two days before, and Reese had sounded so enthusiastic. But what if it *had* slipped his mind? If that was the case, then he was a jerk. Especially since coming uptown was out of the way for her. A few choice Sicilian curses bubbled at the back of her throat, eager for voice, but she squelched them.

Another possibility—something had happened to him. Something bad. He'd slipped in the shower and cracked his head. He was lying in the tub right now, blood and water mingling as they trickled down the pristine white porcelain towards the drain. *Oh, God!* Panic rattled her until she convinced herself she was giving in to her overactive imagination. Imposing calm, she tried to construct more rational, less violent explanations for Reese's absence.

He was in the shower and didn't hear the doorman buzz.

He was on his way home from an errand that had run late.

He was so distracted crossing the street on his way home from his late-running errand that he'd been struck by a psychotic cab driver.

She reined in her thoughts, taking notice of where she was. She'd walked to Fifth Avenue and was standing in front of the Guggenheim. She had to stop spinning scenarios and *do* something. She could go into the museum and distract herself in the gift shop, or grab an overpriced cup of coffee in the cafe. Or, she could try calling Reese herself. *Bingo.*

Whipping out her cellphone, she dialed his number.
It was busy.

Mild relief pulsed through her. See, he *was* home. He must've been in the shower when the doorman buzzed. Or, maybe he'd been out running errands and they'd just missed each other. Theresa dialed her own number to see if he'd left some kind of message. He hadn't. Clearly he was still expecting her. Proud of her powers of deduction, she turned and started walking back toward Reese's building.

The breeze was blowing across her face now, but she minded it less, finding its touch invigorating. She was tempted to sprint the remaining distance to Eighty-ninth and Park, but didn't want to risk turning an ankle in her heels, or worse, appearing overeager. What if he happened to look out the window and saw her jogging up to his building? No, slow and steady won the race. Besides, there was no reason to hurry. He was there; that was all that mattered.

Reese's building was a magnificent old limestone edifice, clearly prewar. Breezing back into the lobby, Theresa ignored the irked look that flitted across the doorman's face and marched right up to him. "I'm here to see Reese Banister," she said, repeating word for word the statement she'd made less than twenty minutes earlier. "My name is Theresa Falconetti."

"I'm afraid I haven't seen Mr. Banister come in since you were last here," the doorman replied in a condescending tone.

"No, but he and I spoke on the telephone," Theresa lied. "Please buzz him." *And wipe that supercilious look off your face while you're at it.*

The doorman did as he was told. Theresa was gratified to see his surprise when Reese responded to being buzzed and told him to send her up.

"He's on the fifteenth floor," the doorman said with a small frown. "Apartment A."

Thanking him, Theresa rode the elevator up. The doors opened onto a roomy marble foyer decorated with a large oval table flanked by two Queen Anne chairs. Atop the table sat a beautiful bouquet of fresh flowers. To the right was the door to Reese's apartment. To the left, the door to the only other apartment on the floor. Theresa tried not to think about how the furniture in Reese's hallway was nicer than the furniture in her living room and rang his bell. Tiny sparks of anticipation kissed her skin, making it tingle. A second later, Reese answered, clad in a bathrobe, hair tousled. Theresa's sparks fizzled away.

"Reese?"

"I'm so sorry you came all the way up here. I've been trying to reach you."

"What's the matter?"

"I'm coming down with the flu or something, I'm not sure. I'm afraid I can't go with you tonight."

"Oh." Theresa worked hard to keep the disappointment she was feeling from showing on her face.

"Don't be mad," said Reese.

"I'm not," Theresa insisted. Her hand moved to massage a pain that had suddenly appeared in her neck. "I just wish you'd called me."

"I tried to leave a message, but there's something wrong with your answering machine. It won't pick up."

Liar. "It does that sometimes," she said, trying to remember if it ever had. Unsure of what else to say, she looked down at her shoes.

"Theresa?"

She lifted her head. "I'm sorry. I was looking forward to tonight, that's all."

"Me, too."

She paused, waiting for him to invite her in for a moment. When he didn't, she boldly took the initiative.

"Since I'm here, couldn't I see some of your pictures?" she suggested. "I won't stay long."

Reese looked uneasy. "I don't think that's a very good idea. I don't want to get you sick."

"I understand," said Theresa, even though she didn't. She backed up slightly. "Well, I'll be on my way."

"I'm so sorry," Reese apologized again.

"Don't worry about it," Theresa told him. "Feel better."

"I'll try." He reached out, giving one of her curls a tug. "Okay if I call you Monday?"

As let down as she was feeling, this small, affectionate gesture lifted her spirits a bit. "That would be great."

"Okay, then. Well, have fun at the party. And give my apologies to the hosts."

"I will."

"Bye now," he said softly, closing the door.

Numb, Theresa stood in the foyer. Something was *wrong*. Yes, that was the word. Something felt wrong with this whole scenario but she couldn't quite place what it was.

No, she knew.

She just hated that she was thinking it.

She took a step forward with the intent of pressing an ear to his door, then stopped. *She would trust him.* Walking back to the elevator, she pressed the button to go down. The doors peeled back instantly and she stepped inside, the trip to the lobby a slow, harsh ride down to reality. She could feel the doorman's superior gaze as she left the building and headed back outside to—what?

Theresa checked her watch. Half an hour until the party, if she arrived promptly at eight. Right now she didn't want to arrive at all. Who wanted to be the lone single duck in an apartment full of couples? Dejected, she slumped against the side of the building.

If she didn't show, she would never hear the end of it from Janna.

• • •

"I swear on Nonna's eyes, Mikey. You leave now and I'm gonna cut your greasy heart out. We had an agreement."

Michael tried to take the glinting tip of the filleting knife Anthony aimed at his chest seriously, but it was hard. His mind was on fire, burning bright with just one miraculous word: Theresa.

Theresa. Theresa. Theresa. Finally!

Ty had tracked him down at Dante's and asked if he wanted to come to a dinner party at his house tonight. As he strained to hear above the noisy din of the restaurant, the hairs on the back of his neck had stood up. Ever since he'd seen his cousin, he'd been carrying the moonstone around in his pocket like some kind of good luck charm. Just two nights earlier, he'd given in and lit the candles she'd given him, feeling like a total jackass. Now look what had happened: That woo woo crap Gemma had talked him into had worked!

Even though it was a last-minute invite, he'd accepted. It was a small gathering, and Theresa would be there—Ty had said so. That could only mean one thing: He was wearing her down. He knew Theresa. There was *no way* they would have invited him if she hadn't agreed to it. Which meant she had. In fact, maybe she had finally come to her stubborn senses and specifically *requested* he be there. Hurriedly jotting down the address on a napkin from the bar, he'd promised to be there in forty-five minutes.

It wasn't until he hung up that he'd realized he'd forgotten about one very moody, quick-to-anger obstacle.

"C'mon, Ant," he cajoled. No one on the kitchen staff blinked twice over the fact their boss was brandishing a knife at his own sibling. Obviously, they were used to his

brother's dramatics. "I've been waiting two years for this. *Two years!* Cut me some slack here. And lower the knife while you're at it."

"Suppose the woman of my dreams called me and wanted *me* to leave?" posited Anthony bitterly, putting down the knife as requested. "Would *I* be able to just run out?"

"Don't bust my balls, all right? You know it's different."

"You're a co-owner of the restaurant. You have a responsibility."

Michael could feel his teeth clenching. "It's one night."

"Which will turn into two, then three . . ." Anthony folded his arms across his chest and shook his head gravely, a gesture so like their mother's that Michael felt himself going cold with goose bumps. "This is why I told you to stick to hockey, Mikey. It's all or nothing in this biz."

"Look." Michael was growing impatient. Every minute he spent debating Anthony was a minute less he'd spend with Theresa. "I'll do anything you want, okay? Anything."

"*Any*thing? You swear?"

"Any*thing.*"

"Okay. From now on, if you're in town on a Sunday morning and you don't have practice, you take Nonna to Mass."

Michael could feel his face fall.

"You said *anything,*" Anthony reminded him, wagging an annoying finger in his face.

Bit by deliberate bit, Michael realized, Anthony was dismantling any semblance of a life he had. It was his own fault: He never should have agreed to spend his nights off at the restaurant. The guys on the team had already started poking fun at the way he was only allowed to "come out and play" after road games. Man about town? Ever since he began working on Anthony about PR, effing maitre d' was more like it.

But this bargain involved Theresa. Anthony had him by the short and curlies, and knew it. "*Fine,* I'll take Nonna to Mass," Michael capitulated. "Now can I get the hell out of here?"

"Sure," Anthony assured him. "No problem. Remember: Nonna prefers the eight A.M. Mass to the one at ten. Pick her up around seven-thirty or so tomorrow—"

"Tomorrow?"

"Tomorrow's Sunday, Mike."

"Right, right, right," Michael grumbled. "You were saying?"

"Pick her up at seven-thirty," Anthony continued calmly, "because she likes to get to church early to get *her* seat on the aisle, third pew on the left. Afterwards, bring her to Aunt Gavina's."

"Third pew, Aunt Gavina, got it. Anything else?"

Anthony's mouth twitched into a smirk. "Have fun tonight."

"I will. And Ant?" This was the truly hard part, but Michael knew he had to do it.

"Yeah?"

"Thanks."

Theresa, finally. Theresa, finally.

That's all he could think on the drive over. Eyes momentarily leaving the road, he quickly glanced down to make sure what he was wearing was okay. Chinos, nice blue blazer, striped shirt, tie . . . yeah, that worked. Good thing he'd been working the front of the house, greeting customers and making sure everyone was satisfied. He drove on a bit more before abruptly raising his left arm to his nose and sniffing, fearful he might show up smelling like a plate of fried calamari.

Thankfully, he smelled just fine.

He wondered if he'd feel weird being at the coach's house. He'd socialized with Ty before, all the guys had, but never at his own place. He wondered if any of the other guys from the team would be there. Gilly, probably. No, definitely. Ty and Gilly were best friends; they went back years. He pressed his index finger to his lips, then touched it to the St. Christopher medal dangling from his rearview mirror that his mother had given him when he'd first earned his license. *Thank you, God.* Next he gave the moonstone in his pocket an extra rub for luck. What the hell? It couldn't hurt to have all the bases covered.

Theresa had to hand it to Janna: When it came to creating a relaxed atmosphere, she was a master. She'd covered nearly every flat surface with candles of all different sizes and shapes, suffusing the room with a warm, intimate glow. Quiet, classical music provided a subtle, relaxing undercurrent to conversation, while the food was laid out on the dining room table buffet style, allowing guests to pick at will and sit where they pleased.

Which was good. Since she was alone.

Theresa knew full well that although Janna said nothing when she arrived without Reese, at some point in the evening her best friend would drag her off to some remote corner and ask what the story was. Well, the story was simple. Reese was sick. Would Janna believe it? *Did she believe it herself?* What she needed was a nice glass of wine. And some food. She'd stay for an hour and head out.

She approached the dining room table, trying to decide whether to be good, and pile her plate high with salad, or be bad, and cut a big slab of lasagna. Considering Reese punted on her at the last minute, she felt she deserved the lasagna as a consolation prize. She had just started cutting when the doorbell rang. The voice she heard call out greetings in the living room made her freeze mid-slice.

Michael Dante.

Panicking, she picked up her empty plate and made a beeline for the kitchen, where Janna stood at the counter, serenely arranging a plate of crudités.

"I want a divorce," Theresa announced.

Janna glanced up at her. "What?"

"I want a divorce. You're not my best friend anymore. It's over."

Bemused, Janna put down the matchstick-size carrot in her hand and turned to her friend. "What's going on, Terry?"

Theresa began to explain but was silenced by the sudden appearance of Janna's sister, Petra, who had stuck her head around the kitchen door.

"Got any ice?" she asked. Her eyes lit on Theresa. "Hey, Terry! Long time, no see. How's it going?"

"Great," Theresa replied. She couldn't remember the last time she'd seen Janna's sister. "You?"

"Busy." She reached out for the ice bucket Janna handed her. "Grab a plate and come sit with me and Denise."

"Will do," Theresa promised.

"You were saying?" Janna continued when it was back to just the two of them.

"Do you know who just walked through your front door? *Do you?*"

"Ed MacMahon? The cookie monster? Who?"

"Michael Dante," Theresa announced dramatically.

Janna shrugged. "Oh." She went back to piling carrots on the platter.

"Oh?" Theresa echoed incredulously. "You invited him and you didn't *tell* me?"

"I thought you were going to be here with Reese," Janna said lightly, tearing open a bag of celery with her teeth. "I didn't think it mattered. Besides, it wasn't my idea, it was Ty's. Something to do with team unity." With the care of an artist, she arranged the celery on the platter. "So what are you going to do? Hide in here all night?"

"Maybe."

"Too late," Janna murmured beneath her breath as Michael Dante appeared in the kitchen doorway.

"Hey, Janna, Theresa."

He gave Janna a small peck on the cheek. Theresa tensed, waiting to see if he'd try to do the same with her. She was glad when he didn't—although seeing him brought back her dream and with it, an embarrassing, unexpected rush of heat to her body. She turned away, pretending to study Janna's spice rack.

"Everything smells great," said Michael.

"Thank you," Janna replied.

"Need help with anything?"

Theresa rolled her eyes, glad he couldn't see her face. *Need help with anything?* she mimicked in her head. What was he, a freaking Boy Scout? He was always so nice and helpful.

"No, everything's set," Janna said.

Theresa turned back around just in time to see her friend lift the fully adorned veggie platter from the counter and hustle it through the kitchen door, leaving her alone with the last person on earth she wanted to be left alone with.

"So," Michael began casually, taking a step towards her. "What are you doing in here?"

Hiding from you, she almost said, but decided against it. He hadn't really *done* anything. Why be mean? Instead she answered, "Talking to Janna." She eyed him carefully. "You know, I almost didn't recognize you without your pinky ring and toothpick."

Michael chuckled affectionately. "Starting early tonight, huh?"

"*We're* not starting anything," Theresa snorted.

"Oh, no?" Michael raised an eyebrow. "Then why am I here?"

"What are you talking about?"

Michael winked. "Let's just say I know."

"You know what?"

"I *know*," Michael repeated, more portentously this time.

"Well, *I* don't," Theresa said, taking a small step back as he moved towards her.

"C'mon, Theresa," Michael admonished as he drew nearer. "I know you had something to do with my being invited tonight."

"What?" Theresa said, astonished. "Are you out of your mind? I had *nothing* to do with it."

Michael frowned. "Yeah, right."

"Believe what you want," Theresa said, shaking her head. "Ty invited you because he wants you to bond with your teammates or something, *maleducato*."

"God, I love when you call me names in Italian," Michael murmured, putting his hand over his heart as he feigned a swoon.

"I can call you worse," Theresa smiled, warming up.

His eyes flashed wickedly. "You sure you want to do that? Someone might walk in and think you're an Italian girl from Brooklyn. Can't have that."

Theresa gasped. "You are *such* a jerk."

"And *you* are enjoying every minute of flirting with me like this, but you'll never admit it." Michael sighed, cocking his head to one side as he studied her. "Tell you what. Let's call a truce. You stop calling me names and I'll stop teasing you. Deal?"

"Deal," Theresa muttered, hating her own transparency.

"So now what?" Michael asked.

"I guess we should join the party and try to have some fun."

"You sure you remember how to do that?"

"Wouldn't you like to know," Theresa replied in a mock purr. *Shit! I did it again! God, what IS it with him?* She adjusted her glasses. *One hour,* she told herself as she gestured toward the door, then breezed past him out of the kitchen. *She'd stay one hour, then she'd leave.*

With Michael following, she went to the buffet table, put together a plate of food, mostly salad, a small piece of lasagna, then headed for one of two large, overstuffed chairs perpendicular to the couch where Petra and Denise sat, careful not to spill anything as she sat down.

Just as she knew he would, Michael settled in the other chair after briefly talking to Ty, Kevin Gill, and some very young, adolescent-looking blond man.

As politely as she could, Theresa introduced Michael to Janna's sister and her partner. Aware of Michael's ability to charm any audience, she wasn't surprised when he soon had them engaged in a lively conversation about the law, since both women were lawyers. What did take her aback was his bold willingness to say "I don't know what you're talking about" when he didn't understand something. Most men she knew, starting with her own father and brother, would play along rather than admit a gap in knowledge. Studying his strong profile in the candlelight, Theresa couldn't help but be impressed by the confidence it took to be so honest. God knows if it were her, she'd be nodding her head off, pretending she understood what was being discussed even if she was clueless.

She watched with curiosity as the blond boy, whom Ty had been holding court with most of the evening, sauntered over to Michael. "Still here, huh, Dante? This must be way past your bedtime."

Michael ignored him.

The blond's eyes flicked lasciviously to Theresa. "Who ya got here, your granddaughter?"

Michael didn't even bother to look at him. "Right," he replied, bored.

Van Dorn looked down at Theresa, seemingly unaware of the silence that followed his initial statement. "Into old guys, huh?"

"Watch how you talk to her," Michael warned.

Theresa could feel her ire rising. "Who are you?" she asked van Dorn coldly.

Petra and Denise both sniggered but van Dorn carried on, oblivious. "I'm Paul van Dorn. I'm the one who's going to force this old guy"—he glanced at Michael—"into early retirement. Ain't that right, Mikey?"

"Right," Michael repeated, yawning.

"Were you raised by wolves?" Theresa asked. Clearly Michael was used to this young jackass needling him, but that didn't mean the rest of them had to listen to it—or like it.

Van Dorn laughed and nervously glanced around at the others, rolling his eyes as if to say "Is this chick nuts or what?" When no one responded in kind, his face turned pink.

"What?" he asked.

"What the *hell* makes you think you can march up to someone at a party and insult them?" Petra demanded.

"Didn't your mommy and daddy teach you any manners?" Denise asked, almost simultaneously.

Mortified, van Dorn slunk away. Theresa, struck by the thought that they might well have totally emasculated Michael, turned to him apologetically. "I'm sorry. But that kid was *way* outta line."

"Not a problem," Michael replied, looking at her in wry amusement. "Maybe I should hire you as my bodyguard."

"I mean, where does he get off?"

"It's okay, Theresa," Michael assured her, putting a warm hand on her shoulder. Heat shot through her as she noticed the size of his hands. *Big, strong, square. Solid.*

"Sorry," she repeated.

"Don't be sorry," Petra said. "That little twerp had it coming."

"What do you think, can I sue for harassment?" Michael joked.

All three women laughed.

One hour turned to two, two to three, and three to four. Before she knew it, people were saying their good-byes as the party wound down. She'd spent the entire evening in Michael Dante's company and had had a good time. How was that possible?

"Would you like a ride home?"

Michael's question was a simple one, but Theresa stalled. On the one hand, it would save her cab fare. But on the other, she'd be alone with him again, which could be dangerous, especially since he seemed to have an uncanny gift for getting under her skin and making her behave like she was still a wisecracking, flirty Bensonhurst girl. Still, she didn't want to appear ungracious.

"That would be great," she told him.

All night long, he'd been checking his watch. Theresa couldn't decide if it was a personal tick, or if he was bored as hell. But when he did it again as soon as they got in the car, she couldn't hold her tongue.

"I'm sorry you were bored," she said as he drove down Fifty-seventh to First Avenue.

Michael glanced at her, confused. "What?"

"You kept checking your watch like you couldn't wait to get out of there. Are you meeting someone after you drop me off?" *Not that I care.*

"No."

"Then what?"

Stopped at a red light, Michael's hands restlessly tapped out a beat on the steering wheel. "You'll make fun of me."

"I will not!"

"Yeah, right." Michael sighed. "The reason I kept checking my watch—"

"Every five minutes—"

"Get outta here—"

"Ten, then."

"—is because I wanted to make sure I got home in time to get some sleep. I have to take my grandmother to Mass tomorrow morning."

"That's sweet."

"Really." Michael's voice was full of distrust.

"Honest." The car lurched slightly as the light turned green and they continued driving. "Where does she go? Saint Finbar's?"

"Yeah."

"God." Memories flooded Theresa's mind. "Is that nasty Father Clementine still there?"

"Oh, yeah." Michael cracked his window slightly. "You know Clementine?"

"Who doesn't? When I won the third grade spelling bee, he didn't want to give me my prize because the sister told him I talked too much in class."

"So what happened?"

"My mother went up there, threatened him within an inch of his life, and he handed over the prize."

Michael laughed appreciatively. "I can see your mother doing that."

"Mmm." Theresa hated that he knew her mother. It was too close, too intimate. Time to steer the conversation away from Brooklyn.

"So what'll happen Monday in the locker room between you and van Dorn? Will you hang him out to dry?"

"He's not worth the effort." Michael turned left, steering the Mercedes smoothly onto First Avenue. "Annoying little bastard, though, isn't he?"

"That's one word for it. Is he seriously gunning for your spot in the lineup?"

"Yup."

"Does he have a chance?" Theresa asked, feeling, to her surprise, genuine concern.

"Nope."

"Well, that's good." She settled back in her seat, relaxing. She'd had a nice evening. Good food, good conversation, low key, no pressure, no complaints.

Apart from Reese bailing on her on such short notice.

And Michael calling her bluff in the kitchen.

She stole a glance at him; he seemed to be in his own world, his eyes fastened on the road, right thumb still tapping on the wheel. *Is he nervous being with me?* she wondered.

Without warning, he turned and looked at her.

"What?" she asked, warily.

"Nothing."

Since he was still looking at her, instead of the road, she said, "Nice car."

"Let me guess: You were expecting a Camaro. Or maybe a ribboned donkey cart full of mozzarella and oregano plants."

"I'm not that bad," Theresa protested. "And keep your eyes on the road."

"Yeah, you are," said Michael. "But you can't help it."

"Gee, thanks," Theresa retorted. A bit sulky now, she peered out the window. She'd always liked New York late at night. The place still pulsed with energy; but it was more subdued, concentrated, like the ocean in between bouts of breaking waves.

"Almost there," she announced to him. "I'm on Fifty-ninth."

"Got it." The car slowly rolled up to another red light and halted. After a moment or two of silence, Michael again turned to look at her. His eyes were so full of desire that Theresa contemplated jumping out of the car while it was still at a standstill—not because she wasn't feeling the same way, but because she *was*.

Obviously she'd had too much vino.

"I had a really nice time tonight," Michael said quietly.

Theresa looked out the passenger window. "Me, too."

Silence thick as snowfall blanketed the car. Finally reaching her building, Michael eased the car to a halt at the curb. It sat there, idling, while Theresa tensely waited for him to bid her good night. But he didn't.

"I need to ask you a question," Michael said.

"Go ahead."

His gaze was full of tenderness. "Would you mind if I kissed you?"

Theresa's breath caught. This was so out of left field, so unexpected, that for a moment she couldn't speak. *He had asked, not assumed.* She thought about it. What harm was there in one small, friendly kiss? She would be doing him a favor; maybe even get him off her back once and for all.

She lifted her eyes to his. "Okay," she whispered.

Slowly, almost gingerly as if he was afraid of hurting her in some way, Michael leaned over and gently cupping a hand behind her neck, lowered his mouth to hers. Theresa felt a small, internal shudder of resistance—*It's not Lubov, it's not Lubov, it's not Lubov*—then gradually surrendered. The kiss was sweet and lingering, the firm press of his mouth against hers tasting of wine and long pent up desire. She could tell he wanted more, but he didn't push. And she . . . well, she was dizzy with this, her first taste of a man in so, so long. She clung to the moment and reveled in it, was even disappointed when it ended, though she continued to tell herself she'd done him a favor, nothing more, nothing less.

Seemingly contented, Michael settled back in the driver's seat. "So, when do you want to go out for coffee?"

Theresa blinked in confusion. "Excuse me?"

"Coffee. C'mon, Theresa. You just let me kiss you, you let me drive you home . . . are you telling me you're *still* not going to let me buy you *coffee*?"

"This *was* coffee, Michael. This whole evening— *clearly*—was in lieu of coffee. Get it?"

"Ah ha!" Michael exclaimed. "So you *did* ask Ty and Janna to invite me!"

"What color is the sky in your world, Dante? Because clearly, you are living on a completely different planet. On *my* planet, tonight counted as our coffee date!"

"Oh, no. No way." He was shaking his head obstinately. "The rule book states you can't substitute a party for a one-on-one situation."

"Well, obviously you don't have the most up-to-date version. My edition says substitutions are fine."

She could see the hard set of his jaw in the dim yellow lamplight flooding the car.

"You're not playing fair, Theresa."

"I'm not playing *at all,* Michael. The sooner you get that through your head, the better." *The nerve! I let him kiss me and he still has the* cogliones *to assume he's going to get a coffee date as well? Relentless little—*

"It's getting late," Michael snapped, stepping on the gas to make the engine roar.

"Fine," Theresa snapped back. She couldn't wait to get out of the car and be free of this—*baccala.* What the hell had she been thinking?!

Mother of God, *she* was the *baccala.*

Meanwhile, Michael was staring straight ahead, unwilling to look at her. "So I guess the next time we see each other will be to go over stuff for Dante's?" he said through clenched teeth.

"I guess." Theresa opened the car door and stepped out onto the curb. "Have fun at church tomorrow morning."

"Yeah, right."

She went to close the door, but at the last second Michael leaned over, holding it open. "I'm not giving up on you, Theresa," he declared.

Ignoring him, she pushed his arm away, slamming the car door shut.

She meant to tell him to drive safely, but it was too late: He had already peeled away from the curb.

CHAPTER

08

It was so hot in St. Finbar's, and the drone of the priest was so boring, Michael feared he'd pass out and smash his forehead on the pew in front of him.

He'd conveyed Nonna Maria to church by seven-thirty, as directed, but she wasn't the only one there early to stake her claim. Michael counted at least twenty nearly identical old women filing into the church at the same time, all legging it as fast as they could up the center aisle to grab "their" spots. He wondered what would happen if one of them found someone else sitting in their personal seat. Would they all band together and force the interloper to move? The image of a band of rosary bead-wielding grannies menacing a poor, unsuspecting worshipper amused him.

Hell, he needed *something* to laugh about, didn't he?

Arriving home the night before, the first thing he'd done was throw Gemma's moonstone out the window. Next, he tossed the candles in the trash. Even now, the temptation to scowl at the figure on the cross and mutter

"Thanks for nothing" was strong. He resisted, fearing outright sacrilege.

What the hell had happened?

One minute Theresa was letting him kiss her, the next she was telling him their relationship was strictly business. It didn't make sense. *She* didn't make sense. He'd locked lips with a few women in his time, and he could tell when someone was into it. Theresa was definitely into it. Aware of her past, he'd deliberately held back, not wanting to push her. He didn't want to do or say anything to make her feel pressured or trapped. He sensed she appreciated it, though—

Ouch, Madonn'. "Jesus, Nonna!" A sharp poke in the ribs knocked him out of his daydream. Everyone else in the church was on their knees.

"Sorry," he whispered to his grandmother, whose disapproval he couldn't bear.

He knelt down beside her, knowing his knees would regret it later. He was relieved when Nonna closed her eyes and seemed to lose herself in prayer.

Maybe he *had* pushed.

Maybe asking her out for coffee right after the kiss was too much for her to handle. He knew pushiness was a problem of his. Something would stick in his mind and like a dog with a bone, he couldn't let it go. Dogged determination was the reason he'd made it into the NHL. The reason he was still on the third line and that effing—*Sorry, Jesus*—moron van Dorn remained out of the lineup. Truth be told, he wasn't sure he knew how to back off.

But if he wanted to get Theresa, he might have to learn.

A sharp pinch to his arm let him know it was time to sit back in the pew again. Grimacing, he slid back, his knees throbbing with pain. Talk about penance. People were rising from their seats and walking towards the front of the church to receive communion. His grandmother eyed him expectantly but he shook his head no. He knew it disappointed her, but in this case, it was too bad. It didn't feel right, especially since he'd been sitting here feeling angry with God.

He watched the parade of parishioners slowly make their way towards the brass altar railing, where they waited patiently for the priest to feed them their wafer and wine. He *had* pushed, he decided. He'd ruined a perfectly romantic moment by nudging that one extra inch. *Gavone,* he chided himself. *When are you going to learn?* But he'd meant what he'd said about not giving up on her. The tarot cards had explicitly said—*okay, maybe not explicitly*—that she might be The One. It was going to take a lot of time, patience and energy, and there would be lots of obstacles to overcome. Maybe this was just one of the minor setbacks predicted in the cards; the universe telling him "Cool your jets, buddy boy, take it slow."

"Psst, yo Mikey."

The stage whisper made him turn. There was Theresa's brother Phil and his two oldest kids shuffling up the aisle. Not wanting to disturb other parishioners, some of whom were obviously deep in contemplation, Michael just winked. "Meet me outside after," Phil continued, his daughter rolling her eyes at her father's irreverence during a solemn moment. Michael nodded yes, waving to little Vicki, who happily waved back. He waited for his grandmother to return to her seat.

The rest of the service passed in an interminable blur.

"Phil, Little Phil, Vicki, I want you to meet my grandmother, Maria Grimaldi."

After a pointed barb from Father Clementine about how happy he was to see "this young man" back in church, Michael was finally able to escort Nonna outside, where Phil and his kids were waiting. Phil politely shook Nonna's hand while the two kids stood there, smiling nervously and backing away slightly, unsure what to do.

"We go to Gavina's," Nonna said impatiently.

"I know," Michael soothed. "It'll just be a minute."

As if she didn't hear him, Nonna started toddling away, up Benson Street to where the car was parked.

"What's up?" he asked Phil hurriedly, keeping an eye on his grandmother.

"What are you doing two Sundays from now?"

Michael ran through the team's schedule in his head. "We're home. We've got an early afternoon game against Toronto. Why?"

"Why don't you stop by after the game for coffee and dessert? Debbie and I are giving Mom and Dad a break. Theresa's going to be there."

Michael hesitated. "I don't think Theresa would be too happy to see me there. She didn't react too well last time."

"Don't let her scare you. She's all bark and no bite. Whaddaya say?"

It didn't take long for Michael to make his decision. "Sure, why not? I'll call when it gets closer so you can tell me what I should bring."

Phil clapped a hand on his back. "Good man."

"I gotta run, Phil, my grandmother is trying to get into someone else's car."

Waving his good-bye, Michael jogged off in the direction of Nonna, shouting for her to wait. Maybe accepting the invite was a mistake. Maybe it was pushy.

Or maybe Phil's being in church today was divinely ordained.

Pointing Nonna in the direction of his own car, Gemma's admonition to "have faith" seemed to resonate. He felt lighter, more confident; all previous traces of soul wrestling vanished into the frosty morning air. Once he'd dropped Nonna off at his aunt's, he would swing back to

his place and check the gutter to see if maybe the moonstone had rolled into it.

Then he'd fish those candles out of the garbage.

Monday morning. Theresa had contemplated calling in
sick to avoid Janna's third degree. But she couldn't. They
had too much work. Plus, it was simply postponing the inevitable.

The sooner she spilled, the sooner she could forget the
whole evening.

Forgetting was high on Theresa's "To Do" list.

She'd spent most of Sunday working at home, putting
the final touches on a press kit for an actress on *Jailbirds,*
a new network comedy taking place inside a women's
prison. The show might not last, but if Theresa did her job
right, interest in her new client would. Revising the press
release, she'd picked up the phone to call Reese a half
dozen times, always deciding at the last second not to go
through with it. Conversely, every time her phone rang,
she tried not picking it up on the first ring to keep from
seeming desperate.

Unfortunately, all that did was give her three-second
respites from talking to her mother, her brother, and four
different solicitors.

So much for self-restraint.

Arriving at work, she was surprised to find Terrence
absent. The world's nosiest man was usually there before
both she and Janna, tidying his desk and sharpening his
barbs. Meandering down the hall, she could hear Janna's
fingers flying furiously across the computer keyboard.
Her door was open, so Theresa walked right in. Janna's
fingers went silent as Theresa plopped down in the nearest
chair.

"All right," said Theresa. "What do you want to know
first?"

"Did you have a good time?"

"Yeesss," Theresa replied slowly. She was surprised; she thought Janna's first question would be "Have you heard from Reese since Saturday?"

"So, have you heard from Reese since Saturday?" Ah. It was the second question. Janna wasn't slipping.

"No."

Janna tapped a pen on the edge of her desk.

"Refresh my memory. What was wrong with him again? A bad case of bullshititis?"

"Not funny."

"C'mon, Terry, lighten up."

"People do suddenly get sick, you know." *Though I didn't believe him either.*

"I know," Janna allowed. She stopped tapping and put her elbows on the desk, cupping her chin in her left hand. "You and Michael seemed to be having a pretty good time together."

Theresa remained silent.

"Even Ty noticed it," Janna continued, with a sly smile. "He thought you and Michael looked cute together."

"So did Spanky and Alfalfa. That didn't mean they were a love match."

"Why are you so touchy about this?"

"You *know* why." A great jet of frustration was hissing up inside her. "Why does everyone treat me like an idiot who doesn't know her own heart and mind?"

Janna looked baffled. "What do you mean?"

"You, my mother, Michael—you all think he's The One for me and I'm too stupid to see it!" Hot, angry tears threatened. "I'm sorry," she choked, trying not to cry. "I'm just tired of everyone thinking they know what's best for me." *I'm tired of thinking I've found a nice man only to have him turn around and kick me in the teeth.*

Janna slid out from behind her desk and, crouching beside Theresa's chair, wrapped a loving arm around her shoulder. "This is about Reese Banister, isn't it?"

"No!" Theresa yelped. "I—okay, I was disappointed he didn't come with me, all right? I really wanted you to meet the *real* him."

"When did the *real him* call you to cancel?" Janna asked pointedly.

"Does it matter?" Theresa sniffled.

"Ladies?"

Theresa and Janna both turned to see Terrence standing in the doorway, holding aloft a gorgeous spray of flowers and a huge, gold box of Godiva chocolates.

"These arrived seconds ago for a certain Ms. Falconetti." He rattled the chocolate box. "Come and get it, girl."

Theresa flew from the chair and fetched the flowers and candy from Terrence. She opened the tiny white envelope pinned to the flower arrangement, all frustration and doubt fading away as she read aloud: *"Theresa. Sorry about Saturday night. Will call soon and we'll have dinner. Reese."*

"Well," Terrence purred. "What's all *this* about?"

"Thanks," Theresa said, ignoring his curiosity. "You can go now."

"Would you like me to put those in water for you?" he asked politely.

"Oh." *Flowers. Water. Right.* "Sure." She handed them back to him.

"That'll be one Godiva chocolate, please."

Theresa grinned. "Later. If you behave."

"Define *behave*," Terrence replied brazenly.

"Good-bye," said Theresa loudly, smiling as she pushed him out the door. She turned back to Janna, beaming. "See? See how nice Reese is?"

When Janna simply nodded, Theresa knew she was holding her tongue, but didn't care. Let Janna think what she wanted. *She* knew what a wonderful person Reese was, and if Janna chose to believe otherwise, that was *her* problem. Once Janna spent time with Reese and saw what a sensitive, intelligent man he was, she'd give up her pathetic campaigning for Michael Dante.

"Want a chocolate?" she asked.

The mood in the Blades locker room was more pumped up than usual as the players began dressing for their game. They were playing Dallas, who were leading the Western Conference. It would be a real test for the team, and the sellout crowd would be especially stoked.

Fastening his lucky shoulder pads with the same old lucky skate laces he'd used for five years, Michael mused on his new superstitions. Not only had he managed to retrieve the gemstone, but it was in his locker, hidden in the pocket of his pants. *Who knows?* he thought, sitting down on the bench to affix his shin guards next. *Maybe it will bring luck on the ice as well.*

His metaphysical reverie was broken not by backup goalie Denny O'Malley cranking up the pre-game music to an almost deafening level—though that was annoying—but by a preppie thorn in his side.

"You sure you're up to playing tonight?" van Dorn asked. "I thought you might have thrown your back out over the weekend, attempting to get it on with that girl from the party."

Michael ignored him and continued dressing.

"No answer," van Dorn observed aloud. "Hmm. Maybe he doesn't have his hearing aid turned on."

Pissed but self-controlled, Michael regarded his nemesis pitifully. "Do yourself a favor. You're in the pros now. Start acting like it."

"Right on, Mikey," said defenseman Barry Fontaine, whose locker was beside Michael's.

Embarrassed, van Dorn sneered and walked away.

"Still gunnin' for ya spot, eh?" asked Barry.

"Guess so," said Michael. Slipping on his padded pants and tying down his sweater, Michael found himself getting worked up. With van Dorn breathing down his neck, Anthony breaking his balls and Theresa screwing with his head, it was a miracle he hadn't landed in a mental hospital. He could fully imagine himself behind bars after murdering van Dorn with his bare hands. *Arrogant little shit.* Did he really think insults were going to rattle him? Mr. Ivy League obviously hadn't heard the kind of trash talk dished out on the ice in the minors. Lacing up his skates, he vowed that from now on, nothing the little twerp said would get under his skin.

On the ice, Michael transformed his anger into aggression. On his first shift, he nailed one of Dallas's defensemen in the corner with a punishing body check. On his second shift he broke up a cross-ice pass that could have easily turned into an odd man rush against the Blades. His energy wasn't lost on Ty, who gave him more ice time during the second and third periods than he'd seen in a year, double-shifting his line. Inspired, Michael made another great defensive play, stealing the puck and flipping a perfect saucer pass to Kevin Gill, who was just off the bench. Gill went in alone and scored the game winner.

After the final horn, as the team gathered around goalie Pierre LaRouche, Michael finally allowed himself to relax. He couldn't remember the last time he felt so high, so invincible. He'd played the entire game "in the zone" and was named one of the "Stars of the Game," along with LaRouche and second-line center Thad Meyers. He reveled in the adulation of the Blades fans, especially those way up in the blue seats chanting "Mikey D, Mikey D," when he stepped back out onto the ice after the game.

These were his people. God, he loved New Yorkers.

In the locker room afterwards, he basked in the compliments of his teammates: "You were on fire out there, Mike!" Gilly shouted. "Over the hill my ass!" yelled fellow vet Nick Roberts. Their appreciation was made all the more sweet knowing that Golden Boy heard every word of it.

Emerging from his shower relaxed, yet still energized, Michael found himself being flagged over to the coach's office by Ty.

"You played a helluva game out there tonight, Mike."

"Thanks, coach."

He winked at Michael. "You must have been inspired, huh?"

Michael laughed ruefully, vigorously toweling his head. "Pissed off was more like it."

"Things not going well with Theresa?" Ty asked.

"Things aren't going, period."

"Want to talk?" Ty offered.

Michael hesitated. It embarrassed him, spilling his guts to Ty, especially after already talking to Kevin. Whenever he'd had "girl trouble" in the past, he'd been able to figure things out on his own. But this was different. This wasn't just any woman, this was The One. "You sure?" he double-checked, stalling. "Don't you have to talk to the media?"

"A few minutes wait won't kill them. Go on."

As briefly as he could, Michael filled Ty in, emphasizing how he had followed Kevin's advice on wooing, but omitting his visit to Gemma. He couldn't believe he was telling all this to his coach, but what the hell. Good advice often came from unexpected places. When he told Ty about Theresa's brother asking him over for dessert, Ty's response was immediate.

"You're going, right?"

"I said yes, but . . ." Michael frowned uneasily.

"But what?"

"I'm worried about looking pathetic, you know?"

"You won't look pathetic," Ty assured him. "You'll look determined."

"Yeah?" Michael wasn't so sure.

"Yeah. Look: Why are you in the NHL?"

"What?"

"Why are you in the NHL?" Ty repeated patiently. "Why are you in the pros when so many other guys with more natural ability never made it out of the minors?"

Pride burgeoned in Michael's chest. "Because I don't give up."

"That's right. You're a warrior, Michael. You do whatever it takes. That's what you have to do with Theresa."

Michael nodded slowly. "Yeah. I guess you're right." It was comforting to hear his coach echo the revelation he himself had had in church the previous weekend. In the end, it all boiled down to determination, didn't it? Determination to win the game. Determination to get the girl.

And faith. He couldn't forget about that.

But there was still something gnawing at him.

"Why did she let me kiss her, then freak out when I asked her out for coffee?"

"I think Theresa might have a lot of issues around intimacy after what happened," Ty said carefully, his gaze seeming to penetrate Michael's in an effort to make sure he knew what was being referred to. "I wouldn't take it personally."

"It's kind of hard not to."

"I know, but you have to realize that she's probably scared shitless by the thought of being vulnerable to you in any way. Go slow. Be patient."

"I can do that."

"Then go for it," Ty encouraged. He picked up his sports jacket and swung it up onto his shoulder. "Anything else?"

"You could give me more ice time from now on," Michael joshed.

"Keep playing like tonight and I will. Have a good night, Mikey."

"You, too, Ty."

"I have an idea," Theresa said enthusiastically. "Why don't we go out back and play wiffle ball until your mom calls us for dessert?" Though she loved spending time with Vicki and Little Phil, watching the same movie over and over was not her idea of fun. Hitting the remote, she stopped the video.

"Cool," said Little Phil. He was off the couch in a shot. Vicki didn't look so sure.

"What's the matter, sweetie?" Theresa asked.

"Philly's gonna hit me with the bat."

"Philly will not hit you with the bat, I promise," Theresa said, rising from the couch and extending a hand to her niece. Together they walked through to the kitchen, where Theresa's mother and sister-in-law were busy loading the dishwasher and getting out the tableware for dessert.

"We're going to go in the back for a while," Theresa announced.

"Sure, anything to get out of KP patrol," Debbie teased.

"It's good for her to play with children," Theresa's mother declared.

"As opposed to burning them at the stake like I usually do?" Theresa offered.

"We'll call you for dessert," Theresa's mother continued, deliberately ignoring Theresa's comment. "What's Daddy doing? Is he still asleep?"

Theresa peered back through the kitchen doorway to look at her father, who was indeed asleep on the far end of the couch. Watching the slow rise and fall of his chest, Theresa's own breath hitched. He had once been such a robust man. But now he was little more than a shell, his skin gray, his body stooped and failing. *He's dying from the cancer,* she thought. The truth of it made her throat close to the size of a pinhole. *Not yet, God, please,* she prayed.

Collecting herself, she turned back to her mother. "Still sleeping," she reported.

Her mother glanced up at the clock. "Remind me I have to give him his pills at nine."

"I will." She peered down at her niece, smiling. "Ready to go?"

"Yup."

Vicki skipped out the back door and down the back steps, running to join her brother in the yard. Theresa followed at a slower pace, watching them. She couldn't believe how big they were. Wasn't it just yesterday she was visiting them in the hospital? She remembered their tiny pink faces were serene with contentment as she held them tightly in her arms, then lifted them to her nose and inhaled deeply, intoxicated by their pure, innocent baby smell. Tears threatened and she shook them away. Jesus, what was wrong with her? It felt like anything could set her off these days. Reese, her father, the kids . . . maybe she was having a nervous breakdown.

"Okay, you two," she called, joining them. "I'll pitch and you can take turns hitting. Phil, clock your sister with that bat and you're a dead man, got it?"

"Yeah," Phil muttered.

Both kids complained of the cold, but Theresa wasn't having any of it. It wasn't cold at all; they were just so used to sitting slack-jawed in front of the TV they'd forgotten the joys of brisk, invigorating exercise. When she had kids, she'd sure as hell make sure they got some fresh air once in a while.

When she had kids.

Theresa felt the bottom of her stomach drop. It had always been *if,* not *when.* Yet looking at Vicki and Phil, who were busy now squabbling over who would get to hit first, Theresa was overcome with a hollow feeling inside. *Where is this coming from?* she puzzled, frightened by how real and deep the feelings of longing were. Yes, she'd always dreamed of getting married, but kids had always been an abstract concept. Clearly, this was somehow related to Reese. Or—

No.

Genuinely unsettled now, she focused her energies on being an aunt. Her brother stuck his head out the back door and called the three of them in for dessert. Walking back towards the house, she was actually looking forward to losing herself in adult conversation.

But when she entered the dining room she found Michael Dante sitting there.

He was surrounded by her family, all smiling like cats who had swallowed canaries.

"Let me guess," she sighed. "You were walking by and decided to stop in."

"I invited him," her brother confessed.

"Look, Terry, Michael brought cannolis from Dante's for dessert," her mother interjected, clearly hoping to forestall World War Three from erupting between her two children.

"Gee, cannolis. Well, that makes it all right, then," Theresa said sarcastically.

"Who wants coffee?" Debbie asked with false cheer.

"I'll have some," Michael said politely, holding his cup aloft. His eyes sought Theresa's but she refused to look at him.

Coffee poured, Michael engaged in small talk, to which Theresa's family eagerly responded. She couldn't get over how much they liked him. The beatific smile on her mother's face when she looked at him . . . And her father! *Madonn',* telling him things about other relatives he hardly ever talked about outside the circle of the immediate family. How could they do this to her? *Good old, stupid Theresa, doesn't know when a man is good for her. Let's invite Michael over without her knowing and see if she finally gets it.* After the tenth or eleventh time her brother referred to Michael as "Mikey D," her last frazzled nerve gave way.

"Will you stop calling him that?" she snapped. "He's not one of the Back Street Boys, for Chrissakes."

"That's his nickname," Phil said defensively. He looked to Michael for confirmation. "Am I right or am I right?"

"You're right," Michael said tepidly.

"It's moronic," Theresa insisted.

"What?" her brother jeered at her. "You can come up with something better?"

Theresa laughed ominously. "You don't want me to go down that road, okay?"

"Go down it," Phil challenged.

"Drop it, *cidrule,*" their father commanded.

Theresa rose and started clearing the table. Well aware she couldn't avoid Michael forever, she followed him out to his car when he left, knowing that behind the lace curtains in Phil and Debbie's front window, her whole family was watching them talk.

"I don't believe you," she began, crossing her arms across her chest as she parked a hip against the hood of his car. "You think I *like* being ambushed?"

"It wasn't my idea," said Michael. A breeze rippled past, and Theresa caught a whiff of what she assumed was his aftershave, a clean, woodsy scent that she quite liked. Or would have, if someone else was wearing it.

"I don't care *whose* idea it was," she countered. "You should have said no."

"I told you," Michael said stubbornly. "I'm not giving up."

"And I told you: You're wasting your time."

"Time's all I got, Theresa." Michael's mouth eased into a slow, confident smile. "I'm in no hurry."

Of all the stubborn, pigheaded, obstinate . . . he wasn't going to take the hint, was he? It was futile. Useless. He would keep at her until she finally broke down. *Unbelievable.* Keeping her expression bland, she regarded him.

"*If* I go out for coffee with you, will you get off my case?"

"How about dinner?"

"How about a swift kick in the pants?"

"Is that a yes?"

Theresa's jaw dropped. "You are one *pushy* SOB, you know that?"

"I'll take that as a compliment," Michael replied, actually looking pleased.

"Take it however you want!" She could hear her own voice rising in disbelief.

He jingled his car keys in his pocket impatiently. "So, dinner?"

Theresa threw her hands up in the air. "Fine, dinner! Whatever it takes to get you off my back!" She turned towards the front window, cupping her hands around her mouth. "I'VE AGREED TO HAVE DINNER WITH HIM!" she called loudly. "YOU CAN ALL GO BACK TO YOUR OWN LIVES NOW!"

She saw the curtain flutter slightly. She turned back to Michael. "Call me at the office. We'll figure out a date and time."

"Sounds good," Michael murmured.

"Now do you mind if I go back inside with *my* family?"

"Go right ahead. And please, thank your brother again for inviting me. That was really nice of him."

"Phil's a nice guy when he's not meddling in other people's lives."

She made her way back inside, frowning. Her family was gathered around the TV, watching with forced concentration. Seeing them, she almost burst out laughing. Deciding to play along, she sat down and pretended to be absorbed in what was on the screen, too. Finally her mother couldn't take it anymore.

"*So,* when are the two of you going out to dinner?"

"I don't know, Ma," Theresa said, still staring at the TV. "But as soon as I find out, you'll be the first to know."

CHAPTER

09

"This is insane!" Theresa fretted aloud. "How do I know you're not going to slit my throat and dump my body in the Rockaways?!"

"Just relax," Michael commanded, his tone laced with amusement as he eased his car away from the curb. "Where's your sense of adventure?"

"It fled the minute you insisted I put on this blindfold."

"Trust me, okay?"

Theresa flinched when Michael reached out and gave her leg a reassuring squeeze, mainly because she couldn't see it coming. She tried tilting her head back to peek out from beneath the silk that was binding her eyes, but it was useless.

Michael had tied it good and tight.

Okay, she was *intrigued*. No one had ever shown up for a date—wait, wrong word, this was a mercy meal—and asked her to put on a blindfold. Clearly the man had a few creative bones in his body. And maybe a few screws loose as well.

"Is this going to take long?" she asked nervously.

"What, the ride or dinner?"

"Both."

"Ever thought of getting a 'scrip for Xanax? You need to calm down."

"Oh, so now you're a psychiatrist, too," Theresa jibed. "Hockey player, restaurateur, shrink. Is there no end to your talents?"

"That's for me to know and you to find out."

Theresa groaned and concentrated on enduring the ride to God knows where. Two weeks had passed since she'd been ambushed at Phil and Debbie's; close to four since Reese had sent her the flowers and chocolate. She and Reese had talked by phone, but still hadn't managed to pin down a date for dinner. He'd been traveling a lot, to LA, San Francisco, Chicago, Miami. Theresa knew why his work schedule was so busy—almost weekly, she and Janna read in the trades of yet another PR firm fallen to Butler Corporation. Reese always mentioned these buy-outs on the phone, using it as a segue to ask where she and Janna were in terms of selling. Theresa didn't like to think about the subject and increasingly found herself getting defensive whenever the question arose. She hated when that happened.

But she hated thinking about the whole Butler Corporation situation even more.

She and Janna barely spoke about it.

It was as if they'd made a silent pact agreeing that if neither of them mentioned it, it would just disappear. Which was ridiculous. Ted Banister called Janna daily. She and Janna were working hard to drum up business. But so far, it was yielding little.

"This music okay?"

Theresa left her thoughts to focus on the question. She'd been totally oblivious to the music. Now she listened. "Andrea Bocelli?"

"Yup."

She could hear the pleasure in Michael's voice that she had recognized it and sighed dramatically. "You're such a wop."

"It's good music," Michael countered. "It has nothing to do with being Italian. Just relax and enjoy it."

"Is this what you play in the locker room to get pumped up?"

Michael laughed. "Yeah, right. Anthony turned me on to it. He plays it in the restaurant."

"It *is* nice," Theresa admitted. She wondered what other drivers thought, catching sight of a blindfolded woman in the passenger seat of a Mercedes. Probably that it was some sex game. *Or that the driver was going to elaborate lengths to surprise his companion.* The thought made Theresa feel guilty. Michael was going through a lot of effort for her benefit, and all she hoped was that it would be finished and done within two hours.

The ride went quickly because they talked. About the restaurant, mainly. Work. Family stuff. She realized with some surprise that Reese never asked about her family. But that was because they were into discussing culture and ideas. They communicated on a more artistic level.

"Okay, we're here."

Theresa felt her pulse surge slightly as the car rolled to a stop. The temptation to tear off the blindfold was strong, but she didn't want to spoil whatever carefully calibrated plans Michael had laid down. Still intrigued, she let him open the car door, take her gently by the arm, and lead her a few feet towards another door, which he steered her through.

"You can take off your blindfold now," he said.

Swallowing nervously, Theresa untied the strip of silk from around her head.

They were in Dante's. The entire restaurant was empty save for a young woman with long, streaming red hair, who was busy tuning a violin. The table they usually sat at to do business was beautifully set, with a single rose in a bud vase and two long white tapers burning. Theresa turned to Michael, stunned.

"You closed the restaurant just for me?"

Michael nodded, his expression somewhat hopeful.

"Are you *nuts?* We're supposed to be building your client base, not—"

"*Sshh.*" He put his index finger to her lips to quiet her. "Just relax, okay?"

"Okay," Theresa said none too convincingly as she let Michael lead her to the table. "How on earth did you convince Anthony to close the restaurant on a Saturday night?"

"I have my ways," Michael replied mysteriously as he pulled out the chair for her.

"Is he in the kitchen?" Theresa whispered, fearing a scene.

"He's making a special dinner for us."

Theresa clucked her tongue. "Michael . . ." She was touched, her heart filling with tender appreciation for his efforts. It was wrong to compare, completely unfair, but this trumped Reese's flowers and chocolates. This was something she read about in women's magazines, a fantasy scenario that happened to other women, not her.

In the flickering candlelight, the wine flowed and the violinist played, eyes closed and face serene, her slim, nimble fingers coaxing beautiful music that was bewitching. Theresa got to formally meet Anthony as he served their meal. The food was delicious. And Michael . . .

Well, he was a wonderful dinner companion, genuinely interested in everything she had to say. Theresa tried not to fall under the spell of the candlelight, but it was hard: He was a handsome man, and the fact he had gone through all this effort was astounding. It showed he was a romantic, just like she was. As the evening drew to a close, she found herself feeling disappointed that all too soon, it would be over.

"This was wonderful," she murmured, because it was.

Michael's face lit up, warmed by her praise. He folded and refolded his napkin, seeming to stall for time. "Would you like to come back to my place for coffee?"

Theresa hesitated.

"No pressure," he assured her quietly. "If you'd rather I just take you home, I can do that."

Theresa was flustered. How was it possible he could be so pushy one minute and so sensitive the next? Her mind harkened back to their kiss of almost a month before, the sweetness of it. Was it wrong to want to feel that again, that heady, unshakable sense of someone wanting you? If she accepted his offer, was she just being a tease?

She looked at him, really looked. There was no expectation in his eyes, only concern—for her. Her heart gave a small shiver of gratitude. Or maybe it was something else. *Admit it, you like him. You liked when he kissed you. Take a chance.*

His apartment wasn't what she imagined.

She had expected to find herself in a miniature version of her parents' house, complete with a couch protected by plastic slipcovers and huge, velvet, tasseled lamps on the end tables. It wasn't like that at all. It was a duplex in a Park Slope brownstone that he owned, spare and tidy, with Danish modern furniture and a staircase leading up to the second floor. It was obviously an athlete's home: Not only was his coffee table littered with sports and fitness magazines, but the first hockey stick he'd ever used as a peewee player was mounted on the wall, right above a bookcase containing every trophy he had ever won. A pair of battered skates lay at the bottom of the stairs, waiting to be conveyed to the second floor whenever their owner got around to it.

"No pictures of the Pope?" Theresa teased, settling down on the couch. "No Mario Lanza records?"

"I hid them in case you came over." He kicked off his shoes, bidding Theresa to do the same, and lit two big candles, one red and one white. "What do you want to hear?"

"Whatever you have is fine."

Michael crouched down in front of his small CD collection. "I don't have much, to tell the truth. How about if I just put on QXR?"

WQXR, New York's classical radio station. Another surprise. "That's fine," she assured him, taking a deep breath in an effort to stave off anxiety.

Michael flipped on the stereo and asked how she liked her coffee before disappearing into the kitchen. She offered to help, but he assured her he could handle it. Her offer had less to do with an assumption of incompetence than a strong desire not to be left alone with her thoughts. The last time she'd been in a man's apartment . . . *This is Michael. Stop.*

She settled back in relief when he reappeared bearing a tray with two steaming mugs of coffee and some almond cookies.

"Sorry I took so long," he apologized, handing her a warm mug.

"You didn't."

Michael's face was guileless, an open book. "Well, it felt like a long time to me."

Theresa waited for the conversation between them to become awkward and strained. She waited for the moment to arrive when she could politely jump up and put an end to the evening before it became uncomfortable. But it didn't happen. And when he gently reached out to take off her glasses, she let him, unsurprised when, just as he'd done weeks earlier, he asked permission to kiss her. She granted it, certain that all her demons would be laid to rest once and for all.

But she was wrong.

Oh, the kiss was gorgeous. From the very second his mouth played across hers with a teasing brush of the lips, her entire body was taut and tingling with anticipation. Heady pleasure wound its way through her as his tongue slowly parted her lips so he could taste her fully, and she him, each telling the other without words that there was only this, now, a perfect fusion of softness that made her feel as if she were losing the battle against gravity.

But as she felt herself tremble with desire for him, she was overwhelmed with fear.

Feeling weightless was glorious. Feeling unmoored was not. And that's what was happening. Despite the lovely, intoxicating sense of being carried away, she had to end it. Because if she didn't, every image of herself she'd ever created would be called into question. And she couldn't have that.

As gingerly as she could, she eased away from him, fumbling for her glasses.

"I can't do this," she said shakily, standing up. "I'm sorry, Michael, but I can't."

Bafflement clouded the joyous clarity that only a moment ago had shone in his eyes. "What?"

"This was wrong," Theresa said quietly, knowing she was lying. It was anything but wrong, yet her feelings for this man terrified her more than she could even articulate. "Dinner was wonderful, and I enjoy talking to you, but I don't have romantic feelings for you. I'm sorry."

Pain flickered across the handsome face, followed by a stubborn set of the jaw. "I don't believe you, Theresa."

"Michael—"

"Do you have any idea how you were kissing me just now?" he challenged, his expression reflecting the sense of wounded outrage he was trying to contain. "With joy. With passion."

"It was my body responding, Michael. Not my heart. Not my soul."

"Bullshit." His expression softened. "Look, I know you're scared because of what happened—"

Theresa's hand instinctively shot out as if to push his words away. "Don't even go there, because you don't know what you're talking about, okay?"

"Okay," Michael said cautiously.

"I'm going to go home now," she announced.

Michael looked uneasy. "Don't you think we should talk about this?"

"There's nothing to talk about," Theresa insisted. "You promised that if I had dinner with you, you would get off my case. That's what I'm asking you to do."

"So even though you thoroughly enjoyed dinner, this is it, done, *finito*. No more spending time together."

"Not like this."

"Like how?"

"I need to think about it, Michael, okay?" she said lamely.

"Okay." Frustration danced at the edge of his voice. "You think about it. You think about how you're attracted to me, but keep pushing me away."

"I'm going now," Theresa repeated, more to herself than to him.

"She's going now," he muttered to himself. "Great." He looked around the living room almost as if he didn't know where he was and was trying to get his bearings. "Let me just get my shoes on and I'll drive you."

"That's ridiculous," Theresa said, grabbing her purse. "I can take the subway."

"You are *not* taking the subway at this hour."

"I'm an *adult,* Michael, I can do as I please."

"You're right," he capitulated. "But if you won't let me

drive you, at least let me call you a cab for my own peace of mind."

"Fine." She knew she should be grateful for his concern, but she wasn't. Having to wait for a cab meant spending more time in his presence, time he could use to wear her down and make her open up. She wanted to run home, remember who she'd been striving to be and erase this whole evening from her mind. *That's* what she wanted to do.

Thankfully, the cab showed up within minutes. Theresa slid into the back seat, eager for Michael to slam the door and walk back inside. But being Michael, he couldn't.

"You know, one of these days you're going to get tired of running, Theresa. You're going to get tired of denying who you are."

She jerked her head to look at him. "And?"

"You figure it out," he said, finally slamming the cab door and walking back up the steps of the brownstone.

Little did he know that was the *last* thing she wanted to do.

Gemma lived in a studio on East Twenty-fifth and Third. Michael knew his cousin was no Martha Stewart. But he wasn't prepared for the chaos of her small apartment: Arcane books on the occult crowded nearly every surface, while herbs and plants competed for space on the floor and at the windows. Just as in her store, the scent of incense was overpowering. Peeling off his coat, Michael wondered if the neighbors ever complained. If he were her neighbor, he sure would.

"What can I get you?" Gemma asked cheerfully. That was one of the things Michael loved about her: She always seemed to be in a good mood. No making him feel guilty for not being in touch for a while, just, "Sure, come on over, no problem."

"What have you got?" Michael asked.

"Cinnamon apple tea, chamomile tea—"

"How about coffee?"

"Coffee's really bad for you, Mikey."

"I appreciate your concern, Gem, but I didn't sleep too well last night and I could use the buzz."

Her lower lip curled down disapprovingly. "You've never had trouble sleeping before. I'll see what I can find."

She walked over to her small kitchen area, bidding him to follow. Michael leaned against the wall, watching as she fished around in various cabinets until she came up with a jar of instant coffee that looked like it had been buried in a time capsule in 1972 and dug back up again.

"This okay?" she asked.

"It'll have to be."

Gemma tried opening the jar herself, but when it wouldn't budge, she handed it to Michael. "So, what's going on with the restaurant? My mother said you guys have been doing Friday night specials, and you're actually going to do a Thanksgiving Day dinner this year."

He handed the open jar back to his cousin. "The restaurant's doing really well."

"That's great. Any write-ups?"

"Not yet, but Theresa said to be patient. We need strong word-of-mouth first."

At the mention of Theresa's name, curiosity flickered in Gemma's eyes. "How are things going with you two?" she asked coyly, filling the tea kettle.

"A dead man gets more action than I do," Michael replied disgustedly. "Those candles you gave me are worth *bupkus*."

"Uh huh," said Gemma, nodding sympathetically.

"And forget the moonstone! It's brought me nothing but *agita!*"

"Talk to cousin Gemma," she cooed, half teasing him

as she extracted two coffee mugs from a cabinet beneath the avocado green counter.

"Explain to me how the female brain works," Michael demanded.

"In fifty words or less?"

"I'm serious, Gemma. I arrange this wonderful romantic dinner for us, she loves it, we go back to my place for coffee, we're kissing, and the next thing I know I'm being told she's not attracted to me romantically. What's the deal?"

"She's frightened."

"Yeah, no kidding," Michael concurred gloomily.

"She's attracted to you but she doesn't want to be," Gemma declared, putting a tea bag in one of the cups.

"Why? Am I such an ogre?"

"You must represent something that terrifies her."

"Being Italian?" Michael mused aloud. "What?"

"I don't know," Gemma said. "Maybe it's because you're a hockey player."

"I don't know." Michael rubbed his forehead, forlorn. "What should I do?"

Gemma thought. When the kettle emitted an ear-piercing shriek, she hurried to silence it, pouring the hot steaming water into the two mugs. "Well, I can perform a spell—"

"No." Michael was adamant. "No more quackery."

Gemma grinned at him. "Scared?"

"Skeptical."

"I could give you some dried hibiscus flowers to carry in a little pouch," Gemma continued, bobbing her tea bag up and down in its cup. "They're renowned for attracting love, lust and passion."

"Forget all that stuff, okay?" Michael begged. "Just give me some straight advice."

Gemma puffed up her cheeks and blew out, sending a

horizontal stream of steam from her coffee mug. "Don't give up."

"Because?" He took the mug filled with coffee and opening her fridge, pulled out some soy milk. "Do you have any regular milk? You know, the kind that comes from one of those animals that say *moo*?" Gemma shook her head no. "I'll drink it black, then." He took a sip of the putrid liquid in his mug masquerading as coffee. "You were saying?"

"Don't give up. She obviously likes you. If she didn't, she would never have agreed to go back to your place after dinner."

"And the kisses?"

"Same thing. She's got some stuff to work out, maybe even past life stuff and—don't you dare roll your eyes—"

Michael made his eyes behave.

"All you can do is wait it out."

"What if I'm waiting in vain?"

"We've been over this, Mikey," Gemma admonished. "What did I tell you the first time?"

Michael squirmed like a kid who'd been called on in class to answer the same question repeatedly. "Have faith," he muttered resentfully.

Gemma nodded her approval. "That's right."

Michael followed her back out into the living room, where she shifted to the floor a pile of books on alchemy (*What the*—? Michael thought) so they could sit on the couch.

"I would do one thing differently, though," said Gemma thoughtfully as she eased herself down.

"What?" Michael took another sip of coffee, then put the cup down on the floor for good. It was undrinkable.

"Play it cool. Don't make any more attempts at wooing her. I bet you she'll come sniffing around, wanting to know what you've been up to."

"You think?" The idea of Theresa pursuing him was exciting.

"I *know*." She took a long, slow sip of tea. "I'd like to meet her some time. Read her aura."

Michael practiced further eye restraint and said, "She'll probably be at the grand reopening of the restaurant. You can meet her then."

"I'd like that." She peered at Michael with interest. "So what else is going on?"

Michael told her. He told her of his troubles with Anthony and the annoyance of having to deal with van Dorn. About how ever since his "wine, dine and leave you to pine" experience with Theresa, his mind was a mess. How even his coach had noticed that he had the attention span of a gnat, and asked if he was losing his edge. What he didn't tell her was that the criticism hurt, because he feared it was true. Maybe his hockey playing days were coming to an end. *What then?*

In return, he listened avidly to what was going on in her life, mildly envious she seemed so well-balanced. He toyed with the idea of setting her up with one of his teammates, then thought better of it. All he needed was one of them finding out his cousin was a *stregh* and his life would be hell.

Two hours flew by. "Shoot," he said, taking his cup from the floor and hustling into her kitchen to deposit it in the sink. "I should get down to Met Gar."

"Who you playing tonight?" asked Gemma.

"Colorado."

"You did really well against Dallas," she noted proudly.

"Yeah, but not so good against Detroit and Tampa." His brows furrowed. "I have to put all this outside stuff in perspective. It's really messing with my concentration."

"Frosted quartz can help with balance," Gemma told him.

"Frosted flakes?" Michael teased, pretending he hadn't heard correctly.

Gemma smacked his arm. "My cousin, the comedian." She raised up on her tiptoes to give him a kiss. "Give my love to Anthony. Tell him I'll come by soon."

"Tell him yourself. I have to go to the restaurant after the game. Why don't you come with me? You could even come to the game if you want."

"Okay," Gemma said brightly. "That would be fun."

"Just one thing."

"What?"

"No hexes on the other team, okay?"

Gemma placed her hand over her heart. "You have my word of honor," she replied fervently. A mischievous expression played across the soft features of her face. "But if you lose, don't come crying to me."

CHAPTER

10

Scott Strauss was a chunky, handsome man in his early forties. He had been Janna and Theresa's accountant since their days at the network. They liked him because he was smart, direct and personable. Riding the elevator to his office with Janna, Theresa tried to distract herself from thinking about the meeting they were about to have. She found her thoughts drifting to Reese. If he were only a stronger presence in her life, then all this agonizing over her attraction to Michael would be moot.

"Theresa." Scott's handshake was warm and firm as he motioned for her and Janna to sit in the vacant Eames chairs in front of his desk. After they were all seated, his gaze ranged over both women. "Well, I've had a chance to look everything over."

"And—?" Janna prompted. The trip over from their own office had been largely silent, each of them hoping for the best, but not expecting it.

"I have good news and bad news." He flipped open a folder on the desk in front of him and skimmed it. "The good news is FM PR's current revenue covers its ongoing expenses, which, in the best of all possible worlds, means the business would be profitable."

"*Would* be?" Theresa echoed, flashing Janna a look of concern.

"That's the bad news," Scott continued. "Even though you were able to finance start-up costs with cash, you had to borrow two hundred thousand to cover operating expenses while you were lining up clients." He paused, once again studying the paperwork before him. "Your current revenue isn't enough to cover expenses and your accounts payable."

"No?" Janna said, sounding shocked.

Theresa felt a small, hard kernel of fear forming in her gut. Janna had gone to business school. If *she* was shocked, it had to be bad.

Theresa looked at Scott questioningly. "So this means—?"

"You need to bring in more money so you can pay back what you borrowed."

"Or else?" Janna asked.

"You could be out of business within a year if your lenders are strict."

Shocked, doomed silence filled the room.

"Go on," Janna said in a barely audible voice.

Scott sighed heavily, the sigh of a man trapped being the bearer of bad tidings. "Well, you can either pay off the debts with personal funds if you have them, or—"

"We can try to drum up a whole lot of new clients real fast," Janna finished for him in a voice disconcertingly devoid of emotion.

"Exactly. I'd recommend both, actually."

Stunned, Janna and Theresa turned and stared at each other. Theresa thought Janna looked on the edge of tears and lowered her gaze. Janna was the strong one, the level-headed one. If she cried . . . Theresa couldn't even bear to think about it.

But Janna was, as always, the consummate professional, though her voice was subdued as she asked, "We don't have to worry about any of this, though, if we sell to Butler, am I right?"

"Correct. They would assume your debt as part of the deal."

"Is that what you think we should do?" Theresa interjected. She caught Janna's annoyed glance but ignored it. They needed to stop avoiding the subject and start planning. Theresa was simply putting the cards out on the table.

Scott looked uncomfortable. "I can't answer that. It's a personal decision that involves a helluva lot more than just numbers."

"Chicken," Theresa threw back at him affectionately.

"I don't envy you," he admitted. "It's a tough decision."

Another awkward silence arose, but no one had the energy or inclination to fill it. Somber, Janna rose first, leaning forward to shake Scott's hand across the expanse of his desk. "Thanks for shooting straight with us, Scott. We appreciate it."

"Well, my services aren't without cost," he said mischievously.

Theresa smiled. "What can we do for you?"

"Mike Piazza's autograph for my sons?"

"Not a problem," Janna assured him. "I'll be seeing him later in the week. I'll have two autographed pictures sent here."

"Great." Scott's easygoing grin stretched from ear to ear. "You've made my day."

"I wish we could say the same," Janna replied dolefully. She looked to Theresa. "Are we ready to roll, *compadre*?"

"Let's go," Theresa declared with false confidence. "We'll be in touch," she promised, shaking Scott's hand.

They walked in stony silence down the steel and concrete canyon of Madison Avenue, oblivious to the few sad snowflakes swirling from the sky. Unable to face going back to the office, Janna suggested they go to the nearest coffee bar instead. Ducking into a Starbuck's on East Sixty-eighth, they peeled off their coats, ordered drinks and hunkered down at a small table for two.

"Well?" Janna asked, looking and sounding miserable as she carefully blew into her chai latte to cool it. "What do you think?"

"Of what? Be more specific." Theresa was finding it hard to concentrate as conflicting images of their future ricocheted through her already overloaded mind.

"Scott's saying that if we don't pay off our loans out of our own pockets, we'll become another failed business statistic."

"I put all my savings *and* the settlement move into starting up," Theresa said grimly. "I don't have any more."

"I know." Janna broke off a small piece of biscotti, her eyes straying to the enormous square cut diamond on her left ring finger. "But I do have a husband. A very *rich* husband. We could get the money from him."

She lifted her gaze to meet Theresa's.

"Would you be comfortable doing that?" Theresa asked.

"I don't know. I know Ty would give it to us gladly. The problem is my ego," Janna admitted. "We created this company with our own money and our own credit with the bank. The idea of having to go to him for help . . ." Her voice trailed off into silence.

"Feels like failure?" Theresa supplied.

"Not failure, exactly." Janna stared down at the table. "It just feels . . . like it wouldn't be *ours* alone anymore, just yours and mine." She looked to Theresa for confirmation. "Does that make sense?"

"Totally."

Janna looked relieved. Then she asked, "How do *you* feel about us using Ty's money, if it came to that?"

Theresa sipped her double espresso. "I don't know."

Janna asked her what she thought about the Butler buyout. The moment of truth had come, all their weeks of avoiding the subject no longer tenable or practical.

"Honestly, Jan? I don't want to sell. I know it would solve all of our problems, but we dreamed of running our own business for so long. . . ." Theresa found herself getting tearful and lowered her head. "Sorry," she muttered, sniffling.

"Don't be crazy," Janna chided, sniffling back. "I feel the same way."

Theresa's head quickly shot up. "Thank *God!* I was so afraid Scott's news was going to send you over the edge and you'd say we should sell and sell fast." She reached across the table for a piece of biscotti.

"So, I guess the big question is: What do we do now?" asked Janna.

"Figure out how to cut expenses?" Theresa suggested.

"Well, we could fire Terrence, close the office, and work out of my apartment."

Theresa blanched. "Do you really want to do that?"

"No."

"Well, that solves that."

"I don't think we should come right out and tell Ted Banister we're not going to bite on Butler's offer," said Janna, thinking aloud. "If we do, Butler will get very nasty very fast and start trying to steal clients, which is the last thing we need. I say we keep stringing them along while we really bust our butts trying to expand our base."

"I agree."

Expand our base. Cut expenses. Accounts receivable. Accounts payable. *This is why I should have become a writer,* Theresa thought miserably. All this business and money talk gave her a headache. The thought of trying to drum up even more business exhausted her, and she knew Janna had to be feeling the same way. They were both dancing as fast as they could, and there were only so many hours in a day. But if ensuring their company remained just that—*their* company—then they'd just learn to dance faster. It was as simple as that.

"What about the Ty option?" asked Theresa.

"Let's pretend it doesn't exist right now, okay? This is our baby. Let's try to do it our way, with our money, for as long as we can. Agreed?"

"Agreed."

"Good." Looking more relaxed than she had all morning, Janna finished the biscotti, then pressed Theresa to reveal how her "Get off my back" date with Michael had gone.

"It went great," Theresa said forlornly.

"So why the long face?"

"Because he's not what I pictured for myself, okay?" She dug the heel of her palms deep into her eye sockets. "I mean, I don't think he's what I want. I don't know."

"I don't understand," Janna replied impatiently. "For as long as I've known you, you've talked about wanting to meet a nice guy who'll treat you right. Now you have and you're running from him. What's the problem?"

Theresa pulled her palms from her eyes. "It's him. He's so . . . Brooklyn."

"So?" Janna's voice was sharp.

"Don't get annoyed with me, Janna, I'm feeling pretty confused right now."

"Well, so am I," Janna countered testily. "He's so

Brooklyn—what does that mean? Do you have any idea how snobbish that sounds?"

"I know, I know," Theresa groaned, "but I can't help it. I worked my whole life to get away from guys like that—"

"Guys like what?" Janna snapped. When two women at a nearby table glanced over she lowered her voice, but it was still impassioned. "Guys who happen to come from the same place you do? Guys who are nice and stable and care about their families?" She took a quick sip of her latte. "No offense, Terry, but your 'He isn't what I envisioned for my life' spiel is getting old. He's a great guy. He clearly adores you. What's the problem?"

"I don't know," Theresa groaned again, feeling herself shrink under Janna's scolding. "I guess I'm just scared."

"Of what? Of being happy? Of finding out that after all is said and done, what you really crave is love and family and stability, just like everyone else?"

Theresa's gaze drifted to the window, where busy New Yorkers hustled down the broad gray sidewalk to destinations unknown. She recalled her mother once asking if she was ashamed of where she came from. The question had shocked Theresa, because she didn't know how to answer it. It wasn't that she was embarrassed by her family's insularity or working class ethos. It was just that she saw there was so much more out there, and she wanted it. Badly. She wanted the money, and the freedom, and the fast track. She wanted glamour. But she also wanted love.

"I always wanted to be extraordinary," she said in a small, bewildered voice as she looked back to Janna. "I always wanted an extraordinary life."

"Well, you have one. We all do. You, me, Joe the garbage man, Sally the dog walker, everyone. That's the big secret they never tell you in 'You Can Have It All 101.'"

Theresa flinched. "You really think I'm being an idiot, don't you?"

"Yes, I really do," Janna replied without hesitation. "According to you, I've supposedly found the last, good straight man in New York. Well, another one has come along, yet you refuse to go for him for reasons that are completely beyond my comprehension."

"I'm scared," Theresa repeated quietly.

"I know you are, Terry. But you've got to get back into therapy or get over it or *something,* or else you're going to throw up roadblocks every time a nice guy comes within two feet of you."

"I didn't throw up roadblocks with Reese," Theresa pointed out quickly.

"That's because he's a Ralph Lauren ad come to life. He's not real." Janna leaned forward. "Who has treated you better so far: Reese or Michael?"

Theresa's face froze in displeasure.

"Answer me," Janna insisted.

"Michael," Theresa muttered into her coffee cup.

Janna leaned back in her chair triumphantly. "I rest my case."

"So what am I supposed to do, then?"

"Well, how did you leave things with Michael?"

Theresa frowned. "Not well. He told me that one of these days I was going to get tired of running away from myself."

"So call and tell him you're tired of running."

"I don't know if I can."

"Then be confused and alone," Janna replied irritably. "What do you want me to say?"

"I know," said Theresa, scrambling to defuse Janna's frustration, which she knew was justified. "I know I'm driving you crazy. I know it's time to give up this fantasy that when I meet The One, it will be like being hit with a lightning bolt. Just be patient with me, okay? I'm trying to sort things out, I really am."

"Well, sort quicker. Michael's not going to wait for you forever."

With what looked to Theresa like a final glare of annoyance, Janna drained her paper cup. Chastened, Theresa did the same. She knew everything Janna said was right. She just wished Janna weren't so blunt. Then again, there were times when she'd been equally honest. That's what real friends did for each other: They cut to the chase, no matter how painful. She made a vow right there and then: *I will try to sort things out as fast as I can. And when I'm sure about what I want to do, I'll take action.*

"DANTE!"

The anger in Ty's voice was made all the more ominous by its echoing off the high dome of the practice arena. Skating over to the bench where his coach stood, Michael knew what was coming. He braced himself.

"Coach?" he asked.

"You got lead in your skates or what? My grandfather skates faster than you and he's been dead for twelve years."

"I know," Michael muttered. There was no jump in his legs at all this morning. "I'll pick it up."

"You better. Where's that guy who was on fire a few weeks back?" asked Ty, snapping his gum.

Michael stuck his chin out. "He's here."

"He is?" Ty looked to his left and to his right. "That's funny, 'cause I don't see him."

Michael's grip tightened around his hockey stick. "You made your point."

"Don't let me down. I need your level of play to be where it was a few weeks ago, Mikey, and I need you to keep it there."

"I will," Michael swore, itchy for the reprimand to end so he could get back out on the ice and finish practice.

"Good," said Ty. "Everyone here is dealing with crap of one kind or another off the ice. It's no excuse for slacking off."

"I'm not slacking off," Michael replied irritably. "Can I get back out there to show you?"

Ty's head bobbed approvingly. "Be my guest," he challenged.

Michael rejoined his teammates, who had just started their two-on-two drills. *Screw Theresa Falconetti,* he thought angrily, as he and Barry Fontaine staved off an offensive rush from Kevin Gill and Tully Webster. *Screw Anthony. And screw van Dorn while we're at it. Screw everyone.*

Ty's admonition pissed Michael off so much he remained fired up for the rest of the day, and well into the Blades game that night against the Rangers. By the time the third period rolled around, Michael had been a physical presence on both ends of the ice. The Blades held a slim, one-goal lead with the clock ticking down slower than seemed humanly possible.

Ty had Michael on the ice for a defensive face-off with less than a minute remaining. There was a mad scramble in front of the Blades crease and the puck squirted out to the point. Michael saw Rangers defenseman Pascal Noel winding up to take a slap shot; reflexively, Michael dove to block it, the puck hitting him squarely on the right side of the helmet as his body crumpled to the ice. He felt his eyes roll up in the back of his head as he grimaced against the pounding pain beating at his temple. A white, hissing sound seemed to fill his ears, blocking out the sound of the final horn as he closed his eyes.

When he opened them, there were four Kevin Gills standing over him.

"Mike?"

The hissing sound had ebbed away, replaced by that of a phone that seemed to be ringing from deep inside his head. He blinked, fighting to focus. The multiple images remained. The ringing sound now hummed in a perfect circle around the perimeter of his skull.

"Mike? You gonna be okay? You need help getting up?"

He nodded, causing a surge of nausea deep within him. He allowed Kevin and Tully Webster to help him to his feet. Skating toward the bench, he barely heard the praise of his teammates. Rather than stopping, he headed straight for the bathroom in the visiting team's locker room, where he puked his guts out. Looking up, he found Dr. Linderman, one of the team's physicians, staring at him.

"How you doing, Michael?"

"Okay," Michael replied, loping over to the nearest bench to sit down.

"You dizzy?"

Michael nodded weakly, then regretted it. He should have lied. The more symptoms he displayed, the longer he was likely to be off the ice. He knew guys whose brains were scrambled because they insisted on playing through a head injury. He didn't want to be one of them, but at the same time . . . shit . . .

He blinked furiously as the doctor shone a light deep into his eyes. "All right, we're going to do an X ray here, and then we'll shoot over to the hospital. They'll probably want to keep you overnight for observation. Looks like you have a concussion."

"No kidding."

Peeling off his helmet, Michael groaned. The room was moving to and fro and the urge to throw up again was strong. With deliberate slowness he stood, trying hard not to appear too woozy. Having been through this before, he already knew he'd be out for at least three days.

And he knew who Ty would put in to replace him.

● ● ●

The next day, the back page of the *New York Post* screamed BADABOING! MIKEY D HAS CONCUSSION, while the *Daily News* declared, ONE FOR THE TEAM: MIKEY D TAKES SHOT TO THE MELON. Concerned, Theresa pressed Janna the hockey expert for details. When she learned that Michael had to be symptom free for at least forty-eight hours before he'd be allowed to play, she realized his injury provided her with the perfect excuse to pay him a visit and apologize for the disastrous ending of their dinner date the week before.

She'd decided Janna was right.

She *was* cutting off her nose to spite her face by being so rigid in the parameters she'd set for her dream man. She was still attracted to Reese, and if he called and asked her out she'd certainly join him. But she was done thinking of him as the answer to her cosmopolitan prayers. Her new M.O. was to be open-minded to whatever and whoever the world decided to throw in her path.

And that included Michael Dante.

Two days later, she was on the subway, halfway to Brooklyn to surprise him, when it dawned on her that she had no idea where he lived, apart from the fact it was in Park Slope. They'd been so busy talking on the way there she'd paid no attention to where he was driving and she wasn't in the room later when he made the call to the cab company to pick her up. She called Janna from her cellphone, hoping Janna could in turn buzz Ty and get back to her. But Janna's phone was off.

Which left Theresa with one option.

She couldn't decide whether Anthony looked horrified or terrified when he opened the door of the restaurant to her.

"Mikey's not here," he announced soberly, clearly hoping she would turn around and leave. When she didn't, simmering resentment crept into his already suspicious brown eyes.

"I know that," Theresa replied. "I need his home address." Anthony looked unmoved. "I need to talk to him about something important," she added, hoping the additional gravitas would yield an answer.

"Mikey's unavailable," Anthony declared.

Theresa was unsure how to take this. Was he referring to the concussion? Or was he making a veiled comment about their failed date? Maybe Michael had poured his frustration out to Anthony, who was really telling Theresa to take a hike and leave his brother alone. Maybe Michael *wanted* her to leave him alone? She hadn't even thought of that.

"Look, Anthony, I really need to talk to him," Theresa repeated.

"If it's about the restaurant, you can talk to me," Anthony declared, folding his massive forearms across his chest.

"It's not just about the restaurant," Theresa informed him, drawing her scarf tighter against her throat. "Though something has come up."

"What?" Anthony growled.

"There's a local cable show called *Italian Cooking and Living*. Ever heard of it?"

"No."

"Well, they got the press kit and called, wanting to know if you might be interested in being a guest chef."

"No, thanks."

"Anthony—"

"Do I look like Molto freakin' Mario to you?" He glowered. "Do I?"

No, thought Theresa, *you look like you should be in a straight jacket, pumped full of Thorazine.* She took a deep breath and tried again.

"Anthony—"

"You want Mikey's address or what?"

"That would be great," Theresa replied politely. Michael was right: Talking to Anthony was like talking to a slab of granite, especially if he didn't care for what you were saying.

"It's 212 President Street."

"Thank you."

"Don't get him worked up," Anthony warned. "He's supposed to be resting."

"I won't get him worked up," Theresa promised, thanking him profusely while wondering if *worked up* meant something sexual in Anthonyspeak.

Turning onto Michael's brownstone-lined street, Theresa felt her mouth go dry. Suppose she buzzed to be let in and he wouldn't see her? What then? Fingers crossed, she climbed the high steps leading to his front door and pressed the bell.

The intercom crackled. "Hello?" It was Michael.

Theresa cleared her throat and nervously leaned in closer to the intercom. "Michael, it's Theresa. Can I come in?"

She released the button and waited, worrying a hangnail on her left index finger. He was going to politely tell her to take a hike. He was going to read her the riot act, calling her a psycho and every other choice name in the book. He was—

"Come on up."

Buzzed through the front door, Theresa found him waiting at his apartment door, looking tired and a little worse for wear in a pair of blue sweatpants and a softly faded red flannel shirt.

"Hey," he said quietly. He had a severe case of bed head. Obviously he'd been lying down.

"Hey," she returned, peering into his face with considerable concern. "How are you feeling? I heard you took a puck to the head."

"I still have a headache," he admitted, ushering her inside. "And if I get up too fast from lying down, the whole room spins. But apart from that . . ." He held out a hand. "Take your coat?"

"Thanks." She slipped off her trench coat and handed it to him, watching as he went to hang it on a nearby coat rack, his steps slightly unsteady.

"Michael, why don't you lie back down on the couch and I'll make us something to drink? It doesn't look like you should be on your feet."

"I'm fine," he insisted stubbornly.

"Michael."

He shrugged. "Okay. You want to play nursemaid while I lie on my butt, who am I to argue?"

Theresa waited until he'd eased himself back down on the sofa before perching on the edge by his feet. "You look miserable."

"I am miserable. I can't play. I can't even practice."

"Who's replacing you?" she asked, seeing immediately it was a mistake as his eyes flared with contempt.

"That little shit you met at the party, van Dorn. Don't you read the papers?" he asked bitterly. "In the space of two games, he's turned the third line into a scoring line and brings lightning speed where before there was only steely determination."

Theresa winced. "Is that a direct quote?"

"Yeah, from the *Times*. Like that *la fava* LaPointe knows a thing about hockey."

Theresa laughed. "You Dante boys need your mouths washed out with soap."

"Yeah, well, if the epithet fits . . ." Michael grumbled. He raised himself up slightly, adjusting the pillows behind his back. "I may not be the most riveting conversationalist today. My head hurts and this whole thing with van Dorn has put me in a pretty bad mood."

"That's okay," Theresa assured him. The urge to touch his tired face, brush her knuckles against the day-old stubble gracing his cheek, was strong. She opted instead for a friendly squeeze to his foot, since she was sitting right next to it. "You want me to make you some coffee or something? Tea?"

"Nah, I'm fine. But if you want to make yourself something, go ahead."

"I'm fine, too." She glanced around the living room, which seemed a bit messier than the last time she'd been there. Newspapers were piled up on the floor and a ratty old afghan lay crumpled by Michael's feet. "So, what have you been doing to entertain yourself?"

"Watching *The Wild and the Free*. Reading."

"What do hockey players read?" she asked. "No, wait, I know. Your favorite book is . . ." she closed her eyes, deep in concentration, "*Of Ice and Men*." Her eyes sprang open. "Favorite play? *The Iceman Cometh*."

"Is that your idea of hockey humor?" Michael asked in a voice laced with pity.

"It was pretty good for off the top of my head." She grinned.

"Well, it's funnier than *Happy Gilmore,* but it's no *Slap Shot*."

"Thank you," Theresa said. "I think."

"So, what brings you to Park Slope?" he asked, his eyes quietly searching her face.

"You."

"Uh huh," Michael replied cautiously, his expression giving away nothing. "You have some restaurant stuff we need to go over?"

"I already handled it with Anthony."

Michael stiffened in alarm. "You talked to Anthony?"

"Just briefly. I told him the local cable show *Italian*

Cooking and Living wants him as a guest chef. He said he has no interest."

Michael closed his eyes, sighing. "Don't listen to him. He'll do it."

"What are you going to do, put a gun to his head?"

"Just trust me on this, okay? Get me the details, and I'll make it happen."

"Okay," Theresa replied dubiously. She shifted her weight, fearful she might slip off the edge of the couch onto the floor. "This might sound nosy, but does Anthony have a girlfriend or anything?"

Michael's eyes slowly opened. "Why?" he asked harshly. "You interested?"

"What?" Theresa exclaimed. She tried to picture herself even touching Anthony and burst out laughing. "Are you nuts?"

Michael looked suspicious. "Then why do you want to know?"

She stopped chuckling. "Because he seems so self-contained. Alone. I just wondered if he had anyone."

"Other than the Virgin Mary? No." Michael scratched absently at the stubble on his chin. "There was this hostess at the restaurant for a while named Loretta. He had a crush on her, but I don't think he ever did anything about it." He frowned. "What can you do? That's who he is."

"I guess," she concurred. *And I think I'm starting to figure out who I am. I think.*

Discomfort crept onto Michael's face. "So, you're here because—?"

"I needed to talk you."

"About—?"

"Last Saturday night."

"Okay." His tone was guarded.

Fearing she might end up nervously kneading his toes, Theresa got up, strolling his living room as she spoke. "I've been thinking a lot about what you said when you put me in the cab—you know, that stuff about me denying who I am." She looked at Michael: "I think you're right. That's what I've been doing." She paused, turning over in her hand a battered old puck she found atop one of his bookshelves. "I've been afraid of getting close to someone with a background similar to mine, since I've spent my adult life trying to get away from that whole Italian thing." She looked to him uncertainly. "Do I sound nuts?"

"No more than usual," he assured her.

Theresa smiled. "Good." Her grip around the puck was tight. "I know I've behaved like a complete schizo—" She caught Michael's amused grin and shyly smiled back. "And I'm sorry. But if you're willing to give me another chance, I would love to spend some more time with you, Michael. Because I really like you."

There. Speech done. Surprised to see her hand was trembling somewhat, she put the puck back down and waited for him to say, "Sorry, but I already have a deranged brother and I don't think I can handle another lunatic in my life." Instead, all he said was, "C'mere."

Theresa looked at him. "What?"

He patted the couch beside him. "I said, c'mere."

Theresa walked towards him and sat down. Taking her right hand, Michael tightly laced his fingers through hers. "Of course I'd like to spend more time with you. What would you like to do?"

With that, he gently brought her hand to his lips and tenderly kissed it, the warmth of his mouth climbing like a slow fever through her body.

No one had ever raised her hand to his mouth and kissed it before. No one. She felt like a fine, beautiful, medieval lady being courted by the most honorable and chivalrous of knights. What had she done to deserve this kindness? This patience?

"I . . ." She swallowed, struggling to collect herself. "Do you like to dance?" she blurted.

Michael reared back slightly, insulted. "Excuse me, but you seem to forget all the women were fighting to dance with me at Ty and Janna's wedding. All except you, of course."

"That's right," Theresa murmured, pinking with embarrassment as she remembered her repeated refusals to dance with him. She recalled watching him, surprised someone their age was so good when it came to the old, slow dances. Most guys were lucky if they could execute a basic box step.

"Can *you* dance?" Michael asked pointedly.

"Yes," Theresa replied, pretending to be miffed.

"Then let's do it. Ever been to the Rainbow Room?"

Theresa smiled and shook her head. "Only for work. Never for pleasure."

"Then that's where we'll go."

The Rainbow Room. Theresa nearly swooned. Ever since she was a little girl, she had dreamed of going there on a date—not that she'd ever admit it to any of her friends besides Janna, since they would tease her mercilessly about it being "*So* bridge and tunnel." But any time she'd been there for a PR function, she'd been entranced. There was the slowly spinning, circular dance floor . . . couples dancing the night away in each other's arms . . . and the twinkling lights of Manhattan viewed from the floor-to-ceiling windows. It was wonderful, maybe too wonderful. Theresa frowned.

"Don't you have to make reservations weeks in advance?"

"Not if you're Mikey D. Just tell me if it's where you want to go."

Theresa could barely find her voice. "It is."

"Then it's a date." There was no mistaking the meaning in the directness of Michael's gaze. *"Right?"*

Theresa returned his gaze with a genuine smile. "Right."

CHAPTER

11

She had to be dreaming.

Theresa had been to the Rainbow Room before, but nothing prepared her for the sensation of stepping out of the elevator on the sixty-fifth floor of Thirty Rock with a handsome man by her side, one who was clearly looking forward to doting on her all evening. She found herself transported to another world, one of glamour and sophistication. She was back in the days when women in gorgeous, glittering gowns were tangoed, dipped and twirled by men in ties and tails.

Holding Michael's hand, she took it all in as if viewing it for the first time: The floor-to-ceiling windows offering a breathtaking, panoramic view of the city; the glossy, parquet patterned, revolving dance floor with its starburst design in the center; the mirrored pillars reflecting back the image of the diners, dancers and the twelve piece orchestra. Awestruck, she remained silent as a captain in tails conveyed them to a table for two on the edge of the dance floor. When a waiter arrived and asked if they wanted drinks, Theresa barely heard him; she was too busy staring at the giant sparkling crystal chandelier hanging above the dance floor.

"Theresa?" Michael gently prompted.

She tore her gaze from the ceiling. "Hmm?"

Michael looked amused, probably because she was still starry-eyed. "Would you like anything to drink?" he asked.

"Champagne would be wonderful," she murmured.

Michael looked up at the waiter. "Bring a bottle of Piper-Heidsieck, please."

The waiter nodded and left, leaving Theresa alone with her amazement and the man who had made it possible. "It's *so beautiful* in here. I'd almost forgotten."

"Isn't it?" Michael glanced around the room admiringly. "Here, come with me a minute. I want to show you something."

Intrigued, Theresa rose, following Michael's lead as they slowly made their way around the ring of windows circling the room. The night winter sky was clear and beautiful. From this high above the city, they could see down to the Battery and up through Central Park. Theresa had never paid much attention to the Empire State Building before. But viewed from the Rainbow Room it looked beautiful, almost mystical, bathed in colored lights which gave it a magic all its own.

"Impressive, huh?" said Michael.

"Amazing," Theresa whispered.

They returned to their table, awaiting the arrival of their champagne. Theresa was struck by how she and Michael seemed to be the youngest ones there. Most of the couples were her parents' age or older. Many of the older men wore tuxes. Theresa turned to Michael, appraising his attire. He looked quite handsome in his jacket and tie, although Theresa had a feeling that given the choice, the tie would be off in five seconds.

"You look nice," she told him.

Michael nodded appreciatively. "So do you."

Theresa allowed herself to bask in his compliment. She'd picked what she wore carefully, making sure it was not too sexy but not too conservative, either. Alluring yet modest. Judging by Michael's reaction, she had chosen correctly.

"So I have to ask you something," she began.

"Shoot."

"Have you brought other women here?" Seeing the discomfort that flashed across his face, she hastily added, "It's okay if you have, I swear. I'm just curious."

"Just one," he said stiffly. "A long time ago."

Theresa nodded. "Okay. That's all I wanted to know."

The waiter returned with their champagne and two menus. Theresa was about to bring her flute to her lips when Michael stopped her. "Wait," he said.

"We need a toast," Theresa finished his thought. "You do it."

"Hmm. Let me think." His demeanor turned serious as he contemplated what to say. When he finally had it, his expression softened. He was not a man prone to stoicism, Theresa noticed. Everything he felt, everything he thought was telegraphed across his face.

"Hold up your glass," he urged.

Theresa held up her glass.

"To here and now," he said quietly.

"To here and now," Theresa thoughtfully echoed, clinking her glass against his before taking a sip. Michael was right. There was only here and now, second by wonderful second. All she could do was savor it, because it would never, could never, come around again. It was a feeling she vowed to hang on to.

As if on cue, the orchestra, fronted by a buxom, curvy female singer, began playing. Theresa concentrated, sure she recognized the tune. Then it came to her: It was

"Begin the Beguine," a favorite of her grandmother's. Recognition brought a lump to her throat as she remembered her Nonna, now long gone, listening to old records while cooking Sunday dinner for the family. *Here and now,* Theresa reminded herself. *Be here now.*

Her gaze drifted to the dance floor, where couples were dancing, their expertise obvious. Theresa watched in mute admiration as a man who had to be at least seventy executed some fancy footwork with his wife. She turned to Michael, mildly panicked.

"We can't go out there. We'll embarrass ourselves."

"Gedouddahere," Michael scoffed, teasing her with his wiseguy voice. "You're with Mikey D, the Dancing Wonder."

"But you're with Flat Foot Falconetti, who's lucky if she can get through her kick boxing class without falling over."

"Just relax," Michael soothed in his regular voice. "You'll be fine. People always worry that other people are watching them." He looked comically to the left and then to the right. "But the truth is, no one gives a damn what anyone else is doing."

"I hope you're right."

Mercifully, he waited through a rumba and a lindy before offering her his hand and taking her out to the dance floor for a slow torch song. She was stiff at first, the feeling of his large hand resting against the small of her back generating a small fire within her that was completely unexpected. But as the dance wore on, she allowed him to guide her and began relaxing enough to enjoy being so close to him. Michael was light on his feet, his movements fluid yet commanding, filled with confidence.

Theresa looked up into his eyes, which were fixed on hers with a tender gentleness that brought the lump back to her throat. When was the last time anyone had looked at her like that? Come to think of it: *Had* any man ever looked at her like that? She cleared her throat, eager to cover the emotion she was feeling. "Confession time," she said as he twirled her past the orchestra. "Where did you learn to dance?"

Amusement sparkled in Michael's eyes as he shook his head. "It's a secret."

"Anthony?" Theresa teased.

"My mother." His hold on her tightened ever so slightly, sending a small rush of pleasure through her body. "My dad hated to dance and my mom loved it, so she would dance with me and Anthony."

"Anthony can *dance?*"

"You should see him samba."

"Get out of here!" Theresa couldn't believe it. What was next? Talking cats?

Michael, though, that was another story. She could imagine a pint-sized version of him being led around the living room and loving it. In fact, she could imagine him pushing his mother to teach him everything she knew, and the poor woman being exhausted. A smile crept over her face that did not go unnoticed.

"What?" Michael asked.

"I was imagining you as a little boy, demanding that your mother teach you all the dances she knew."

Michael chuckled. "That pretty much sums it up."

When the song ended, Theresa did her best to cover her disappointment. The night was young, after all, and there was champagne to drink, caviar to relish, filet mignon to eat—and dancing, hours and hours of it in his arms, where she hadn't realized she wanted to be until she was out of them.

"Are you having fun?" Michael asked her over dessert, his face lighting up with delight when she said yes. *Here and now,* she kept reminding herself. Here and now she was sharing a meal with a good man whose strikingly handsome face she longed to caress in the flickering candlelight. Here and now she was dancing with a man capable of making it seem as if the room around them had faded to lavender mist and it was only the two of them out there on the slowly revolving dance floor, their contented sighs saying more than words ever could. Theresa didn't want it to end, this sense of wonder and timelessness that had enveloped her. Enveloped *them*.

And so, when the restaurant closed, she asked him if he wanted to come back to her place for coffee. Michael agreed.

"Nice place," *Michael* noted approvingly, gravitating toward the windows looking out on the Fifty-ninth Street bridge. "Do you watch the marathon from here?"

"Actually, I run the marathon."

He turned back to her, impressed. "You do? That's amazing."

Hoping music might take the edge off her nerves, Theresa switched on the television, choosing the "Singers and Standards" channel on Music Choice. "As Time Goes By" was on, Theresa quietly mouthing along "You must remember this/ A kiss is just a kiss . . ." as she adjusted the volume. She turned back to Michael, who stood on the plush oriental rug in the middle of the room. His expression was inviting as he held a hand out to her.

"Would you like to keep dancing?"

Theresa blushed. "Michael."

"What?" He came towards her.

"I feel stupid."

"Why?" he asked as he wrapped her in his arms, swaying slowly in time to the music as he laid his cheek against hers. "No one can see."

He was right. No one could see. Intoxicated by the nearness of him, she let him lead her around the living room in a slow, sensuous dance. Body melded against body as need, primal and urgent, made itself known to Theresa. When Michael stopped moving but did not release her, Theresa held her breath, want of him pumping through her system like blood, like oxygen, vital and alive. And when he whispered her name as he reverently let down her hair and removed her glasses, she felt herself tremble, conscious and needful of what she hoped was to come. His hands tenderly framed her face. Then he barely, almost imperceptibly, skimmed his mouth over hers.

Sighing softly, Theresa closed her eyes, desperately wanting to be taken wherever he cared to lead next. There was a split second of suspended silence before his mouth returned to hers, hot, drugging, insistent. Theresa's mind reeled; it was surprising and new as a first kiss, pure in its desire yet desperately needy at the same time. Stirred by the demanding press of his mouth, and by the fluttering deep within the pit of her own stomach, Theresa opened her lips beneath his, a parched flower in need of rain and replenishment. *Here and now,* she thought, as his arms slowly twined around her and they staggered over to the couch, neither wanting nor willing to break contact.

Here.

Now.

The kiss deepened, Michael's hands roaming the terrain of her back—soft, exploratory, his caresses leaving her wanting more. Long, so long it had been since a man had been so attentive, making her feel as if magic was indeed alive and well in the world.

And yet.

There on the dark edge of her consciousness . . . a shadow.

She pressed hard against Michael, wanting to lose herself in his taste, in his scent. Michael responded by moving his lips to her neck, planting a careful trail of hot, nipping kisses designed to torment. Theresa could hear his desire in his ragged breath, could feel it through the heat of his fingertips as they tenderly grazed her collarbone. She fought to respond in kind, to climb to the next level of burning, glorious need with him, but she couldn't. Something was in the way, black, immovable, looming larger. *This is Michael,* she reminded herself desperately, body shivering as he playfully nipped at her earlobe. *It's not him. Not Lu . . . Relax. Relax, goddammit.* Determined to control it before it controlled her, she wrapped her arms around Michael's neck and in a move that surprised them both, let out a long, sensuous moan before biting his bottom lip, hard. Michael inhaled sharply, pain clearly mixing with pleasure as he read her signal and buried his face deep within her hair, serenading her with sweet murmurs. But for Theresa, there was only pain. The past that had hunted her down now had her in its grip, convincing her that any second now, kisses would turn to kicks and caresses to ravenous gropes and—

No!

She pushed Michael away, gasping, the room around her reduced to the suffocating blackness of her own mind, where joy and pleasure curled up and died when faced with it—him—the shadow.

"I can't," she whimpered, shaking uncontrollably. "I can't."

"Theresa?"

Michael's bewildered voice seemed to be coming from far away. Embarrassed, she lifted her head, shocked by the helpless expression on his face.

"Baby, what can I do?" he asked, sounding pained.

Theresa just shook her head, groping for her glasses.

"Talk to me," he coaxed in a concerned whisper. "Please."

Theresa choked back a sob. "I thought . . . I was ready. I thought . . ."

"Sshh." He went to take her in his arms, then stopped

himself. "Can I hold you?" he asked softly. "Is that all right?"

Theresa nodded mutely as he slowly, almost gingerly, wrapped his arms around her. *You're safe now,* she thought. *Relax.* But she couldn't and began to cry. "I'm so sorry," she sobbed into his chest.

"Don't be silly," Michael chided, holding her fast.

"It was fine," she said, talking more to herself than him as he stroked her hair. "Everything was fine. I was enjoying it so much. And then . . . it was like I was back there again, and he was shoving me down onto to the couch and tearing at my blouse . . . the fringe of his straight black hair hanging in his face . . . not hiding his leer . . ." She broke off, unable to continue.

"Motherfucking little bastard," Michael railed beneath his breath. Theresa could feel the anger fanning through him, sensed his struggle to keep his ire in check. She waited for him to relax, overwhelmed with relief when he carefully drew her even closer. "Just let it out, angel. It's okay. No one can hurt you now. Not while I'm here."

Grateful, Theresa remained nestled in the shelter of his arms, her frantic heartbeat gradually returning to normal as he gently rocked her. Feeling better, she slowly straightened up, swiping at her eyes which she was sure were now ringed with smeared mascara. "Still want to date me now?" she asked bitterly.

Michael angled his head, looking completely baffled. "Of course I do."

"Oh, really?"

"Of course." His fingers found her hair, pushing the few stray strands away from her face. "Why wouldn't I?"

"Because I'm damaged goods, Michael. I'm emotionally crippled. I haven't dated since it happened and judging by tonight, I'll never be able to handle a relationship again."

"You are not damaged goods," he countered ferociously. "You're someone who had something horrible happen to them and you're frightened. I understand that."

"Do you understand it might be months before I'm ready for anything more intimate than a kiss?"

"Yes, I do." His hand found hers. "And I can deal with that, Theresa. My main concern is you. That you feel safe and happy. That you're not afraid."

"Why?" she demanded, her entire body inflamed with confused anger. "Why are you so good to me? Why are you so patient and kind? Any other guy would have been out the door ten minutes ago."

"I take it you haven't figured out yet that I'm *not* any other guy."

"Why?" she repeated, tears threatening to erupt again. "I'm not worth it. I—"

"Stop." His index finger flew to her lips to still them. "I don't want to hear you putting yourself down, okay?"

Theresa nodded. Exhaustion overtook her, making her feel as if someone had filled her brain and body with wet, heavy sand. All she wanted was to crawl into her bed and sleep for years. "I'm tired," she said in a small voice.

"Me, too. It's pretty late." Michael searched her face. "Is there anything I can do, Ter? Here? Now?"

Theresa shook her head.

"Are you sure? I could sleep on the couch if you're scared of being alone. I swear on my mother's grave I won't try anything funny."

Despite all that had just happened, Theresa found herself smiling. "I know that, Michael. No, I'll be okay." She reached out to caress his cheek. "You're so sweet."

"Uh oh," Michael replied guardedly. "*Sweet* is just one cut above *nice*. Sounds like the big brush-off is coming."

"Not at all," Theresa swore, looking at him earnestly. "I had a wonderful time tonight and I would love to see you again—if that's what you want, after, you know . . ."

She looked away, face hot with a sense of shame she couldn't quite get a handle on.

"I would love another date."

Relief gentled Theresa's body, momentarily appeasing the heaviness that had her fighting to keep her eyes open. "I really like you," she hesitated. "And I—"

"You don't have to explain," he cut in gently.

"I'm going out to my folks' tomorrow. My dad's not doing too well. Do you want to come?"

"I can't," he said. *Damn.* "The 'Hunks On Ice' benefit is at Wollman Rink and I have to go. How about this? He pressed her hands between his. "You call me Monday and maybe we can catch a movie during the week? That sound good?"

"That sounds great."

"Okay. It's a deal then." He rose. "Are you sure you're going to be all right?" he asked, slipping his jacket on.

"I'll be fine," she swore. Seeing him to the door, she was glad he was such a trusting soul.

Because if he wasn't, he would have known she was lying.

It had been a long time since she'd been afraid to go to sleep.

Months, maybe even a whole year.

Yet every time she felt herself nodding off, some impulse would jerk her awake, protecting her from the nightmares she feared would ensue if she succumbed to her subconscious. The fact that it was happening again unnerved her, but at least she understood why.

The hard part would be dealing with it.

She spent the next day with her parents, working hard to cover the distress she felt over her father's deteriorating

condition and her own confusion. One minute she was
certain she could handle her intimacy problems on her
own; the next she was mentally rearranging her schedule
to make time for an appointment with her former shrink.
The thought of returning to that earth-toned office and
being asked to *remember* things, and how she *felt* about
them, was unnerving.

Another night of tossing and turning ensued, resulting
in her oversleeping for an important meeting she was
slated to handle on her own.

The previous week, she and Janna had received a call
from the manager of Notorious Devil D, requesting a
meeting. Notorious was sniffing around for new representation. The call should have been perceived as a godsend,
in light of the recent meeting with their accountant. But
both she and Janna hated Notorious Devil D's music. All
his lyrics referred to women as "ho's" and "bitches." Not
that anyone else seemed to notice or care; the public
couldn't get enough of him. Janna and Theresa agreed
they'd be idiots not to take the meeting. Theresa would be
handling it alone since Janna was meeting with Roberto
Alomar, who Mike Piazza had steered their way.

And now she was running late.

Fueled on adrenaline rather than her usual caffeine,
Theresa came flying through the office door at breakneck
speed.

"Are they here?" she asked Terrence breathlessly, *they*
being Notorious and his manager, Albert Groveman.

"Thankfully for your late ass, they just got here a few
minutes ago," Terrence informed her. "I told them you
were still at a breakfast meeting, gave them both coffee
and sent them to your office."

Theresa nodded, grateful, tugged her skirt down and
raked a hand through her hair, which was still damp. "Do
I look okay?"

"You look fine," Terrence replied quickly. "Listen, before you go in there, you might want to take a look at today's paper. There's—"

"I'll look at the paper after," said Theresa, starting down the hall.

"Theresa—"

"After," she called over her shoulder. Arriving at the closed door of her office, she took a deep breath before plunging inside. There, sitting behind her desk, was Notorious Devil D himself, playing with a rubber band. Across the desk from him sat Albert Groveman, a nervous, mousey man who rose politely when Theresa entered the room.

"I hope you don't mind," he said, gesturing at his client whose collection of necklaces probably cost more than the GDP of some small country. "But D always goes for the most comfortable seat in the house."

"No problem," Theresa lied amiably. Shaking both men's hands, she took the seat next to Groveman. "What can I do for you gentlemen?"

"D is unhappy with his current publicist," began Groveman. "Isn't that so, D?"

D nodded.

"Who's repping him now?" Theresa asked.

Groveman named a large entertainment conglomerate which, ironically, had just been purchased by Butler Corporation.

"And what's the problem?" Theresa continued, leaning forward to snatch a legal pad and pen from her desk.

"D doesn't feel they're doing enough to push his image in Hollywood. Ice-T, Snoop Dogg, Sean Combs, Eminem, Kid Rock, Mark Wahlberg—they're all movie stars now. D wants a piece of that action, too. Am I right, D?"

D nodded.

"I see," said Theresa as she took notes, wondering if D realized that in order to be a movie star, you had to talk. "Go on."

"D was also unhappy with the lack of damage control surrounding his recent divorce."

Theresa chewed the tip of her pen thoughtfully. "He tried to get out of the prenup by saying they weren't legally married, because the wedding was performed by a Samoan wrestler/priest, correct?"

"It wasn't legal!" D exploded, lunging across the desk. "I told that bitch from Day One—"

"D!" Groveman barked. "Let me handle this, all right?"

D nodded, slumping down behind Theresa's desk muttering.

"The case *was* somewhat controversial," Groveman admitted smoothly as he regarded Theresa, "but it would have been less so had D's PR people handled it differently."

"Certainly," Theresa said. "Well, let me begin by explaining to you how we work here, and what I think we can offer you."

With as much enthusiasm as she could muster, she gave Groveman and his client the standard "Why you want FM PR to work for you" spiel. Groveman actually seemed to be listening. D, on the other hand, had returned to teasing his brain with the rubber band. When she was done, she asked if they had any questions.

"A few," said Groveman. "Question One: Do you have any other musicians on your roster?"

"We do." Theresa named two, an alterna-chick who was currently in heavy rotation on MTV, and an aging British heavy metal band experiencing a resurgence in their fan base thanks to the inclusion of three of their songs in the latest Cameron Crowe film. Groveman nodded, impressed.

"So you don't just devote yourself to hockey players?" D asked with a smirk.

"Uh, no," said Theresa curtly, caught completely off guard.

"Well, that's good," Groveman cut in. "Would it be possible for you to put in writing what you just laid out for us, along with an estimate of what your services will cost?"

"I'd be glad to. When would you like it by?"

"Is the end of next week all right?"

"That's fine. I'll have it to you by the beginning of next week."

Groveman turned to Theresa's desk. "D?"

D nodded.

"Then it's a wrap," Groveman declared, standing. Theresa rose at the same time he did. She couldn't wait for them to leave. Keeping a pleasant smile plastered on her face, she escorted them to the elevators. Reentering the office, Terrence accosted her immediately.

"Well? How did it go?" he asked anxiously.

"Fine, if you ignore some non sequitur about hockey players." Terrence winced. "How is it possible that Notorious Devil D is a gazillionaire and I'm not?" Theresa wondered aloud.

"It's one of those mysteries of the universe, hon, like, 'How many face lifts can Joan Rivers endure before she starts resembling a hammerhead shark?'"

"Mmm." Despite his delightfully forked tongue, Theresa noticed he looked distinctly troubled. "What's the matter?"

"Here's why they made a crack about hockey players," Terrence said, slowly pushing his copy of the *New York Sentinel* towards her. "Read it and scream," he sighed, pretending to busy himself with some paperwork in front of him.

Heart in throat, Theresa opened to the *Sentinel*'s notorious gossip page, "Eye Spy." She scanned it, stopping when Michael's name jumped out at her in bold letters:

"Spotted Canoodling at the Rainbow Room: New York Blades' own **Mikey D** with publicist Theresa Falconetti. Two short years ago, Falconetti won an out-of-court settlement in a case of alleged sexual assault against one of Mikey's former teammates, **Alexei Lubov.** Looks like Miss F just can't resist men on skates."

Theresa closed the paper. She stood still, mouth filling with sand while invisible talons dug deep into her chest, making it hard to breathe. She pushed the paper back towards Terrence.

"Are you okay?" he asked uneasily.

Theresa opened her mouth to say something, but the right words wouldn't come. In fact, no words would come. It was as if the conduit between her brain and her mouth were blocked.

"It's bullshit, Theresa, you of all people should know that," Terrence said fiercely. The phone rang. "Oh, shit. Let me get that."

Theresa nodded. While Terrence took the call, she quietly folded up the newspaper, then grabbed a piece of scrap paper on his desk and began scribbling. When she was done, she handed it to him. "I'm going out, but I'll be back after lunch," it read. "There's something I need to do."

CHAPTER

12

"Michael. How's it going?"

Exhaling slowly as he released his left leg from a standing quad stretch, Michael turned to see Ty standing beside him. This evening would be his first game back following his concussion, and everyone, from the trainers to the coaching staff to his teammates, was keeping a careful eye on him. Michael appreciated their concern, but there was no need: He'd gotten clearance to play from both the team doctor and a neurologist.

"It's going well," he told Ty.

"Good. Don't want you to push it if you're not feeling one hundred percent."

"I'm feeling great," Michael answered.

"You sure?"

"Yes."

"Good," Ty repeated. He patted Michael's shoulder before crossing to talk to Kevin Gill. Michael tried not to stare as the two of them conversed, occasionally turning their heads to glance back at him. It was another minute or two before they separated and moved on to talk to other players.

Chest tight, Michael squirted a shot of Gatorade into his mouth and sat down on a mat, resuming his stretches. He wasn't an idiot. In the space of one week, van Dorn had seized his opportunity and had dazzled the shit out of everyone. He was a better skater. He was better with the puck. He scored goals. Obviously Ty and Kevin were deciding who to dress for tonight's game.

Resentment roiled through him, though he knew it was misplaced. He'd been a professional athlete long enough to know this came with the territory. It was an old story: A veteran player gets hurt, a rookie waiting in the wings finally gets the chance to show his mettle and—*bam!*—before you know it, the vet finds himself crying into the bubbly at his retirement party at the advanced old age of thirty-five. Just thinking about it made him grind his teeth. He'd be damned if he'd let it happen to *him*. He still had two, maybe three good productive years left if he maintained his focus and drive. No way was he going to roll over and die for Dennis the fucking Menace.

He was midway through his second set of one hundred stomach crunches when the sound of Tully Webster's voice cut through his fantasy of boarding the little bastard.

"Yo, Mikey. There's some girl out there who wants to talk to you. Says it's urgent."

Gemma? Theresa? Puzzled, Michael grabbed his towel and draped it over his neck, ignoring the catcalls and off-color comments of his teammates as he strode across the weight room. He found Theresa waiting for him out in the hallway, leaning against a concrete wall.

"Hey, you," he said, bad mood dissipating at the mere sight of her. He leaned in for a small peck to her cheek, then thought better of it, slick as he was with perspiration. His sweaty appearance embarrassed him, but there was nothing he could do about it, apart from toweling off as best he could and praying he didn't have killer BO. He pressed his towel first to his face, then to his neck. "This is a surprise."

"I know." Theresa's expression was grim, her hands dug deep in her coat pockets.

"Everything okay?"

"No."

"Is it your dad?" He remembered she'd gone out to Brooklyn the day before specifically to spend some time with her old man. Maybe he was in the hospital?

Appreciation flickered briefly across Theresa's face. "My father's fine." She smiled wanly. "I mean—relatively. You know." Peering past him, she gazed anxiously up the long, neon-lit corridor. "Look, is there somewhere a bit more private where we can talk?"

"Sure." Michael paused to think. "Follow me."

He led her to the players' lounge, careful to use the alternative entrance circumventing the actual locker room. He knew a couple of the guys might wander in and out in towels, picking at the muffins and fruit laid out on the long banquet table adjacent to the huge ceiling-mounted TV, but there was nothing he could do about it. Short of asking Ty if he could use his office, the players' lounge was the best he could manage on such short notice.

Eager to put Theresa at ease, he gestured towards the table. "Coffee?" Theresa shook her head.

"Muffin?"

"No, thank you, Michael."

Her voice was overly polite. Cautious now, he peered at her, attempting to decipher her expression while trying not to give anything away with his own. Her demeanor was tense and businesslike. In fact, it was downright standoffish. Michael's guts began to churn.

Since she didn't want anything to eat or drink, the only thing left to do was sit. He escorted her to the couch closest to the TV. Distracted by the chattering voices of women coming from the set, he turned it off before sitting down beside her.

He forced a smile, determined to sound upbeat. "What's up?"

Theresa was uncharacteristically poker-faced as she extracted a copy of the *New York Sentinel* from her brief-case and handed it to him. Confused, Michael's eyes scanned the page until he spotted his own name in bold type, carefully reading what was printed there. When he was through, he handed the paper back to her.

"Everyone knows half the stuff that's printed in that column is bullshit. Don't let it get to you." Seeing his words had no effect, he gently pried the paper from her fingers, dumping it in the trash.

"You don't get it, do you?" Theresa stared at him. "Not only does that witch Lynette Homes insinuate that Lubov might not have assaulted me, but she makes me sound like a goddamn puck bunny!"

"So?" Michael repeated. He couldn't believe she was getting bent out of shape over what some low life, muck-raker had written. "Who cares what this bimbo says?"

"I do! Janna and I are trying to expand our business," Theresa said in frustration. "We're trying to drum up new clients. What do you think the odds of us succeeding are if the public thinks I'm some slut who brings frivolous lawsuits and bangs jocks for fun?"

Michael blinked with incredulity. "Who's going to think that?"

"Anyone who reads that column!" Theresa railed. "*Jesus*, Michael!"

Her voice was loud enough now to draw the attention of a couple of his teammates, who poked their heads around the door in curiosity. When Michael leveled them with a look that could curdle milk, the heads disappeared. He turned back to Theresa. "What's going on?" he asked.

His aim was to sound patient, but he could hear the

edge in his voice, defensive, challenging. Theresa's eyes grazed the floor, the opposite wall, anywhere but his face. "Look at me, Theresa," he commanded. Every muscle in his body tensed as he waited for her to force her glistening eyes to his.

"I'm really sorry, Michael, but I can't go out with you right now. My career's at stake, and I just can't risk it."

"You're kidding, right?"

Theresa squirmed uncomfortably. "Michael—"

Instinctually, his left hand shot out in a gesture meant to silence her. It worked. The only sound in the room was that of their breathing.

Michael just stared. Theresa's face seemed to break up right in front him. Fragments of eye, delicate nose, sensuous lips—all of it broke apart like a puzzle being slowly dismantled while behind his eyes, the red of anger pushed at the sockets, insistent, threatening to blow his head open.

"Career—?"

He couldn't even finish the sentence. Maybe she hadn't said it. Maybe his mind had manufactured it. He narrowed his eyes, trying to put her face back together again, trying to hold back the red baying for blood, but it was no use. Something inside him broke, and it wasn't just his heart. It was the dam holding back months of frustration at being told to wait, being told to woo, being told that no matter what he did, whether on or off the ice, it simply wasn't good enough.

He began laughing. Quietly, at first, then loudly, uproariously, the sound harsh to his own ears, tinged as it was with a hint of mania. He was laughing so hard tears rolled down his face; so hard he thought his sides would split open. "My career's at stake!" he howled, barely able to breathe as he punched the words out. "Oh, that's good! That's the best one you've come up with yet!"

"Michael."

He forced himself to look in the direction of her voice, watching as her face reassembled itself. She was staring at him with frightened eyes that said *You're behaving like a lunatic*. Well, maybe he was. Maybe this was what months of being repeatedly kicked in the balls did to a man. Even so, in the interest of civilized conversation, he thought it might be wise to try to get his rage under control.

"What?" he said, angrily panting his way back to normal breath. He wanted to hear what she had to say, really he did, but when she opened her mouth to talk he was surprised to hear his own voice coming out instead.

"Wait, let me guess: You changed your mind and now you *can* go out with me?"

Theresa looked away, shamefaced.

"What, did I say the wrong thing?" Michael challenged. "Did I say the *right* thing? Because, with you, I never know whether I'm going to get kissed or kicked."

She turned back to him, her expression pained. "Listen to me, Michael."

"No, *you* listen to *me*." A hot stream of long unspoken words shot up his throat, impossible to ignore. "First you won't go out with me because I'm a *toothless gavone*. Oh yeah, I *heard* you say that at Ty's wedding. *Then* you won't go out with me because I'm Italian. Now you won't go out with me because it'll screw up your career. *Do you have any idea how fucked up you are?*"

He knew he was shouting, but he didn't care. Righteous indignation was screaming through his veins, and he was determined to give it full vent. After all she'd put him through, *months* of watching and waiting and behaving, and for what? *For this?* "You know what your problem is, Theresa?" he asked, as he jumped up from the couch. "You're a head case."

"Michael." Her voice was trembling. "Let me just—"

"Explain?" he finished for her contemptuously as he

paced back and forth like a caged beast. "Explain what? You're a mess. You don't know who you are, you don't know what you want, and you don't know where you're going." Out of the corner of his eye, he saw some of his teammates still hovering nervously in the doorway, but he didn't care. They wanted to see a show? They craved some drama in their lives? Well, they'd come to the right place. "I thought that if I was nice enough, and romantic enough, and patient enough, that eventually I'd win you over." He slapped himself in the forehead. "*Ubatz!* What the hell was I thinking? Why couldn't I see what was right in front of my face? You might be beautiful, but *Madonn'*, you are batshit crazy!"

He heard some chuckles but ignored them. Theresa, meanwhile, was slowly turning red, her normally beautiful face—a face he had tenderly cradled in his hands just two nights before—twitching with mounting humiliation.

"I am not crazy, Michael," she hissed up at him through clenched teeth.

"No?" He stopped pacing and rounded in on her. "You're not? What's the word you would use to describe someone who swoons in your arms one minute and two days later tells you they can't see you?"

"Confused," Theresa tossed back angrily.

"Confused." Michael rocked on his heels, mulling this over. "Hmm. Someone who does that to you once might be called confused. But twice?" He shook his head. "Sorry. *Confused* is not the word that comes to mind. Try cruel. Try crazy."

"I never meant to be cruel, Michael. Honestly."

"I don't give a damn what you did or didn't mean, Theresa." He snorted. "I thought the concussion I suffered last week left my brain scrambled. But you know what? That was *nothing* compared to the mind games you've been playing with me. You don't want to see me?" Michael shrugged. "No problem. I need you like I need an effing hole in the head. We can deal with each other on a purely professional basis. Otherwise, I don't want to see you, I don't want to hear from you, I don't want to know you. *Capisce?*"

Theresa nodded shakily.

"Glad we understand each other." Nothing left to say, he stalked off in the direction of the locker room. His eavesdropping teammates remained clustered around the doorway, watching wide-eyed as he approached them. "What the hell are you bozos looking at?" he snarled, shoving past them.

No one answered.

Back in the locker room, Michael's heart was still pounding. He took a few deep calming breaths, working to ignore the irrational feeling that everyone was staring. Now that he'd unloaded, all he wanted to do was hit the shower and get the hell out of Met Gar as quickly as possible, the better to get his head back on straight before tonight's game. But no sooner had he made it to his locker than van Dorn came slinking over, his smug face incandescent with scorn.

"Girl trouble, huh?"

Michael's mouth twitched. *Ignore him,* he told himself, humming a happy tune in his head in an effort to distract himself. *Don't get into it with the little prick.*

"What, she come down here to ditch you?" van Dorn needled.

"*Vaffanculo,* eh?" Michael returned, refusing to even make eye contact.

"Riiiight. Whatever the fuck that means in Wopspeak." Van Dorn took a step closer, giving Michael a knowing, fraternal nudge in the ribs. "That girl in the players' lounge—you know, the one you were just yelling at? Isn't she the chick who sucked off Lubov? Too bad we're not playing his team again this season. You two could compare notes."

Michael wasn't sure what happened next. One minute he was staring at his shampoo bottle and humming. The next his right fist was connecting with van Dorn's jaw, sending him sprawling backwards over the bench. If van Dorn had any intention of fighting back, it was never realized. Michael was on him so fast, punching him so furiously, that it took three guys to tear him away.

"WHAT THE HELL IS GOING ON HERE?"

Kevin Gill's voice boomed through the locker room, rendering it instantly silent. Still being restrained by his teammates, Michael spat on the floor and looked away, knowing all the captain had to see was van Dorn's bloodied lip and rapidly swelling eye and he'd know what had gone down, though not necessarily why.

"Gentlemen?" Kevin went to van Dorn first, helping him up onto the bench. "Get him a towel," he commanded no one in particular. A clean white towel appeared, courtesy of Tim Halifax, which van Dorn pressed to his mouth.

"What happened?" Kevin demanded.

"Nothing," van Dorn replied blankly.

"Dante." Kevin's voice rang with disapproval. "You want to tell me what the hell happened here?"

"Nothing," Michael replied, glaring down at van Dorn in disgust as he folded his arms angrily across his chest. The locker room was dead silent as he, along with everyone else, waited to hear what Kevin had to say. The captain seemed to be taking care to make eye contact with both Michael and van Dorn as he spoke.

"I don't give a damn about what started this, okay? What I care about is the team. You two just undermined everything we're trying to create here. I won't have it. And neither should you." He looked to the other players. "Just in case it has slipped some of your minds, let me remind you all: What goes on in this locker room stays in this locker room. I don't want to open the paper tomorrow and read about a fight between two members of the New York Blades. Am I making myself clear?"

The team muttered its understanding. When Kevin's gaze flicked specifically to Michael, he jerked his head in an approximation of answering yes. There was small comfort when Kevin did the same with van Dorn, whose response was to simply stare down at the floor.

"Good. I'm glad we're all on the same page. Now let's get some rest. We have an important game tonight."

It seemed to Michael as if no one moved or spoke for the longest time. They all appeared rooted to the spot, embarrassed not only by the reprimand but by what had caused it. Irritated by the lingering silence, Michael picked up his shampoo bottle and soap and headed for the showers, eager for the release hot water beating down on his body would bring.

That afternoon, while back at his apartment "resting," as if he could, Michael thought about Theresa. He was upset with himself for losing control. But what the hell did she expect? She'd ambushed him at work, for Chrissakes. Ambushed him on the heels of a Saturday night spent dancing in his arms. Not only had she caught him unaware, but at the worst possible time. His entire morning had been one long, unmitigated disaster from start to finish.

Maybe he should call and apologize for wailing on her that way? No. He'd meant what he said. He just wished he hadn't expressed it so colorfully.

His mind flashed on the news item she'd shoved beneath his nose. Two stupid sentences in a gossip column and their romance was over before it even really began. It was astounding, the more so when he considered what she did for a living. Shit, half the time *she* was the person feeding this kind of junk to the media just to get her clients' names in print! He was no shrink, but he knew fear when he saw it, and Theresa was afraid—of herself, of what other people thought, of getting close, of her own fucking shadow.

Maybe he'd done them both a favor by reading her the riot act, because now she could go get her head shrunk or whatever the hell it was she wanted to do to help herself, and he could concentrate on hockey and the restaurant, period. What had happened between them was actually *positive,* then.

Yeah. Right.

It was getting dark when he arrived at Met Gar at four-thirty for the Blades game against Toronto. His team-mates, even those closest to him, regarded him cautiously, as if one false look might set him off. Their unease made him realize the damage he'd done.

Tradition held that after the pre-game warm-up, the team returned to the locker room to learn the lineup and listen to whatever words of wisdom and inspiration Ty cared to share. Tonight, Ty's notes for the team were few: Watch out for the long center ice passes Toronto is famous for; don't let up on the forecheck. He didn't say a word about the fight. Michael worried that Ty might keep him off the ice, but he was to resume his usual spot on the third line, relegating van Dorn to his former status as thorn in his side and permanent threat.

He waited until Ty had finished before asking if he might say something to the team. The sense of shock rippling through the warm locker room was palpable.

"Go ahead," Ty urged.

Acutely aware that all eyes were on him, Michael paused to collect himself before he opened his mouth. He wanted to make sure he had the words straight in his head. When he was finally ready, he drew a deep breath of air. Then he started talking.

"One of the things I love about being a professional hockey player, apart from the money, of course"—that brought a few laughs, easing his nerves—"is that it brings together twenty guys who might not have anything else in common apart from their love of hockey. Guys who might even hate each other's guts. But when they get out on the ice, they'll risk their necks for each other."

He swallowed, surprised at how quickly his mouth had become dry. "I owe all of you an apology. I was wrong. It won't happen again."

The room was silent. Then, one by one, they each took their sticks and began tapping them on the floor as a show of support as Michael walked toward van Dorn and extended his hand. The younger player looked momentarily stunned before returning the gesture, the two enemies stiffly shaking hands as the tapping continued. Michael felt a huge weight lift from him as he strolled back to his locker to put his helmet on. He might not have handled things well with Theresa, but at least he had repaired what damage he could here. For that, he was grateful.

CHAPTER
13

She hated needing to be here. The soothing, familiar cadence of Dr. Gardner's voice should have put her at ease. Instead, she was tense as her old therapist asked her why she was back. *Isn't it obvious?* she longed to scream. Theresa leaned forward to keep from sinking into the plush recesses of Dr. Gardner's couch. "I'm here because I'm a mess," she declared, shocked at how quickly tears threatened.

"How so?" Dr. Gardner wanted to know. A stout, motherly woman with a taste for tweeds, her face was open, yet impassive. Theresa wondered if she ever secretly wished her clients would just shut up and get a grip.

"I . . ." Theresa halted. Where to begin? With Michael's pursuit and her initial refusals? Her post-Rainbow Room meltdown? The business? Her dad's cancer? Her continuing attraction to Reese, who was due back in New York in two weeks' time? Flummoxed, she waited for a definitive answer to present itself.

Dr. Gardner also waited.

No prompting. No helpful clues about where to start.

Theresa decided to start with Michael's upbraiding. *I'm not going to cry,* she told herself, but the minute she started to speak, her eyes began watering. Before she knew it she was jamming tissues to her dripping nose. "I'm sorry," she whispered as she told the therapist what had happened. Her narration was punctuated with unavoidable sniffles and sporadic silences.

Throughout it all, Dr. Gardner smiled benignly with her trademark detachment that always amazed Theresa. Eventually she asked, "What upsets you the most about your run-in with Michael?"

Theresa bowed her head, the crumpled tissue in her hand reduced to the size of a pellet as she crushed it repeatedly while mulling the question over. "That his anger at me was completely justified." She wiped her nose on her hand thoughtfully. "And that I didn't think before I acted."

Dr. Gardner looked intrigued. "What do you mean?"

Theresa shifted on the couch. "I shouldn't have charged down there and thrown the newspaper in his face. I should have thought about how I wanted to talk to him about it."

Dr. Gardner's voice was gentle. "So, why do you think you did that?"

"I don't know."

"Do you think you saw the news item as a way to get out of your relationship?"

"Why would I want to do that?" Theresa answered too quickly. Even as the words shot from her lips, she knew Dr. Gardner had hit on something. The newly forming knot in her shoulders told her so. So did the headache coming on behind her right eye, sharp and hot as a firecracker. Tensing, she mounted a defense.

"If Michael had let me get a word in edgewise, or had listened carefully to what I was saying, he would have noticed I said 'I can't go out with you *right now.*' Not 'I can't see you ever again.'"

Dr. Gardner folded her hands in her lap. "You were trying to convey to him that your rejection was just temporary?"

"Yes."

"And you expected that when this current crisis blew over, he would be there waiting for you?"

Theresa said nothing. She didn't want to admit that yes, that was exactly what she'd been thinking, unstable, unfair bitch that she was. Dr. Gardner must have been reading her mind, because her next question was "Does that seem fair to you?"

"No," Theresa admitted reluctantly in a voice just above a whisper. The pain in her head was getting worse. She closed her eyes, hoping the momentary plunge into darkness might help. When she opened them, Dr. Gardner was looking at her curiously.

"Do you care about Michael?"

"Yes." Her response was immediate and rang true. There was relief in that, in this one brief spasm of clarity.

"Then why do you think you keep sending him mixed messages?"

Theresa reached for a new, fresh tissue as her eyes began seeping again, sending the Rothko print behind Dr. Gardner's head into even softer focus. "Because . . . I'm frightened."

"Of—?"

"Getting too close."

"Because—?"

This time Theresa let the tears come full force. They were hot and nasty, leaving a trail of salty streaks that ran down her cheeks and fell in fat, indelicate drops off her chin. She told Dr. Gardner about the shadow, and the sleepless, nightmare-filled nights. About her family and how they loved her too much, so much that she often felt she wanted to get away from them. She talked until the blink of her eyelids felt like sandpaper against her eyes, until there were no words left to say. When she was done, Dr. Gardner had one question left to ask her.

"What do you hope to achieve by returning to therapy, Theresa?"

Finally, an easy question. "I want to stop running. I want to stop feeling afraid. I want to be in control of my life."

Dr. Gardner smiled.

"You've come to the right place," she said.

Back at work, the pain in Theresa's skull was so severe she was forced to lie down on the couch in Janna's darkened office while she waited for her to return from lunch. The therapy session had drained her more than she thought possible. She'd forgotten about that: how tired you were afterwards, as if spilling your guts were a strenuous activity. It had been months since she'd had a migraine this bad. Like an idiot, she had forgotten to bring her pills with her in her purse. The slightest movement of her head made her feel as if a spike were being jabbed into her eye, and the accompanying nausea didn't help. As soon as she filled Janna in on her accounts, she was going to crawl home and die.

A few minutes later, she heard the office door click open and Janna softly call her name.

"I'm on the couch," Theresa moaned. The mere act of speaking had her wincing.

"Oh, Terry." Janna's voice rang with sympathy as she sat down on the couch near Theresa's head. "Do you want a massage?" she offered. "Would that help?"

Theresa nodded, though it pained her to. She concentrated on relaxing as Janna slowly, deeply, began massaging her temples.

"You missed your calling," Theresa said.

Janna chuckled appreciatively. "Ty says the same thing. He thinks if I ever decide to switch careers, I should become a massage therapist."

"He's right."

"What brought this on?" Janna asked, concerned.

"Therapy," Theresa answered, her body loosening ever so slightly as Janna's fingers worked their magic. Initially, the small circular motions Janna employed seemed to make the pounding worse. But then the pain receded ever so slightly, granting Theresa some leeway to expand on her answer without fear of throwing up. "I'm seeing Dr. Gardner again."

"Oh." Janna sounded neither shocked nor surprised. "First session?"

Theresa nodded, regretting it immediately as daggers of pain sliced through her head.

"Those are always the worst," said Janna.

"Tell me about it," Theresa murmured.

"Is it because of what happened at Met Gar the other day?" Janna asked.

Theresa remembered something Janna had told her ages ago: Jocks were the worst gossips on earth. Word of her verbal altercation with Michael must have traveled around the locker room at lightning speed. By the time Ty got home from the game that night, he must have told Janna everything. "Yes. But that was three days ago, Janna," Theresa pointed out quietly. "How come you didn't mention it until now?"

Janna's answer was simple and direct. "I figured if you wanted to discuss it, you'd bring it up."

"I appreciate that."

"You know that if you ever need to talk to me about anything, I'm here, right?" she reminded Theresa.

"I do know that. And I appreciate it, believe me."

"Good."

She could feel Janna's own relief coming through the pads of her fingertips as they relaxed their pressure. The massage was working: The pain in Theresa's head was beginning to abate. Now if the nausea would only follow suit.

"Are you up to talking business?" Janna asked gently.

"I can try."

"Then shoot."

"First up, Notorious Devil D. When I'm feeling better, we should probably talk about whether we really want to take him on or not."

"Okay," Janna agreed.

"What's up with the Mets' Alomar?"

"I think he's about to join the FM PR family," Janna said confidently.

"Great."

"I know." Her fingers carefully kneaded their way back and forth below Theresa's hairline. "Reese Banister called here twice for you this morning."

Theresa almost sat up. "He did?"

"Yup. Didn't want to talk to me. Only wanted to talk to you."

Theresa flushed with pleasure. "I guess I better call him."

"I guess so."

There was an edge to Janna's voice Theresa didn't care to dwell on. Pressing hard, Janna slowly ran both her thumbs the length of Theresa's jawline and back up again, stopping to massage the space right below her ears. "How's the Dante's account going? If it would make things easier, we could switch. I could take that account and you could take Piazza."

"No, I'll be fine," Theresa assured her. "I can handle seeing Michael."

"No kidding, " Janna said knowingly. "The question is: Can Michael handle seeing you?"

• • • •

Five minutes. That's all Michael was going to give Anthony before he hopped in his car, drove over to the house and dragged the giant *idiota* down to the restaurant by his ears. Yeah, it was early. Six A.M. on a Sunday morning was very early. But if Michael could be on time after playing a game *and* closing out the restaurant the night before, and Aunt Gavina could rouse herself to take Nonna to Mass as a favor to "you boys," then there was no reason Anthony couldn't get his sorry ass down to Dante's, too.

Two weeks earlier Theresa had called him with some incredible news: the Food Network was doing a special called "Mangia: The Joy of Italian Cooking," and she had convinced the producers to include Dante's. The plan was for Anthony to cook one of the restaurant's signature dishes on camera before he and Michael were interviewed about it and the restaurant. Hearing the enthusiasm in Theresa's voice had made him tense; not only because he missed her, but because he knew he'd have to convince Anthony to do it.

When Michael related the good news, Anthony yelled. He snarled. He threw pots and pans, imploring various dead relatives to help him avoid this personal hell. Michael waited for the theatrics to finish before pulling out his ace-in-the-hole. In the five months since they'd hired Theresa, bookings had nearly doubled. They'd had to add more tables for which they'd barely had room, since the renovation wasn't slated to start until the following month. They'd been written up in the *Daily News* and had received a positive on-air review from WOR's Joan Hamburg.

Sure, there had been a few rough spots.

Anthony still hadn't forgiven him for keeping the restaurant open on Christmas Eve to serve the traditional Italian fish feast, referring to it melodramatically as "Black Christmas," even though it was a huge success. And the inclusion of two younger, hipper waiters hadn't gone down too well with the older wait staff.

But just as Michael had hoped, Dante's was beginning to earn a real reputation across the city. More importantly, they were turning an incredible profit. "You never complain about *that*," Michael pointed out to his brother, who muttered incomprehensibly then stormed away. When he returned, he agreed to do the shoot on one condition: He would not cook in some "fancy, schmancy Manhattan studio." He would only cook in the restaurant kitchen. Much to Michael's chagrin, the special's producers agreed.

Checking his watch yet again, Michael watched as the film crew carefully laid out the ingredients Anthony would be using on one of the long stainless steel tables in the kitchen. Anthony had decided to make osso buco in bianco, or tomatoless braised veal shanks. "Does it take long to cook?" the director asked. At least Michael assumed it was the director, since he seemed to be the guy telling everyone else what to do.

Michael shrugged. "I don't know."

The director turned away in disgust.

Certain he was in the way, he went out to the dining room, surveying the sea of empty tables with their shining cutlery and perfectly starched white napkins. He didn't want to think about how much time he spent here now. This was his life: the restaurant and hockey.

He picked up a random glass off a table for four, checking it for spots. The Blades were past the midpoint of the season now, and all across the league, it was becoming clear which teams were locks for the post season and which teams were not. The Blades were not. The team needed to kick it up a notch if they wanted into the playoffs. That was why Kevin and Ty had come to him shortly after New Year's to tell him they were shifting him to the fourth line. "We need van Dorn's speed on the third line, Mikey," Ty had explained, never one to candy-coat. "We need his scoring." Being a professional, Michael understood. But it still hurt. The only thing that stopped him from choking on his own resentment was throwing himself into the restaurant.

The front door opened. *Finally,* thought Michael. But it wasn't Anthony, it was Theresa, the tip of her nose red with cold as she hurried towards him.

"Sorry I'm late," she said.

Michael felt a small pang of longing knock against his ribs as he watched her unwind a silk scarf from around her neck and toss her jacket over a nearby chair. Though they'd had occasion to discuss business on the phone—always polite, always detached—they hadn't seen each other since that day in December when she'd lowered the boom on him. Seeing her now, all his frustration came flooding back.

Pulling a clipboard out of her briefcase, she motioned toward the kitchen. "The crew setting up?"

"Yup. There's just one problem." Theresa froze. "Anthony's not here yet."

"Have you called him?"

"Twice."

Theresa's expression was grim. "Tell me this isn't happening."

"He'll be here," Michael assured her. Tentative, hands in the pockets of his pants, he approached her. "So, how have you been?"

Theresa looked up from where she was peering at the clipboard. "Fine," she said quickly. "You?"

"Good, good." He cleared his throat. "How's your dad?" he asked, even though he knew. He had become friendly with Theresa's brother Phil, and thus knew almost everything there was to know about the Falconettis.

"He's hanging in there," Theresa replied politely, clearly not wanting to talk about it. "I'll tell him you asked about him."

"Thanks."

Silence descended, awkward and obvious, a pink elephant of discomfort stampeding into the room.

"I'm going to go in with the crew," Theresa announced.

Michael nodded as she strode purposefully through the swinging doors of the kitchen, leaving him alone with his ache for her and what he'd been so convinced should have been, but was not. He remembered the shock of pleasure on her face when he'd taken off her blindfold, the child-like wonder in her eyes as she danced in his arms. All dust now, all past.

His dejection lifted somewhat when finally—*finally*— Anthony appeared, whistling jauntily in a way that made Michael's nerves twitch.

"Where the hell have you been?" Michael demanded. "The film crew's all set up in the kitchen and waiting for you!"

"Sorry," Anthony replied, though it was obvious he wasn't. "I was at Angie's last night. I overslept."

Michael's head thrust forward in disbelief. "Angie Calabrese the cop?"

Anthony nodded, smiling slyly.

"You and she—"

"You got it," he purred, adding a wink for good measure.

Michael stepped back, dumbfounded. His nightmare had come true: Anthony was now the one with a life; he, Mikey D, had squat. *Sweet Jesus on the cross.* The only thing left to do was off himself.

Stunned, he followed his brother into the kitchen, trying hard to ignore the tension level which rocketed from zero to fifty the minute Anthony saw the way the ingredients were laid out. He and Theresa exchanged worried glances. Michael was positive it would take the intervention of a platoon of saints for this shoot to come off. But surprisingly, Anthony quickly rose to the occasion. He even seemed to be enjoying himself. *Amazing what a good screw can do,* Michael thought bitterly.

By the time Anthony was done cooking and the crew was ready to begin filming the segment about the restau-

rant, Michael got the feeling that the last thing the former
Phantom of the Double Boiler wanted to do was share the
spotlight.

"I can handle the segment on my own, Mike."

"No, that's okay," Michael replied testily. He sat where
the director told him to sit, at a small round table in the center of the restaurant with his brother. They were instructed to
look casual and relaxed while Sonia, the skinny blonde host-
ing the show, plied them with questions.

"So, how long has Dante's been around?" she asked,
doing the best imitation of someone genuinely interested
Michael ever saw.

"Fifty years," Anthony boomed proudly.

"No, forty years," Michael corrected as Anthony's
massive head slowly turned to challenge him. "Do the
math, Ant: You're thirty-six and Mom and Pop opened it
four years before you were born. That's forty years."

"Whatever," Anthony muttered.

"And why is that veal dish you made so special to
Dante's?" Sonia chirped.

"I'll take this one, Michael," answered Anthony
quickly. He turned to the camera, smiling broadly. "The
recipe is one that's been in the family for close to seventy
years. It was handed down from my paternal grandmother
to my parents long, long ago."

"No," Michael found himself saying again, "the recipe
came from Mom's mom, Anthony."

But Anthony was obstinately shaking his head. "You're
wrong, Mikey. I distinctly remember Mom telling me
Grandma Dante gave it to her when she got married."

"Yeah?" Michael gave a curt laugh. "Well, I remember
Pop saying the recipe was the only freebie Nonna Maria
ever gave away in her life."

"Cut!" Whipping off his headset, the director approached them. "Can we cut the Cain and Abel act and get
this in the can, please?"

"Maybe we should just talk to the cook," Sonia suggested delicately. She looked at Michael, addressing him like he was a four-year-old. "Does that work for you?"

"Sure, it works for me," Michael managed through clenched teeth. He turned to his brother. "Does it work for you?"

Anthony chuckled affectionately. "I told you, Mike. Stick to the ice. This is my domain."

"Right." Michael bounded out of the chair and proceeded to watch the rest of the shoot from the sidelines with Theresa.

"He's doing really well," Theresa whispered to him at one point. For the first time all morning, she really looked at him. "Are you sure you're all right with Anthony being the star?"

"Oh, yeah," Michael lied. He was fine with Anthony being the star. And with being demoted to the fourth line. And with Theresa shattering his heart. He was fine with all of it. Fuck, he was Mikey D, right? Not sure he could stand a minute more of Anthony's sucking up to the camera, he stood. "I'm going to take off."

Theresa barely seemed to hear; her eyes remained fixed on Anthony. "Okay. As soon as I know when this is going to air, I'll give you a call." Suddenly, she craned her neck to look at him, and for a split second, Michael thought that maybe she was going to say something like "Hey, let's go for a coffee afterwards" or "I really miss you, let's do dinner." But instead, all she said was, "Take care."

"Yeah, you, too," he replied dully, struck by how casually people used the phrase without really stopping to think about its meaning. Did he really want her to take care? God, yes, with all his heart and all his soul. But did she want the same for him? He would never know.

CHAPTER

14

How did it feel seeing Michael again, Theresa?

Sitting at a small table in Cafe Des Artistes, Theresa imagined the deliberately neutral calibration of Dr. Gardner's voice. She imagined her own response. *I felt tense. Sad. Uncomfortable. I felt . . . desire.*

Speaking to Michael on the phone was one thing.

But coming face-to-face with him at the "Mangia" shoot was another. She was unprepared for the conflicted feelings that poured out of her when she walked into Dante's and there he was, all alone in the chilly dining room, inspecting a glass from a nearby table. How handsome he looked, much more rugged than the picture she'd been carrying of him in her mind's eye. Desire for him had rippled through her like an unexpected breeze kicking up on still water, catching her by surprise. Peeling off her coat, she had tried not to be too obvious about checking him out. But even the most furtive of sidelong glances revealed to her how sad he looked. All she could think was: *You did this to him. You kicked him in the teeth, and now look at him.* But then she'd remembered Dr. Gardner saying guilt was anger turned inward, and she started to get mad.

It wasn't her fault that things ended with a bang, it was his.

Wasn't it?

Seeing him at the shoot, she had zigzagged madly between extremes of emotion. She didn't want to talk to him. She wanted to spill her guts. She wanted to ask who the hell he thought he was, humiliating her at Met Gar. She wanted to apologize for jerking him around. She pictured her emotions as a waterfall in reverse, feelings flowing back into her where she could dam them up once and for all.

Unfortunately, it wasn't that easy.

She got the impression that seeing her was hard for Michael as well. Usually assertive, he was tentative, his amiability turned down a few notches. Theresa thought that had she been warmer in her responses, Michael would have loosened up and they might have had a friendly conversation. But she had kept him at arm's length. So that neither of them would get hurt.

Besides, there was Reese to consider.

Ever since he'd returned to New York, they'd been seeing a lot of each other, though physical contact between them was minimal. He rarely did more than hold her hand, or press his lips lightly to her forehead at the end of an evening. Since she was still grappling with the shadow, this was fine with her. "Taking it slow" was Reese's motto. But after eight weeks, shouldn't they be taking their relationship to the next level? Maybe that's why he called today, and told her to meet him here, at one of the most romantic restaurants in the city, saying he had something important he needed to discuss?

She massaged the back of her neck and checked her watch. Reese was always late. Her parents would say it showed a lack of respect; that it was a sign he didn't care enough to get there on time. But her folks didn't understand how easily someone with an artistic temperament could get caught up in something else. She knew he worked too hard, and that his head was often in the clouds, thinking about photos he wanted to take.

Even so, she'd been sitting alone for forty minutes.

Peering through the subdued, romantic lighting at one of the lush, gorgeous wood nymph murals, a thought appeared like a flash on a blank screen: *Michael would never make you wait for forty minutes.* These comparisons happened all the time. Theresa did her best to get rid of them, especially since they always favored Michael. Why did the man who'd yelled at her in public and pushed relentlessly always fare better? Dr. Gardner would claim Theresa knew the answer. And maybe Dr. Gardner was right. But Theresa knew one other thing: Reese could provide her with the life she'd always dreamed of.

Whether it made emotional sense or not.

Fifteen minutes later, Reese came strolling into the dark-paneled room, his blond hair wind-whipped, the shoulders of his camel hair coat dusted with snow. In his left hand he carried a single white rose. Theresa watched as he deposited his coat at the cloak room and deftly made his way through the maze of closely packed tables buzzing with discreet conversation.

"I know, I know, I know," he sighed regretfully, handing her the rose. "We had to finish up the last minute details of an acquisition."

"I was about to abandon all hope." Theresa lifted the delicate bud to her nose. What mattered was he was here now—and he'd been considerate enough to bring her a flower. A rose, no less. Surely that canceled out his tardiness?

"What are you drinking?" Reese asked.

"Merlot."

"I guess I'll get the same."

He flagged down a waiter, got his drink, and raising the glass to his lips, drank deeply. "Mmm. That hits the spot." He looked around the room, eyes carefully taking in the other patrons as well as the lush, playful murals before his attention came back to her.

"So, how was your day?"

"Boring," Theresa replied.

Which was true. She'd spent much of it catching up on E-mail and making follow-up phone calls to press kit recipients, both chores she hated. She preferred meeting with clients or the challenge of putting together a campaign.

"Maybe this will help," Reese offered, reaching down into his ever-present leather satchel and presenting her with a small silver box tied with a red ribbon.

"Reese." Theresa's voice was gently chiding. Perhaps to make up for the lack of time they were able to spend together, he was always buying her gifts. Last week it had been a hand-tooled leather journal with her initials on it. The week before, an original first edition of *Wuthering Heights*. When he was out of town, he sent flowers so often that Janna joked the office was starting to smell like a funeral parlor.

"Open it," he urged, eyes crinkling up as he gave that crooked, boyish smile that she adored.

Theresa tugged clumsily at the red ribbon, holding her breath as she lifted the lid of the box. Inside was a beautifully wrought, sterling silver cable bracelet.

"Do you like it?" Reese asked anxiously. "It's David Yurman."

"I *love* it," Theresa murmured, slipping it on her wrist and admiring it.

"Good." He sounded relieved. "I noticed you wear silver a lot, and the bracelet reminded me of you, it's so delicate."

"Thank you," Theresa whispered, overcome. "You know, you don't have to buy me presents all the time."

He sweetly chucked her chin. "Maybe I like to."

She blushed. "I'd better start returning the favor."

"Don't be ridiculous. Being able to spend time with you is present enough for me."

Reese's expression was watchful as he took another sip of his wine. "So, not to change the subject too abruptly, but I was wondering: Have you given any further thought to . . . ?"

He didn't finish, because he didn't have to. It had become somewhat of a running joke between them, his asking about the buyout and her refusal to discuss it.

"I thought we agreed that subject was off limits," Theresa reminded him.

"Just looking out for your interests," Reese murmured, cracking open his menu.

"Janna and I are big girls. We can look after ourselves."

Opening her own menu she wished to God the waiter would come by with some bread, crudités, anything. She was dying of starvation.

And curiosity.

Why were they here?

Reese made her wait through dessert before explaining, and by the time coffee was served, she was too nervous to even taste her apple tartin.

"So, the big announcement." There was a hint of self-deprecation in his voice.

She braced as his hand reached across the table for hers. Warmed from wine and, she hoped, good conversation, his flesh was soft, supple, his long, tapering fingers curling around hers with confidence. *His hands are so delicate,* Theresa thought to herself. *Not like Michael's, which were strong, broad—Stop.*

She waited.

"I know we've been spending a lot of time together," Reese began, his thumb nervously tracing back and forth over hers. "And I know you've been wondering what, exactly, is going on between us."

Theresa felt a small blush rising to her cheeks as she recognized how easily she'd been read.

"Well," Reese said, pausing to take a slow, deep breath. "I brought you here tonight because I wanted to say that I think I'm falling in love with you."

Theresa pitched back slightly, colliding with the hard wood of her chair. His words felt swift as a blur, impossible to get a hold of. *In love?* She had expected something else, a declaration of intent, maybe, but not this.

"I know what you're thinking."

She disliked when people said that, especially men, especially in the context of a serious discussion. "What?" she challenged.

"You're thinking 'How can he say he loves me when he's barely touched me?' "

Theresa's eyes dropped down to the table. Either Reese was a mind reader or she was transparent as glass. Perhaps it was a bit of both. Looking back to him, she was surprised to note his expression seemed unusually blank. Was he afraid she was going to bolt if he betrayed too much emotion? Or was he waiting for a gesture, an acknowledgment of what he'd said so far, before he continued?

Surprised to find her hand trembling slightly, Theresa reached for the security of her coffee cup.

"You're right," she admitted quietly. "Go on."

The coffee was lukewarm, but she drank it anyway. She would have gulped down Drano if it promised to quell the feeling of unreality burgeoning inside her.

"I haven't touched you *because* I'm falling for you," Reese explained ardently, the fervor in his voice snapping Theresa to attention. His free hand tapped out a nervous

beat on the table. "I have an aunt named Letitia Mac-
George; she's a psychotherapist. I assume you've heard of
her?"

Letitia MacGeorge . . . the name sounded vaguely familiar to Theresa, but for some reason an heiress kept
coming to mind, not a therapist. Theresa shook her head.
"No. Haven't heard of her."

Reese looked surprised, but continued. "Well, be that
as it may, when I started to develop feelings for you, I
spoke with her about what happened to you."

A lump came to Theresa's throat. "You talked to your
aunt about me?"

"Yes." His eyes scanned hers for approval. "I knew
you'd been traumatized, and I didn't want to risk doing
anything that might make it worse."

"I see." She could feel her voice slipping away in the
undertow created by impending tears and fought to hang
on to it. "And what did your aunt, the famous psychotherapist, say?"

If he caught the touch of defensiveness in her voice, he
didn't let on. "She said I should let you tell me when you
were ready, or needed, to be touched."

"And—?" Theresa prompted. There was more. There
had to be.

Reese sighed. "And that it might be months, maybe
even years, before you were whole again."

She was struck by the words he chose. *He understands
a part of who I am was stolen. He sees I need to heal, to
be restored. Reese cares so much he actually spoke to a
professional about me.* In other circumstances, such a discussion might have infuriated her. But given how Reese
claimed to feel, it was clearly a gesture of love. She stared
at her lap, warding off tears. "I don't know what to say."

"Say that even if you don't feel the same right now,
you'll keep the door open."

"I will," Theresa promised. She lifted her head and

reached out to touch his cheek, surprised when he flinched slightly. "What?" she asked, concerned.

"I don't want you thinking you *have* to touch me."

"I *want* to. Honestly."

He gave silent assent as she repeated the gesture, his cheek a natural fit in the cup of her hand. This time he seemed to relax into it. This was what she wanted, had wanted, all along. Everything happens for a reason, her mother often claimed. Well, this was the reason she and Michael Dante didn't work out.

Slowly, almost reluctantly, she lowered her hand.

"Are you all right with all this?" he asked, reaching for his coffee cup.

"It's a bit overwhelming," Theresa admitted. "But I can handle it."

"Good." He scanned her face, seeming to look for doubts. "So now what?"

Theresa broke into a slow smile. "Now you meet my family."

As she sat at her parents' dining room table two weeks later, trying to ignore the quiet disapproval emanating from her mother, it occurred to Theresa that she should have lied to Reese about what time he was expected.

She'd told him three.

What she should have done was fib and tell him two-thirty.

That way he'd have made it on time. Better yet, she should have arrived *with* him, thus insuring punctuality. But no; she'd been so excited about showing him off that when her mother insisted they come to dinner, and Reese said he was so nervous he could only handle coffee, she didn't think twice about going out to Brooklyn before him. The way she saw it, it would give her a chance to talk him up before he actually arrived.

226 *Deirdre Martin*

Now he was fifteen minutes late.

And with every minute that passed her family liked him less.

"So," her mother began, the word clipped as she pulled the ciambella she'd made for the occasion towards her. "Doesn't Mr. Wonderful own a wristwatch?" Without asking, she began slicing up the cake.

Theresa clenched her teeth. "He'll be here, Ma." *He'd better be,* she added to herself.

"What does he do again?" her brother Phil asked, reaching right in front of her to grab the first piece of cake.

"He's a lawyer," Theresa repeated patiently. "And a photographer."

"What does he take pictures of?" Phil crowed. "All the clients he bleeds dry?"

"Jesus, Phil." Theresa's sister-in-law turned to her apologetically. "He's such a retard."

"Speak for yourself," Phil retorted, digging into the cake without waiting for anyone else to be served. "A lawyer and a photographer," he garbled with a full mouth. "What, a professional athlete isn't good enough for you?"

Theresa caught the look of warning that flashed across her mother's face.

So. She and Michael had been discussed, probably often. Well, *good.* It was good they all realized it wasn't going to happen, no matter how many novenas they prayed, or Sunday afternoon ambushes they planned.

"Does he make a lot of money?" Debbie asked, indicating with her fingers that she wanted Theresa's mother to cut her a bigger slice of cake.

"I don't know," Theresa said, because she really didn't, though she suspected the answer was "Yes."

"Of course he makes a lot of money," her brother the expert told his wife. "He's a lawyer. That's what they do: They take other people's money."

"Why is it in this family," Theresa asked as she accepted a piece of cake from her mother, "success is something to mock rather than admire?"

"What?" Phil asked plaintively, looking back and forth between his wife and mother imploringly. "What mock?"

"Never mind." Theresa stood up, certain she'd lose her temper if she didn't get away from the table. "I'm going to peek in on Poppy and see how he's doing." Excusing herself, she padded up the thickly carpeted stairs to her parents' bedroom. She knew Phil: He would keep making snide comments until she either exploded or their mother yelled at him to stop. Better to absent herself.

Her father spent most of his days in bed now, too weak to make it up or down the stairs. Entering the room, Theresa's spirits sank. The air was stale with the smell of sickness, her father's shrunken form propped up against a small mountain of pillows. His bedside table was littered with plastic pill bottles. Phil had set up a small TV for him to watch on a snack table. Ironically, it was tuned to a hockey game.

"Hi, Poppy," Theresa said, sitting down beside him.

With what appeared to be great effort, her father turned his head in the direction of her voice. Seeing who it was, he smiled, slowly moving a hand out from beneath the thick layers of covers to clutch hers. "Just can't tear yourself away from your sick old Papa, huh?"

His voice was weak. The voice that once sang at the drop of a hat, yelled when homework wasn't done, barked orders at construction crews—now thin and reedy, fading. Theresa's eyes began to well.

"Can I get you anything?" she asked, gently stroking the fine silver hair which, up until recently, he had maintained religiously with a weekly trip to Ruggiero the Barber. It dawned on her that she'd never done this before. She'd been alive for thirty-three years and never, in all that time, had she touched her father's head. Regret bubbled up, thick and lung clogging. She'd been so rigid, sticking to her once-a-month schedule of seeing the family, even as her father grew sicker. Now she could see she'd squandered the chance to spend more time with him.

Her father shook his head, refusing her offer of dessert.

"You sure?" Theresa continued. "Mommy's cutting the ciambella. I could bring you a little piece with some espresso if you wanted."

"No, sweetheart, I'm fine. I have no appetite anymore, anyway." A bitter laugh gurgled its way up his throat. "Bet you thought you'd never see that day, eh?"

Despite herself, Theresa smiled. That was just like her father, making jokes while he lay dying. Up until now, she'd successfully warded off the reality of his situation, telling herself that he would improve, that he would beat it. But when her mother quietly mentioned hospice care while they set the table together, Theresa was forced to admit her fantasies of her father getting better were just that—fantasies. *Everything happens for a reason,* she thought angrily. *Everything but this.*

Her father's once bright eyes, now dulled to a lackluster brown, were studying her. "Something is bothering you. Tell me."

"It's nothing," Theresa lied, staring at the ornate silver crucifix hanging above her parents' bed that had been there for as long as she could remember. She turned back to her father. "I'm just worried about you."

Her father made a pooh-poohing motion with his hand. "Don't be ridiculous. I'm tough as an old mountain goat."

"And twice as nasty," Theresa teased lovingly.

From downstairs, she could hear the doorbell ring. *Reese. Thank God.* She squeezed her father's hand excitedly. "My new boyfriend is here. Are you up to meeting him?"

"No, no," her father wheezed. "I don't want him seeing me like this."

"Dad, he knows—"

"No, *cara mia*. Let a man have his dignity. Please."

"Okay," Theresa promised, backing off. It disappointed her, but she understood. If there was a just God, Reese would meet her father another time. She kissed her father's hand. "I guess I should go downstairs." *And head Phil off at the pass.*

"Go," he urged.

"All right." Leaning over she tenderly kissed his forehead. "I'll come back up before I leave."

Eyelids drooping, her father nodded. Theresa was halfway across the bedroom when she heard him weakly call her name. She turned.

"Yes, Poppy?"

"He's late," her father rasped. "I don't like that. It means he doesn't respect you enough."

"I'll tell him that," Theresa returned quietly, making her way back down the stairs. She hated that he was dying, and that he might be right.

Madonn', could it get any colder? Turning up the collar of his bomber jacket against the slicing February winds, Michael hurried along Eighty-sixth Street on his way to the Falconettis. The Sunday before, when he was again stuck taking Nonna Maria to the early bird Mass because Casanova had spent the night with Police Woman, he'd run into Phil, who told him the old man wasn't doing too well. He decided then and there that he would surprise the family with another box of Anthony's fresh cannolis. There was no possibility of running into Theresa, since she visited her folks the first Sunday of every month, which was still a week away. A week in which Dante's would close its doors for a month of renovation.

Seeing her at the "Mangia" shoot had been tougher than he thought. Until then, he was pretty sure he had a handle on his feelings. But after the shoot, there was a big black, Theresa-sized hole inside him that he didn't know how to fill. It bugged him that she barely gave him the time of day. Maybe she was pissed he hadn't apologized for ripping into her at Met Gar? Well, she could stay pissed until hell became the fifty-first state. Her excuse for ditching him was bullshit and he'd meant what he'd said.

So how come he missed her so badly his guts actually hurt?

He bounded up the front stoop and rang the doorbell, hoping he wasn't interrupting their Sunday meal. There was a slight delay before the door swung open and Phil appeared.

"Hey, Phil." Michael held up the box of cannolis. "I thought I'd surprise your mom, see how your dad is doing."

"Uh . . ." Phil glanced behind him uncomfortably. "This isn't really a good time, Mike."

"Philly? Who's at the door?"

Mrs. Falconetti was heard before she was seen, elbowing her way past her son to see who he was talking to. "Michael! How wonderful to see you! Come in, come in. It's been too long."

Stepping inside, Michael hugged Theresa's mother before handing her the box. "These are for you, some cannolis from the restaurant."

"You're so considerate, Michael," Mrs. Falconetti beamed. "Such a good boy. Take off your coat."

Michael obeyed, wondering what the hell was wrong with Phil. He hadn't moved from his place at the door and was gesticulating wildly while mouthing things behind his mother's back. "What?" Michael hissed when Mrs. Falconetti momentarily stepped away to hang up his coat.

"Theresa's in there," Phil hissed back. "And she's got some putz with her, a real *esoso*."

"*Merda*." Before Michael had a chance to escape, he was being dragged by the wrist into the dining room, barely given a chance to say hello to Phil's kids who were sprawled on the sectional couch in the living room watching a video. There at the table, looking as uncomfortable as Michael was feeling, sat Debbie, Phil's wife, juggling the baby whose name he could never remember on her lap; Theresa, who looked like she'd just been whacked in the head with a shovel; and some sun-kissed blond preppie whom Michael disliked immediately. He was like an older version of Paul van Dorn.

"Look who decided to stop by," Mrs. Falconetti cooed, pulling out a chair for Michael.

"I don't believe you," Theresa said to her mother. She turned to Michael. "I don't believe *you*, either."

"I didn't know you were here, Theresa." Michael noticed the blond guy's face was handsome, but cold. He appeared to be detached, an observer holding himself above the fray, politely watching the theatrics. Wanting to get it the hell over with, as well as find out who he was, he extended his hand to the stranger.

"Michael Dante."

"Reese Banister." He narrowed his eyes in scrutiny. "Your name sounds very familiar to me."

"I play for the New York Blades."

"Soccer?"

"Hockey," Michael corrected, trying not to sound annoyed.

Reese shrugged, absently twirling a coffee spoon. "I'm not a sports fan."

"That's too bad," replied Michael.

"I've never felt as if I were missing out on anything."

"Well, you are."

Reese lifted an eyebrow. "Sorry, what's your connection to this family?"

"Michael is a friend of Phil's," Theresa interjected pointedly, her eyes burning a message into Michael's. "Aren't you, Mike?"

"Michael and Theresa used to go out," Mrs. Falconetti revealed before Michael could answer.

"Really." Reese turned to Theresa questioningly. "When was this? Back in high school?"

"No, in December," Michael answered.

Theresa looked like she wanted to kill him but he didn't care. She'd already stomped on his heart and now, sitting here with this snooty, tight ass *gavone*, she was kicking him in the teeth to boot. What was the worst she could do? Cut him out of her life? Surprise: She already had.

Reese, meanwhile, seemed taken aback by Michael's statement. He studied Michael as if he were a bacterial specimen under a microscope. "You don't seem Theresa's type," he pronounced slowly.

"Neither do you," Michael shot back.

"Stop!" Theresa hissed.

"Coffee, Mikey?" Mrs. Falconetti trilled.

"Mikey?" Reese echoed disdainfully.

Phil jutted his chin out defiantly. "Yeah, Mikey, as in Mikey D, one of the best wingers in the NHL."

Theresa put her head in her hands. "Enough."

"It's all right," Reese assured her, wrapping a protective arm around her shoulder.

The sight of it made Michael want to puke. He felt as if someone had cranked the thermostat in the room and he was smothering, a molten band of tension and pain tightening around his head. Phil was right: This guy was a major *cafone*. He was obviously upper class, and arrogant, and he was with Theresa.

That was the part he couldn't get over.

Michael hated him.

She'd dropped him like a hot potato for *this?* If his ego wasn't already in the sewer, it was headed down the toilet now. What the hell was wrong with her? Couldn't she see what a *poseur* this guy was? At least she wasn't hanging on his arm and cooing in his ear. There was comfort in that—that, and the fact her mother had obviously dragged him in here on purpose with the intention of getting under this guy's skin. He could see Mrs. F and Phil disliked Fleece or Meese or whatever the hell his name was as much as he did. Which begged the question: What the hell had gotten into Theresa, that she would hook up with a *sfacciato* like this?

Well. It wasn't his place to ask her. Nor was it his place to be here, either. Michael rose from the table.

"Look," he said to Theresa's mother apologetically, "I shouldn't have just dropped by. I'm sorry for disrupting your dinner. I'm gonna take off, okay?"

"I think that would be a good idea," Reese said.

Mrs. Falconetti drew herself up imperiously. "Excuse me. This is *my* house."

Reese looked mortified. "I—"

But Mrs. Falconetti wasn't listening. She was beside Michael's chair, her hand on his shoulder. "Stay," she implored. "At least have a piece of cake."

Michael's eyes darted to Theresa's. *Go,* they begged. *Please.*

"I think I should go," Michael said quietly. He gave Theresa's mother a peck on the cheek. "Give my regards to Mr. F. Either Anthony or I will stop by during the week with a nice plate of ziti and gravy for him, okay?"

Mrs. Falconetti nodded, crestfallen.

Though it killed him to do so, Michael regarded Reese. "Nice meeting you," he said. Reese said nothing.

"Good-bye," Theresa said politely, looking grateful.

Michael gave a quick nod in response.

With Theresa's brother in tow, Michael walked through to the living room to pick up his coat.

"Jesus Christ, Mikey, I'm sorry," Phil was blubbering. "I tried to tell you at the door—"

Michael clasped his shoulder. "I know. Don't sweat it."

He was halfway into his jacket when Theresa appeared.

"You should have called," she said, walking him to the door while Phil skulked away, clearly afraid of the fireworks.

"Yeah," Michael said ruefully. "Sorry about that." He zipped up his coat. "So this *boyfriend* of yours—I guess being linked in the gossip columns with him might *help* business?"

Theresa was silent. He pushed open the front door. "Take care of yourself, Theresa."

"I'll call you before the grand reopening to review strategy," she said.

"Whatever," Michael replied, walking down the steps. He heard the door close softly behind him and then he was alone, on the sidewalk, walking back up the same street he'd hurried along fifteen minutes earlier.

Sometimes that was all the time it took for your life to go under.

CHAPTER 15

"Sounds like it was a total disaster, Theresa."

Janna had been listening patiently about the previous day in Brooklyn. They were in her office, going over their schedules for the week. After Michael left, things went from bad to worse. Prior to his arrival, her family didn't want to give Reese a chance because he was fifteen minutes late and he wasn't Italian.

After, they froze him out because he wasn't Michael Dante.

Her mother blamed Reese for Michael's departure and sulked theatrically, conveniently forgetting that Michael had shown up without an invitation. Phil rabidly seized onto Reese's lack of interest in sports with the intensity of a terrier and tried to start an argument with him. By the time she and Reese left, Theresa was furious as well as mortified. Her family knew how important Reese was to her. Couldn't they have at least *tried* to be gracious?

She considered Janna's statement carefully before responding. "I wouldn't say it was a total disaster."

"No?" Janna looked surprised as she sorted the mound of papers on her desk into neat piles. "What was good about it?"

"Well." Theresa paused thoughtfully. "The family did get to meet Reese—"

"And they hated him."

"They didn't *hate* him," Theresa insisted, irritated by Janna's penchant for hyperbole. "They just didn't warm up to him."

"Theresa." Janna's voice was chiding. "It sounds like they hated him."

"They didn't give him a chance," Theresa continued, refusing to cast the day in such black-and-white terms. "Especially after Michael appeared."

"Poor Michael," Janna murmured sympathetically.

"What do you mean, poor Michael?" Theresa retorted. "How about poor me? Do you have any idea how awkward it was when he showed up?"

Janna appeared cautious. "It doesn't sound like Reese was very nice to him."

"Michael wasn't very nice to Reese, either."

"Can you blame him?"

Janna was her best friend, but sometimes . . . *How could she defend Michael's being rude to Reese, but not Reese's right to be rude in return?* Rather than risk a discussion she didn't want to have, Theresa steered the conversation toward business.

"Let's talk about Notorious Devil D."

"Let's," Janna agreed, with relief. "What do you want to do?"

"Well, what are the pros and cons? Pros: He's a major artist; it would up our profile considerably; it would bring in the bucks."

Janna nodded in agreement, adding, "Cons: He's a misogynist pig whose lyrics are morally reprehensible."

Theresa leaned forward, elbows on knees, chin cupped

in the palm of her left hand. "Do we have the right to be in an ethical dilemma about this?" she wondered aloud.

Janna looked at Theresa with interest. "What do you mean?"

"I mean we're publicists, Janna. People pay us money and we peddle them to the public. D's willing to pay us *a lot* to peddle."

"But do we want to peddle someone who appears to condone violence? Whose lyrics seem to say it's okay to hit women and call them names? Do we want to be associated with that?"

"No," Theresa said without hesitation, "we do not."

"So that settles it, then. We're not going to take the account."

They both fell silent for a moment. Then Janna asked, "Right?"

Theresa started. "What do you mean, *right?*"

"Right we don't want to take on this account even though it would be mega. Right?"

"Right," Theresa reiterated. She bit her lip. "I mean, I guess," she added lamely.

Janna let out a groan of frustration. "What do you mean, you guess?"

"You know me Janna, I could write up a campaign to make this guy sound like a boy scout if I wanted to. But I'm not sure I do."

"You know what we need to do? We need to listen to our guts. My father always said the only time you ever go wrong in life is when you don't listen to your gut. So let's try to do that."

Once again silence descended. Theresa even went so far as closing her eyes, the better to still the swirl of voices in her head clamoring for attention. She breathed deeply, waiting for them to die down. Finally, a clear voice emerged.

"Let me guess. You're both communicating with your spirit guides."

Theresa opened her eyes. It was Terrence.

"Have you forgotten how to knock?" Janna asked.

"Begging your pardon, Miz Scarlett, but the door was *open.*" He held up a sheaf of papers, waving it at Theresa. "I pulled together all those names and addresses you wanted for the invites to the Dante's opening. Any other unpaid work you want me to do?"

Janna and Theresa exchanged guilty glances. "No, that's fine. You can leave the list on my desk."

Terrence bowed deeply and disappeared.

"We need to give him a raise," Theresa suggested tentatively, as soon as she was sure he was out of earshot.

"Using what?" Janna replied. "Monopoly money?" Worry clouded her eyes. "I know you're right. I just can't think about it right now."

"I know."

"So," Janna resumed hopefully, "did you get any message from your gut?"

"Did you?"

"Yes."

"And—?" Theresa had a feeling she knew what Janna would say, but she was on tenterhooks waiting to hear it anyway.

"I think we should pass."

"I agree."

"You do?" Janna looked taken aback. "I thought for sure you were going to say the opposite."

"Why, because a few minutes ago I played devil's advocate?" Theresa turned solemn. "No. When we started this company, we decided our motto would be 'Integrity and Ingenuity,' remember? Taking on Notorious Devil D flies in the face of integrity if you ask me."

Janna's shoulders sank in relief. "So do you want to call his manager or should I?"

"I'll call him, since I'm the one they met with. I'll tell him we've decided there's a conflict with an existing client and we can't take him on." She sighed. "I think we're making the right decision, Jan. I know it means we have to hustle even more, but I don't think I could live with myself if we took him on."

"Me, too. We'll be fine," Janna declared confidently.

There was no guarantee of that, Theresa realized. But they couldn't afford to think otherwise.

A week later, Theresa stood in her kitchen doing something which months earlier would have been unfathomable: She was cooking for a man. Tired of always eating out, she'd invited Reese over for dinner.

Issuing the invitation was easy; preparing for the actual evening was not.

She and Dr. Gardner had spent an entire session on why she was so overwrought about the prospect of cooking a simple meal, what she was afraid would go wrong, and what concrete steps she could take if something did go awry. Theresa left the therapist's office convinced she had everything under control, an illusion which evaporated the minute she got home and actually started to prepare the meal.

"After the stew has been cooking for an hour or so," she read aloud from the cookbook Janna had lent her, propped up on the counter by the stove, "add the onions. Continue cooking the stew, leaving it uncovered."

"Hmmm. I can handle that." She reached for the small white bowl of onions she'd already chopped and tipped them into the stew pot, giving the mixture a good stir. The aroma that wafted up to tickle her nostrils was hearty, making her stomach growl. She checked that the flame was on low, then glanced up at the clock. Reese was due in about half an hour, meaning she really had at least forty-five minutes. She still had time for a shower.

The shower felt good, the perfect way to unwind from a day spent steeped in domestic pursuits: shopping for food, cleaning the apartment, cooking. Janna had offered to cook something that could be popped in the oven shortly before Reese arrived—a casserole, maybe, or a quiche—but Theresa decided she wanted to make a meal for him from scratch. Going through Janna's cookbook collection, which she'd never once explored in all the years they'd lived together, she settled on a beef stew, with a sweet potato puree on the side and brownies for dessert. The brownies were already baked, and the puree, which had been a royal pain in the ass to make, sat within the microwave waiting to be warmed.

Everything *was* under control.

She was hustling from the bathroom to the bedroom when the shrill, unexpected ring of the phone stopped her dead in her tracks. *No. Please don't be canceling.* Holding her towel with one hand, she picked up the phone with the other.

"Hello?"

"Theresa? It's Michael."

Theresa closed her eyes, hanging her head in defeat. The universe *would* arrange to have Michael Dante call her while she was running around trying to get ready to entertain another man. It was too awful.

"What's up?" she asked.

"I ran into Danny Aiello last night at a fund-raiser, and he said he'd be willing to come to the reopening."

"That's great!" Theresa enthused. The more Italian celebrities they were able to line up, the better. But she didn't really have time to talk about it. "I'll get in touch with his people and arrange everything. Thanks, Michael."

She hung up the phone. She knew it was rude, but she

couldn't help it. She still had to dress and make up and make sure the stew didn't burn before Reese arrived.

An hour later, Reese showed up. He seemed distracted as well as edgy. But he'd been traveling all week, so Theresa tried not to take it personally. She poured him a glass of shiraz and sat down with him on the couch, doing her best to appear relaxed when in reality, her mind was on when she should microwave the puree to make sure it was done at exactly the same time as the stew. She barely registered Reese's question about how work was going.

"What?" she asked distractedly.

Reese frowned with impatience. "I asked if anything exciting happened for you this week," he repeated.

"Well, Janna and I stuck to our guns on an integrity issue," she said proudly. She told him about Notorious Devil D. That was when she noticed the vein in Reese's right temple throbbing wildly.

"Let me make sure I'm getting this straight." His voice was eerily calm. "You and Janna turned down a major account any other PR firm would kill for because *you don't like his lyrics.*"

"It's not *that* simple."

"It *is* that simple," Reese shot back. "How stupid *are* the two of you?"

Theresa slammed her wineglass down on the coffee table, the perfect aural exclamation point. *"Excuse me?"*

"Does what you did strike you as making good business sense?" Reese asked heatedly. "Does it?"

"Sometimes there are more important things than making money, Reese."

"This isn't about making money, Theresa. It has to do with prestige. Visibility. This would have put your firm on the map."

"We are on the map," Theresa insisted angrily.

"What map would that be?" Reese snorted derisively.
"The map of boutique agencies headed for extinction?"

"Bucone!" Theresa snapped, snatching up her wine-glass and storming into the kitchen.

Heart pounding, she gazed around haplessly, knowing Reese was going to appear any second wanting to continue their "conversation." *Well, Dr. Gardner,* she thought franti-cally, *we certainly didn't plan for this, did we?* She couldn't believe the way he'd reacted. Especially since they had talked about issues like integrity way back when! She re-called him saying he sometimes felt he didn't have any, working as he did for his uncle—maybe it hit too close to home? Reminded him of his own feelings of selling out? But to say what he said . . . *Jesus.*

Utterly rattled, she moved back and forth between the stove and the microwave, trying to figure out what to do. As anticipated, Reese appeared in the kitchen doorway, looking mildly perturbed.

"Did you just curse at me in Italian?"

Theresa ignored him. Her slip embarrassed her—even though he deserved it.

"Look, I'm sorry for what I said. I didn't mean it to come out that way."

"No?" Theresa stirred the stew furiously, flecks of brown spattering the stovetop. "Then what *did* you mean?"

"That maybe you and Janna could use some guidance," he explained. He came toward her, resting a reassuring hand on her shoulder. "This is just one more example of why I think it would benefit you to *sell.* You'd be under the wing of a large corporation experienced in handling this kind of thing."

"Janna and I made the right decision." Theresa jerked her shoulder away. "And if you bring up the Butler offer one more time, I'm going to ask you to leave."

"Whoa." Reese stepped back. "Someone's quick on the trigger tonight."

"Someone's tired of the man who says he's falling in love with her always twisting the conversation around to business."

"Do I?" Reese looked genuinely surprised.

"Yes."

"Well, I don't mean to. Sorry." Clearly wanting to get off the subject, Reese leaned forward, sniffing the stew. "Smells good."

"It'll be a few more minutes," Theresa replied begrudgingly, afraid that if she didn't get her still pounding pulse under control, she'd work herself into a migraine.

"Is it a family recipe?"

"No. I got it from Janna."

"How *is* your family?" he inquired.

Theresa, now at the microwave, glanced back over her shoulder. There was something in his voice, in the way he had emphasized the word *is* that irked her. But his face was guileless. Perhaps she was being oversensitive.

"They're alright. I may go back out there tomorrow to give my mother a break, you know? She's been run ragged taking care of my dad." Her gaze turned hopeful. "Want to come? Keep me company? It would give them another chance to get to know you."

"No offense, Theresa, but if I want to watch a family overeat and attack each other, I'll turn on *The Sopranos*."

This time Theresa turned around fully, unable to believe what she'd just heard. His words couldn't have hurt her more if he'd punched her squarely in the gut. "How dare you?"

Reese laughed, confused. "What?"

"How dare you insult my family that way?"

"Oh, it's all right for *you* to insult them," Reese pointed out with a chortle, "telling me how much they smother you with that whole 'Italian thing.'"

"That's right," Theresa cut in angrily. "Because that's different."

"Is it?"

"You know it is. It's my family. I can say what I want. You can't." She went back to the stew pot and turned down the flame to give herself something to do, lest she really let him have it.

"I have an idea." Reese's voice rang with false cheer. "How about if I go outside and ring the doorbell and we start the evening all over again?"

"Fine," Theresa agreed.

She waited while he went outside and rang the bell. When she reopened the door to him, he was standing there with a big smile.

"Hello, gorgeous."

Theresa rolled her eyes. "Get your butt in here. Dinner's almost ready."

On the surface, their "Take Two" tactic seemed to work. She served dinner, and Reese seemed to enjoy it. But those two insults in less than ten minutes at the start of the evening cast a pall over the meal. Theresa could feel both of them straining as they attempted to keep conversation light and interesting.

"So, should we check out the Matisse/Picasso show when it comes to town?" Reese asked.

"Yes. Of course."

"Good." Reese paused. "You like both of them, I take it?"

"Yes." Theresa smiled, in spite of herself. She'd always dreamed of finding someone urban and sophisticated with whom she could discuss art and culture. And now here he was. But things flared up almost immediately when she mentioned he didn't seem to be complaining as often about the work he was doing for the law firm.

"What's the point?" he snapped. "I made my bed and now I have to lie in it."

"Reese?"

"Mmm?"

"Is something wrong?" she asked. "I mean—with us?"

Reese blinked. "No. Why would you think that?"

Theresa groped for the right words. "I don't know. I just feel like no matter what we talk about tonight, we just keep rubbing each other the wrong way."

"You're being silly."

"Am I?"

"Yes. Come here," he said, getting up and motioning towards the sofa.

A wave of excitement surged through Theresa as she followed him and they sat down next to each other. *Now, finally, one of the gaps between us will be bridged, bringing us closer. . . .* She inhaled slowly, wanting to savor the moment. But the lack of enthusiasm in his embrace, as well as in his prolonged, closed-mouth kiss, was disappointing. Theresa held on, waiting for the kiss to deepen and for his arms to draw her in safe, but she waited in vain.

"Reese, are you *sure* there's nothing wrong?"

"I don't understand why you keep asking that," he replied in frustration.

She had to tread carefully. She didn't want to make him think his prowess was sub par . . . "You seem preoccupied," she began. "It felt like you weren't really into it."

Reese sighed. "I was trying to restrain myself, Theresa. I want you so badly I'm afraid if I give in to it, I might not be able to control myself. Can't you see that?"

She hadn't thought of that. *He cared about her, wanted to protect her.* "I'm sorry," she murmured, feeling silly.

Cleaning up the kitchen after he left, she was plagued by a feeling of unease.

Here was a man who seemed to embody everything she thought she wanted, with an impressive pedigree thrown in to boot. So why wasn't she happier? Why couldn't she shake the sense that his words were out of sync with his actions? Was it possible the incident with Lubov had affected her so deeply that even the simplest signposts were hard for her to follow? This dinner was supposed to help her clarify things. Instead, she felt more confused than ever.

The next day, Theresa went out to Brooklyn, and wound up staying overnight so her mother could go to the movies for the first time in months with her Aunt Toni. On Monday, she arrived at the office to find a bouquet of flowers from Reese, thanking her for dinner. On Tuesday, she sat on the big, squishy couch in Dr. Gardner's office trying to make sense of her own discontent.

"It's not like I don't enjoy being with him, because I do," she explained, sipping demurely at the piping hot chamomile tea Dr. Gardner's secretary had prepared at the beginning of the session. They'd already covered her weekend with her family, the Notorious Devil D decision, and most of Friday night's dinner with Reese, including his insulting her. They had now come to the part of the fifty minutes Theresa hated most: the part where they really dug down deep.

"But—?" Dr. Gardner prodded.

Theresa noticed Dr. Gardner looked very nice. She noticed lots of things today: the new fountain pen Dr. Gardner was holding, the fact that the blinds were closed rather than open, all of it part of her brain's grand effort to avoid self-analysis. She stalled for as long as she could, and then, with a defeated sigh, she succumbed.

"He doesn't seem as open as he used to be. When we first met, we talked about everything. But now I get the sense that certain topics are off-limits."

"And that bothers you."

"Yes." *Of course it does,* she added in her head. *Why else would I be talking about it?*

"Does it bother you that he doesn't touch you?" Dr. Gardner asked.

Theresa felt her stomach roll. "Yes," she admitted.

"Why?"

Theresa swallowed. "Because it makes me feel unattractive."

Dr. Gardner nodded carefully. "What do you think he'd say in response?"

Theresa clasped her tea cup tightly between her hands. "He'd say that he's very busy at work, and that he's trying not to push me, to give me space."

Dr. Gardner's gaze was direct. "And do you believe him?"

No. Oh, God. Where did that come from?

"No," Theresa admitted aloud.

"Why not?"

Now Theresa squirmed. She hated this. The questioning, the probing, the endless why, why, why. "I'm not really sure," she answered slowly, which was the truth. "I can't put my finger on it. It's just a sense I have that something about this whole thing isn't quite right."

"Do you think he's using you?"

"No." Theresa visibly bristled, an action she regretted since Dr. Gardner picked up on it immediately.

"You seem upset by the suggestion," Dr. Gardner pointed out, her eyes straying momentarily to the small digital clock on the Plexiglas table between them.

"Well, wouldn't you be?" Theresa countered, wondering how much time she had left. "I'm not stupid. I think I'd be able to tell if he were using me."

"Okay."

Much to Theresa's relief, Dr. Gardner seemed to accept her explanation. But she wasn't off the hook yet.

"Let's get back to what you were saying about feeling things were not quite right."

Theresa prepared herself.

"What attracted you to Reese in the first place?"

"That's easy: He's intelligent and artistic." She paused. "He's sophisticated. He makes good money."

"Uh huh." Dr. Gardner's voice was patient. "But he also insults you and makes you feel unattractive. So why do you want to be with him?"

"It's safe," Theresa blurted. Her gaze darted around the room almost as if the voice had come from somewhere else. She couldn't believe she'd said it.

"Safe how?" Dr. Gardner prompted gently.

Theresa hated the drowning feeling that welled up inside her whenever she and Dr. Gardner struck emotional gold. Struggling not to go under, she sought the right words. "Safe emotionally." She put the mug of tea down on the table and locked her hands together in her lap, tightly. "When I was seeing Michael, I felt so vulnerable." She licked her lips nervously. "My feelings were right here on the surface, all the time. It was scary. But with Reese, I feel . . . protected."

"From?"

"I don't know."

"True intimacy, maybe?"

Theresa's gaze fell to the floor. The suggestion shook her, because she suspected it was true. Here she'd been telling herself she wanted to bring her relationship with Reese to another level, but did she, really? If she were able to make her fantasy match reality, would her confusion disappear? Would she be happy then? She longed to sort it all out, really she did, but she wondered if she had the energy to deal with everything that needed to be dealt with.

It was exhausting, not to mention terrifying.

She wanted to say as much. But when she lifted her gaze, Dr. Gardner gently informed her that her time was up. She'd have to wrestle her demons alone for another week.

CHAPTER

16

Crunch time. The ball-busting end of the regular season.

Like most players, Michael loved and loathed it. It was time to prove what you could do out on the ice, but the pressure to perform was intense. With less than a week left in the regular season, the Blades were clinging to a berth in the playoffs. If they won two of their next three games, they'd clinch a spot. If they lost, they'd be cleaning out their lockers and wishing each other a good summer even though it was only April. In order to be completely ready for the playoffs, Michael needed more ice time than he was currently getting on the fourth line.

He needed to talk to Ty.

He waited until practice was over and his teammates were drifting out to the parking lot in groups of two's and three's to drive back to the city. Ty, who usually left the practice rink with Gilly, was on the phone in his office when Michael popped his head in the door.

Feet up on the desk, Ty motioned "come in," asking

whoever was on the phone to hold while he covered the mouthpiece. "What's up?"

"I need to talk to you about something," Michael explained.

Ty checked his watch. "I'm going to Maggie's Grill to grab some lunch. Want to join me?"

Michael shrugged easily. "Sure."

"Meet you there in fifteen minutes." With that, Ty resumed his phone conversation. Judging from his tone of voice, whoever was on the other end was giving him a hard time.

Michael had never been to Maggie's. It was a post-practice tradition for Ty to eat there with Kevin Gill, but Kevin, out with back spasms, had missed practice. Michael didn't mind being second choice. Entering the dark-paneled grill filled with happy, chatting locals, he was struck by how much he noticed about restaurants now: the layout of the dining room, the appearance and attentiveness of the wait staff, the design of the menu. Crazy, but these were the kind of things keeping him up at night. Dante's grand reopening was two days away, and every minute he wasn't practicing or playing hockey, he was in Bensonhurst with his surly brother, getting ready for what he hoped would be a night to remember.

Over one hundred invitations had gone out, many to prominent food critics. Theresa warned him they might not show up. Even so, Michael was hopeful they would garner a review, especially since the "Mangia" special had recently aired on the Food Network and the restaurant was being deluged by calls. Danny Aiello and James Gandolfini had promised they'd come, thrilling Theresa since it might get them mentioned in the entertainment mags. She'd arranged for a photographer to be on hand. Michael was hemorrhaging money for all this PR but he didn't care. If it put Dante's on the map, it was worth it.

Seated at "Ty's table," he waited for the man himself to show, surprised to find he was feeling nervous. When Ty finally appeared, ten minutes late, Michael noticed the way he casually waded through the dining room, exchanging pleasantries with diners who clearly knew him as a regular and as a New York sports celebrity. It seemed everyone who dined there loved him.

"Sorry I'm late," Ty apologized, pulling up a chair. "It took me forever to get off the phone."

"You didn't sound too happy," Michael observed.

Ty frowned. "It was Capesi, trying to talk me into some interview for *Sports Illustrated* on coaching styles."

"Are you gonna do it?"

"My ass," Ty griped. "I'd rather lop off my left ball than sit down to an interview." He flashed a chagrined smile. "Can't blame the guy for trying to do his job, though."

A pert waitress appeared, wanting to know where Kevin was.

"Back spasms," Ty murmured with a grimace. He motioned toward Michael. "This is Michael Dante, Ginger. He plays for the Blades as well."

Ginger smiled, friendly. "Hello, Michael." Her gaze bounced back and forth between both men. "Do you know what you want for lunch?"

Michael looked to Ty for guidance. "What do you recommend?"

Ty sank back in his chair. "Everyone raves about the burger and onion rings but if you ask me, it's the grilled salmon that takes the prize."

"Grilled salmon, then," Michael said. "And onion rings."

Ginger scribbled on her pad. "Two grilled salmons."

She tapped Ty's shoulder with her pencil. "The usual salad?" Ty nodded. "And to drink?" she concluded.

"Two Heinekens," Ty answered, eyes catching Michael's to make sure that was acceptable.

Michael nodded.

"You got it," said Ginger, walking away.

Anxiety mounting, Michael glanced around the dining room. "Nice place," he said with an approving nod.

"Yeah, it is. So, what's on your mind?" Ty asked, cutting to the heart of the matter.

Since Ty never beat around the bush, Michael decided to return the favor.

"What do I have to do to get more ice time?"

Ty said nothing as he reached for the bread basket at the center of the table. "Go on."

"You know me," Michael declared simply, glad when Ginger quickly reappeared with their beers. It gave him something to occupy his hands, which he tended to wave around when he was speaking, especially if the subject matter made him emotional, which this did. "You know what kind of a player I am. For me to really be my best, I need ice time. That's not happening on the fourth line."

Ty took a long, slow sip of his brew. "You haven't been having the greatest year."

"I know that," Michael admitted. "The concussion was a setback."

"It wasn't just the concussion," Ty continued bluntly, breaking off a crust of hard, seeded bread.

Michael looked away. This was harder than he thought. "I know I've been distracted, and I know my play has been erratic. But we've been through two playoff runs together. You know that in the playoffs, I'll do whatever it takes."

Ty seemed to be considering Michael's words carefully as he swallowed down a chunk of bread. His brown eyes were probing, direct. "What are you asking for, Mike?"

"I want back on the third line."

Michael tried not to be deflated by Ty's lack of immediate response. He waited with mounting unease as Ty stared at him through narrowed eyes, assessing him. Finally, after an interminably awkward silence, Ty spoke. His voice was grim.

"I know you're a pro; that's never been in doubt. If you really want back on the third line, you have to forget about your broken heart and your restaurant, and concentrate on hockey. Every spare second you have, you're out at Dante's. I heard you on the cell phone in the locker room the other day ordering flowers for the reopening."

Michael jolted with embarrassment. "So?"

"It's a distraction you can't afford." Frustrated, Ty leaned toward him, his voice one notch above a passionate hiss. "April's here, Mikey. You need to *live* hockey. You have to eat it and breathe it. It has to be the only thing you think about. The only thing you *dream* about."

"Right," Michael muttered, fighting mounting restlessness. Everyone in the league knew Ty's "Live, eat and breathe" hockey speech by heart. It was the NHL equivalent of the Gettysburg Address. Michael wasn't sure he could sit through it again. Yet he knew without the kind of singularity of focus Ty insisted upon, there was no hope of winning the Cup. And, apparently, no hope for him to regain his place on the third line. He was about to tell Ty he was well aware of what he needed to do, but Ty wasn't done talking.

"It's do or die time, Michael. Not just for the team, but for you personally."

"What do you mean?"

"I mean," said Ty, pausing politely as Ginger deposited their meals in front of them, "that you need to decide whether you want to be a professional hockey player or a restaurateur. You can't do both." He cut into his salmon, the intense expression on his face momentarily melting away as he put a forkful in his mouth, clearly relishing it. He waved his fork at Michael. "Try it. It's fantastic."

Though Michael's appetite had vanished, he forced himself to eat a piece of fish. Ty was right. It was good. It could have used some rosemary, though. He gave Ty the thumbs up.

Spearing a forkful of salad, Ty continued, "Look, I was once where you are now, okay?"

Michael's curiosity was piqued. "How so?"

"Two years ago, when we won that second Cup, I was at the top of my game. But I had also fallen in love with Janna. I had to make a decision: keep playing hockey or have a personal life." He downed another mouthful of beer before continuing his extemporization. "Some guys can do both. Look at Kevin: He's got a wonderful wife and kids, *and* he's a great hockey player. But me? I could never split my concentration like that. And unless I'm wrong, neither can you. You need to focus on one thing, either hockey or the restaurant. You can't do both."

Michael sighed, acquiescent. "I hear you," he murmured, knowing that Ty had spoken the truth.

"Good," Ty said. His furrowed brows finally relaxed, indicating to Michael that the serious part of their discussion was over.

They talked golf over the rest of the meal, but Michael's mind was elsewhere: on his level of play, and, unavoidably, on the restaurant. He cursed himself for being an idiot. He should have waited until *after* the re-opening to have this discussion with Ty. Now he would spend the next few days stressing about both. He scolded himself as his appetite slowly returned. *You can juggle both for just forty-eight hours more, can't you?* Confident he could, he dug into his lunch.

His teammates were right. The onion rings were amazing.

* * *

Standing in the middle of Dante's expanded dining room an hour before the grand reopening, Michael felt as though he'd taken speed as adrenaline sizzled through his system like demon electricity. He was tense and snappish. He wanted everything, from the placement of the flower arrangements to the final check of basic china and silverware, to be done better, faster, *now.* He could hear the wait staff bitching about him behind his back, but he didn't care. He wanted this night to go off without a hitch. He wanted it to be perfect.

And if that meant riding their asses, so be it.

His nerves weren't helped by his family.

Anthony, never calm under pressure, had become preternaturally silent. He reminded Michael of a volcano whose benign surface belied chaos and destruction roiling beneath. And then there were the rest of them, calling his cell phone every five minutes to question his seating arrangements. Nonna Maria and Aunt Gavina weren't speaking. Gemma wanted to sit with Nonna, but Gemma's mother, Aunt Connie, was afraid Gemma would wear a pentacle and give Nonna a stroke. So now Gemma and her mother weren't speaking. Plus, cousin Robbie wanted to know if he could bring his Honduran girlfriend, and Uncle Jimmy needed a special chair for his back. On and on it went until Michael wished he'd been raised in an orphanage.

A poor day at practice didn't help, either. Hard as he tried to concentrate, he was distracted, his mind going over lists of last minute preparations when it should have been focused on the drills. Ty saw it, too. Michael tried not to feel abashed, but it was hard. He was fucking up and he knew it. He comforted himself with the fact it was just temporary.

After tonight he'd be back on track, hockeywise.

Finally, there was Theresa. His guts twisted in abject

misery when she came strolling into the restaurant.
Dressed in black from head to toe with ankle high stiletto
boots and a sharp red leather bag that made Michael think
of his own heart, she was a vision of urban sophistication
and aplomb. She soon made it clear that as the publicist,
she was running the show. She was so smart and witty,
gorgeous and spirited—and she didn't want a thing to do
with him. Instead, she'd chosen Little Lord Fauntleroy,
who thankfully appeared to be MIA. Every time Michael
saw her, he felt a stab of regret over the way things had
played out. Worst was the pain of remembering how mag-
ical it felt when he was able to break through her defenses
and get her to laugh or smile. So beautiful. So scared.

"Michael."

He turned as the object of his daydream tugged urgently on his arm.

"What?"

"Go change into your tux and hang out in the kitchen
until I need you."

"Why?"

Theresa pulled a face. "You're driving me and everyone else out here nuts. You're behaving like a crazy person, barking orders and moving things around. It's not
fun."

"So you want to get rid of me?"

"In a word? Yes."

"Where's Preppie Boy?" he asked, unable to resist.

Theresa pressed her mouth into a hard line. "Out of
town on business."

Michael studied her face, hard and defensive now after
his unwarranted barb. "You happy?" he asked softly.

"Very. Now go." Grabbing him by the shoulders, she
gently turned him in the direction of the kitchen.

Resigned to his fate, he obeyed, shuffling through the
swinging doors. The heat of the kitchen smacked him like
a steaming towel to the face. But the smells . . . He perked

back up, unable to decide which was more enticing: the aroma of bread baking, the tart, aromatic smell of fresh basil being chopped, or the comforting, familiar scent of the family sauce simmering on the stove. He tried to be as unobtrusive as possible as Anthony and the rest of the kitchen staff chopped, baked and stirred. Almost unconsciously, he found himself edging toward his brother. Anthony took one look at him, glared, then went back to filling the cannoli shells he had laid out on a papered tray.

"What's the problem?" Michael asked, coming to rest against the steel table where his brother was working.

"Get out, Mike," Anthony commanded. "I'm very, very busy."

Ignoring him, Michael dipped his finger in a nearby bowl of cannoli filling. Anthony growled something about unsanitary practices under his breath but continued filling the pastries nonetheless.

Michael frowned. "We open in less than an hour, Ant. Can't you get someone else to fill those?"

"No."

"I'll do it," Michael offered. If he had to stand around doing nothing while Theresa ran the show out front and Anthony was boss back here, he'd lose his mind.

Anthony's left eyelid twitched. "Get the hell out of here before I murder you, Mike."

"I can't," Michael informed him. "I've been banished from the dining room until further notice."

"Then keep out of my way."

Michael slunk to the nearest stove. Grabbing a clean wooden spoon, he dipped it into one of the large vats of simmering sauce and took a taste, pausing to get the full flavor. He took another small spoonful. Something was missing.

"I think this needs more sugar, Anthony."

"GO FUCK YOURSELF, MIKE!" Anthony barked loudly. The kitchen staff laughed nervously.

"I mean it, Ant," Michael said seriously. "I think it needs more sugar."

"You think it needs more sugar?" Anthony repeated. "*You* think it needs more sugar? Fine. I'll add more sugar."

He disappeared into the supply room, returning with a five-pound bag of sugar. Violently tearing open the top, he dumped the entire contents into the pot of sauce, his mouth twisted in a perverse smile. "How's that, Mike? That enough sugar?"

Michael's mouth fell open.

"Are you out of your fucking mind?" he yelled.

"Yeah, I am!" Anthony shouted back, the lid blowing off the anger he'd been trying to control all day. "I'm out of my FUCKING MIND to have agreed to let a HOCKEY PLAYER tell me what to do with *MY* RESTAURANT!"

"*Your* restaurant?" Michael thundered. "Listen, you SOB, who's laid out all the money for PR, who paid for the renovation, who—"

"Who asked you to?" Face mottled purple with rage, Anthony tore off his apron, hurling it at Michael's feet. "You want the big, new, improved restaurant? Take it. It's yours. I QUIT."

With that, he stormed out the back door of the kitchen, kicking it once for good measure before disappearing completely.

No one was laughing now.

"Fuck," Michael whispered to himself. Face burning, he swallowed hard, crouching down to pick up the apron before braving a glance at the petrified kitchen staff. "Uh, carry on," he said lamely, sounding like a mortified monarch. "I'll be right back."

Carrying the crumpled apron in his hand, he followed his brother out the back door. He found Anthony behind the restaurant dumpster, puffing furiously on a cigarette.

"Fuck off," he snarled.

"Anthony." Michael approached him carefully, the way you would a rabid animal. "I'm sorry. I didn't mean to step on your toes."

"You've been stepping on my toes since September, Mike. And I'm fucking sick of it."

"I know, I know," Michael apologized. As discreetly as he could, he glanced at his watch. Forty minutes until Theresa opened the doors. *Jesus H. Christ.* Sweat began beading on his brow as he imagined the disaster that would ensue if Anthony refused to return to the kitchen. There was only one thing to do: grovel.

"Please don't quit," he begged his brother. His request was met by stony silence. "Dante's needs you."

"I don't know, Mike," Anthony replied, drawing obstinately on his cigarette. "I don't know if I can take you acting like you're the one who's been cooking for twenty years, like you're the one who knows how to run a restaurant."

"Anthony, please."

"We've got some issues, Mike," Anthony prattled on. "Stuff I've been holding in that I don't think I can anymore."

Michael looked down at the ground, praying for patience. *He wants to have a heart-to-heart NOW? Be cool, Mikey. Say and do whatever needs to be said to get him back in his friggin' apron.* Michael slowly lifted his gaze to Anthony. "I hear what you're saying," he told him calmly. "And I promise you we will talk about this. But right now, I need you to come back and cook. Please. I swear on Mom and Pop's graves that I will keep out of your hair and that I will listen to everything you have to say. But please . . . go cook."

For a split second, it looked as if Anthony's top lip was ready to curl into a sneer, the prelude to turning down his brother's desperate request. Instead, he tossed his ciga-

rette to the ground, crushing it beneath the toe of his shoe.
"All right," he agreed sullenly. "But on one condition."

Michael was so thrilled he would have agreed to cas-
tration. "What's that?"

"You never fucking tell me the sauce needs sugar
again."

Michael put his hand over his heart. "Done."

"And."

"What?" Michael bit out impatiently. He couldn't believe there was more.

The scowl faded from Anthony's face as he clasped an
arm around Michael's shoulder. "You take a freaking chill
pill and try to enjoy yourself. This is our night, buddy
boy. Let's knock 'em dead."

It had been drummed into Theresa's brain in Catholic
school that the deadliest of the seven deadly sins was
pride. But tonight, watching the ecstatic faces of the
crowd as they stuffed themselves with the best food
they'd ever tasted, she didn't care if she was sinning. She
couldn't have been more proud if she'd owned the restaurant herself.

Women who normally picked at their food looked like
they might lick their plates. The men ate heartily, un-
abashedly, as the wait staff circled the room, impeccably
professional and attentive. Theresa couldn't believe she'd
ever been nervous about putting together a PR campaign
for a restaurant. If the bottomless appetites of the partygoers were any indication, she had a bona fide success on
her hands.

She couldn't take complete credit, of course. None of
this would have been possible if Anthony wasn't a dyna-
mite cook, or if he and Michael hadn't been willing to follow the plan she'd drafted back in the fall. She took
another look around the room. They had maintained the

same decor despite the expansion, with pictures of Popes, gondoliers and prominent Italians beatifically beaming down on the diners from the red walls. She was glad they hadn't gone with her initial impulse to go more upscale.

She wished Reese were here to witness her success, but he was in Chicago, closing yet another deal on behalf of Butler Corporation. She took a sip of her bellini; he'd be back tomorrow, and she could share the good news with him then. She knew he wasn't much of a celebrity watcher, but maybe even he would get a kick out of the picture of her between Danny Aiello and James Gandolfini.

She continued scouring the room, checking to make sure everyone was having a good time. Her mother had insisted on staying home with her father, but there was her idiotic brother Phil, red sauce splattered on the white napkin tucked beneath his chin while he virtually inhaled ravioli . . . Ty and Janna, laughing and joking at a long table set up especially for some of the Blades and their wives . . . and Michael, tucked away discreetly in a corner with a petite, curvy woman whom Theresa had never seen before.

His arm was around her shoulder.

His head was ducked down to listen to what she whispered in his ear.

Whatever it was, it was hilarious—Michael threw his head back and laughed while the woman gazed up into his face affectionately. He drew her even closer.

That was when Theresa felt a wrecking ball hit her gut.

I don't care, she thought feverishly, forcing her eyes away. She had rejected him, and he had a right to get on with his life, just like she had. But the sight of him with this woman made her feel frantic. *Who was she?* Burning with curiosity, she scoped out the room once more, zeroing in on Anthony, who was taking a break from the kitchen and was talking with a waiter so ancient Theresa was sure he'd witnessed the Fall of Rome firsthand.

Sliding gracefully off her bar stool, she moved toward him, trying to figure out how to initiate a conversation and work it around to what she wanted—*needed*—to know. She and Anthony had never really gotten along. At first it had to do with his resistance to her publicizing the restaurant, but now she was sure that in his mind, she was the unstable bitch who'd ripped his brother's heart out. By the time she reached him, she had come up with her opening gambit. Smiling sweetly, she tapped him on the shoulder.

"Anthony?"

She made sure she sounded tentative and needy as he turned around, surprised to see her there.

"Theresa." His voice was formal. "What can I do for you?"

"This is the first chance all evening I've had to tell you how amazing the food is," she gushed. "You must be very, very proud."

Anthony cleared his throat nervously, clearly uncomfortable. "Yes, well, thank you."

"I know you're shy, but would you let me make a big announcement and introduce you to the guests so they can all give you a round of applause?"

"Well . . ."

Theresa could see that he loved the idea but was trying to appear modest.

"Please?" she cajoled.

"All right," he capitulated graciously as if she were twisting his arm.

"Great. Would you like to do it now, or in half an hour or so, when people start ordering dessert?"

"Later is good."

"Terrific." She squeezed his arm. "By the way," she

asked casually, "who's that woman Michael's talking to? I don't think I've seen her before."

Theresa's hand tightened around her sweating glass as Anthony trained his eyes on Michael and the woman in the corner. The gaze he returned to Theresa was bored, almost nonchalant.

"Oh, that's Mikey's new girlfriend." The edges of his mouth tilted upwards into a slow, lascivious smile. "Hot, isn't she?"

"I guess," Theresa mumbled, numb. She was glad the restaurant wasn't lit brightly enough for Anthony to see the twin flames now consuming her cheeks. *Michael's new girlfriend* . . .

"You okay?" Anthony asked.

"I'm fine," Theresa assured him, forcing a smile. She would not give rein to the upset pinching at her. She would focus on work. "I'll introduce you before dessert," she repeated, making her way back to the bar. A few minutes ago she'd felt like the Queen of the Universe, triumphant, successful, invincible. But now?

She was all too aware of being human.

Closing the door of Dante's as the final partygoers departed, Michael was struck by a sense of accomplishment that far outweighed his exhaustion. It reminded him of the way he felt after playing a great game: wrung out but inspired. Despite a rocky start, the evening had been an unqualified success. Everyone said so, including Theresa. Apart from what the staff had saved to eat later on, all the food was gone. Aldo, the waiter who had worked for his parents for forty years, had pulled him aside at one point and with tears in his tired eyes, whispered fervently, "Your parents would be so proud, Mikey."

That was all he needed to hear.

Rubbing the weariness from his eyes, he plodded

across the room and slid onto a bar stool beside Anthony. The sag in his brother's shoulders told him Anthony was as tired as he was, probably more. Still wrapped in his apron, he sat quietly puffing on a cigar and drinking Sambuca. Soon they would have to start cleaning up. But for now, both felt entitled to sit for a few minutes and just rest.

Anthony pulled another cigar out of his pocket and held it out to Michael, who waved it away disdainfully. "Get outta here. You know I don't smoke."

Anthony put the offending object back in his shirt pocket with a shrug.

"Since when do you smoke cigars?" Michael wanted to know. He knew Anthony had been smoking cigarettes since he was twelve, introduced to them, perversely, by Nonna Maria, a master of blowing smoke rings. But stogies?

"Angie turned me onto them," Anthony revealed, puffing contentedly.

"Angie the cop smokes cigars?"

"A lot of women do nowadays," Anthony replied knowingly. "It's very chic."

"Pop would kill you if he saw you with a cigar," Michael pointed out, hopping off the stool to slip behind the bar and fix himself a Dewar's on the rocks. "Remember? He always said that was what killed Grandpa Dante."

Anthony made a disparaging face. "Old age killed Grandpa Dante, not cigars. He was, what? Ninety-six? C'mon."

"Still."

"Don't lecture me on health, Mikey, 'cause I'll cut your greasy heart out, I swear to God I will."

"You've been threatening to do that for years."

"Doesn't mean I won't make good on it one day."

Michael laughed easily as he sat back down beside his brother. His first sip of Dewar's went down nice and smooth, coating his throat and stomach with soothing warmth. He'd have to watch it, though, drink it slow. He was already feeling punchy with weariness. If he drank too fast he'd wind up snoring with his head on the bar.

"So." He peered down into his drink, ice cubes tinkling as he shifted the glass restlessly. A sense of inevitability had hung over his head all evening. Now he was going to bring it to its needed conclusion. "You want to talk?"

Anthony shot him a sidelong glance, wary. "About what?"

"Don't yank my chain, Anthony, I'm too tired."

"Fine, we'll talk," Anthony muttered resignedly.

All night long, while eating, schmoozing and trying hard not to be acutely aware of where Theresa was every second, Michael had rehearsed this speech to his brother in his head. But now that the moment was finally here, and with it Anthony's obvious reluctance to discuss what couldn't be avoided any longer, all the fancy words and explanations he'd so meticulously thought out fell away. It was down to honesty, pure and simple.

Which unnerved him.

He and Anthony had never, truly, had a heart-to-heart.

"I'm sorry I've been stepping on your toes," Michael began. "That was never my intention."

"You made me feel like a moron, Mike." Anthony's voice was terse with repressed emotion. "You made me feel like I was an idiot for being content with the way things were."

Michael looked away with a grimace, not knowing how to deal with the pain in his brother's voice. Men in physical pain, he could deal with. But this was psychic pain, the kind men spent their whole lives trying to cover up, *especially* men like himself, who made their living trying to prove their invulnerability. How was he supposed to deal with *that?*

"I never intended to make you feel stupid," he murmured, feeling the inadequacy of his response. Being open and honest with his brother was so much harder than he thought.

"What *did* you intend?"

Their eyes met in the mirror behind the bar. Anthony's gaze was confused, expectant. Michael struggled to come up with words that would appease as well as explain.

"All I wanted . . . was Dante's to be the best it could be. I'm a professional athlete, Anthony. I compete for a living. I strive to be the best. I can't help it. It's who I am. It's *what* I am." He looked at Anthony hopefully. "Remember how Ma always said that? 'Be the best you can be.' I knew we were sitting on a winner here and that with a little PR, we could turn Dante's into the gold mine it never really was for Mom and Dad."

"But—"

Anthony halted.

"What?" Michael prodded. "You can say it. C'mon."

"It wasn't yours to decide that, Mike." Anthony sounded resentful. "I mean, yeah, I know, legally the restaurant is half yours. But you're not the one who's put his guts into it. While you were in juniors, I was here, day in, day out, seven days a week, learning to cook from Ma. Dad taught me the ropes while you traveled around in the minors. By the time you made it into the NHL, *I* was the one running this place." He stubbed out his cigar. "This isn't a hockey game, Mike. It's a restaurant, and it's my life. The way you just came in here and imposed your will . . ." He shook his head, unable to continue.

Michael looked down at his feet, ashamed. "I did it because I was scared, Anthony."

There. He did it. Finally said aloud what he'd been feeling but was too afraid to give voice to, even to himself. But now that he'd put it out there, he felt a burden lifted, accompanied by a sense of clarity that was liberating.

Anthony peered at him in bewilderment. "Huh?"

Pain settled on Michael's chest, real as someone kneeling on it. "If I'm lucky, I've got two, maybe three years left to play, and then I'm through." He looked around the restaurant: at the table he used to do his homework at after school; at the picture of JP2 his mother had bought at a church rummage sale. "Dante's is my *future*. That's why I wanted the expansion and the prestige. I wanted it to be the best because this is where I'm going to wind up."

"Yeah, but you're not here *yet*," Anthony pointed out. "What the hell are you worrying about that shit now for? Focus on hockey, for Chrissakes."

"I intend to," Michael replied, fully aware of the irony of Anthony's words. He took a sip of Dewar's. "From now on, you're not going to have to deal with any of the selfish, self-motivated crap I've been laying on you for the past eight months."

"Yeah?" Anthony looked doubtful.

"I promise. I'll pop in like I always did, schmooze, bring the guys back here for meals, whatever. But for the rest of the season, I am officially out of your hair. That is, if you'll release me from our agreement."

"Hell, yeah," said Anthony, polishing off his Sambuca.

"I do need to know one thing, though."

Anthony's eyes hooded with suspicion. "What?"

"Now that we've expanded, and you've been featured on TV, and we've run the weekly special, and we're finally *making a real profit,* aren't you glad I was such a pushy pain in the ass?"

Anthony muttered something indistinguishable, prompting Michael to cup a hand behind his right ear.

"What was that? I couldn't make out what you said."

"Yeah, I'm glad," Anthony barked.

"I thought so."

Anthony smiled with self-deprecation. "You know how

I am, Mike. Set in my ways. The last thing I wanted was you changing things around. But now that you have . . ." His eyes traveled around the restaurant wistfully. "I see that change can be good." He wagged a warning finger in Michael's face. "But I still don't want you hanging around here all the time."

"I won't." He wrapped his arm around his brother's shoulder affectionately. "Dante's is yours, Anthony. It's half mine in name, but the restaurant is truly yours. And always will be."

Anthony coughed, choked up, as he grabbed his brother in a bear hug. "Thank you, Mike." Breaking apart, a wicked smile pierced Anthony's solemn demeanor. "Hey, I just remembered you owe me."

"What?"

"Remember when you were in the corner talking to Gemma?"

Michael nodded. Gemma had been telling him a hilarious story about some guy who'd come into her store wanting information about putting a hex on John Tesh, for whom he had an irrational hatred.

"Well," Anthony continued confidentially, "Theresa came over to me, and she was very curious about who you were talking to. *Very* curious."

Michael's weariness suddenly faded. "And—?"

"I told her Gemma was your new girlfriend."

Michael was silent for a second. Then he began to laugh.

"Did she look upset?"

"I thought she was gonna toss her clams right there on the floor," Anthony related, giggling madly like a schoolboy.

Michael raised his left hand, slapping Anthony's in a high five.

"I was happy to be able to twist the knife a little after the way she treated you," Anthony added.

"I always knew you were a good brother, Ant."

"I try," Anthony concluded philosophically, sliding off his seat with a sigh. "Time to clean up."

"I'll leave that to you."

"Not unless you want me to cut your greasy heart out."

"Well, in that case . . ."

CHAPTER

17

"Oh. My. God!!!"

Sitting in the sun with Reese on a blanket in Central Park's Sheep Meadow, Theresa was eagerly perusing the local papers for restaurant reviews. "Listen to *this*!" She shook Reese's arm as she read aloud from the *Post*.

> "Dante's offers magnificent dining at affordable prices . . . family atmosphere and traditional menu belie a sophistication that would tantalize even the most jaded palate . . . osso buco outstanding . . . cannolis defy description . . . worth the trip to Brooklyn."

She put the paper down, covering her face with her hands while excitedly fluttering her outstretched legs.

"Are you all right?"

The disapproval in Reese's voice made her lower her hands from her face.

"Do you understand how important these reviews are?"

"Yes," said Reese. "But there's no need to have a seizure."

"Oh, boo to you," Theresa frowned, sticking her tongue out at him. "They just gave Dante's three and one half stars! Out of four!" She picked up the *Sentinel* and quickly looked through it. There was nothing about Dante's, the bastards. Thumbing through *Newsday*'s "Eats" column, she found another review that said Dante's had, among other attributes, "a pleasant and casual atmosphere offering quality, authentic cuisine." Buzzing from the praise, she whipped out her cell phone and called both Michael and Anthony. She got their machines. She left a message for Janna, too. And Terrence. Her parents' line was busy.

"I wish you'd been there," she said to Reese, lying down on the blanket.

"So you've said."

"Now I just have to wait to see if that picture of Aiello and Gandolfini makes it onto *New York's* 'Scene' page, or even *People's* 'Star Tracks.' "

"That would be good," Reese murmured, sounding distinctly disinterested.

Theresa turned her head to look at him, her eyes hidden behind sunglasses. He sat cross-legged on the edge of the blanket, engrossed in the latest issue of the *National Review*. Did he really not care? She was tempted to say, "I'm carrying an alien's baby" to see if he was paying attention, then thought better of it. He would say she was being immature. Maybe she was. A tiny breath of desire for him whispered through her, at least when she looked at his face. His legs were another matter. They were more spindly than she had hoped. Between that and the blond hairs, they looked almost adolescent. Theresa liked men with strong, muscled legs. Athletic legs. *Michael probably has good legs,* she thought.

She turned her face up to the sun. Michael had been on

her mind more than she'd care to admit. Perhaps it was because so much of her energy and attention had been focused on Dante's. But she kept returning to the image of Michael talking to his girlfriend, their happy, laughing faces haunting her mind. The worst part was seeing the ease with which the woman interacted with his family. Michael's grandmother had grabbed the girlfriend's face in her hands and kissed it repeatedly. Clearly they'd all met her and had liked and approved of her. *How serious are they?* Theresa wondered uneasily. *Is he thinking of marrying her?*

Disturbed, she turned back to Reese. "Am I ever going to meet your family?"

"Mmm?" His nose was still buried in his magazine.

Theresa heaved a sigh of frustration. She repeated herself, only louder this time. "Am I ever going to meet your family?"

"Eventually."

"Do you think you could put the magazine down? You're giving me an inferiority complex."

Reese appeared initially not to hear. Annoyed, Theresa was about to reach over and snatch it from his hands when he finally closed it, putting it down on the blanket beside him. "There. Done. You were saying?"

"I was wondering when I was going to meet your family."

"And I said eventually."

"What's the delay?"

Reese contemplated a distant line of trees as he pushed his slipping sunglasses back up the bridge of his nose. "I guess there isn't any, really," he said, sounding reluctant.

"You don't sound too enthused," Theresa noted. *What was his hesitation?*

"You know I like to tread carefully when it comes to these things," Reese explained.

Theresa looked over the top of her sunglasses. "These things being—?"

"Serious things."

Like affection, Theresa thought. She nodded her understanding, noting Reese's tacit, almost relieved, acceptance of her response. *Is he embarrassed by me? Am I not good enough?* These questions set off alarm bells in her head. But no sooner had she silenced them than an even more disturbing question appeared. One Dr. Gardner had asked her: *Why are you with someone who makes you feel badly about yourself?* Determined to avoid an answer, Theresa turned over onto her stomach and propped herself up on her elbows to people watch.

Nice weather seemed to trigger a primordial response in New Yorkers' brains to go outdoors. In adolescence, she'd feel guilty if she curled up inside with a book when the sun was shining, her mother acting as if she were committing seasonal treason. Now she watched as a man about twenty paces away twisted himself into a variety of yoga postures, his suppleness both awe-inspiring and disconcerting. Closer, a woman in a thong bikini lay basking, her head bobbing up and down in time to her Walkman.

Theresa could smell her tanning lotion.

The scent triggered memories of taking the train out to Long Beach for a day by the ocean with her family. She could still feel the pure joy of sitting on a blanket beside her mother, sipping Hawaiian Punch from a Dixie cup and munching on an Oreo. The sun baked wet sand onto her feet and a stiff breeze would cause a momentary chill, prompting her to draw her beach towel tighter around her drying shoulders. Those were good times. Innocent times. She missed them.

As if reading her thoughts, Reese stretched out on the blanket beside her. "It'll be beach weather soon."

"You like the beach?"

"Love it. Love the beach, love the ocean, love to sail."

"I've never been sailing," Theresa admitted, feeling oddly embarrassed. Maybe it was the casual way Reese had said it, as if sailing automatically went hand in hand with the ocean.

"Really? You've never been sailing?" Reese was peering at her in surprise.

"I'm from *Bensonhurst,* Reese. We don't sail. We eat and fight, remember?"

"I'll have to take you, then."

Theresa smiled. "That would be nice."

Her cell phone rang. Excited, certain it was Janna or one of the Dante brothers responding to her ecstatic messages, she practically sang "He-lllloo-oh!"

But it wasn't.

It was her brother Phil, bawling as if his heart would break.

Their father was dead.

"*Terry? Are you* all right?"

The light, almost timid touch of her sister-in-law's hand forced Theresa back into her body. They were standing just inside the door of the room where her father was laid out, greeting visitors who had come to pay their respects.

Theresa nodded slowly. "I'm okay, Debbie," she murmured.

A little over twenty-four hours ago, she'd been lying on a blanket in Central Park, fondly remembering past trips to the beach and imagining future sailing expeditions. Now she was trapped in the present, holding back an ever-threatening avalanche of tears at Ricci and Brothers Funeral Home. The intervening hours had been surreal: a frantic discharging of necessary tasks interspersed with jags of all-consuming grief. If she didn't need to be strong for her mother, Theresa wouldn't be here. She pictured herself tied to a bed and being given a shot to stop her screaming.

Following her brother's phone call, she and Reese had rushed to Bensonhurst. By the time they arrived, the ambulance had come and gone, removing her father's body. Phil, Debbie and the kids were there with Theresa's mother. Theresa took one look at her mother's grief-crumpled face and proceeded to break down. She and her mother sat together sobbing on the sofa until Aunt Toni, her mother's sister, arrived to take her place.

It was no comfort that her father had died at home in his sleep. He was dead. Never again would he tenderly call her *"Cara mia."* Never again would she make a special trip to Balducci's for him to buy the Pernigotti nougat he loved. No more teasing about finding a husband, no more needling about being too big for her britches and abandoning her roots.

Her poppy was gone forever.

The world would never, ever be the same.

Reese's presence was more a hindrance than a help. He was as uncomfortable being there as her family was having him. Theresa cut him loose, promising to call him when she returned to the city later that night. Escorting him to the door, she tried to ignore the relief in his eyes where she had hoped to see sympathy.

There was so much to do. Phil appeared unable to cope with any of it. Given the luxury of time, Theresa would have been annoyed. But they didn't have that luxury. The only thing Phil could handle was calling Dante's to arrange for the post-funeral catering. Everything else was up to Theresa and Debbie.

After deciding which funeral home to use, Theresa took her mother down to make the arrangements. She didn't believe in out-of-body experiences, but she was certain she'd had one in the sitting room of Ricci Brothers. From a vantage point high near the ceiling she watched herself sitting stiff-backed with her mother, while Fabio Ricci, who looked like an aging Frankie Avalon, talked to them about embalming and music and mass cards and viewing hours and rosary beads and flower arrangements. She saw herself trying not to gasp when Ricci quoted casket prices to them and watched her own eyes wince when her mother said she wanted fat, mean Father Clementine to perform the funeral Mass at St. Finbar's.

They decided on a two-day wake, with both afternoon and evening viewing hours. Her mother chose a solid oak casket with natural finish and a tan crepe interior for $3,500.00. *Whatever Ma wants,* Theresa kept repeating to herself, trying not to imagine what the markup on the coffin had to be. *Whatever Ma wants.*

Back home, there were calls to make, directions to give, obituary information to feed to the paper. Theresa was profoundly grateful Debbie was there. As useless as Phil was, that's how helpful Debbie was. It was Debbie who called relatives and friends and arranged for a double plot while Theresa helped her mother pick out what her father would wear.

Opening the door to his closet, Theresa's knees weakened as the familiar, lingering scent of her father, still clinging to his clothing, filled her nostrils. She clenched her jaw hard, determined not to break down. "The blue suit?" she suggested, her voice little more than a croak. Her mother simply nodded then sat down, dazed, on the bed, her hand lovingly smoothing the indentation in the pillow where just hours before her husband's head had rested.

That night, by the time she got back to the city, all Theresa wanted to do was sleep—for days, months, years. But she couldn't. Overtired and knotted up with grief, she called Reese as she had told him she would. He said he couldn't make the wake, but would be there for the funeral. Theresa was too tired to protest or ask why. She knew why. He would be off on business, happily destroying small start-ups like her own.

She spent the rest of the night trying to get her mind to stop racing. Sometime around 4 A.M., her body surrendered and she plunged into sleep. Yet when she awoke four hours later, it was as if she'd had no sleep at all. She showered, dressed and drove straight back to her mother's house. When the time came for all of them to go over to Ricci's for the first viewing, her mother broke down, saying she just couldn't bear it. Phil and the kids stayed behind with her while Theresa and Debbie went to the funeral home.

And now here she was, lying to her sister-in-law about her mental state and thinking she might suffocate from the overpowering scent of the floral arrangements ringing the room. Faces swarmed in and out of focus, their mouths expressing grief, sorrow, sympathy and regrets. So many different words, all inadequate. Theresa heard herself thanking them but it was someone else talking, someone who was calm and composed. Feeling almost drugged, she let Debbie lead her to a nearby couch.

"I'm going to get you a glass of water, okay?" Debbie whispered. "You look awful."

Theresa nodded listlessly while Debbie slipped away. That was when Michael Dante appeared.

"Hey, Theresa." Voice gentle, he sat down beside her on the couch, taking her hand. The warmth of it shocked Theresa. Up until that moment, she hadn't realized how cold she was. "I'm so sorry about your dad," he murmured sincerely.

Theresa squeezed his hand. "Thanks." She lifted her eyes to his. The compassion that had been missing in Reese's shone in Michael's, his green-blue eyes moist with genuine sorrow.

"Phil called about the catering. Anthony and I want you to know it's on the house."

"Michael—"

"No Michaels. Your father was a loyal customer of Dante's for years. This is something we want to do out of respect for him. Don't worry about picking the stuff up, either. We'll swing by the house while you're all at the funeral and set up."

Theresa nodded gratefully. "Okay," she whispered.

Debbie reappeared, bearing a glass of water in a plastic cup. "Here, Theresa, drink this. It'll do you good."

Theresa took the cup unquestioningly and drank. Debbie was right. The water made her dry throat feel better. "Thanks," she murmured, handing the cup back.

"No problem. Hey, Michael." Debbie leaned over and kissed Michael's cheek. "Thanks for coming."

"No problem."

Debbie regarded Theresa. "I just heard from Phil. He, Ma and the kids are on their way over." With that she left to greet a new arrival.

"You okay?" Michael asked, concerned, his thumb unconsciously rubbing hers.

"No," Theresa admitted, not wanting to look at him. She was afraid that if she did, she would burst into tears. That was the last thing she wanted to happen, especially with her mother on the way. She needed to be strong.

Michael tightened his grasp of her hand. "What can I do?"

"You're doing it," she told him. "Just by being here."

Michael glanced toward the front of the room. "Will you be okay if I go and pay my respects for a minute?"

Theresa nodded, forcing herself to watch him go. Since arriving, she had assiduously avoided the open casket. To her, the body on display at the front of the room wasn't her father. It was a husk, a wax replica. That wasn't how she wanted to remember him. And yet, she felt somehow disloyal avoiding him.

Michael kneeled on the small, velvet prie-dieux before the casket and made the sign of the cross. Theresa was about to turn away, but then something caught her eye. She squinted; there was a hot orange price tag stuck to the bottom of Michael's left shoe. Biting her lip to stifle a smile, she waited for him to rejoin her on the couch.

"You forgot to take the price sticker off your shoe," she whispered.

"What?" Looking around to make sure no one was watching, Michael lifted his left foot and peeled off the offending item, rolling it into a tiny ball and shoving it into the pocket of his jacket. "Thanks," he said, looking mortified.

They settled into silence, Theresa rising to greet two distant relatives who arrived.

"Helluva lot of people here," Michael eventually observed.

Theresa's eyes began to well up.

"Your father was loved." Without asking, he reached into his pocket and pulled out a hanky. "Here."

Taking it, Theresa pressed it to her eyes. She did not want to lose control in front of Michael. She did not want to lose control in front of anyone. Yet what Michael had said was true. Her father *was* loved. The room was packed, and the number of flower arrangements bordered on the obscene. She could have done without the giant crosses made of rosebuds and the stopped clocks, but it was the sentiment that counted, not the tastefulness of the arrangement.

A commotion out in the hallway caught her attention. Children's voices, her brother's voice admonishing. Phil was here with the kids and her mother. Theresa stiffened. *Be strong.*

Rising, she excused herself and went to her mother. Seeing Theresa, her mother collapsed wailing in her arms.

"It's okay, Mama," she whispered, struggling to hold her up. She shot an imploring glance at Phil for help, but he himself was sobbing in his wife's arms. As best as she could, Theresa maneuvered her mother into the sitting room. Michael Dante jumped to his feet to help her.

"It's okay, Mrs. F," Michael soothed. "Whatever you need."

Together, Theresa and Michael tried to lead her toward one of the couches along the wall, but she shook her head vehemently. "No. I need to talk to my Dominic."

Theresa felt her chest constrict as they helped her mother toward the front of the room. She tried to block out the looks of sympathy and pain and the sound of snuffling tears. *Thank God for Michael,* she thought.

As gently as they could, Michael and Theresa helped her mother into a kneeling position in front of the casket. Theresa could no longer avoid looking at her father. He was inches away, his face peaceful, his large, calloused workman's hands folded serenely on his chest with a string of rosary beads entwined in his fingers. Her breath hitched, and she went to move away. But her mother had other plans.

"Bambina, please kneel with me."

Trapped, Theresa knelt beside her suffering mother while Michael faded away.

"Look how peaceful he looks," her mother noted tenderly.

"Yes," Theresa managed.

Groaning with anguish, her mother reached out to touch the cold cheek before her. *"Ti amo,"* she whispered passionately, caressing her husband's still face. *"Il mondo e vuoto senza di te."*

Choking back a sob, Theresa translated in her head. *My love. The world is empty without you.*

"He loved you," her mother told her. "He was so proud of you."

Theresa stared at her mother through watery eyes. "W-what?"

"I know he gave you a hard time about leaving the neighborhood and teased you about getting above yourself. But he'd tell anyone who'd listen: 'My daughter graduated NYU. She runs her own business. We did a good job with that one, Nat,' he'd say to me. Your poppy loved you, *cara mia*."

"Mama—"

She couldn't finish. Before the words were out, the sobs she'd been holding back erupted. Blinded with tears, she rose from the prie-dieux and fled.

Watching Theresa hurry from the sitting room, her beautiful face smeared with tears, Michael struggled with whether or not to jump up and go after her. Maybe she wanted to be alone, and the last thing she wanted to deal with was him hovering? But something inside him wouldn't let him just sit there. She needed him. He could *feel* it. He excused himself from his conversation with Phil and went in search of her.

He found her sitting in her car in the funeral parlor parking lot, the windows rolled up and the radio blasting to drown out the sound of the sobs rattling her body. Not wanting to startle her, Michael gently tapped on the driver's side window.

No response. He tapped louder.

Swiping at her eyes, Theresa rolled the window down a crack. "Go away, Michael," she pleaded. "Please."

"Forget it. Not when you're this upset."

"I'm fine."

"Yeah, and—could you turn the radio down? It's louder than a jackhammer."

Sniffling, Theresa turned the radio off.

"Thank you. As I was saying, I'm not leaving you alone when you're this upset."

"I'm fine," she repeated, with a pathetic smile. She went to roll the window back up but Michael thrust his left hand into the small gap.

"C'mon, Theresa. Let's take a walk. You'll feel better."

Like a child, she reluctantly got out of the car. "Where do you want to go?" she asked woodenly, rubbing her arms.

"Let's go to Eighty-sixth Street," Michael answered.

The temperature had dropped over the course of the afternoon, the cheering rays of the sun now obscured by mean, swift-moving clouds that threatened rain. Taking off his jacket, Michael draped it over Theresa's shoulders, half expecting a yelp of protest. None came.

Silent, they began walking, past store windows both of them had grown up peering into.

Where the hell's Fleece? Michael wondered to himself. *He should be here, taking care of her, comforting her. What the hell kind of a boyfriend is this guy?*

"You staying at your mom's tonight?" he asked, trying to make conversation.

Theresa nodded numbly. "'Til after the funeral."

"That's good. Anthony said he'd be at the second viewing later tonight."

"That's good."

"You want to talk?"

"What's there to talk about?" Theresa asked quietly. "My poppy's dead. End of story."

Michael hesitated, trying to come up with appropriate words of comfort. "I know the pain feels so big right now that it will never go away. And in a certain way, it never does. But you learn to deal with it. Believe me."

Theresa swallowed. "Thank you."

They walked on. Michael reached for her hand, surprised by how thin and cold it felt. He stopped, and taking both her hands between his, began rubbing them vigorously to warm them.

"You want to go back?"

The misery that flashed in her eyes made his heart catch. She looked so scared and vulnerable, not at all the smart-mouthed, wisecracker she often seemed. *If I could,* he told her silently, *I would take all your pain away.*

Theresa looked down at her feet, then off into the distance. "You know what my mother told me?" she asked into the wind. A storm, a bad one, was definitely on the way.

"What?"

Her face contorted with grief. "She told me my father was proud of me."

Pulling her hands from between his, she covered her face and began to sob.

"*Sshh,* c'mere, it's okay."

As gently as if he were coaxing a skittish colt, Michael drew Theresa into the safe haven of his arms. Her body was stiff at first, almost as if she were determined not to succumb to the protection being offered. But Michael held on tight, stroking her hair, whispering any words of comfort he could think of. *Can't you see how much I love you?* he asked her silently, her anguish ripping him apart. *That I would do anything for you?* He wished he could say the words of his heart aloud. Let her know that as long as he drew breath, she would never be alone, or afraid, or neglected.

But it wasn't the time.

"I'm so stupid," Theresa wept, giving herself over to the pain consuming her. "I thought my parents were so provincial, so Brooklyn, so simple because they never wanted anything more out of life than to love each other and raise a family. *I'm* the one who's pathetic. The books you read, your zip code, going to art shows, none of it matters. What matters is your family. The people who love you." She turned her tear-streaked face up to his. "Why couldn't I see that? Why?"

"You're seeing it now," Michael murmured tenderly, carefully wiping her tears away. He drew her closer. "It's .okay," he promised, gently rocking her where they stood. "Everything is going to be okay."

"Don't let go," she pleaded.

"I'm right here," he whispered in her ear as the first rain drop fell. "And I'm not going anywhere."

CHAPTER

18

Theresa stormed past the spluttering receptionist at Banister & Banister and ploughed straight into Reese's office. She found him on the phone, laughing jovially. Seeing her, his eyes went wide and his face turned the color of chalk. He reminded Theresa of a cartoon character.

"Sutton, let me get back to you, all right? *Ciao.*" His voice was smooth as untrammeled silk. *Like always,* Theresa thought bitterly.

Hanging up the phone, he sauntered out from behind his desk. "This is a surprise."

"So was your absence at my father's funeral yesterday."

The pain of the statement lodged in her throat. He had promised to be there. She left him a detailed message with the time, place and directions. Yet he never showed. Phil, when he wasn't sobbing, had asked repeatedly where her "hot shot boyfriend" was. Michael didn't say zip about it, even though he must have been wondering, too.

It was Michael who helped keep her mother upright beside the open grave.

Michael who acted as her rock when it should have been *Reese.*

Before Reese could respond, the receptionist, a barrel-shaped older woman, appeared in the doorway with a security guard. "There she is," she declared, pointing dramatically at Theresa.

The guard's concerned eyes sought Reese's. "Everything all right, Mr. Banister?"

"Everything's fine, Raymond. You and Elinore can get back to what you were doing." Clearly deflated that Theresa wasn't going to be arrested, Elinore disappeared behind the massive bulk of the guard, who failed to close the door.

Theresa did it for him.

She stared Reese down. "Well?"

Reese was cool. "Well what?"

"Why weren't you at my father's funeral? You said you'd be there. I needed you. What happened?" She was fighting to keep her voice level, but she wanted to curse and throw things.

"Didn't you get my message?"

"The one that said you were delayed in Miami?" she jeered. "Yeah, I got it."

He shrugged. "Well, there you go, then."

"*There you go, then?*" Theresa echoed incredulously. "Reese, you left that message *while* I was at the funeral, even though you knew what time the funeral was. Are you telling me you didn't do that on purpose?"

His mouth folded into a frown. "You're being ridiculous, Theresa."

"There are more important things than business, Reese. This was one of them." She shook her head. "You know, for someone who claims to hate what he does for a living, you sure as hell go above and beyond the call of duty."

"Doing things right is important to me," Reese returned coldly.

"Really? And what about doing the *right thing*?" Her heart was spasming in her chest, an erratic, rapid-fire rhythm. They were headed toward the moment of truth. "Reese?"

He leaned against his desk, feet casually crossed at the ankles, arms folded across his chest as a look of bored resignation played across his face. "You want to know the truth, Theresa?"

"Yes, please. I would find it a refreshing change."

"The truth is that work is more important to me than some two-bit, goomba funeral."

Theresa blinked as she sank down in a chair. She was beyond stunned. She was stupefied.

Reese was watching her intently. "Is that a satisfactory explanation?"

Theresa looked at him, at the cool, blue eyes she had once imagined her children inheriting, at the sandy blond hair that fell so boyishly across his brow, and she felt her insides turn to ice. "You've been using me," she said, knowing suddenly that it was true. "You thought that if you wooed me long enough, you'd eventually wear me down and talk me into selling FM PR."

"*Very* good." Reese slowly, tauntingly, applauded her.

It all made brutal sense now: the foot-dragging, the evasiveness, the lack of affection. "How long were you prepared to carry on with this charade?" she forced herself to ask.

"As long as it took."

"Didn't you think I would have figured it out eventually?"

"Who knows? It took you this long," was his snide reply.

"And that night I came to your apartment before Ty and Janna's party and you said you were sick—?"

"What do you want to know? Her name, or how long we've been together?"

It took every ounce of self-control she had not to flinch. Or cry. Jesus, how she longed to cry. But she'd be goddamned if she'd give this bastard the satisfaction.

Reese slid back behind his desk. "I have work to do."

There were a million questions crowding her brain, all of them jostling for attention, while in her heart, pain and anger vied for dominance. She looked hard at him, at this stupid fantasy man of hers that she'd spent hours deluding herself about, and felt nothing but cold, pure hatred.

"I want to know something. I want to know how you came up with this plan. I want to know why you picked the strategy you did."

He looked put out by her question. "My uncle and I are professionals, Theresa. We thoroughly research every company we help Butler acquire, searching for weaknesses and ways to make inroads. Our research on you turned up the Lubov case."

Theresa tensed. "And so—?"

"So we focused on you."

"Why?" Theresa demanded sharply. "What inroad did you see in *me?*"

"Someone successful but over thirty and still single, and therefore open to being romanced. But carefully, because of her history of abuse."

Theresa's head was spinning. "You heartless, unethical SOB," she yelled, winging the bracelet he'd given her at him. "How can you stand yourself?"

Reese looked unperturbed. "All's fair in love and war. And when it comes to corporate acquisitions, it's war." He chuckled lightly. "Although in your case, I must say I went 'above and beyond the call of duty,' to quote you."

"How so?"

"Meeting your family?" He sucked in his lips. *"Please."*

"I know," Theresa agreed, in a sarcastic voice. "Don't

they realize there's more to life than family dinners? Why, they don't even sail! Philistines!"

Reese narrowed his eyes. "Are you mocking me?"

This time, Theresa was the one applauding. "I'm mocking you, your values, your shallow existence—"

"An existence *you* aspired to," Reese pointed out with a condescending smile. "Which made you such an easy target."

"You're right," Theresa admitted. "I did aspire to it. But you know what? I had a revelation the other night at my father's wake. I'd rather be at a Sunday dinner at my mother's house, playing with my nieces and nephews and listening to my mother and brother fighting, than swanning around Manhattan, making sure the right people see me. My family are kind, loving human beings, which is more than I can say for you. You're *pathetic*. You weren't fit to cross my parents' doorway, never mind sit down at their table and break bread—"

Reese yawned. "Are you done?"

"Almost." Theresa crossed to his desk, her splayed hands firm on his neat little piles of papers as she leaned forward to get into his face. "Research this, asshole: FM PR will never sell out to Butler. Never. You got that?"

"Then you'd better be prepared to be battered into bankruptcy, because that's where you're headed." He picked up his phone. "Butler will bury you."

Theresa smiled. Tossing her hair, she strode toward the closed door of Reese's office and flung it open wide.

"Bring it on."

Theresa's bravado began fading within minutes of leaving Reese's office, just as she feared. She contemplated going in to work despite having taken the day off, but in the end decided against it. Instead, she spent the day at the library, a haven of her childhood and still one of her favorite places in the city. She read newspapers, magazines, journals. She watched people come and go as the sun faded and the day drew to a close. Finally, driven by hunger, she went home and fixed herself some dinner.

When she was done, she started walking.

She walked all the way from her apartment at Fifty-ninth and First down to Times Square, then back up again. Several times, seeing but not seeing, she banged into people on the street. "Sorry," she'd murmur hastily, then keep walking.

"Crazy bitch," one man called after her.

She was walking to save her sanity. She was certain if she walked long enough, she would begin to feel numb. That was preferable to the despair she carried inside her. If she stopped moving, she would be forced to confront the painful truth head on: that deep down in her heart, she'd known all along that Reese's feelings for her weren't genuine. She'd forced herself to believe otherwise, because she was so determined to make all her girlhood fantasies about big city romance come true. She'd thought herself too smart for such delusion, but clearly that wasn't case.

She was as capable of self-deception as the next woman.

And she'd let a good man, maybe the right man, slip through her fingers.

She'd been out for more than three hours when it started to rain. She walked anyway, not caring that her drenched clothing clung to her body or that her hair lay pasted to her head. All that mattered was putting one foot in front of the other until she became so exhausted she couldn't move. At that point she would call a cab, go home and collapse into the oblivion of sleep.

She walked two more hours.

Eventually, she forced herself to take in her whereabouts, noting she was back in midtown. A quick check of her watch revealed it was a little after midnight. Surprising herself, she walked to Ty and Janna's.

The night doorman didn't want to let her in.

Theresa dug into her purse and produced her business card, pointing out Janna's name on it, too, along with the name of their company. The doorman reluctantly capitulated. She was let inside and he buzzed upstairs. Looking like he couldn't quite believe it, he told her she was cleared to go up to Ty and Janna's apartment.

They were both waiting at the door in their bathrobes. Janna looked sick with worry as she hustled her inside.

"Oh my God, Theresa." Janna quietly closed the door and asked Ty to get her some towels as well as his spare bathrobe. When he disappeared, Janna reached up and touched Theresa's cheek. "Talk to me, honey."

Theresa began shivering. "I'm sorry," she whispered to Janna, though she wasn't quite sure what she was sorry for. She forced herself to focus. "I'm sorry to disturb you so late at night."

"Don't be ridiculous."

Ty reappeared with the towels and bathrobe and Janna led Theresa to the bathroom. "Dry off and change. I'll go put on some water for tea. What kind do you want?"

"Got any cyanide instead?"

Janna didn't react.

"That was a joke, Jan." She closed the bathroom door.

Her clothing was so wet it was dripping onto the floor, making little puddles on the marble. Theresa stole a look at herself in the mirror. No wonder the doorman didn't want to let her in; she looked like a madwoman, her supposedly waterproof mascara a dark, angry bruise beneath her eyes.

Now that she was no longer moving, she began to feel. Cold. Humiliated. Angry. How much time had she wasted feeding false hopes? How much work would she have to do now to rebuild her self-esteem? *Dr. Gardner's going to have a field day with this,* she thought ruefully as she donned the oversized bathrobe, tying its sash tightly around her waist.

She wanted to hide in the bathroom.

If she went out into the kitchen, she'd have to talk about what had happened, and she wasn't sure she could do that. But then she thought: *Why else would you have shown up here, if not to talk?*

Gathering her dripping clothes into a bundle, she reemerged. Janna took them from her and promptly loaded them into the dryer. Then she forced Theresa to sit down on the couch. Ty was nowhere to be seen.

"Where's your husband?"

"He's in the bedroom, giving us our privacy."

Theresa ducked her head, grateful.

"Talk to me, Terry. What's going on?"

Just as she had in Reese's office, Theresa simply blinked. She didn't know where to begin. With her conversation with Reese? With the realization she'd had at the funeral? With how safe she'd felt in Michael Dante's arms the first night of the wake, when he'd followed her out into the parking lot? For some reason, the image of him kneeling with the price tag stuck on the bottom of his shoe flashed in her mind and she laughed.

"Theresa?" Janna asked, alarmed.

"Don't worry, I'm not losing my mind," Theresa assured her. She peered down at her bare feet. They were waterlogged, shriveled. She knew she had to stop stalling. "Reese was using me," she began.

She lifted her eyes to her best friend's. Like a dam breaking, the words started pouring out of her, furious, unstoppable. She told Janna every horrible detail, from his reluctance to touch her to the details of his wooing plan. Janna listened intently, requesting Theresa pause only once, when she went to the kitchen to fetch their tea.

Theresa talked until her jaw hurt and there was nothing left to say.

And when she was done talking, she began to cry.

Blowing her nose into tissue after tissue, she wondered if it were possible to run out of tears. She'd cried more in the last four days than all the days of her life combined. Whether she was crying for her father or herself, she didn't know. Maybe it didn't even matter. "I'm sorry," she apologized again, winding down.

"Don't be," Janna chided. "You've had terrible emotional shocks on two fronts." She clucked her tongue disgustedly. "That slimeball. I thought he was up to something." She put her arm around Theresa's shoulder, giving it a loving squeeze.

Theresa's bruised heart swelled. It would have been so easy for Janna to say "I told you so." But she didn't, and Theresa knew she wouldn't, because that's not what true friends did, and Theresa had never, ever had a truer friend than Janna MacNeil.

"I'm such an idiot," Theresa lamented tearfully.

"No, you're *not*."

"Yes, I *am*," Theresa insisted. "Only an idiot would have let Michael Dante go. Only an idiot would have chosen style over substance."

Janna reached forward for her teacup. "It's not too late."

"Yes, it is. He's got a girlfriend."

"He does?"

"Yes," Theresa said, tearing up again. "Didn't you see her at the reopening? A little redhead, even shorter than you." She winced. "Sorry, that was a really mean thing to say."

Janna waved her hand dismissively, asking, "Are you *sure* she's his girlfriend?"

"Yes," she said miserably. "I saw them canoodling in the corner." The memory still smarted.

"Hmmm." Janna contemplated this. "Well, maybe it's

not serious. Who knows?" She took a sip of tea. "I think you should call him."

"Oh, right." Theresa shook her head. "And say what? 'Sorry I jerked you around, but guess what? I've finally come to my senses and realized what a great guy you are. Can I have a second chance?' "

Janna's gaze was steady. "Why not?"

"Because, believe it or not, even after this debacle with Reese, I do have some pride."

"I think you're being ridiculously stubborn," Janna declared.

"Would you call Ty if you'd treated him like garbage *and* you knew he was involved with someone else?"

Janna looked uncomfortable. "Well . . ."

"The answer is no, you wouldn't. I think I have to hop on board the reality train, and you should join me."

"But Michael still cares about you. It was all over his face at the wake and funeral."

"That was kindness you saw, Janna." Theresa put her head in her hands. "Michael's a good person. He saw I was in pain and he wanted to help. End of story."

"I don't know," Janna rebutted.

"I do." She looked up at Janna with pain in her eyes. "I blew it."

She regarded Theresa sympathetically. "So now what?"

"I throw myself into work and contemplate joining a religious order?"

"Don't give up on men. They're not all bad, you know." Janna motioned with her head towards the bedroom.

Theresa smiled wanly. "I know." She craned her neck in the direction of Janna's laundry room. "How much longer, do you think?"

"It's after one in the morning, Ter. Why don't you just crash in the spare bedroom?"

"Are you sure?" Theresa asked. "I've been enough of an imposition already."

"Of course I am. I want you to sleep in, too. In fact, I think you should take the rest of the week off. It's only three days. Terrence and I can pick up the slack."

Work. Theresa's heart sank as Reese's final, vituperative words came back to her. "We need to talk about the business, Jan."

"Not tonight." Janna stood. "Don't get up if you hear movement in the kitchen around five-thirty or so. Ty's got an early morning flight to Ottawa for the first round." She leaned over and kissed Theresa's cheek. "Please try to get some rest. And don't ever apologize for coming to me when you need help. You're my best friend."

With that, she disappeared into the bedroom. Theresa finished her tea and headed for the spare room. Her head barely touched the pillow before she was asleep.

Shoot it! Shoot it!

Shit. Michael's heart sank along with the rest of the players' on the bench as Ottawa's goalie poke-checked Paul van Dorn before he could get off a shot. With three minutes left in the game, the teams were tied at 1-1. A quick glance around the Corel Centre revealed it was filled to capacity, the crowd holding its collective breath as the clock wound torturously down. Two nights before, in the first game of the first round, the Blades had humiliated Ottawa on its home ice, 3-0. But tonight, Ottawa had come out battling. Michael and the fourth line had seen only spot action.

He watched as the third line, still on the ice, cycled the puck in the offensive zone. For a split second, it looked as if one of Ottawa's defensemen might wrest the puck from right winger Barry Fontaine. But Fontaine maintained control, flipping the puck behind the net, van Dorn skating in

after it. The blade of his stick had barely touched it when—
BAM!—he was boarded by the thuggish Ottawa defense-
men Ulf Torkelson, one of the chippiest players in the NHL.
Van Dorn's head snapped back, and then he was down. At
first there was silence. Then, half rising off the bench,
Michael and the rest of the Blades began screaming.

"That's a hit from behind!" Michael shouted.

"What are you, fucking blind?!" Ty yelled at the ref.
"Call that!"

Play had stopped, but Samuelson hadn't been penal-
ized. In fact, he took the opportunity of van Dorn's injury
to slowly skate by the Blades bench.

"Looks like the little rookie isn't so pretty now, eh?"
he jeered.

"You're a dead man!" Michael shouted.

"What are you gonna do, hit me with a spaghetti pot,
Mikey?" Samuelson taunted, circling back to Ottawa's defensive zone.

Out on the ice, two of the Blades trainers were helping
the dazed van Dorn to his feet and then to the dressing
room, his bloodied face covered in a towel. Ty, who had
been warned he was in serious danger of a bench minor,
tapped Michael on the shoulder. The fourth line skated out
onto the ice.

New York won the face-off, and just as Michael had
envisioned, the puck slid into the corner. Both he and
Torkelson hustled after it, Michael leaving his feet and
slamming into the big Swede with everything he had. But
before Michael could get to the loose puck, Torkelson elbowed him in the face with all his might, sending a blinding pain cracking down Michael's cheekbone.

Retaliating, Michael shoved his gloves in Torkelson's
face. "C'mon, big man! Let's see how tough you are face-
to-face!"

A scrum of players from both sides quickly formed

around the two of them as the linesmen fought their way into the pack, pushing Michael and Torkelson apart.

"Both of you! Out of here!" the helmeted referee yelled at them. "Number Eight, Ottawa, two minutes for elbowing. Number Thirty-three, New York, two minutes for roughing."

Michael lost it. "If you're not gonna keep him honest, then we have to!" he yelled at the ref. "What, you didn't SEE the hit? Were you too busy getting ANOTHER DOUGHNUT?"

The ref ignored him, and Michael was forced to skate, glaring, to the penalty box. The left side of his face felt like it was on fire, the flesh throbbing and swelling as he sat there. Play resumed with the teams skating four on four. A minute later, Ottawa scored, putting them up 2 to 1 with less than a minute left.

The horn blew signifying end of play, and Michael bolted from the penalty box, heading straight for Torkelson. But he was blocked by one of the linesmen who grabbed him by the arms.

"Game's over, Mikey. Let it go for tonight."

"You fucking coward!" Michael shouted past the linesman at Torkelson. "*No way* am I done with you!"

"Mikey, get off the ice!" the referee yelled.

Frowning with dismay, Michael jerked his arm out of the linesman's grasp while Torkelson disappeared into Ottawa's locker room.

"You need your eyes checked," Michael muttered to the referee, skating off the ice. His left cheek had ballooned up so far, so fast, that he could almost see it in front of his left eye. Gritting his teeth against the pain, he went to join his teammates.

"*How's the face* feel, Mike?"

Michael tried not to blink as Dr. Linderman shone a

penlight deep into his eyes, their noses close enough to touch. Obviously he was worried about another concussion. Michael wasn't. Any pain he was feeling was in his face.

"My head feels fine," he told the doctor.

"Well, your face is killing me," the doctor laughed, amused with his own joke. "Sorry, I couldn't resist." He switched off the penlight. "Put that ice pack back on your face."

Michael complied. The anesthetizing cold helped him block out both the endless throbbing and the anxiety in the room. Ty and Kevin were both there, nervously waiting to hear what the doctor had to say. Judging by Linderman's deep sigh as he showed them all the X ray, Michael knew it wasn't good.

"There's a hairline fracture to the left cheekbone. Here." Linderman's finger traced the thin line along the X ray.

Ty, looking displeased, regarded the doctor. "So, what's the prognosis?"

"If he sits out, it heals and is as good as new in two months. If he gets hit there again, he'll need reconstructive surgery."

"Fuck," Ty muttered.

Michael peeled the ice pack away from his face. "Fuck is right," he echoed loudly. "No way am I not playing."

Linderman chuckled as he lightly grasped Michael by the elbow and steered him toward a nearby mirror hanging on the white concrete wall. "Have a look at yourself and then see what you think."

Michael faced his reflection in the mirror. The entire left side of his face was swollen and bruised, the skin turning varying shades of yellow, purple and black. Michael's response was a shrug.

"I look like a hockey player."

Kevin chuckled, but Michael failed to see the humor.

He could feel the season slipping away from him. "I've got two days to ice it. By the time Wednesday rolls around it won't look half this bad."

"You really should avoid contact," Dr. Linderman reiterated. Michael ignored him. All his attention was focused on Ty and Kevin, off in the corner talking. Michael hoped to Christ they weren't going to pull the rug out from under him. Dante's had reopened and was up and running. He had rededicated himself to hockey. If he couldn't play, he didn't know what the hell he'd do with himself. The thought was unbearable.

Ty and Kevin approached him.

"What about wearing a shield, Mikey?" Kevin suggested with concern.

"No fucking way," Michael spat.

Ty took a step toward him. "Michael—"

"No shield! I've never worn one in my life and I'm not about to start now. It's not my eyes we're talking about here, it's my face. You make me wear a shield and you may as well hang a billboard that says 'Dante is injured.' They'll be going after me all night. We'll ice it," Michael maintained stubbornly. "It'll be fine. No shield."

"Jesus H. Christ." Ty blew out a breath, shaking his head as he looked to Kevin. "What do you think?"

Kevin looked Michael in his one good eye. "Promise us you won't drop your gloves."

Michael looked at both of them. "I promise."

He waited, Ty and Kevin exchanging quick glances before Ty gave an almost imperceptible jerk of the head. Then he spoke.

"You'll dress. No shield."

CHAPTER

19

The room was small and solidly beige. Several tiny white tea lights flickered, while ethereal sounding harp music was pumped in. Theresa inhaled deeply, intoxicated by what smelled like lavender tinged with another fragrance, perhaps tangerine. As the massage therapist administered a long, deep stroke down her spine, she felt herself drifting away into the ether. She closed her eyes, her body quietly humming with contentment.

"This," Theresa sighed, "was a very good idea."

"So, I was thinking," Janna mumbled, lying on a table next to her.

"Mmm?"

"We should use Ty's money."

"You sly fox," Theresa accused dreamily while the massage therapist worked on her left shoulder blade, pushing and pulling at the knotted muscle there. "You deliberately brought me here to relax me so you could bring this up."

Janna laughed. "Am I that transparent?"

"Yes."

"Well, what do you think?"

Theresa paused, enjoying the sensation of being fully in her body, appreciating a delicious sense of weightlessness. Janna was smart; now *was* the perfect time to talk about their business, when both their minds were relaxed and uncluttered.

"I don't know," Theresa admitted. "I feel badly your husband has to bail us out. That you—he—are going to pour more money into the company, and I won't be contributing anything."

Janna gave a languid sigh, her response delayed, Theresa supposed, by the pleasure she was currently experiencing as her own therapist worked on her neck. "Who put up most of the seed money for the business from her settlement?"

"Me," Theresa said reluctantly.

"So why can't we take money from my husband? It all evens out in the end."

"I guess." Theresa mulled this over as her shoulder muscles slowly, miraculously loosened. Without an infusion of cash, Reese's nasty prediction would come true: Butler would bury them. Ty's money would pay off their debts and also give them a financial cushion. They'd be able to keep Terrence on, perhaps even hire another publicist to handle smaller accounts.

"Have you talked to Ty?" Theresa asked, realizing immediately it was a stupid question. Of course she'd talked to Ty. Knowing Janna, the papers had already been drawn up and were just sitting at the bank waiting to be signed.

"He said we could use as much as we want."

Theresa whistled softly. "Does he realize how dangerous a statement that is?"

"I don't think we'll need that much, as long as we continue to grow the business. Now that we've done restaurant PR, we could expand in that direction. Our focus has been too narrow. We need more restaurants and small businesses on the roster."

"You're right," Theresa agreed. The success of her Dante's campaign made her confident she could branch out beyond repping celebs.

"So is that a yes?" Janna sounded hopeful.

"Yes."

"Good," Janna crowed. "We'll show those bastards at Butler."

But Theresa wasn't so sure. "The minute we tell them we're not interested in their offer, they're going to start stealing clients," she predicted.

"Let them try. We can handle them. We're the best, remember?"

"I remember." Theresa smiled to herself, surprised to find her eyes getting moist. When she and Janna worked together at the network and managed to pull off a particular PR coup, they would often high five each other and say, "We're the best." Because they were. *Let Butler come sniffing around our clients,* she thought defiantly. *We'll give them a run for their money.*

"We should probably give Terrence a raise," she murmured, tensing slightly as the therapist gently pushed up the sheet covering her lower body to begin working on the back of her legs.

"I agree," said Janna. "Let's tell him tomorrow."

"And then make him take us out to lunch."

They both laughed.

Long . . . slow . . . deep. The therapist's hands glided over Theresa's calves with ease, pausing to work out a kink just above the back of her knee. "I'm beginning to see why you have this done every week," she said to Janna.

"Sometimes coming to Karma for a massage is the only thing that keeps me from murdering Ty."

Theresa gasped with feigned shock. "You mean he's not perfect?"

"Not when I have PMS," Janna returned. "Speaking of Ty . . . the Blades . . ."

Theresa groaned. "What?"

"Have you thought about getting back in touch with Michael?"

"No," Theresa said emphatically.

"Well, you should. Maybe he's not serious with the redhead. Maybe he's just with her because you were with Reese."

"Maybe we'll never find out because I refuse to humiliate myself." The therapist deepened the pressure, causing Theresa to sigh with pleasure.

"It can't hurt to let him know you're available."

"And how do you propose I do that?"

"The team will be back in town tomorrow night to play Ottawa at Met Gar. You and I could visit before the game, say hi."

"Won't Ty get pissed? I thought pre-game was when he got them all revved up and ready to fight. We'll be committing puckus interruptus."

Janna chuckled. "We'll go down before they dress, when they're all working on their sticks and skates."

Theresa thought a moment. Saying hello couldn't hurt, could it? She felt so good . . . so relaxed . . . blissful . . . positive. . . .

"All right," she agreed easily, feeling herself being carried away on a wave of well being. Right now, anything seemed possible.

Perhaps even getting Michael back.

"I'm leaving."

Theresa's declaration was met with a firm grasp of the wrist. "Don't be an *idiot*. All you have to do is say hi, how

are you, and then we'll go to our seats and watch the
warm-up."

"You promise?"

"I promise. Here, we'll say hi to Ty first."

Her wrist still in Janna's clutches, Theresa found herself being dragged along the fluorescent-lit, labyrinthine
corridors beneath Met Gar toward the open doorway of an
office.

"Hello, my love." Janna dropped Theresa's wrist and
headed toward the desk behind which her husband sat.

"Hey."

Hovering uneasily in the doorway, Theresa watched as
Ty rose to kiss his wife. She felt awkward and self-
conscious in front of him; the last time Ty had seen her, it
was after midnight and she was shivering and drenched to
the bone in the foyer of his apartment. He must have
thought she was nuts. Still did, probably.

"Hi, Theresa." Ty's gaze was overly sympathetic as it
lit on her. "How's it going?"

"Fine." *God, he does think I'm nuts. Maybe I am.
Being here is insane. Michael has a girlfriend. And she
isn't me.*

"Theresa and I thought we'd pop in and say hi before
the game. Where's Kevin?" Janna inquired. "Down with
the rest of the guys?"

"Yeah." Ty looked mildly suspicious. "Why?"

"I just want to say hello," Janna replied perkily. She
stood up on tiptoes and kissed her husband's nose. "Win
tonight, okay?"

"Don't distract the guys for too long," he called after
them as Janna once again grabbed Theresa and headed
back down the corridor. "They have to dress soon!"

"I know," Janna called over her shoulder.

Theresa shook her hand free of Janna's. "I'm *really* not
sure this is such a good idea."

"Too late."

They had rounded a corner, and there, at the far end of the corridor taping the blade of his stick, was Michael. Theresa's heart lurched. It should be easy to stroll up to him and start a conversation. After all, it had been his arms she cried in at the funeral home, his strength that had prevented her from totally breaking down beside her father's open grave. But grief tended to suspend the rules of reality. Now that they'd each returned to the "real world," Theresa felt sure they'd resume their roles within it.

"I'm going to talk to Kevin," Janna murmured, veering off into the locker room.

Before Theresa could protest, Janna was gone. Taking a deep, steadying breath, she continued walking towards Michael, whose head was bent low in concentration. Lifting it, Theresa saw the left side of his face looked pulverized. She gasped, drawing Michael's attention. Seeing her, his face broke into a huge, if lopsided smile.

"What are you doing here?" he asked pleasantly.

"I'm watching the game with Janna and thought I'd say hi." Theresa grimaced. "What happened to your face?"

Michael shrugged dismissively. "It's nothing."

"It doesn't look like nothing." Her hand was halfway to his cheek before she realized what she was doing and checked herself. "What happened?" she asked again.

"One of Ottawa's defensemen elbowed me. Not a big deal." Finished taping the stick, he slowly spun it left, then right, admiring his own handiwork. He lowered it to the floor, lifting it back up to eye level before putting it down again.

"What are you doing?" Theresa asked.

"What?"

She waved her hand in the direction of the stick. "What's the tape for?"

Michael looked amused. "You really want to know?"

"No, what you do with your stick is your business,"

Theresa answered, suppressing a smile. This felt good, teasing him like this. This was within her comfort zone. This she could handle.

Michael laughed. "Well, I'm going to tell you anyway. It gives you more feel for the puck."

Theresa nodded as though she understood, even though she really didn't.

"So, how's your mom doing?" Michael asked.

"Good," Theresa answered quickly. "She's doing good." She could feel awkwardness beginning to creep into the conversation, making her tense and twitchy. *It's just Michael,* she reminded herself. *Just be normal.*

"So . . . um . . ." She heard herself sounding uncomfortable and tried to remedy it. "I just wanted to thank you for all you did during the wake and funeral," she said softly. She felt shaky inside, tender. "I couldn't have gotten through it without you."

His eyes caught hers before looking down at his stick, which he mindlessly twirled. "Anytime," he murmured.

What should I say now? Theresa thought desperately. She felt overwhelmed by her own ineptness and flustered that what should be a simple conversation seemed so uncomfortable for both of them. She was frantic to keep the flow going, desperate to fill the silence that felt like drowning. And so, unthinking, she blurted, "How's your girlfriend?"

Michael slowly returned his gaze to her, seeming to ponder the question. "She's okay."

Theresa's pulse picked up expectantly. Now he would ask how her boyfriend was, the jerk who didn't show up for the wake and funeral, and she'd tell him they were finished, and he would nod, maybe even say he's sorry, but he would also understand the message she was trying to give him.

But Michael didn't ask.

Since there was no way she was going to casually vol-

unteer the information that she and Reese had split, for
fear of looking desperate, she just stood there like a big
twit, saying nothing. Michael stopped twirling his stick,
cleared his throat and checked his watch.

"I should probably head into the locker room soon."

Theresa understood dismissal. She braved a smile. "It
was good to see you," she told him, trying to sound as
pleasant and undevastated as she could.

"You, too. Take care."

He leaned in, chastely kissing her cheek. Theresa
barely had time to catch his scent before he was off down
the hallway to join his teammates. She watched him walk
away, the broad shoulders that had sheltered her when she
was most vulnerable, squared and strong, his stride slow
but sure.

I've lost him, she thought.

Overcome with sadness, she waited for Janna to join
her so they could go upstairs and watch the game.

"Jesus, Mary and St. Joseph," Michael groaned to
himself on the bench as the Blades gave up another quick
goal to Ottawa, putting them down 2 to 0 at the bottom of
the second period. They were now down two games to
one, Ottawa having mopped the ice with them two nights
before, winning 4-1. The home crowd at Met Gar had actually booed them, a phenomenon Michael understood but
didn't appreciate. He himself had only seen one shift per
period during that game, and even then, it was only after
penalty kills when the other forwards needed breathers.
He noticed Ty never put him on the ice at the same time
as Torkelson.

They should have come out tonight energized, ready to
wreak havoc. Instead their game was flatter than soda left
standing overnight. Were it not for their goalie, Pierre
LaRouche, the Blades would be out of it completely.

Thanks to his "standing on his head," Ottawa only scored twice despite an endless flurry of scoring chances.

If they lost tonight . . . Michael didn't care to finish the thought.

The crowd, as restless and frustrated as the players, groaned loudly when one of van Dorn's shots hit Ottawa's goal post rather than sailing into an open net. Michael hated giving the little bastard any credit, but he *was* generating energy. The whole third line was. He watched as van Dorn and his two former linemates endlessly cycled, trying to create scoring chances, only to be kept on the perimeter by Ottawa's defense. When the horn blew at the end of the second period, Michael followed his dejected teammates off the bench and back into the locker room, where Ty yelled at them using language strong enough to blister paint.

Back on the bench at the top of the third, the mood in the building was tense. Ty started the third line. New York won the face-off and dumped the puck in the Ottawa zone. Van Dorn skated into the corner to dig it out. That was when Torkelson cross-checked him into the boards.

"SON OF A BITCH!" Michael yelled in disbelief, his shout blending with those of his irate teammates and indeed, the entire Met Gar crowd, who were howling for justice at the top of their impassioned lungs. The Blades bench tensed as they waited to see whether the referees would call it this time, or let Torkelson get away with the cheap shot.

"Number Eight, Ottawa, two minutes for cross-checking."

The crowd erupted in a roar of pleasure.

"Asshole!" backup goalie Denny O'Malley yelled at Torkelson as he was led to the penalty box located to the far left end of the Blades bench, where Michael was sitting. Michael refused to even look at him.

Instead, he kept his attention on the ice. This was it.

With Ottawa down a man while Torkelson sat in the sin bin, this was probably the Blades best chance to come back. Michael watched, tense, as the power play did everything short of selling their souls to the devil to score. But the Ottawa penalty killers played smart. By the time the power play came to an end, the Blades had failed to get off even one shot.

"All right. Time's short," Ty growled. He tapped Michael on the shoulder. "Get out there and keep your gloves *on*, you hear me?"

Michael nodded, eager for his chance on the ice. His face still hurt, but most of the swelling had gone down, though severe bruising remained. Ty had been true to his word: He hadn't made him wear a shield. Skating into Ottawa's zone, Michael made a beeline for Ottawa defenseman Thad Durgin, who was desperately racing after the puck as it skittered along the boards. Using the full force of his weight, Michael gritted his teeth and checked him. The crowd went berserk.

Michael dashed after the loose puck, centering it to Guy La Temp, who deflected it wide. This time the crowd didn't boo; they cheered. Michael and his line were doing exactly what Ty had sent them out to do. They were bringing some life back into the building and inspiring their teammates to a higher level of play.

Their shift ended and they skated, panting, back to the bench. No sooner had they mopped the sweat from their brows and squirted some cold water into their mouths than Ty sent them back out a minute later. This time Torkelson was on the ice. A frisson of excitement crackled through Michael as he jumped over the boards. He heard Ty's voice in his mind—*Keep your gloves on!*—as he waited for the puck to be dropped. Ottawa won the face-off and shot the puck into the Blades zone.

Michael skated along the blue line as Blades defenseman Barry Fontaine dug the puck out from behind the net, sending it along the boards into the neutral zone where Michael picked it up. He hustled toward the Ottawa's zone, looking for someone to pass to. But a spear to his side from Torkelson caught him up short, causing him to cough up the puck.

Furious, Michael whipped around and hooked Torkelson between the legs so he couldn't get to the puck. The whistle blew as players from both teams seemed to stream in from all directions, surrounding the two adversaries.

"Hey, goomba, nice face," Torkelson taunted.

"Stay cool, Mikey." Barry Fontaine's voice was more a plea than a piece of advice.

But Michael couldn't stay cool. He was pissed, and he was sick and tired of Torkelson's antics. The Swede needed to be taught a lesson. "Fuck it," Michael rasped, dropping his gloves.

Chuckling, Torkelson did the same. Michael could hear the blood beating in his ears, a loud whooshing noise that seemed to come from deep within his head. The two squared off, slowly circling each other as the arena fell silent and the players and officials gave them space.

Torkelson launched a right. Michael, expecting it, stepped inside and connected with two short, quick rights of his own. As Torkelson grabbed on to his jersey, Michael could hear the crowd at Met Gar roaring their approval, their cries of support and blood lust ringing in his ears.

He and Torkelson were locked together now in a violent embrace. Both were exhausted as the two linesmen finally broke them apart. Out of the corner of his eye, Michael could see his teammates standing along the bench, banging their sticks in unison against the boards in support of him. Both referees glared at him, then Torkelson, their displeasure obvious as one blew the whistle.

"Number Eight, Ottawa, two minutes for spearing, five minutes for fighting, and a game misconduct. Number

Thirty-three, New York, two minutes for hooking, five minutes for fighting, and a game misconduct."

The crowd booed the call, choice words sailing down from the blue seats to the ref's ears or so they hoped. Shaking off the linesman still holding him back, Michael skated off the ice, heading not to the bench but to the locker room, where he had been banished for the rest of the game.

"Where the hell are your brains?" Dr. Linderman yelled as soon as he spotted Michael coming down the hallway. "In your ass?"

Michael ignored him, heading straight for the locker room so he could watch the rest of the game on TV. All he wanted was to be left alone to watch in peace. But Linderman followed him.

"Didn't I tell you what could have happened if that goon punched you in the face? The left side of your face could have shattered! Your entire summer would be spent getting reconstructive surgery! Tell me: Was it worth the risk?"

Michael looked directly at the doctor.

"Yes."

Muttering something beneath his breath, the doctor stormed away, leaving Michael alone. Pulling off his skates, Michael watched as Ty put the first line back out on the ice.

"C'mon," Michael urged, his eyes glued to the set. "*Do* something."

His teammates appeared to have heard him. Within ten seconds of the puck being dropped, New York scored. They were finally on the board. Anxious, Michael watched the momentum build as the Blades fought to tie it up, every man appearing to pull the urge to win from deep within himself. But it wasn't enough. In the last two minutes of play, New York pulled their goalie for an extra skater. Within forty-five seconds a turnover in the neutral zone led to an Ottawa empty net goal. The Blades lost the game 3-1. They were down in the series by the same score. If they lost the next game, they'd be out of the playoffs.

Dejected, Michael awaited the return of his teammates. Everyone's face told the same story. Exhausted, embarrassed silence prevailed as the players listlessly undressed, no one seeming to have the energy or inclination to speak.

The locker room door creaked open, and Ty stepped inside. Tension rippled through the room as Michael and his teammates anticipated their well-deserved dressing down.

"Gather around." Ty climbed up on to a bench as the Blades numbly, dumbly, did what they were told. "I want you all to look around at every other player in this room so that in years to come, you'll remember who you shared this night with. This was a game New Yorkers will talk about for years.

"Tonight you saw what a real hockey player is made of. Michael's left cheekbone was fractured in game two in Ottawa. But did that stop him from going after Torkelson? No. When we were challenged, he didn't stop to think. He stood up for us. He didn't worry whether he'd wind up having to get a new face. He thought only of *the team*. You want to lift the Cup? Then play like Michael Dante. The man has the heart of a lion."

Ty stepped down from the bench. The locker room remained momentarily silent. Then a French Canadian voice called out, "The heart of a lion but the breath of a baboon!"

Everyone laughed, Michael included. It was Pierre LaRouche, breaking the awestruck tension in the only way he knew how. Michael was glad of it. Ty's speech had been completely unexpected, moving him more deeply than he thought possible. *I'm back,* he thought triumphantly, every cell in his body pulsing with life and a sense of revitalization. Ty clapped him on the back before leaving the players' midst. "Fuckin' A, Mikey," said fellow vet Guy La Temp, voice thick with admiration as he made his way toward his own locker.

"Uh, Mike?"

Michael turned at the sound of Paul van Dorn's voice. "Yeah?" What the hell did the little prick want with him?

Van Dorn nervously licked his lips, his gaze bouncing off the nearby players. "I guess you're not ready for the retirement home yet."

"Fuck you too, kid," Michael lobbed back with a big, happy, self-satisfied smile he'd been holding at bay. *Goddamn, life was good!* He had no complaints except one, which was a helluva lot less than most people had. Feeling relaxed for the first time in weeks, he grabbed a towel and went to take a shower, pausing once to check his reflection in the mirror. He had to admit, the left side of his face still looked pretty bad. But his place on the team and his ego had both been restored. Definitely worth it.

CHAPTER
20

Either Dante's was robbed, or it had burned to the ground. Those were the only reasons Anthony would call on the spur of the moment and ask if he could stop by. Something had to be wrong. If someone in the family had died, Anthony would have told him straight out on the phone. Putting up the coffee he knew his brother would want to drink, Michael sighed. He and Anthony would either have to handle the insurance or fill out a police report. Either way, it would probably end up in a big, heated debate.

But he wouldn't let it bother him. No, he was still feeling too good about Ty's speech the night before. No more distractions, no more worries about the restaurant unless it was a pile of ash. Now it was just him, using his talents to play the game he loved, pure and simple. The only thing missing in his life—and he felt like a selfish bastard even dwelling on it because so much of his life was blessed— was love.

Helping Theresa through her father's death had been a

mixed bag. It gave him the chance to show her what a good guy he could be, especially compared to that *testa di merda* boyfriend of hers. But holding her close and helping her cope had been rough on him, too. There were times during the two days of the wake and funeral he had longed to pull her aside and say, "I'm sorry I yelled at you and called you a psycho. I take it back. Forgive me and let's give this thing another chance."

But he didn't.

His pride wouldn't let him.

She's moved on, he'd reminded himself, *and thinks you have, too.* Hadn't she asked him about his girlfriend yesterday, before the game? What was he supposed to do? Admit Anthony had made her up? He should have said they'd broken up, but that didn't cross his mind until afterwards. He'd deliberately refrained from asking about Fleece, because he didn't want to know. He was livid the bastard wasn't there for her when she truly needed him, and he was royally pissed Fleece was the one who got to hold Theresa night after night when he, Michael, was the one who truly cared for her. "Ah, fuck it," he muttered to himself, getting two mugs out of the cabinet. What was done was done. No use getting his guts in a twist over it.

The buzzer sounded and he hustled to let his brother in. Anthony didn't *look* particularly distraught, so maybe the restaurant was all right, after all. They hugged, Anthony taking a step back to peruse Michael's face.

"Jesus. I didn't think you could look any uglier, Mikey, but obviously I was wrong."

Michael held his tongue. He'd already heard this joke countless times from his teammates.

"Does it hurt?" Anthony asked.

"Not as badly as it did."

"Don't let Nonna see you. She'll have a heart attack." He scoped out Michael's living room. "Nice place," he murmured approvingly.

"If you'd come by more often, you'd have known that," Michael ribbed.

"Yeah, I know," Anthony admitted, embarrassed. "Time gets away from you, you know?" His eyes continued traveling the room, stopping to linger on the large white and red candles sitting on Michael's coffee table. Startled, he turned to his brother. "Uh, Mike, where did you get those candles?"

"I don't remember," Michael lied.

"Did you get them from Gemma?"

"I might have," Michael said carefully. "Why?"

Anthony looked mortified. "'Cause I have the same ones."

Michael looked at the candles, then his brother, then back to the candles. "What do you mean you have the same ones?" he asked suspiciously.

"Don't laugh, okay? But when I was first starting to like Angie, I went to Gemma to see if she could give me some advice. She gave me the same candles as you've got over there."

"Wait a minute." Michael's mind was reeling. "You took candles from Gemma? *You?* The man who used to make the sign of the cross when she entered the room?"

"I was desperate, Mikey," was Anthony's plaintive reply.

"Did she read your cards?"

"No." Anthony looked horrified. "She wanted to, but I wouldn't let her. That's devil stuff, bro."

"Oh, but burning candles to attract love isn't?" Michael shook his head and asked the next, inevitable question, even though he felt sure he already knew the answer. "Did she give you a moonstone, too?"

Anthony nodded, and Michael sighed in resignation. "Well, I'm glad her hoodoo voodoo worked for one of us." He gestured toward the kitchen. "Joe?"

"Sure thing."

Leading the way, Michael walked with Anthony into the kitchen. He felt pissed at Gemma. Did she hand out the same candles and rocks to every poor, lovelorn *schnook* who came boohooing to her store? He was under the impression—mistaken, obviously—that Gemma had selected the moonstone and candles to work specifically for *him*. The fact she gave the same talismans to Anthony made him feel faceless, somehow. Generic.

He poured their coffee, trying to ignore the way Anthony's gaze was crawling over every surface of the kitchen. He knew what his brother was thinking: that he didn't utilize space well. That he needed a bigger stove and the cooking implements he kept in a ceramic jug on the counter were woefully inadequate.

"What?" he finally asked, sounding irritated as he handed his brother a mug.

"This is a really nice kitchen, Mike."

Jesus. Anthony was just full of surprises these days.

Anthony took a sip of his coffee, his lips disappearing into a thin, disapproving line. "What kind of coffee is this, if you don't mind me asking?"

"Starbuck's."

"You don't go to Miraglia Brothers?"

"Anthony," Michael replied patiently as they headed back out into the living room, "I live in Park Slope. Miraglia Brothers is in Bensonhurst. No offense, but I'm not making a special trip for coffee, especially since I'm not around a lot of the time."

"I'll buy it for you," Anthony offered, sitting down. Michael did the same. "I get it at a discount for the restaurant."

"Whatever." If his brother wanted to buy him coffee, that was fine with him. Whatever floated his boat.

"So." Michael gingerly opened his mouth, sipping some coffee. It wasn't only his cheek, but the whole left side of his face that still hurt, right down to his jaw. "What is it you wanted to talk about?"

"It's Angie," Anthony replied portentously.

"Yeah?" Michael prompted, starting to get worried. The gravity in his brother's voice . . . Was she sick? Pregnant? Shot in the line of duty?

Anthony peered down into his coffee mug. "I think I'm going to ask her to marry me, Mike."

"Holy—" Michael put his mug down and clapped his brother on the back. "That's great, Anthony!"

Anthony looked uncertain. "Yeah?"

Michael was incredulous. "What do you mean, *yeah*?" He did an imitation of Anthony's sad sack face. "What's the problem here?"

"No problem," Anthony hastened to assure him. "I just . . ." He shrugged.

"What?"

"I wanted you to be the first to know," said Anthony. "But I felt kinda nervous about telling you, since things aren't going too hot for you in the romance department right now."

"So? That doesn't mean I can't still be happy for you!" He clasped an arm around Anthony's shoulder, pulling him close and causing coffee to slosh over the edge of the cup. "Shit. Don't worry about that. This is great news, Anthony!"

Anthony still appeared dubious. "Yeah? You really mean it?"

"What do I have to do to convince you, stand on my head and spit wooden nickels?"

Relief rushed to Anthony's face. "I'm so glad you're okay with this, Mike. I was really afraid you'd be upset."

"Don't be a jackass."

But Michael *was* upset.

His brother's news, though he refused to show it, made him feel as if his insides were a slowly deflating balloon.

Gone were the feelings of elation over Ty's speech. They were replaced by an overwhelming sense of inadequacy and envy. The one thing lacking in his own life, his brother now had. *It wasn't supposed to happen like this,* he thought stupidly. *I'm the successful one, the social one, the famous one, the good-looking one. It should be me celebrating, not him.* His meanness of spirit surprised him. Yet he *was* genuinely happy for his brother. How was it possible to feel two conflicting emotions so strongly at once?

"So when's the wedding?" he forced himself to ask.

Anthony looked like a rabbit trapped in headlights. "Geez, I don't know, I mean I haven't even asked her yet. I haven't even gotten her a ring."

"You better hop to it, then."

"If she says yes, you'll be my best man, won't you?"

Michael felt his throat constrict with emotion. If he didn't watch himself, he'd get teary, and Christ knows that was the last thing he wanted, because it would set Anthony off. Before you knew it they'd be the Amazing Weeping Dante Brothers of Brooklyn, New York.

"Of course I'll be your best man," Michael managed, trying not to get choked up. "It would be an honor."

"There's one more thing."

What else could there be? Michael wondered. Maybe Angie *was* pregnant. Or maybe Anthony was one of these people who wanted to get married in a hot air balloon or something crazy like that. He waited.

"I was thinking of asking her to live with me."

"So?"

"You don't mind? I thought you might have a problem with it, you know, it being Mom and Dad's house and all."

Michael couldn't believe what he was hearing. Was he some kind of monster, that Anthony worried he'd have a fit over stupid stuff like this? He couldn't care less if they lived together. He supposed Anthony was just trying to be supersensitive to his feelings. Michael couldn't fault him for that, even if his fears were completely misplaced.

"Anthony." Michael grasped his brother's shoulder tightly. "It's not Mom and Dad's house. It's your house. And if you want to invite Angie to move in before you get married, I think that's great. Maybe you'll finally redecorate the place."

A smile crept onto Anthony's face. "Maybe. Angie's got good taste."

"Well, that's good."

"Now we just have to find the one for you, Mike."

"Yeah," Michael agreed wistfully. There was no point telling his brother that he'd found The One then lost her. It was too complicated. Too painful. So he kept his lip buttoned, trying to enjoy his brother's happiness instead.

As if his brother's impending engagement wasn't bad enough, Michael got the phone call he'd been expecting from Ty: He'd been given a one-game suspension. Still, he flew with the rest of the team to Ottawa the next day for Game Five. He watched from a skybox with the rest of the players who hadn't dressed for the game, gratified to see the Blades fly out onto the ice pumped and ready. From the second the puck was dropped, it was clear his teammates were giving it their all.

But Michael noticed, as did everyone else, that the third line wasn't performing as well as before. They were perpetually a step slow or a second late. They weren't winning the battles in the corners or controlling the loose pucks. van Dorn in particular was out of sync. In the end, it didn't matter: Goalie Pierre LaRouche stole the game for them, shutting out Ottawa 1-0. New York had clawed their way back and were now trailing three games to two.

Still, if they didn't win the next game, they'd be eliminated from the playoffs.

Two days later, circling the ice during the pre-game skate, Michael could feel the nervous energy crackling through the building. The pressure was on. The players' usual joshing and bantering in the locker room was unusually subdued. Skating past the bench, he saw Ty and Kevin call van Dorn over. The younger player nodded his head yes, and then it was Michael they were calling. Puzzled, Michael approached them.

"What's up?"

"You're playing the third line tonight," Ty informed him. "I'm shifting van Dorn to right wing and giving you back your old spot on the left. Any questions?"

"Nope."

Michael rejoined his teammates gracefully gliding around the rink, wondering if the elation he felt inside showed on his face. *One shift at a time,* he kept saying to himself. *We just need to win one shift at a time.*

By the time the game began, Michael was pumped, especially when Ty decided to open with the third line. Taking to the ice to the crowd's heady chant of "Mikey D! Mikey D!" he watched in near breathless anticipation as the puck was dropped at center ice. Then he was flying, weightless, his body pure motion, making it impossible for him to tell where he left off and the ice began.

Getting a regular shift, he felt like he was in the zone. He hit, he back checked, he scrambled fearlessly into corners. Six minutes in, he dug out a cross corner dump-in by defenseman Alfie Shields and threw it to van Dorn in the high slot for a one-timer. The crowd roared as one as the first goal of the game blazed on the electronic scoreboard.

The Blades kept up the pressure, but were unable to score for the rest of the period. Michael could feel the building growing restive as Ottawa came out for the second period clearly loaded for bear. They played their hearts out, eventually tying the game 1-1 after a mad scramble in front of the Blades net.

Both teams were playing it close to the vest, not wanting to make any stupid mistakes or take any unnecessary penalties. Michael felt he and van Dorn were meshing well on the ice, so well that Ty short-shifted them twice. Their line was out on the ice at the end of the second period when an Ottawa player took a slap shot from the point. The puck deflected off defenseman Alfie Shields's skates, caroming into the Blades net.

Ottawa was ahead 2-1.

Michael tried to hold his pessimism at bay. *It ain't over yet. One shift at a time,* he repeated to himself, his words echoing Ty's as the coach tried to whip the enthusiasm back into his players in between periods. By the time the Blades returned to the bench for the start of the third period, Michael was convinced he and his teammates could turn the game around.

"Let's win this period," Ty roared at them.

Every time he stepped out onto the ice, Michael played full tilt, knowing their backs were against the wall. Van Dorn had a good chance to score, but his deflection went wide. Ottawa's goalie was on fire, warding off shot after shot as the Blades tried desperately to put another number up on the board.

With a minute left in the game, Ty pulled their goalie LaRouche. "Get on the ice," he barked at Michael. "Crash the net." When the puck was dropped, Michael fought his way to Ottawa's crease and camped there, doing his best to screen the red hot net-minder. But before he knew it, the horn sounded.

The season was over.

The Blades were out of the playoffs.

Exhausted, Michael and his teammates comforted each

other. They stood on their side of the red line, dejectedly leaning on their sticks as they quietly watched Ottawa celebrate. When they were done, both teams lined up for the traditional end-of-series handshake. No matter how long he'd been playing the game, it always hurt like hell to lose, and tonight was no exception. Sucking up his disappointment, Michael extended his hand to each Ottawa player who came down the line, pleased when some of them praised his play and even kidded him about his ugly mug needing plastic surgery. When it came time for him to shake hands with Torkelson, he was gratified when the hulking Swede put one hand behind his head and pulled him close. "You're one tough *guido,* Mikey. Always have been."

"Good luck, Ulf," Michael returned warmly.

Van Dorn, standing behind Michael, was dumbfounded. "You two know each other?"

"We were in juniors together. We go way back."

van Dorn blinked uncomprehendingly. "But . . ."

"The game comes first, Paul," Michael explained to him. "The game *always* comes first."

"Everybody doing okay? You have enough to eat and drink?"

Circulating the banquet room at Dante's, Michael wanted to make sure all his teammates and their wives were having a good time. Ever since he'd returned to New York, it was an end-of-season tradition for the Blades to finish up with a meal at Dante's. Coming off the ice after their defeat with Ottawa, no one wanted to discuss the depressing prospect of returning the next day to clean out their lockers and say their good-byes for the summer. Instead, they talked about how they couldn't wait to get to Brooklyn to stuff themselves with pasta. Michael had forewarned Anthony they might be coming the next night if they lost the game, so Anthony was prepared for the on-slaught. Even so, he complained loudly when they all walked in. Michael knew it was all guff. If there was one thing Anthony loved, it was cooking for an appreciative audience.

Satisfied that the first table of players and their fami-lies were all happy with their meals, Michael moved on, pausing behind Abby Gill with a friendly hand on her shoulder. "Your lasagne okay?"

Abby rolled her eyes in mock ecstasy, tapping her fork on the edge of her plate. "I want this recipe."

"I don't know," Michael teased good-naturedly. "It's a family secret. You might have to sell one of the kids to my brother."

"Done," said Kevin. Everyone at the table laughed as he pulled up an empty chair. "Mikey, why don't you sit down and enjoy yourself?"

"In a minute," he promised.

He checked with the next table, and the next, always getting the same answer. The food was great. They had enough to drink. Why didn't he sit his butt down and relax?

Finally, he took their advice. Sliding into the empty chair beside Paul van Dorn, he tucked into Anthony's fa-mous lasagne with mushrooms and ham, listening intently to the debate being waged over whether a certain sports-caster's toupee was tacky or convincing. Van Dorn turned to him.

"You're brother's a great cook, Mike."

Michael smiled. "I'll tell him you said so."

Van Dorn shook his head disgustedly. "I can't believe that deflection went wide."

"Let it go," Michael advised. "Season's over. You'll drive yourself nuts if you dwell on that stuff."

"I guess." Van Dorn pushed a half-eaten piece of ravioli around his plate. "So, will you stick around the city for the summer?"

"On and off." Van Dorn's attempt at making small talk touched Michael. "I've got a place on the Jersey shore I try to get to as much as possible. You?"

Van Dorn looked forlorn. "I don't know. I guess I'll head up to my family's summer place in Sharon and figure out what to do from there."

"Well, some of the guys sometimes come down to the shore. If you ever want to come down, or use the house on a weekend I'm not, feel free."

Van Dorn flushed, grateful. "Thanks, Mike."

"Glad to see you two *putzes* are finally bonding."

Michael and van Dorn both turned to see Ty standing behind them, beer stein in hand.

"How's it going, coach?" Michael asked jovially.

"Tell your brother that anytime he wants to drop off an order of scungilli at my house, he should feel free." He took a sip of beer. "It's important you two get along. You're going to be spending a lot of time together next year."

Michael's pulse spiked. "Coach?"

"I'm giving you back your spot on the third line, moving Paul here to right wing full-time. You two worked well together out on the ice."

Michael turned back to the table, stunned. His old position back on the third line . . . *Madonn'*.

"Coach?"

Ty, walking away, turned back.

"Thank you," said Michael humbly.

Ty nodded and continued on to his table. But Michael was transfixed. In his mind's eye he was already imagining next season. He saw himself whipping the puck to center Barry Fontaine and Fontaine scoring . . . saw himself hustling towards the net on a breakaway, the red light above the goal flashing on after he'd gone five hole and scored.

"Michael?"

Janna's voice snapped him out of it. Sheepish, he stood, leaning down to kiss her cheek. "Hey, Jan. Sorry I haven't had a chance to come to your table yet. I was eating my dinner."

"Hockey player and maître d'. You're a talented man," Janna quipped.

"I'm just a hockey player, thank you very much."

"A good one, too." She tugged distractedly at one of her earrings. "So, where's your girlfriend? I was hoping to meet her."

"She's out of town," flew out of Michael's mouth, prompting immediate regret. *That was your chance to say you'd broken up. What the hell is wrong with you?*

Janna looked sympathetic. "That's too bad." She sipped her drink, eyeing him thoughtfully. "Theresa and *her* boyfriend just broke up, you know."

"You mean the Invisible Man?" Michael replied, trying not to sound angry. "Nice, the way he showed up for the wake and funeral."

Janna's mouth tilted down into a frown. "I know. I'm so glad she dumped him. She could do so much better, don't you agree?"

There was no mistaking the not-so-subtle subtext in Janna's voice.

Michael nodded. "I do agree."

"Well, you go finish your dinner." Janna smiled. "And the next time your girlfriend's in town, let's all get-together."

Michael swallowed hard. "Sounds great."

Watching Janna return to her place beside Ty, Michael wondered, *Does she know the girlfriend story is bull? Is she baiting me? Why can't women just be direct? Hell, for that matter, why can't I? Shit.*

So Theresa was free. Now what? He knew the answer before his brain even had a chance to fully formulate it.

He would talk to Gemma.

"I've got a bone to pick with you."

Michael's voice was stern yet affectionate as he approached Gemma, who was sitting behind the counter at the Golden Bough. It was Saturday morning, but he'd been up and about for a while. He had stopped by Met Gar to clear out his locker and say good-bye to teammates leaving New York for the summer. Then he'd headed up to the Blades practice facility in Armonk, to pick up the rest of his stuff there. By the time he made it back down to the Village, he'd been obsessing about Theresa for three hours. He was relieved to see Gemma's shop wasn't crowded.

"That's a nice way to greet your favorite cousin." Gemma smiled.

Michael slipped behind the counter and after a quick peck to her cheek, perched on the stool beside hers. "I'm not sure you're my favorite anymore."

"No? What did I do?"

"Those candles you gave me? The moonrock?"

"Moon*stone*," Gemma corrected.

"Whatever. You gave the same things to Anthony!"

Gemma shrugged, unruffled, while her eyes carefully followed a skulking teen in black Goth gear. "You were both seeking to attract love."

"But I thought that stuff was a special prescription you cooked up just for *me*."

Gemma cast him a sidelong glance. "I never said that."

"True." Michael sighed, his eyes on the teen now as well. If he needed proof he was getting old, this kid was it. Black nail polish, black eyeliner, spiked hair—how the hell could this kid's parents let him walk out of the house like that? "Kids today," he muttered.

Gemma laughed. "You sound just like your father."

"Yeah? Well, I'm starting to think he had a point."

Sensing he was being watched, the Goth slunk out of the shop.

Gemma breathed a sigh of relief, turning to Michael. "I was so sure he was going to steal that dragon flagon."

"Yeah, everyone needs one of those," Michael observed.

Gemma pinched him then said, "You didn't come here to bitch about candles."

"No, I didn't," Michael confessed. He hesitated.

Gemma peered at him, her gaze concentrated. "Theresa?"

Michael nodded. He felt pathetic.

"She's jealous of you," Gemma announced. "Her aura was pulsing red at the reopening."

Michael swallowed, not wanting to dwell on the idea of Theresa pulsing in any way. "You got your cosmic wires crossed. She wasn't jealous of me," he informed his cousin miserably. "She was jealous of *you*. Anthony told her you were my girlfriend."

Gemma drew back, baffled. "Why?"

"To make her jealous."

"Well, it worked."

"Yeah, but now there's a problem."

A customer interrupted them. Michael waited until the store was empty before continuing. "Theresa was dating someone else then, so I was glad Anthony told her I had a girlfriend. But now she's free."

"So?"

"I want to ask her out, except it will mean telling her Anthony lied."

"Why? Just tell her you broke up with your girlfriend."

Michael shifted his weight uncomfortably on the stool. "And what happens if she and I get back together, and we're all at a family gathering, and she finds out you're my cousin? What do we do then?"

"Hmmm." Gemma looked stumped. "I guess you have to tell her the truth."

"She's going to think I'm a loser," Michael lamented, "lying about having a girlfriend just to make her jealous."

"Maybe. Or she might be flattered."

"So what you're saying is, it could go either way?" Michael contemplated this. "I could tell her the truth and she might think I'm a loser, or I could tell her the truth and she could be flattered."

"Why are you making that face, Michael?"

"What face?"

"The face a moron makes when he's concentrating *really, really* hard." Gemma shook his arm. "This is not brain surgery, Mikey. Tell her the truth. She might think it's pathetic but *still* be flattered. Ever think of that?"

No, he hadn't. He was obsessing about Theresa thinking he was a loser. Hadn't she thought he was a loser the whole time he was pursuing her, using everything from biscotti to Bocelli to woo her? It hadn't bothered him then. Difference was, he hadn't lied to her. That was the crux of the problem here. The lie.

"What if she can't deal with my lying to her?"

"Michael, look." Frustration was creeping into Gemma's voice. "The woman cares about you. If she didn't, she wouldn't have gotten jealous." Gemma hopped down off her stool to change the music she was playing. The keening sound of bagpipes now filled the store. "Just tell her the truth, Mikey."

"Can we see what the cards say?" he asked shyly.

Gemma clucked her tongue affectionately. "You're unbelievable, you know that?"

"Not unbelievable enough. We lost."

"I told Anthony you would months ago," Gemma replied. "I had a dream about it."

"Oh, yeah?" Michael was skeptical. If his dreams ever came true, he'd be married to Sela Ward *and* Melina Karakaredes at the same time and he'd be able to fly. "So why didn't you tell me? It would have saved me a lot of heartache."

"It would have influenced your play," Gemma said breezily, as she pulled her tarot cards out from under the counter and handed them to Michael. "By the way, tell Anthony he owes me fifty bucks."

Michael's mouth fell open, insulted. "You bet against us?"

"Just shuffle the cards and concentrate on a question."

Michael peered down at the worn cards in the palm of his hand, thinking hard. *Will Theresa forgive me for lying to her and take me back?* He repeated the question aloud, then shuffled the deck seven times, since July was his birth month. Quelling anticipation, he turned over the top card. It was a picture of six guys holding swords, and it was upside down. His eyes darted to Gemma. She looked vaguely green around the gills. Michael's shoulders sank.

"What?"

"Well, it's not great, but it's not totally horrible," she began.

"Just tell me."

"Six of swords reversed means—*can mean*—a stalemate. It means there won't be an immediate solution to present problems."

"Great." Michael pinched the bridge of his nose. The incense smell in the shop, his own plummeting mood and the wailing of the bagpipes were all making him feel on the verge of a headache.

"Let's try again," Gemma urged, handing him the deck.

Too tense now to dream up a new question, Michael posed the same one. This time the card he turned over was one of two figures beneath a blazing hot sun. It, too, was reversed.

"Hmmm." Gemma sounded uneasy.

"Let me guess. I'm going to walk out of here and get hit by a garbage truck."

"Not quite," said Gemma, studying the card. "But it does indicate a clouded future." She lifted her eyes to her cousin's. "Loneliness."

"Great," Michael repeated dully. "I'm glad I came here today. You've really lifted my spirits."

"Hey, you're the one who wanted to read the cards." Gathering them up, she slipped them back into their purple velvet bag and returned them to the space beneath the counter. "You're just having a bad day, giving off negative energy that's affecting the reading. That's all."

"Sure."

"I mean it." She ran her fingers through her long tangled mop of hair. "You could ask the same questions tomorrow and get a different answer. All this means is you probably shouldn't approach Theresa today."

"Or ever."

"Now you sound like Anthony."

At least Anthony's got a girlfriend, Michael thought gloomily. Gemma was right. He *was* filled with negative energy, especially now that the cosmos seemed to be

telling him he was going to be alone, at least for the fore-
seeable future.

"This music sounds like a dying animal," he said irritably.

"It's Celtic."

"It's awful."

Gemma leaned forward, cupping his face in her hands.
"Promise me you're not going to throw in the towel before you've even tried," she begged him gently.

"I won't," Michael promised, delicately removing his
head from her grasp. It reminded him of when he was a
little boy and his grandmother would smother him in
kisses. Not wishing to dwell on his probable misfortune,
he moved on to a different subject. "Are you going to
cousin Paul's party out in Commack next weekend?" he
asked.

"I'm not sure." Gemma hesitated. "Last time I was
there, his wife made some crack about sacrificing chick-
ens that I didn't appreciate. Are you going?"

"Yeah. You should come. Nonna would love to see
you. That's all she could talk about after the reopening:
how good it was to see you."

"Really?" Gemma's face lit up. "Maybe I will, then."

"Come. Please. Anthony can't make it, so I need someone there I can talk to."

"Bring Theresa," Gemma suggested slyly.

"Enough Theresa for today," Michael admonished.

If he and Theresa were a couple, then of course he
would bring her, so all the family could see what a wonderful girl he'd finally found. But first, he had to tell her
he'd lied. It wasn't a conversation he looked forward to.
What if he told her the truth and she simply didn't care?
What if she still wasn't ready, especially on the heels of
her relationship with Fleece? What, then? He tried to
shake himself out of his gloom but it was hard, especially
with the bagpipes squealing in his ears. Taking leave of

his cousin, he headed back to his car, blasting a Stones CD all the way back to Brooklyn. He *would* talk to Theresa—eventually. But for now he would leave things alone.

According to Mick and Keith, time was on his side.

"Theresa?"

Theresa leaned forward from where she sat behind her desk, straining to hear Terrence's muffled voice on the intercom. He sounded as if he were calling from deep within a closet.

"Yes?"

"Some woman who raided Stevie Nicks's wardrobe is here to see you. What should I do?"

"What's her name?" Theresa snickered. "And speak up!"

"I can't. She'll hear me," Terrence insisted in a breathy whisper.

Theresa closed her eyes and shook her head. "Her name?" she repeated.

"She won't tell me. She just says it's urgent."

"I'll be right there."

Theresa swung out from behind her desk and started up the hall. The last thing she wanted to deal with was some wacko who had gotten her name and now wanted representation. Or worse, a job in PR, thinking it was all about hobnobbing with stars and going to fabulous parties. She was all set to give her "I'm sorry, we're not hiring now" speech, when rounding the corner of the lobby, she was struck dumb.

The woman waiting was Michael Dante's girlfriend.

"Um . . . hello." Trying to hide her confusion, Theresa extended her hand. "I'm Theresa Falconetti."

"Gemma Dante. I was wondering if I might have a word with you."

"Certainly." *Gemma Dante?* Theresa's heart plummeted to her feet. *Oh, God, he married her. Oh my God. Oh. My. God.*

Trying to remain calm, Theresa walked with Michael's—Michael's *wuh—her*—back to her office, the strong scent of patchouli assaulting her. It was a scent Theresa associated with college, when a roommate had dragged her to a potluck dinner at the Women's Studies department. Everyone sat around eating tofu and beans, talking about Georgia O'Keeffe and making friends with their own vaginas.

"Here we are." Ushering Gemma into her office, Theresa bade her sit down. She hated to admit it, but the woman had style. A funky, hip earth-mother kind of flair. And she had nice eyes. Soft, big and brown. But no wedding ring. *Maybe, because they married on the spur of the moment, it's not ready yet? Maybe it's a gorgeous platinum band ringed with small diamond baguettes . . .*

"Michael doesn't know I'm here."

Theresa jerked herself back to attention. *Oh, great. She's here to tell me to keep away from her man.*

"He's crazy about you, but he's afraid you'll think he's a loser because he lied to you."

Theresa blinked rapidly, completely confused. "What?"

Gemma smiled, a lovely, warm smile. "Anthony told you I was Michael's girlfriend, right?"

Theresa nodded fearfully.

"I'm not. I'm his—their—cousin." Gemma frowned. "They're both such jerks. Anyway, Anthony told you that to make you jealous, and Michael didn't tell you the truth because you were seeing someone else and he wanted you to think he'd moved on with his life. Which he hasn't." Gemma laughed.

"Oh." Theresa put a hand to her chest, as relief washed over her. *Not his wife. His cousin. Thank God.*

"You look pleased," Gemma noted.

"I am. I mean—" Theresa colored, not sure what to say next.

"Do you like Michael?" Gemma asked softly.

Theresa nodded shyly. "Yes," she managed, feeling overwhelmed. "A lot."

"I'm glad. Michael's a wonderful man, and he's been waiting *so long* for you to come around."

Theresa felt awkward. "He's talked to you about me?"

"We're very close. Have been since we were small."

Theresa wracked her brain, trying to see if she could recall Michael saying anything about a female cousin. Then it hit her. "You're the *stregh*," she blurted.

"Yup."

Embarrassed, Theresa's hand flew to her mouth. "I'm sorry," she apologized. "I didn't mean to just—"

"It's all right," Gemma assured her. "No offense taken."

So this is the witch. Theresa wasn't sure what she'd expected, but Gemma certainly wasn't it. She'd never met a witch before and assumed Michael's cousin would be somehow dark and mysterious.

"What is it?" Gemma coaxed, reading Theresa's perplexed expression. "You expected me to make my entrance on a broomstick?"

The hairs went up on Theresa's arms at the thought that Michael's cousin could tell what she was thinking. "I guess. Sorry," she said again.

"No need to apologize," Gemma reiterated.

Theresa smiled, beginning to relax. "So Michael's willing to give me another chance?" she asked hopefully.

Now Gemma looked confused. "I thought it was the other way around: You were giving him another chance."

Theresa waved a hand in the air, feeling excited. "Either way. He told you that? He wants to see me?"

"Yeah, but like I said, he's a big chicken. So I had an idea."

Theresa leaned forward, eager to hear what Gemma had to say. "What?"

"There's a big family barbecue at my cousin Paul's next Saturday, and I know for a fact Michael is going to be there. Would you like to come with me?"

This wasn't quite what Theresa expected. "I don't know," she hesitated. "Won't it freak him out, me just showing up unexpectedly?"

"*Michael?* Are you kidding me? He'll be thrilled."

"Are you sure?" Theresa was plagued by a vision of Michael taking one look at her and heading straight for his Mercedes, leaving her standing in a cloud of dust as he peeled out of a suburban Long Island cul de sac. But Gemma assured her otherwise.

"Believe me, I know my cousin. He's not going to be freaked out in the least."

"Well, if you're sure."

Gemma reached out, warmly clasping Theresa's hand in her own.

"I'm sure. Trust me."

By the time Theresa arrived in Commack, she was certain of two things. First, that she liked Gemma. She was warm, funny and extremely smart. Second, Gemma should never be allowed behind the wheel of a car.

During the ride in a red Beetle bearing the bumper sticker MY OTHER CAR IS A BROOMSTICK, Theresa found herself invoking the protection of every saint she could remember. Gemma drifted between lanes, cut cars off on the Northern State Parkway and generally failed to pay attention. When they reached Commack, Theresa was thankful to be alive and had to restrain herself from opening the car door and falling to her knees to kiss the pavement.

Apart from a summer share on Fire Island five or six years before, Theresa's experience of Long Island was minimal. She vaguely remembered her family taking a drive out east one summer Sunday and passing some kind of giant wooden duck. From what she could see, Commack didn't have a Main Street or a downtown. Instead, it appeared to be a series of pleasant, tree-lined neighborhoods developed around strip malls and schools. Cousin Paul's street was a bit like her parents' street in Brooklyn. All the houses were of the same design, except here they were aluminum-sided ranches, rather than two-family brick houses. They all had perfectly manicured front lawns, too, but they were larger than in Brooklyn, and none of them boasted statues of the Virgin Mary or St. Francis. Because of the party, the street was completely lined with cars. Theresa and Gemma had to park a block away and walk.

"Are you nervous?" Gemma asked, carrying a big bowl of macaroni salad she'd made.

"A little," Theresa replied.

She was nervous about seeing Michael, whose Mercedes she spotted parked between an Acura and an Excursion. But the true source of her anxiety was allowing herself to be truly *seen* for the first time in a long time. She'd deliberately shed her glasses and sleek ponytail in the hopes of sending a clear message that she was done with disguises, done with pretending to be someone she wasn't. But she felt confident she'd feel comfortable around a big, boisterous Italian family like her own. In homage to her father, whom she was missing terribly today, she'd brought some Pernigotti nougat with her, remembering her mother's instruction never to go to a guest's house empty-handed.

Cousin Paul's house was a ranch with red shutters and

two gleaming black Audis parked in the drive. The front
window as well as the front door was open. Theresa could
hear animated conversation and laughter coming from inside. Following Gemma up the front steps, Theresa felt
the flutter of nerves in her stomach increase.

Michael's in there, she thought.

Overly polite and reserved greetings met them as
Gemma introduced Theresa around the crowded room. In
fact, a subcurrent of tension seemed to follow in their
wake. Theresa couldn't believe that Michael would have
bad-mouthed her to his whole family. Would he have? Or
maybe Anthony had? But then she caught sight of two of
the older relatives eyeing them and whispering, while sor-
rowfully shaking their heads.

And it dawned on her.

They think Gemma and I are a couple. Shit!

Helping herself to a glass of iced tea in the kitchen as
instructed, she pulled Michael's cousin aside. "They think
we're *gay.*"

"What?"

"Your relatives," Theresa whispered urgently. "They
think we're a couple."

Gemma's eyes circled the room. Then she began to
laugh. "Oh my God. You're right. They do!" She laughed
even harder.

"This isn't funny!" Whereas a moment before Theresa
had been feeling nervous at the prospect of seeing
Michael, now she was seized with the burning desire to
stand on a kitchen chair and loudly proclaim, "I am not a
sister of Sappho!" This was Michael's *family,* for God's
sake. How on Earth were they ever going to accept her
with *him* if they thought she was Gemma's lover?

Michael. Where is he? She asked Gemma if she had
any idea where her cousin would be.

"Knowing Mikey, he's out back with the kids."

Theresa nodded, put down her iced tea and headed for

the back door. Gemma was right. There, on his hands and knees in the grass as two little girls and three little boys attacked him, was Michael. Theresa stood on the back stoop, watching. Apparently, they were playing some kind of game where the children were trying to steal Michael's "power" which resided in the numerous little pink barrettes he was wearing in his hair. Theresa forgot her plight for a moment and wished to God she had a camera; the sight of Michael sprouting pastel barrettes was priceless.

"You will never beat me, for I am the King of Commack!" Michael roared, sending the little girls screaming and the boys lunging into a fresh volley of attacks. Theresa loved that he was oblivious to her, as well as the man she assumed to be cousin Paul, who was manning the grill. Theresa squinted. It had to be Paul: She recognized the pinky ring and the huge gold bracelet from when Michael borrowed them to make his point to her about stereotyping Italian men.

It was obvious Michael loved playing with the kids.

Obvious he loved kids, period.

Watching him roughhouse, Theresa was unexpectedly hit with the same sense of deep, primal longing she had that day in her brother's backyard, playing baseball with her niece and nephew. *I want a family,* she thought, *and I want it with Michael Dante.* Almost as if the mild breeze filtering through the huge maple trees had borne her silent thoughts to his ear, Michael looked up, finally aware of her presence.

In his slow smile, Theresa saw the beckoning of love she had dreamed of her entire life.

"Okay, kids, time for a break, the King of Commack is tired."

Gently removing one little girl from where she hung around his neck, Michael rose to his feet, brushing the dirt and grass from his knees and his hands. The kids hopped around him, frantically protesting the end of play, but

Michael was adamant. "We'll play again after we eat, I promise. Right now, Uncle Michael needs a rest."

Disappointed, the children scattered. Michael walked over to where his cousin Paul stood at the grill and cracked open a cooler from which he extracted two Heinekens. Popping the lids, he took a sip, then sauntered over to the stoop to join Theresa, his face mildly sweaty but his expression delighted.

"This is a surprise," he said, handing her a bottle.

"It was supposed to be."

"Where are your glasses?" he asked.

"I don't need them anymore," Theresa replied shakily.

"I see."

Sitting on the bottom step, he patted the maroon-painted concrete next to him. Theresa walked down the four steps to the bottom and joined him.

"Let me guess," said Michael. "Gemma called you."

"Even better: She came to my office."

Michael's head whipped around in disbelief. "Jesus. I'm sorry."

"I'm not," Theresa declared. "If she hadn't, who knows how long I would have had to wait before you finally told me she wasn't your girlfriend."

Michael ducked his head, embarrassed. "She spilled it all, huh?"

"No stone was left unturned." She took a sip of her beer, wondering how long it would take him to realize he was sitting here talking to her with a head full of barrettes. Apparently forever.

"I don't want to alarm you," she whispered, "but your power is still intact."

Michael looked momentarily baffled before it dawned on him what she was referring to. Grinning, he raised his hand to his hair, but Theresa stopped him.

"Allow me."

Tenderly, she removed the clips one by one, secretly

enjoying the feel of his thick, dark hair against her finger-tips.

"Tell any of the Blades you saw me like this and you're doomed," Michael threatened.

"Why?" Theresa asked softly, removing the final bar-rette. "I think it's wonderful. You were great with them."

"Yeah?" Michael looked pleased as he quickly ran a hand through his hair in an attempt to smooth it. "Well, sometimes being with the kids is more fun than being with the adults. At least the kids don't ask you when you're going to win another Cup or find a nice girl and settle down."

That reminded Theresa. "Unfortunately, all your rela-tives think Gemma *has*."

"Has what?"

"Found a nice girl she's settled down with. They think I'm her girlfriend, Michael."

Michael stared at Theresa a moment, then burst into uproarious laughter. "That is *great!* I love it!"

"It's not funny," Theresa admonished, playfully slap-ping his bare knee. Unlike Reese, the sight of Michael Dante in shorts was pleasing. His legs were sculpted and muscular, the hair dark but not too thick. An image of what she imagined his bare torso must look like flashed in her mind but she blocked it with a long pull at her beer. "I'm going to have to set them straight at some point."

"Don't worry," Michael assured her. "Things will take care of themselves."

Knowing what he referred to, or at least hoping she did, Theresa blushed. Silence descended, peaceful yet not awkward. Together they sat watching cousin Paul as he stacked the burgers high on two huge platters, whistling to himself.

"So," Michael ventured, rolling his beer bottle between his palms, "how come you dumped Fleece?"

"Reese. Because he was an asshole."

"I could have told you that."

"I wouldn't have listened."

Michael looked impressed. "That's quite an admission."

"There's a lot I'm willing to admit," Theresa said quietly.

Michael cocked his head sympathetically. "Like what?"

"Like—" Sighing heavily, Theresa put down her beer, pressing the heel of her palms into her closed eyes. "I've been such an idiot, Michael."

Michael pulled away the hand closest to him, and held it in his own. "We've both been stupid, okay? I'm sorry I yelled at you that day and called you a lunatic. You didn't deserve it."

"Yes, I did," Theresa replied, looking at him now. "Because I *was* sending you mixed messages and I *was* jerking you around." Her gaze flitted from his. "I was scared. I was feeling things for you I didn't know how to handle. The thought of being vulnerable terrified me."

"And now?"

Theresa swallowed hard as she met his eyes. "Now I want to handle them. I want to cultivate them and watch them grow. That is, if you—"

He silenced her with a quick kiss. Theresa drew back, pleased. Never before in her life had she so enjoyed being told, in essence, to shut up. Breathless, she squeezed his hand tightly, and in a move that for her was both bold and terrifying, she leaned in to him, covering his mouth with hers.

Pleasure shot through her, heated and sure.

How could something experienced before feel so wondrous and new? Michael's free hand reached up to gently cup the back of her head, drawing her even closer. Theresa was beginning to understand why religious converts yearned to shout their good news from the rooftops.

Kissing Michael, she felt reborn, the sensation of his mouth against hers both holy and sweet. Emboldened by the intoxicating sense of warmth snaking through her, Theresa let the tip of her tongue slide between his lips, her heartbeat quickening as he did the same, his tongue on a quest all its own, teasing and twining. All the fear she carried within her evaporated, replaced by an overwhelming yearning.

This was what she'd wanted all along but had fought so hard against.

This was what all the great poets and writers down the ages rhapsodized about.

For the first time, Theresa felt she understood what it was to be *in* love. To be immersed in it, body and soul, to feel it was at the very core of your reason for being. The kiss deepened. Theresa sighed contentedly, thoroughly drunk on contact with him.

Somewhere in the far recesses of her mind, she thought she heard the sound of someone clearing their throat. Forcing open one eye, Theresa was greeted by the sight of cousin Paul standing in front of her, burger platter in his hand.

He was politely waiting for them to finish kissing so he could go up the back steps.

Blushing furiously, Theresa gently broke apart from Michael, her eyes darting instructively in the direction of his cousin.

Embarrassed, Michael apologized. "Sorry, Paulie."

"No problem," Paul assured them as they moved apart to let him pass. "I remember what that was like," he joked. The screen door slammed shut behind him as he disappeared into the kitchen.

, "I don't think you need to worry about my family thinking you're with Gemma anymore."

Theresa giggled, then reached for her beer, in need of some cooling. "So now what?"

"Now we go inside with the rest of the family and eat, and when the day is done, you come home with me," Michael quietly suggested, his hand reaching up to tenderly stroke her cheek. "But no pressure. I want you to be sure about this."

Theresa let her eyes drift shut as she held his hand fast against her face. "I'm sure," she murmured.

CHAPTER

22

After their kiss, staying for the rest of the barbecue had been torture. Touching as discreetly as possible through dinner and dessert, they were like two overheated teenagers. Michael's relatives were still confused, but Theresa placed faith in Michael's belief that everything would take care of itself in the end as she joined him in bidding everyone a hasty good-bye.

Adding to their agony, they hit bumper-to-bumper traffic.

The only thing that made the ride from Commack to Park Slope bearable for Theresa was that she was with Michael. Every time she looked at his profile, her stomach fluttered in anticipation and disbelief. He was so handsome, so wonderful, and he was *hers.* She could scarcely believe it. Michael's eyes met hers dozens of times during the course of the ride, followed always by that slow, easy smile of his that made her want to melt. Twining the fingers of her left hand through his, Theresa talked: about work, about her family, about her sessions with Dr. Gardner.

The time for hiding was over.

Arriving at his place, standing in front of his open apartment door, she was nervous. Michael must have sensed it; his grip on her hand tightened in a way she found infinitely reassuring. *He wants me to know I'm safe with him,* she realized. *And I want him to know I'm aware of that.* She showed him by squeezing his hand in return.

In the car, time had felt endless, like a distant horizon she would never reach. But now time began unfolding itself in a more serene, inviting way. It was as if the universe itself was holding its breath, waiting to see what would happen next.

Locking the door behind them, Michael moved to her, his hands gently rubbing her shoulders before reaching up to cup her face in his strong, warm hands. "If you're afraid, or have any doubts at all, I'd be happy just to hold you."

The unabashed tenderness in his eyes brought a lump to Theresa's throat. "I'm not afraid," she whispered as her hand grazed the bruise still shadowing his left cheek.

Michael touched his forehead to hers. "You sure?"

"I'm sure," she said as he drew her into an embrace, the feel of her body against his the most natural thing in the world. Here was safety. Here was true harbor. Theresa felt like a clenched fist whose fingers were slowly unfurling to reveal a long hidden, precious jewel. The jewel was her authentic self. Cradled in Michael's arms, she felt radiant.

They walked slowly up the staircase leading to Michael's bedroom, arms linked around each other's waists. Crossing the threshold, Theresa wondered if he would turn on the light. But he didn't. Instead, he walked over to the window and pulled back the curtains. Pale moonlight washed the room, bathing its contents in a hushed, peaceful glow. Michael turned Theresa to him. Then he skimmed his lips over hers, gentle and soft.

"Do you know how long I've dreamed of this?" he asked, voice thick with emotion.

Theresa nodded, too overwhelmed to speak as tears of happiness welled up behind her closed eyes. The longer he held her, the more alive she felt. A slow fire was beginning to smolder deep within her, her own longing for him the kindling. As if the warmth steadily beating through her body weren't enough, Michael again pressed his lips to hers teasingly before turning his attention to her jawline, gracing it with small, hot kisses. His breath on her cheek was thrilling, inflammatory. "Tell me you want me, Theresa," he murmured against the pulse quivering madly at her throat. But before she could answer, he was hungrily nipping his way back to the edges of her mouth.

There was no time for hesitation, and no need. "I want you," Theresa replied as fervently as repeating a vow. Sweet heat jolted through her at the sound of her own confession. Until now, she hadn't realized what it was to literally ache with desire. Now she knew and bore the exquisite suffering willingly.

"Lie down with me," Michael coaxed.

Trembling not with fear but with need, she followed Michael's lead as they moved toward his bed. Theresa watched as he lovingly folded back the crisp white sheets that would soon be receiving them. Far off on the edge of her consciousness, a dark shadow loomed, but Theresa ignored it. Love had reduced its power over her. Trust would see it banished forever.

"Here." Michael sat on the edge of the bed, bidding Theresa to join him. His gaze was quietly seductive as he reached up to stroke the long, curling tresses of her hair, silent appreciation informing his handsome face. Theresa closed her eyes, reveling in the soothing repetition of his touch. He laid her back upon the pillow as if she were the most precious object in the world. She could feel her hair spilling around her like a halo.

Touching his lips to hers with a lightness that belied
his desire, Michael lay down beside her; his movements
were careful, designed not to startle or scare. Gratitude
swam up from deep within her, followed by a greed she
hadn't known she possessed. Moaning softly, she reached
up for him, her hands bunching in his hair as she dragged
his mouth down to hers. She would show him the tor-
ments of the past were gone. She was free to love him as
he deserved to be loved.

As she *wanted* to love.

The kiss was long, deep, soporific. Desire warm as
heated honey languidly pumped through her. Tentative,
Theresa moved her hands beneath his shirt to explore the
solid terrain of his back. Michael's skin was hot and
smooth, the muscles tensing as she continued her explo-
rations farther down, lightly caressing his hips. Hearing
his breath catch, she knew instinctively he was doing battle with himself, fighting the urge to swiftly take what he
had waited for for so long. If going slow was important to
him, then that's what she would do. But not before she
kissed him once again. Not before she memorized his
taste. Dizzy with need, she again crushed her mouth to
his.

Moaning, Michael reared up, rolling atop her. Smiling
as he pushed the now damp tendrils of hair off her forehead, he looked down into her face lovingly.

"Hi," he whispered.

"Hi," Theresa whispered back. She let her eyes drift
shut, her body's pliancy the perfect foil to his pulsing
hardness. Delirium caught her in its fevered grip as
Michael's mouth went to her throat, feasting there. She
wanted. God, how she wanted. And so, when he raised
himself up slightly to begin unfastening the buttons of her
blouse, she mouthed no protest. She knew the slow shuddering of her body as she lay beneath him said more than
words could ever convey.

Her mind fogged as his fingers, strong and sure, lazily traced the twin swell of her breasts through the lacy cotton of her bra. *More,* she pleaded silently. *Do more.* Reading her mind, Michael allowed his fingers to creep beneath the elastic, his fingertips teasing and circling the erect nipples beneath. Theresa groaned, her pleasure mounting. She thought she heard him chuckle as his free hand reached around to unhook her, but she wasn't sure. Maybe it was delight burbling up in her own throat as his hands continued to exert just the barest touch on her breasts. The sensation was as delicious as it was maddening.

"Michael." She sighed, his name a prayer as she twined her arms around his neck. He answered with a hard, fierce kiss, his mouth swallowing her gasp of surprise. Peeling away her shirt and bra, the cool night air brought goose bumps to her bare torso.

Tearing his mouth from hers, he drank her in. "Christ, you're beautiful." Theresa opened her eyes in time to catch the dark, deep look in his. Carefully, he lowered his mouth to her breast, teeth gently tugging as wave after wave of pleasure shot through her. Theresa's body arched to meet each masterful flick of his tongue, each cooling blow of his breath upon her heated skin. *Soon,* she thought. *Soon.*

"Is this okay?" Michael asked, pausing to take her romantic pulse.

"Fine." Theresa gasped. All she wanted was for the touching to go on, for the feel of his body against hers to never, ever stop. She would do anything to prolong this moment, follow him anywhere if he promised to always, always touch her like this. Nothing else in the world mattered. Just the two of them here, now, like this.

Desperate, she yanked hard on the hem of his shirt. Michael got the message and rising up, tugged his shirt off over his head. The sight of his bare chest stole

Theresa's breath. His was an athlete's body: The well-defined muscles of his arms complimented perfectly the rock-solid six-pack of his abs.

"You're perfect," Theresa breathed aloud.

Embarrassment flashed across his face before he lowered himself to her again, burying his face in her neck. Reaching out, her arms encircled his back, drawing him in tight. Words were being whispered. Sweet words. Tender words that made her heart swell. His mouth began a descent down her body, lips and tongue skimming her ribs, then her torso. Theresa had never felt so nakedly alive. Tongue on skin, breath on flesh . . . she was unable to stop herself quivering beneath his touch. He was torturing her, and she loved it. Time stopped as his fingers undid the zipper of her pants, tugging them down gently. Then his hands were there below her belly button, barely brushing her hips before his fingertips started trailing up . . . and back . . . the long, smooth length of her inner thighs.

She was burning now, hips rocking as sensation after glorious sensation drummed through her. Behind her eyes was a kaleidoscope of colors, vibrant and alive. Her body was pure liquid sensation, the longing to merge with him, to lose herself in him, overwhelming.

"Make love to me," she whispered.

Michael groaned as he tore off the remainder of his clothing. *He's magnificent,* Theresa thought. There was no other word for it. Overwhelmed, she turned her head away, her fevered body waiting for the dip of the mattress that would let her know he was once again on the bed.

Heat bubbled to the surface of her skin as Michael's hands resumed their slow, tantalizing caress. Breathing became difficult as he teased his way along her lower torso, fingers carefully pausing to cup her between the legs. Theresa held her breath, waiting. Would he continue on? Or would he—? The answer came seconds later as his fingers began slowly to circle her heat, the pressure light at first, then heavier, faster, his fingers frantic to match the signals her body gave him as she bucked beneath his touch.

"Please," she begged as his fingers danced on, white hot pressure building within her. Just when she thought she couldn't endure any more, it happened: blinding, molten release. Roaring filled her head as she convulsed against him, screaming her joy, no longer conscious of time or space or even her own body. There was only this glorious heat pouring through her, new as the creation of the world.

She had barely returned to herself before it started all over again, Michael's forehead pressed to hers as he whispered, "Hold on." Then they were one, bodies locked together as Theresa wrapped herself around him like a second skin and he began moving inside her. Pressure began building within her again; faint at first, then sharp, concentrated. Barely clinging to the edge of reality, she cried out as her body once more broke into a million shimmering pieces. Her screams of pleasure pushed Michael toward oblivion.

Moaning, he plunged hard, his body shuddering with release as she arched up to meet him, and he filled her.

Michael couldn't believe how beautiful Theresa looked, even in sleep. Propped up on one elbow, he'd been watching her slumber for a while now. The slow, steady rise and fall of her breath was more soothing to him than any piece of music. Her face was a mask of contentment, the soft curve of her right arm as it reached up and beneath the pillow utterly alluring to him. Reaching out to make sure she was real, Michael's fingers barely alighted on the velvet softness of her cheek. Theresa murmured, sighed deeply, and slumbered on. She was dreaming.

He lay back down, watching the lights of passing cars crawl slowly across the ceiling. He'd call Gemma in the morning to thank her. Under other circumstances, Gemma taking matters into her own hands would have pissed him off. But in this case, he was grateful. Christ knew he would have dragged his heels, waiting for the "perfect" opportunity to approach Theresa.

Thank God for Gemma and her Dante pushiness.

Theresa murmured again, only louder. Michael glanced at her, amused. Obviously, she talked in her sleep. It charmed him. Everything she did was endearing to him, even the way she hogged the covers. He couldn't remember the last time he felt this happy. Maybe never. He had no complaints, only dreams.

He listened to her breath slowly rise, then fall. Rise, then fall. He had an overwhelming desire to wake her and tell her how much he loved her but he resisted. She looked so peaceful lying there, so content. No, he'd let her rest. He had the rest of their lives to tell her.

Worried his restlessness might disturb her, he quietly slipped out of bed and padded downstairs into the dim living room. His eyes instinctively trained on Gemma's red and white candles sitting like two squat tree trunks on his coffee table. Time to throw them out? He reached for them, then thought better of it, sentimentality and superstition prompting a decision to keep them. He'd tell Theresa about them in the morning. She'd get a kick out of it, especially the stuff with the tarot cards and Gemma giving the same love prescription to Anthony.

Sitting on the couch, Michael took stock of his living room. Was his place big enough for the two of them? Maybe she'd want him to move into her place? They'd have to talk about it. There was so much to think about, so much to do. More awake than ever, he went to the kitchen to make himself a cup of decaf. A quick check revealed he didn't have any food in the house. He'd run to the bakery early before she woke up and buy an assortment of pastries, which he'd serve to her in bed. He loved the idea of surprising and pampering her. She deserved it. She deserved the best of everything. He was pouring his coffee into a mug when he heard a scream and froze. Was someone being attacked on the street? But then he realized . . . the scream had come from his bedroom.

Theresa.

Racing back upstairs he grabbed a hockey stick, bracing himself for an intruder. But no one was there except Theresa, weeping as she sat in his bed, clutching the sheet to her chest.

"Theresa?"

She seemed not to hear. He approached gingerly, not wanting to startle her. He switched on the bedside light, both of them blinking furiously against the lamp's sudden, harsh glow. Theresa slowly turned to look at him, and the fear in her face broke Michael's heart. Slowly, as she became fully conscious, the look faded and she realized where she was.

"Michael," she gasped with relief. "Thank God."

"C'mere." He gathered her up into his arms. "What happened? You have a nightmare?"

Theresa nodded, her lashes wetting his chest. She seemed to be struggling. "It was—"

"I know what it was. You don't have to tell me."

"I'm so sorry, Michael. I didn't mean to wake you up."

"Sshh, you didn't wake me up." He began stroking her hair. "It's okay. You're with me now. You're safe."

Theresa's voice was muffled against his chest. "Tell my subconscious that."

"Your subconscious will figure it out in time. The question is: Does your conscious mind know it?"

"Yes," Theresa answered in a tiny voice.

Aching to take her pain away, he tilted her tear-stained face up to look into his. "Do you know how much I love you?" he asked tenderly, wiping away the wetness beneath her eyes.

"Yes," Theresa choked out with a sob.

"*Sshh,* it's okay." Drawing her even tighter to him, he began rocking her. He didn't care how long it took: He would sit here, rocking and comforting her until she knew, deep down in her soul, that she was safe. An image of Lubov flashed in his mind and his heart hardened. *That little son of a bitch.* The Russian had been sidelined for most of the season with an injury. Michael couldn't wait to see him on the ice next year. He'd kill him.

"Michael?"

"Mmm?"

"I love you," Theresa whispered. She lifted her head to look in his eyes. What Michael saw there made the angry clouds in his heart burst then blaze: It was adoration, pure and simple. No woman had ever looked at him like this.

Michael closed his eyes, rapturous. "Say it again."

"I love you," Theresa repeated.

"I thought that's what you said."

"I mean it," she emphasized quietly. Calm now, she moved her arms out from his rocking embrace and framed his face in her hands. "I still have some stuff to work out, but as long as I have you, I'm not afraid to deal with it. I'm not afraid of anything anymore. You're my rock, Michael."

"And you're mine, *cara,*" he whispered. He lowered his mouth to hers, longing to kiss away her sadness. Her mouth tasted sweet, so sweet his pulse quickened. He couldn't believe how a simple kiss could send him reeling.

"Go back to sleep," he soothed.

Theresa looked shy, almost embarrassed. "Will you hold me?"

"Always," he swore, squeezing her tightly as they lay

back down together. It was a vow he intended to keep for
as long as he lived.

Theresa awoke to the intoxicating aroma of coffee
brewing and the sound of Michael humming to himself
somewhere in the outer reaches of the apartment. She had
no idea what time it was, only that it was light and it was
morning. She felt more rested than she had in months.
Though shaken by her Lubov nightmare, she had meant
what she'd said to Michael. She wasn't afraid anymore,
not of the past or of what the future would bring. As long
as she had Michael, all would be well.

"Good, you're up."

Michael appeared in the doorway, bearing a tray of
pastries and a coffee carafe. He was wearing sweats and
nothing else.

"When was the last time you had breakfast in bed?" he
asked, approaching her.

Theresa thought. "I've never had breakfast in bed," she
said, snuggling into the covers.

"You're kidding me! Well, you're in for a real treat."

Carefully laying the tray down, he slipped into bed beside her. "We've got coffee, croissants, muffins, cinnamon
buns and doughnuts," Michael announced, pouring her a
cup of coffee.

"Michael." Theresa was touched. "You didn't have to
do this."

"I wanted to," he replied. "I want to spoil you. I want
to pamper you."

"And when do I get to pamper you?" she teased.

He smiled at her, handing her a cup. "Anytime."

Theresa took a sip of coffee. "What time is it?"

"Close to ten."

"Ten!" Theresa exclaimed in disbelief. "I never sleep
till ten!"

"Well, you did this morning." Michael's hand reached up to caress the back of her neck. "You must have needed it."

"I guess." Suddenly ravenous, Theresa reached out and broke off the top of a blueberry muffin. "So what do you want to do today?"

"Make love to you."

"And after that?"

"Anything you want."

"Want to go see my family?" Theresa asked hesitantly as she nibbled on her muffin.

Michael's face lit up. "Great idea! Will Phil, Debbie and the kids be there?"

"They always are."

"Let's do it. We'll surprise them. Make their day."

Theresa leaned over and playfully bit him on the shoulder. "Okay. But first you have to make mine."

As on every Sunday, the door to Theresa's parents' home was unlocked. It amazed Theresa how it never seemed to bother her mother that she didn't know whether she'd be cooking for two people or twenty. And no matter how many people turned up, there was always enough food. There was something to be said for learning to go with the flow.

"You ready?" Michael asked keenly.

Theresa could tell he was itching to see the look on her mother's face when they walked through the door together. She took a deep breath. "Ready."

Holding hands, they plunged inside. They were greeted with a familiar scene: Phil was on the couch watching TV. Little Phil was on the floor, swinging two Barbie dolls by the roots of their hair, prompting his sister Vicki to scream as if she were being disemboweled.

"You gonna tell him to stop that," Theresa asked her brother, "or should I?"

"Hey, look who's here," said Phil, reluctantly dragging his eyes away from the TV. He took one look at Theresa and Michael together and a sly, approving smile spread across his face. "Well, well. Finally saw the light, huh?"

Theresa grinned. "Be nice."

"I'm always nice."

Rocking forward off the couch, Phil rose, grabbing both of them in an embrace. "This is a sight for sore eyes, I gotta tell you. Mom's gonna go mental." He turned to his children, still squabbling on the floor. "Philly! Cut that out and give your aunt Theresa a kiss."

Hopping up happily as if their battle had never happened, both kids gave Theresa—and Michael—kisses and hugs. Before Theresa could go in search of her mother, Phil called out, "Hey, Ma! Come into the living room! I got a surprise for you!"

Theresa and Michael looked at each other sideways, knowing what would come next. Theresa's mother appeared in the doorway of the kitchen. Seeing them together, she made the sign of the cross three times and then burst into tears.

"Oh, *dio mio*," she wept, coming toward them. "When I saw you two together at the funeral, I prayed for this, oh, how I prayed."

"Ma," Theresa began.

"I wish to God your father were here. But I know he's looking down from heaven."

Theresa's eyes watered as she let her mother gather her up in an embrace. She too wished her father had lived long enough to see her with Michael. But she knew her mother was right. Somewhere, her poppy saw and was pleased.

Finished hugging Theresa, her mother moved on to

Michael, showering his face with grateful kisses. "My hero," she gushed. "I prayed for this."

"I know, Mrs. F," Michael soothed, gently disentangling himself from her strangling embrace. "We wanted you to be the first to know."

Theresa's mother drew back with a gasp. "You're getting married?"

"Um . . . yeah," answered Michael, beginning to smile as he seemed to warm to the idea.

Theresa rounded on him, wide-eyed. "What?"

"Well, we are, aren't we?" Michael challenged.

"That's news to me!" *If this wasn't the ultimate in Dante pushiness!*

Her mother's face fell. "You're not getting married?"

"No!" Theresa put a hand to her forehead. "I mean— not *now*. Not right away. I'm sure—eventually." She stomped her foot in exasperation. "I don't know!"

"She doesn't know," her mother repeated to Michael sarcastically. "She finally comes to her senses and she doesn't know."

"She's been through a lot, Mrs. F," said Michael by way of appeasement.

"Haven't we all?" Theresa's mother returned. "We need a wedding to get this family feeling happy again."

"Should I break out some champagne?" Phil asked.

"No," said Theresa.

"Yes," said her mother, staring at her with daggers in her eyes. "We'll toast your *eventual* marriage. Is that okay with you?"

"Fine," said Theresa. She knew her mother. She wasn't going to let this go.

Phil disappeared into the kitchen, returning a minute later with a grinning Debbie in tow and a bottle of champagne.

"I just heard!" Debbie exclaimed, kissing both Theresa and Michael on the cheek. "Congratulations!"

Michael beamed. "Thank you."

"Have you set a date yet?"

"Next August," said Michael.

"August is too hot," declared Theresa's mother. "Have it in May."

"May's out. I'll still be in the playoffs," said Michael.

Too stunned to protest, Theresa listened in amazement.

"How about July?" Michael offered.

"Perfect," said Theresa's mother approvingly.

Phil uncorked the champagne and poured it into five glasses he'd extracted from the sideboard in the dining room. "Everyone, lift up your glass." They all held their glasses aloft. "To Michael and Theresa and their eventual marriage. It's about goddamn time!"

There was laughter as everyone clinked glasses. Sipping her champagne, Theresa smiled. Maybe a wedding wasn't such a bad idea. She did want to spend the rest of her life with him, after all.

And have a family with him.

And live happily ever after.

A wedding made sense then. *With a reception at The Plaza . . .*

Her fantasies were interrupted by her mother, who clutched her arm. "I have to ask," she said, her gaze hopeful as she looked at Theresa.

"What?"

"You *are* going to live in Brooklyn, right?"

To which Theresa could think of only one appropriate response.

"Maaa!"

BODY CHECK

Deirdre Martin

0-515-13489-9

She's going to
need a power play
to win this hockey
star's heart.

"Deirdre Martin

er
s)